QUEEN OF THE MOUNTAIN
BOOK ONE

THE LEGEND...
OF ARTHUR'S SEAT

BY
L. J. McGOWAN

ILLUSTRATIONS BY ANDREW DeFELICE

INFINITY
PUBLISHING

All rights reserved. No part of this book shall be reproduced or transmitted in any form or by any means, electronic, mechanical, magnetic, photographic including photocopying, recording or by any information storage and retrieval system, without prior written permission of the publisher. No patent liability is assumed with respect to the use of the information contained herein. Although every precaution has been taken in the preparation of this book, the publisher and author assume no responsibility for errors or omissions. Neither is any liability assumed for damages resulting from the use of the information contained herein.

Copyright © 2010 by L.J. McGowan

ISBN 0-7414-6049-1

Printed in the United States of America

This is a work of fiction. Names, characters, places, and incidents either are the product of the author's imagination or are used fictitiously. Any resemblance to actual events or locales or persons, living or dead, is entirely coincidental.

Published July 2010

INFINITY PUBLISHING
1094 New DeHaven Street, Suite 100
West Conshohocken, PA 19428-2713
Toll-free (877) BUY BOOK
Local Phone (610) 941-9999
Fax (610) 941-9959
Info@buybooksontheweb.com
www.buybooksontheweb.com

To my sister Peggy
and to the grace of God,
which allowed me
to complete this story.

To everyone else, an Irish Blessing...

May the road rise up to meet you.
May the wind be always at your back.
May the sun shine warm upon your face.
The rains fall soft upon your fields
and until we meet again,
May God hold you in the palm of His hand...

God bless,
L.J. McGowan

Contents

◆ One ◆
The Legend of Arthur's Seat ◆ 1

◆ Two ◆
The Campfire ◆ 8

◆ Three ◆
Ballyrun ◆ 19

◆ Four ◆
A Knight's Tale ◆ 34

◆ Five ◆
A Fine Pourin' Hand ◆ 49

◆ Six ◆
Miss Sheliza Lott ◆ 56

◆ Seven ◆
Ballyrun Celtic Folklore Competition ◆ 62

◆ Eight ◆
Nights of the Faeries Ceili ◆ 80

◆ Nine ◆
The Golden Stag ◆ 95

◆ Ten ◆
The Stone of Destiny ◆ 105

◆ Eleven ◆
The Raven's Gate ◆ 115

♦ TWELVE ♦
INTO THE BELLY OF ARTHUR'S SEAT ♦ 132

♦ THIRTEEN ♦
THE SELKIES ♦ 144

♦ FOURTEEN ♦
ST. BERNADETTE'S ♦ 159

♦ FIFTEEN ♦
CYRIL'S LAUNDRY SERVICE ♦ 167

♦ SIXTEEN ♦
GHOSTS IN THE ATTIC ♦ 181

♦ SEVENTEEN ♦
THE DEVIL'S BRIDGE ♦ 195

♦ EIGHTEEN ♦
THE FAERY DOOR ♦ 204

♦ NINETEEN ♦
THE WARRIOR QUEEN ♦ 220

♦ TWENTY ♦
KENDRYCK'S SECRET ♦ 247

♦ TWENTY-ONE ♦
FINALLY, FOUND WHAT I'M LOOKING FOR ♦ 263

♦ TWENTY-TWO ♦
WOODLAND FAERIES ♦ 281

♦ TWENTY-THREE ♦
THE TRANSFORMATION ♦ 296

♦ TWENTY-FOUR ♦
THE STAFF OF DÚCÁIN ♦ 303

♦ TWENTY-FIVE ♦
MÄÄGORD ♦ 313

♦ CHAPTER TWENTY-SIX ♦
DRAGON GIRL ♦ 329

♦ CHAPTER ONE ♦
The Legend of Arthur's Seat

Legend has it, that beyond that 'dere lone Mountain called Arthur's Seat, lays another world, a splendid world of endless mystery and bewilderment. Some naysayers in the past have called it 'the Otherworld,' or even 'the Sidhe,' a land of faeries, myths, and legends, and without a doubt, untold magic; whereas others had even dared to call it 'Tír na nÓg,' the land of youth where no mortal man ever grows old. But here in Ballyrun, we have a different name for this mysterious land and her name is, Aählynéé.

It is said that in this mysterious land of Aählynéé, her mountaintops would soar straight up to the heavens, higher than any bird could ever fly, just to touch the moon's cheek. Her lush emerald trees would drape down her mountain slopes, while blades of grass shimmered in the sun's rays, as they silently slept at her feet. The rivers flickered with a thousand specks of silver and her sky glistened as a sapphire dancing with the morning sun.

The location and whereabouts of Aählynéé, of course, is a complete and utter mystery. No one, that is, no one in this world as we know it, knows of its whereabouts. Even a rare few in this mystical land truly know how to get in or out of Aählynéé.

It is also said in legend that the great Arthur's Seat holds the key to the Raven's Gate, which is the only known entrance into the land of Aählynéé. You see, Arthur's Seat stretches out across many lands. I say the lands, because Arthur's Seat is said to be in our mortal realm and partially in Aählynéé, the realm of the faery folk. No one quite sure knows where Aählynéé begins and our world; the mortal world that is, ends. That's why sometimes the two worlds can get all jumbled together. Things that would happen in Aählynéé may or could happen here in our world and vice-versa.

Now, many years back, before you were born, there sat a grand Castle, on top of that 'dere Mountain, governed by the noble and handsome King Kendryck who presided over his lands dutifully, by the way of the teine criostal. In fact, all of Aählynéé's magic came from the mystical teine criostal, or as some call it, the Fire Crystal, which was once forged from the heart of a double red winged dragon. The heart, which once drummed inside this fierce beast, was now the bond that kept this magical world and all its inhabitants united.

Well now, this noble King Kendryck, he was a nice, peace lovin' man who ruled Aählynéé from the grand Amethyst Court; a room drenched with the finest jewels, gold, and the richest tapestries in all of Ireland. One day, this grand King gazed out from his window's edge and watched the beautiful Hawkmoon rise over the distant Snowden mountain caps. The Hawkmoon illuminated the ghostly horizon of Aählynéé while his steward, Raedan, stood steadfast beside him.

Silently, a single blaze flickered on top of a bubbling waterspout where the mighty teine criostal slept within the Amethyst Court, suspended high up over a pool of crystal clear water. Though the King had all the power of the teine criostal and all the riches he ever wanted for, he had but only one wish, which was to find his one true love.

Now, on this particular night, when the Hawkmoon arose in the distance, the King stood over the teine criostal and made his wish. Closing his eyes and opening his heart fully, like the gates of Heaven when St. Patrick arrived, he asked for his one true love. A single teardrop trickled from his eye down his rosy cheek into the mystical pool of water that encircled the magnificent teine criostal.

Now, of course, with every good legend there's a catch or a twist of fate. In this case, it was a sorceress and her name was Koréna, and this is what happened!

Crack! A thunderous clap pierced the silence followed by a brilliant flash of crimson. Through a burst of smoke and blinding light, a dark silhouette emerged from the shadowy corner and slivered closer and closer to the King and Raedan. As the smoke cleared, it became evident who the figure was. It was Koréna, a wicked sorceress from the land of Llangdon. Koréna crossed the room in her ink black gown, tongues of fiery hair burned over her porcelain face. Around her tender neck was a small, double red-winged dragonfly, burning red hot with garnets of fire; it flittered its wings with each breath she took.

Raedan's pulse quickened and with a quick thrust, he lunged his body in front of the King, guarding him from Koréna as she slowly slinked across the room. A twinkling glow glistened from the teine criostal, which emitted a radiantly bold light onto Koréna's dark eyes.

"Surprised to see me my old friend?" she inquired silkily. Raising her delicate fingers to her mouth, she puckered her lips and smacked them firmly together. A kiss of flames levitated upon her palm, and with a soft breath she blew it away from her mouth. The King and Raedan crashed down onto the icy stone floor as the fiery chain of flames flurried upon him.

Raedan twisted his slender body away from the flames and said angrily, "There's no love for the likes of you, Koréna!"

Koréna pasted a smile on her face.

Bracing himself, the King arose from the assault and commanded, "What is it that you want, Koréna?"

"There's no beating around that little green leafy thing now, is there with you? Husband?" said Koréna brazenly.

"Husband?" retorted Raedan, turning to the King, "Sire?"

"Koréna get to your point!" said the King demandingly.

A sinister smile coiled on Koréna's lips. "I've devised a perfect plan to get... everything I want," she said calmly. "Oh, and you too will get something of significance in return." Snapping her fingers, a single flame appeared, cradling a mirror within it.

Koréna gazed at her reflection as she slithered her cherry tongue across her teeth. "Oh, don't look at me like that Kendryck. I know what you want! Hmmm...?" she said candidly, putting out the flame between her bony white fingers. "A petite feminine thing to keep the other side of the bedding warm and cozy for you, a little woman to tell you how irresistible you are? Or perhaps, someone to tell you how charming you are, while you bore her to tears?" Koréna leaned in, whispering into his ear. "Maybe a little someone to whisper sweet nothings into your ear? Hmmm... Kendryck? A little someone, like me?"

"You're madder than I thought!" exclaimed Raedan.

"Quite the opposite! I know things Kendryck, things that are taking place right now in Aählynéé under your nose. Great Warriors and Kings are sleeping in your valleys. They're planted all around you; sinister alliances and actions are forging against you, waiting for your departure so they can take control. Make an alliance with me, Kendryck," she said passionately. "Together we'll be invincible! You, of course, will have an adorable little woman and I will be able to crush my father once and for all!"

"You're quite the nutter, aren't you?" exclaimed Raedan.

"Quiet! You pug of a man!" snarled Koréna. "Before I turn you into a newt!"

"Really? Is that all you got?" he replied smugly. "You'll turn me into a newt?"

"*Enough!*" commanded the King. "Koréna, it's time for you to leave!"

"Kendryck, love," she said sweetly. "That's no way to converse with your new bride."

"Destroy Dúcäin?" questioned Raedan. "Your father? He has done you no harm."

"Come now, Kendryck, just think how good we'd look together. You, me, the teine criostal," said Koréna endearingly.

Kendryck snapped, "Enough already!" He bowed before the teine criostal and his booming voice resonated throughout the Amethyst Court. Lifting up his arms high to the heavens, he said mystically, "This night when the Hawkmoon sets, Koréna, you shall never set foot in Aählyneé ever again, for one thousand Hawkmoons."

The teine criostal pulsed with a hot white light, radiating a warm hue throughout the Amethyst Court.

Koréna lunged towards the crystal, crying out, "Kendryck! No!"

Raedan lunged at Koréna, her body went crashing down onto the bitter stone. Swiftly she snapped her fingers and a sphere-shaped fiery light appeared in her hand and she hurled it at the King.

Whack! Hit in the chest, Kendryck stumbled briefly and then turned stiff like a statue, crashing to the floor beneath him. Then suddenly, without recourse, the Castle began to quake below them; Koréna watched the rigid stone floor underneath her begin to shake uncontrollably. Raedan staggered forward, his legs quivering before he crashed down to the chilly floor. He wrapped his hand swiftly around Koréna's ankle, causing her to plummet down to the shifting floor with him. She kicked herself free from Raedan's grip, stood up, and fumbled her way towards the teine criostal. Koréna wobbled clumsily across the room before reaching the mystical pool of water holding up the teine criostal. A pearly smile came across her face as she stood before her claim. A roaring shudder echoed through the Castle as chunks of stone, dirt, and debris showered down upon them as the Castle walls began to collapse.

Raedan averted his eyes up, straining to see his King stumbling to his feet, "*Sire!*" he called urgently.

Then Koréna, the evil sorceress from Llangdon, stood boldly before the teine criostal and roared, "Finally, the teine criostal is mine!" Her fingers swept in, closer to her prize, just barely touching it.

More mortar and sharp stones crashed down upon her, tearing deep wounds into her delicate skin. The Castle swayed and grumbled ferociously, her eyes then turned away to see the cracking stone floor beneath her. "*Ahhh!!!*" she screamed, plunging downward in the floor's bottomless fissure, her body suspended between the room's floor and the darkness below. Breathless, Koréna gazed up towards the teine criostal. Another thunderous crack erupted throughout the room. Before her disbelieving eyes, the teine criostal split into three separate crystals.

Another piercing clap of thunder rumbled throughout the Castle and they all shivered with fear. The three teine criostals then plunged deep into the cascading water, disappearing from their sight. Koréna's hand grasped at the crystals, as the cloudy pool of water began to churn, but it was no use, the three new spirits of the teine criostals were swallowed down deep into the belly of Arthur's Seat.

Battering stones rained down faster from the collapsing walls and ceiling. Once again, the King and Raedan scampered to their feet.

"Sire, quickly!" said Raedan frantically, hoisting up the King's injured body.

Koréna, meanwhile, had pulled herself out of the fissure. She knelt wearily down before the empty mystical pool of water. Aghast, she questioned, "What is this?"

A deep powerful voice echoed from above, "Koréna, for many Hawkmoons you have disobeyed me. Now, you shall be accountable for your actions and imprisoned in this Mountain forever!"

It was Dúcäin, Koréna's father, who had caused the great Castle to crumble apart and the teine criostal to split into three separate crystals. Raedan and the King continued their frantic dash towards the exit, weaving in and out of the toppling rain of stones as they scurried out the door. They escaped just in time; a thick colossal stone plunged down behind them and sealed off the exit, leaving Koréna seemingly with no way out. Koréna saw an exit, the thick glass window, which Kendryck had peered out of, only moments before to watch the Hawkmoon rise.

Running from her demise and the ceaseless pelting down of heavy stones, blinding dust, and hailing mortar, she gazed out the window to see the lone Hawkmoon, quietly setting over the horizon. With a snap of her finger, a fiery sphere appeared in her clutch and she hurled the brilliant ball of fire against the window, shattering the glass into a million wee pieces. Koréna clambered up onto the windowsill's pane. Standing there, a smile inched across her face and she leapt into the air. *Smack!* She slammed straight into an invisible wall, which closed the window off from the world outside. She dropped down to what was once a grand Castle's floor devastated.

Kneeling down before the drained pool of water, she cried out, "You can't do this to me... father!"

A solitary voiced bellowed back, "Your lesson, I'm afraid, must be learned again."

"I'll never forgive you for this father! Never!" she wept despairingly, in her lonely tomb.

When Arthur's Seat finished swallowing Kendryck's Castle along with the three teine criostals, folks from every town, village, and county heard the last known wail of Koréna. "*Noooooooo!*" she howled hopelessly as the unyielding Mountain swallowed her and Kendryck's Castle whole and then the legendary Mountain, Arthur's Seat, fell silent, once again.

Now, legend has it, that Koréna still resides inside Arthur's Seat to this very day, waiting for the thousand Hawkmoons to pass and searching perilously for the three parts of the teine criostals, and trying desperately to make them whole, once again. In order to regain Kendryck's magic, defeat her father, and of course, to finally become *Queen of the Mountain*!

♦ CHAPTER TWO ♦
THE CAMPFIRE

A dangerously dark and silent Mountain slumbers in the far distance, while blissful red and orange embers pop and dance, like wee children in the sweet chill of the evening's air. Cascading spirals of white smoke flurry upward from a particularly small campfire. An aged man, who had seen time pass him by one too many times, sits quietly before the crackling fire, a soft silver beard painted over his tattered, blushed face. He stokes the dwindling fire with a weathered branch and glances across the campfire to his two wee grandchildren and says decisively, "Now children, 'dat there is 'da legend of Arthur's Seat."

A wee lass with ragged, dark auburn hair awkwardly pushes up her oversized sleeves. Dazedly, she watches the sparkling lights shoot out from the sizzling blaze. Adjacent to her, a short, chubby lad sits on a stone, his eyes gazing down to the earth, spying on a shiny black beetle. Leaning forward he snatches it up, its legs flaring wildly in the air. Puzzled, he scratches his greasy black hair, wiping the residue furiously on his tatty blue jeans.

The two children sighed, "Wow!" Kathryn and Billy both gazed upward, watching the puffy smoke drift towards the massive Mountain, behind them.

Kathryn brushed away a few of her wayward strands of hair out of her green eyes. "So, Gramps, whatever happened to the King?" she questioned politely.

Grandpa reached into his patched, raggedy old petty coat. "Aye..." he said softly, and pulled out a battered mahogany pipe with a wad of tobacco leaves. Pausing, he smiled mischievously. "You see dat's all part of 'da mystery of Arthur's Seat! Nobody really knows what's happened." Dreamingly, his eyes gazed up toward the night skies. His blue eyes swiftly scanned the dusky sky. "I believe it'll be time 'fer bed 'fer 'da two of you!"

"Wait! Whatever happened to the evil sorceress, Koréna?" asked Billy anxiously, tossing his prey to the ground. "Is she still inside the Mountain?" He sat up straight, his eyes now bulging like two puffed up balloons. "Maybe, she's watching us - *right now!*" he cried, pointing to the quiet

Mountain.

"Yeah," said Kathryn frightfully, "she could be close to finding all three parts of the Fire Crystal," lowering her voice to a soft whisper, "and come down and destroy us all."

Grandpa shook his head dismissively and said, "Oh, stop it now... 'da two of you. You're causin' trouble. Nobody's comin' down 'ta destroy us! Come hell or high water it's just not goin' ta happen, I tell you! It's just a silly legend. She's not real and neither is Aählynéé."

"But, Gramps," sighed Kathryn disappointingly.

Grandpa grasped tighter onto the pipe's bowl and pointed the curved lip towards Kathryn. "And don't get 'ta thinkin' you're gonna find out if it's real or not," said Grandpa scoldingly. "Now, do as you're told and get on 'ta bed!"

"One more story, Gramps... *please!!!!*" said Kathryn beseechingly.

"Please!" implored Billy.

Grandpa cleared his throat.

Kathryn threw a coaxing look to Billy and with a bright twinkle in her eyes she looked at Grandpa. "Tell us about the rare ravens," she said sweetly.

Billy blissfully interjected, "Yeah, what about those crazy fire birds who tell you of the future?"

"*Please!!!*" pleaded Kathryn and Billy together.

Grandpa removed the warm pipe from his lips and tapped it gently against a nearby rock, pulling out a few crispy tobacco leaves from his pouch and stuffing them into the pipe's bowl. "Well, you'd be talkin' about them 'dere red-winged ravens now, Billy," he stated in a matter of fact way, raising the smooth pipe to his plump lips.

"Did you ever see a red-winged raven, Grandpa?" asked Kathryn.

Grandpa grinned and struck a match on the rock while cuffing his hand to protect the flame, gently lowering it down gracefully against the dried leaves as he began to puff smoke from his lips. Shapes of galloping horses and fiery dragons spewed forth from his lips. The sweet scent of Grandpa's pipe lingered across the campfire and tickled the bottom of Kathryn's nose.

Grandpa nodded, a grin crawling across his crinkled face. "But you see, I didn't see all them 'dere seven ravens, as your Grandmother did," he said succinctly, pointing to the west. "On 'dat 'dere old oak tree by her grave," he paused for a moment, taking a deep breath, "God bless her memory!" He then leaned back and took a few more pleasurable puffs on his pipe. Shapes of wailing banshees and angry leprechauns danced through the chilly air from his lips. "Now, how did 'dat old saying go if one were 'ta see these ravens?" Pulling the pipe out of his mouth, a peaceful stillness trickled across his face, "Aye... yes, that's right." He said harmoniously, "If one were 'ta see these exquisite birds. One raven would be 'fer sorrow, and then two 'fer joy, uhhh... three 'fer marriage, four 'fer a boy, five 'fer silver, six 'fer gold, and seven 'fer 'da secret that's never been told!"

"What do you think the secret is?" inquired Billy.

"Maybe it's the secret of Arthur's Seat?" said Kathryn zealously.

"You see children, no one knows what 'da secret really is... Who bleedin' knows? Perhaps it's where you hid Billy's lightnin' bugs two fortnights ago! Aye, Kathryn?" he said with a knowing wink.

"Hey, where did you hide them?" said Billy demandingly, jolting off his rock, "I caught over a hundred in that jar!"

"Ah yes, 'dose lightnin' bugs are from 'da faery folk!" murmured Grandpa, "'dey are, 'dey are."

Kathryn flimsily waved her hand down and said, "They were *wayyyyy* dead when I found them, Gramps. Anyway, those bugs don't live that long Billy."

"Actually," he said calmly, "insects have been around for 350 million years, while we humans have only been around for 10,000 years. So, technically they do live longer than we do."

Kathryn rolled her eyes.

Grandpa grabbed onto his knobby cane and placed his body weight upon the gnarled branch and slowly rose to his feet, "Yes, those 'dere faery folk will getcha every time... they'll come by and just snatcha right up! Come on now, 'tis time 'fer bed and I don't want any aggravation from 'da two of 'ya either!" he said, aiming his crooked cane at the campfire. "Billy, help me 'ta put 'dis fire out and I'll need you 'ta get me some water from that 'dere stream outback. Yes, I will - I will, I'll need ya 'ta do 'dat 'fer me!" He turned to Kathryn. "Kathryn now you go and take 'dat darn stinky rubbish out to 'da shed now. Come on, off with ya now."

Like a commanded soldier, Kathryn stood up and swung around to face a small dilapidated thatched cottage. The years of bustling winds and endless rain had chipped slowly away at the white washed cottage. Holes tore straight through the layers of the decomposing straw that lined the moldy thatched roof. The weathered old homestead had, without a doubt, seen better days.

Kathryn turned the aged knob on the back door all the way to the far right, pressing her left shoulder firmly against it. "Come on!" she cried bitterly, twisting and turning the knob back and forth feverishly. She balanced her weight sturdily against the door and then slammed into it once again until it popped open. The raggedy old cottage walls quivered as Kathryn was hurled down to the grubby stone floor.

"Don't go breakin' 'dat door again Kat!" yelled Grandpa from outside. "Geezzz... I don't have 'da money 'fer a new one!"

Kathryn rubbed her throbbing shoulder and promptly stood up. "I'm fine! Don't worry about me," she mumbled to herself, dusting the muck off her hand-me-down shirt, two sizes too big.

"And don't be gettin' me shirt all dirty, as well!" griped Grandpa. "We're already out of soap and Fiona won't be stoppin' by 'fer a few days."

"Yep, got it!" she hollered back to Grandpa, rubbing her banged up shoulder some more. "Don't mess up," she mumbled under her breath.

Kathryn let out a loud sigh while her eyes studied the grimy room surrounding her; smoke charred walls were cluttered high with dry saltboxes, thick peat bars, and crusty, black iron pots dangling low above the glowing hearth. Against the back wall was a bare pine table with a solitary oil lamp sitting quietly upon it, trying to keep it company. While dust balls, breadcrumbs, and mice droppings collected silently away in the corners.

"Oh yea!" she said dazedly and crossed the room. Finally, she remembered why she had entered the room and leaned down to scoop up a filthy old container. She heaved the heavy trash bin up and stumbled back a few steps, nearly knockin' the wee oil lamp off the poor lopsided table, which was unfortunately one leg too short. Her nostrils flickered as she caught just a whiff of its contents and let out a loud *"Peee-uuu!"* as she squished her face together in disgust.

Now, Kathryn's feet were weighted solidly down to the ground as she wobbled side to side through the living area with her new found treasure in hand. What a glorious feeling of joy she felt in her hands as she passed the great stone hearth, where years of dust and ash piled up high on its wrought iron grate and where warbled logs stood at attention as if they were saluting her as she waddled by. Next to the hearth was an old wooden bellow, hand carved with a terrifying dragon etched into its belly, covered with a year's worth of soot. Up the hearth's wall climbed garbled and twisted stones, which lead to a beautiful portrait of a young woman. Her skin was soft and dewy, not a blemish or scar on it. Her eyes were as green as the Emerald Isle itself, and cascading down her face was her long auburn hair, which drizzled down onto her white dress. Most interesting was the unique seven-tiered citrine necklace, which she wore around her neck.

Kathryn winked at the portrait, for it was her own Grandmother whom had passed away years ago, before she was ever born. Making for the door, she swung it wide open and tottered down a dirt path down to the shed.

Further on down the path sat a single rose bush, lazily twisting and turning its vines and wrapping itself around an old lifeless tree. Beside it sat an old stone Celtic Cross, which looked like it had weathered many storms. Kathryn made her way down the dusty lane lined with a sturdy stone wall. Upon her travels she passed Sheba, a pasty white mare who looked as if she had seen many, many lifetimes herself. Sheba chewed leisurely on bits of hay protruding from her mouth, ignoring Kathryn's presence. The mare's face and cheeks were marked with deep slashes of time.

Out of the corner of Kathryn's eye, she caught a glimpse of a tiny black fly zooming past the old horse's ear. Oblivious to this little pest, Sheba continued to chomp down on her dinner, until the pesky little fly landed on her, causing her ears to twitch.

"Hi Sheba!" called Kathryn amiably, moving closer to the comatose mare and placed her hand on her coarse matted hair. "You must be hungry girl."

Reaching deep down into her pile of rubbish, digging through the wrappers of Cadbury milk chocolate bars, tea bags, a shriveled up bag of McVitie's chocolate covered biscuits, cracked egg shells, a piece of moldy bread, a dozen plastic bags of Walker's crisps (salt and vinegar), and then she finally pulled out part of an old carrot.

"Here," she said kindly, placing the treat in front of Sheba's wet nose.

Sheba gingerly raised her head and let out a blast of air, shaking her head side to side, causing the pesky fly to fly off her head along with a small cloud of dust and dirt. Gradually, the old mare leaned forward, placing her moist lips into Kathryn's hand, and began to chew loudly on the crunchy carrot.

"There you go girl," she said gently, patting her neck firmly.

The fly then circled round and made his new home on Sheba's left rump. With a vigorous wipe of her hand, Kathryn mopped off Sheba's germs onto her jeans and began her descent back down the path. Sheba jolted back, looking towards her left rump, stalking her new victim. With a hard *'clap'*, the unsuspecting fly was squished from its post with Sheba's whip-like tail and with a slight *'neigh'* quibbling from her lips, Sheba lowered her head down into her bed of hay.

Kathryn continued down the old dirt road to a ragged old shed overgrown with weeds and moss. Protruding shingles hung off the roof, barely covering its contents, and rusty tools rested against its walls not knowing if they were ever to be used again. She walked behind the shed, tipped her tin of rubbish into a pile of rotting compost while a quake of restless flies swarmed around its new meal.

Billy was back up the road, busy pouring out the liquid contents of his rotted bucket; the ashes of the campfire sizzled as mounds of smoke bellowed up into his face causing him to cough incessantly.

Grandpa stared down at the wet fire, now smoldering. "Another one will do!" he grumbled.

Poor Billy was pouring with sweat, his eyes blurred with smoke as he sighed wearily and walked back down to the stream. Scooping up another bucket full of water, he said, "Another one will do!" Muttering under his breath, "I'm blind now and... *another one will do!*" He heaved up the heavy bucket. "I'll do ya!" he mumbled. His gaze caught a swift shadow moving under a rock. Well, Billy being Billy now, he quickly reached down to the ground and snatched whatever was lurking under that rock right up! Cupping his furry little friend in his hand he whispered sinisterly, "I have plans for you!"

Kathryn, meanwhile, was too busy strolling back up the path with a whistle on her lips and a bounce in her step as she gazed down into the empty garbage bin. "What's its worth?" she said modestly. "That's a very good question. Hmmm..." Strolling up the dirt road, she rambled on. "Seeing that it's tilled from the finest gold, embedded with thousands of priceless gems," she continued on, ever so delicately holding onto the bin's handles. "Well, these two handles alone are made of diamonds. Very rare, indeed! And of course, within this fine treasure one would find..." Unfortunately, this is when Kathryn made a wee bit of an error as she looked down into the rubbish, she inadvertently caught another whiff of its slimy remnants still oozing down the inside walls. *"Peee-uuu!"* she wailed, pulling away from the container. "Oh my, that's really nasty. Even I can't imagine anything worse! So, the treasure's booty went down a bit, but it's still worth a hefty fortune, and this explorer won't let anyone steal it from her!"

She finally made her way back to the white washed cottage. A soft light glowed from its windows, as Arthur's Seat slept silently in the distance. Being the great adventurer that she was, Kathryn snuck up to one of the cottage's glowing windows and decided to take a closer look. Inside she was amazed at what she saw, for it was her grandfather fiddling around her grandmother's portrait above the hearth. Quickly, she jumped away from the window hoping to hide her presence.

"Another renegade trying to steal my treasure," she whispered playfully to herself, "but he hasn't seen me just yet! I'll bide my time and surprise him when he least expects it!"

Peering back into the window, she watched as Grandpa slowly cocked his head side to side, keeping his movements hidden. He then gently tugged on the portrait's golden frame and it swung open like a door, a secret door to be correct. Reaching into the compartment, his hand disappeared and then reappeared; holding a citrine necklace, the exact same one her grandmother was wearing in the painting.

"What do we have here?" hummed Kathryn, still spying on her grandfather. "Another treasure? Aye!"

Just when things were getting interesting, two hairy legs silently crept up over her shoulder slowly brushing against her hair. Inside the cottage, Grandpa laced his fingers through the necklace and raised it into the light. The hairy legs stepped in closer, while red beady eyes began to glow on her shoulder. Soon, the descent of furry legs crept in slowly, revealing six more as they began to graze Kathryn's cheek.

Well, I'll have you know, at that precise moment, Kathryn screamed so loudly, she was heard all the way to Dublin. She leaped away from the window and began swatting the furry spider off her cheek but wouldn't you know, those thick bristly house spiders legs hooked into her hair and she began to spin round and round out of control. Whacking at her hair and the spider, she dropped the garbage bin, crashing it to the ground, causing quite a bang. Finally, she flipped her head over and shook her hair hard, until the spider fell to the ground.

Billy was in a full-bellied laugh when he decided to quickly sneak a look into the window as well. "What on earth are you looking at?" he asked.

Kathryn swiftly placed her hand over his mouth and pulled him away from the window. "Billy," she whispered, "*shhh...*" as she spied back through the glass, only to see the portrait closed and Grandpa gone.

"That was close," she said releasing her hand from Billy's mouth.

"Puh!!!" he spluttered, wiping his mouth as he began to spit repeatedly with disgust, "*Pwwwt...* Uhhh... man! What did you do? Wash your hands in compost? *Gross!*"

"I told you not to sneak up on me anymore!"

"Is the great explorer," he said pausing once more to spit, "*pwwwt...* In the middle of a treasure hunt again?"

"Don't start!" she warned him, wiping her hands on her trousers. "You're already going to get it for sneakin' up on me like that!"

The two of them almost forgot where they were, ranting and raving to each other that they didn't see Grandpa appear behind them and from the sour look on his face, he wasn't too happy.

"Come on now," he said demandingly, pointing to the door, "You two do as you're told, off 'ta bed with ya!"

Kathryn just rolled her eyes around in her head, turned around and kicked that poor wee house spider. While Billy on the other hand, in one graceful swoop, snatched it back up and then coyly dropped it in his pocket, as they both walked towards the cottage's front door. Now, siblings being siblings, Kathryn whispered into Billy's ear, "This isn't over!"

Just then, a fine mist of rain began to fall softly down upon the three of them.

"Awww... Geezzz.... it's beginin' 'ta rain again, you know what 'dat means, Billy," said Grandpa.

Billy's face froze with terror. "It's just a light, soft mist Grandpa," he said.

"Just a light mist? Just a light mist!" said Grandpa alarmingly. "Well now, how 'bout we leave you outside in 'da light mist? Now, off with ya now and go fetch Lady Sheba. Kathryn you go and make sure 'deres no food lying around and she's got herself enough room to move about in 'da cottage."

Lady Sheba entered the wee cottage; clip-clopping her hooves on the stone floor, which then began to echo throughout the wee cottage. The scent of wet, muddy hay quickly filled the room as Kathryn took a deep breath and scurried up the ratty ladder leading to her bedroom. Sheba rustled her matted hair about, spraying a soft mist of dampness throughout the cozy living room.

"Ah 'dere you are girl," said Grandpa lovingly, tapping his hand upon his sweet mare's neck. Sheba shook her sodden coat again, discharging another round of water onto Billy's face. Grandpa pulled her reins tighter and cautiously hooked them onto a corroded hook jutting out from the wall.

"Grandpa," inquired Billy carefully, "is there any way for us to know?" he paused for a brief moment, looking at Sheba's derriere. "Well, you know?"

"For us 'ta know what?" replied Grandpa. "Come on now boy, get it out!"

"If she... did her... you know? Took care of her business?"

"Awww, 'fer Pete's sake, your mind is filled with mush boy!" said Grandpa hotly, "No! Does 'dat answer your question? 'Deres no way of knowin' if she's done her business! She's a bleedin' animal 'fer goodness sakes! What do you want? Do you want 'ta stand outside and watch her all bleedin' day 'ta know when her next movement will be?"

"Ummm.... No."

"I didn't think so. So, now 'dat we know 'dat we don't know; she may or may not be leavin' us a sweet little surprise in 'da mornin'. I shall wish you a good night! Now, off 'ta bed with yea."

Being the tired man that he was, Grandpa slumbered

over to his boxed-in-wall bed, a small wood frame built into an alcove beside the hearth, a creamy lace curtain draped around it. He kicked off his boots laden with mud first and then slipped underneath the warm covers, beside the glowing fire. Billy carefully walked past grandpa's bed and climbed up his own rickety ladder, which led to an adjacent room from Kathryn's.

Both rooms were just mere cubbyholes created in the loft of the roof. Kathryn and Billy nestled in their rooms and peered across the great divide waiting for grandpa to douse the flame from his oil lamp. Silently, they waited for his first roaring snore of the evening, signaling the beginning of his deep slumber, for they knew he wouldn't wake until morning.

The living area was ablaze with a soft, orangey glow from the peat fire burning ever so leisurely in the soot-covered hearth. Kathryn jerked her head to the left cueing Billy to reach for a small tin can. Now, the two of them were very clever indeed. They had cut out the top part of a tin and on the bottom of it, a small hole was drilled into it where a simple string was knotted inside. The string extended out and tunneled itself through a small crack, passing through the living area into another hole into Kathryn's room, where she in turn held the replica of Billy's can.

"Whatcha want Kat?" whispered Billy into his tin phone.

Kathryn smiled and waved, chuckling into the can. "By the way," she said cheerfully, "it's your turn to pick up the dung, if Sheba goes!"

Billy's face soured and she closed her crooked door, jumped upon her iron bed and tapped her feet together, oh so joyously. Gazing up onto her wall, she had a vast colored map of the world. In which, she had stuck two small thumbtacks, one on Brooklyn, New York, U.S.A., the other on Ballyrun, Ireland; all the places she'd been in her life. Next to her head she had a small crinkled portrait of Indiana Jones with a list below it that read:

The Ten Rules Of A 'True' Indiana Jones Apprentice:

Rule#1: Always be prepared!
You never know when you may encounter a new adventure!
(Some suggestions are: a durable and powerful flashlight, a compass, non-perishable food, a Swiss army knife, plenty of H2O, and a utility belt. Please see page 90 on authentic Indiana Jones items. Also, the authentic Indiana Jones whip and fedora are optional. Please specify size and height on your ordering form.)

Rule#2: Always be one step ahead of your enemy!
If possible, two or three are better!

Rule#3: Always be alert and aware of your surroundings!
This goes for when you are sleeping and eating as well.

Rule#4: It's 'okay' to make a plan as you go!
In fact, it is the Indiana Jones way! So, go for it!

Rule#5: Avoid snakes!
If possible, at all costs!

Rule#6: Speak the native language!
Learn a valuable trait by speaking the native language. Sign language is acceptable and when in doubt, *improvise!*

Rule#7: Blend in with natives!
The ability to blend in with the natives is truly a valuable commodity and is highly recommended to get out of many sticky situations!

Rule#8: Never sweat!
Never show your adversary any pain or even let them see you sweat!
<u>Note:</u> This does not mean to wear excessive amounts of deodorant, it is more a less, a *mental* objective.

Rule#9: Do the unthinkable!
In times of doubt, always do the unthinkable and *achieve it!* Exactly!

Rule#10: Trust your instincts!
Always *trust* your instincts when faced with conflict! Believing in oneself is the primary goal of being a 'true' Indiana Jones apprentice.

Kathryn slid underneath her stiff covers and then snubbed out the oil lamp next to her bed.

♦ CHAPTER THREE ♦
BALLYRUN

Oh the beauty of the emerald green isle, filled high in all its glory with rocks and stones. There, in the wee valley, sits a small white thatched cottage nestled in the arms of Arthur's Seat. As the rain soaked sky begins to wring itself upon this glorious land, in the far distance, glimpses of light poke free from the gray misty clouds which had blanketed the land all day long.

The weathered red door on the cottage suddenly swung open, while the rain danced dizzily on its mud-spattered driveway. Gradually, two swaddled silhouettes emerged from the doorway and a pudgy lone hand reached out to touch the day's rain.

"Ugh! I think we're gonna get just a *wee* bit wet out there Kat," whimpered Billy. "Do we have to go?"

Pushing her brother aside and with a keen look in her eye she peered out the door, cocking her head side to side and then raised one of her eyebrows at the daunting day. "Grandpa needs us to go to the general store," she said.

Now Grandpa was always a true stickler for money and for some particular reason always carried two purses about him. For some reason, he always would grumble on about leprechauns wanting to steal his purses. Strangely enough, one of his purses was made of cowhide, which he kept fastened on his belt buckle. Inside of this purse was a single silver coin. Once it was emptied, magically another one would replace it, just like that! Billy and Kathryn knew better, of course, than to ever ask him why. The other one was a tiny silver coin purse, which hung snugly on a silver rope around his neck, which no soul ever saw. It was glued to his chest like a sailor's tattoo.

"Now, here's 'da money," said Grandpa miserly, stretching out his hand with one polished silver coin, "and 'da list. Now, don't be gettin' any of 'dat fat free stuff, I wants 'da whole stuff, ya hear?"

The light shimmered off of Grandpa's silver coin as he tossed it into the wet air and it floated down softly like a feather into Kathryn's hand. "Whole," she said. "Got it!"

"Later, Gramps!" said Billy, pulling his flimsy black hood

over his head and stepping out into the fine soft day.

"Ta!" replied Grandpa.

Kathryn lifted up the hood of her mangy green raincoat, placing it snuggly over her head. Swiftly, she zipped it up over her mis-buttoned cardigan and dashed out into the rain after Billy, who had already begun his trek down the road. The door of the cottage slammed shut behind her. Sweet Kathryn's brown shoes kicked up high as she danced up and down around the wee puddles of water scattered along the drive.

Shadows of bushy sheep and lethargic cattle, chewing on soggy hay, sprinkled across the rolling green landscape. The road led up to a lovely stone chapel with an isolated tower lingering on a lazy hill. Cold tombstones scattered across its yard and lay fallen like forgotten orphans from a war long ago. Kathryn and Billy continued on hopping along the lane skipping between the murky puddles.

"All it does is rain here. There's nothin' to do. You've got sheep, cows, mud, rain, some dead people buried a bazillion years ago in forgotten cemeteries, churches, and some more sheep!" said Kathryn miserably, following Billy's footsteps. "This is my life of excitement? My life as an Indiana Jones apprentice?" She lifted up her mud covered shoe, "Muddy shoes?"

"Well, there's nothin' stopping you from climbing Arthur's Seat," he replied unexpectedly.

"Just the weather and Grandpa!"

"And maybe a little thing called courage," he muttered.

A cold hard wind roared over the both of them, muffling his words.

"What did you say?" she asked, not hearing what he had said, due to that pesky cold wind.

"Nothin'! Come on..."

Kathryn sprinted up alongside Billy and playfully bumped him, knocking him aside. Billy's weight teetered slightly and once he recovered his balance, he returned the loving shove.

The rains trickled down over their drowned heads. Down the road, a medieval stone bridge arose through the soggy air; its stones speckled with a light green moss and flowering plants of wild thyme and red valerian shooting out in all directions. Soon, they approached the thunderous roar of water raging down a rocky river from Arthur's Seat. Like a multitude of soldiers, the water crashed down upon its enemy in a deafening constant assault, its wrath now silenced by the rain. Up yonder, further up the fierce river surge, sat a wayward island, breaking the pounding river into two. A thousand and one twisted bushes criss-crossed between scarce abandoned trees.

"You see that!" cried Billy pointing up the river to the lonely island.

"What? The island?" said Kathryn.

"Yeah, Mugs says you can walk along the river and then cut over after the island and you'd be back at Gramps in half the time!"

"Really? Cool! We'll have to check that out!"

The two wet rats turned away from the island and gazed through the dense mist of rain. Out of the corner of Billy's eye, he spied some shadowy figures just on the edge of town. "Who's that?" he said curiously.

"Who's what?"

On a low-lying path just on the cusp of Ballyrun, through the thickest air, they could barely make out a thin wiry fellow accompanied by two youngins. "Them over there," said Billy.

"What's he looking at?" questioned Kathryn squinting her eyes tightly together. "Seems he's holding an instrument? Is that Mr. Hewson?"

"Nah, Mr. Hewson is all old and such!" replied Billy.

"Hmmm. Whatever! I'm freezing! Can we go?"

Kathryn and Billy ignored the stranger on the edge of town that gloomy morning not knowing why he was hunched over and speaking to two children, pointing his finger at Ballyrun. It was just another tourist rolling by, or perhaps it was a tinker telling stories about Arthur's Seat, earning a quick quid for his pocket, but that day they would never know.

It is said that folklores are not only handed down by boisterous Seanachaí, a traditional Irish storyteller, but they are also handed down through songs, words and music. Perhaps that is why Kathryn and Billy had always sung the silly songs their mother Laurel had taught them when they lived in Brooklyn. Or perhaps, it's because they missed her so much, but nonetheless, they sang them anyway, any chance they got.

"Two feet Susie!" giggled Kathryn taking two steps forward.

"Three feet Willie," Billy took three steps.

"Four feet early!" she waddled four steps ahead.

Then they both screamed, "*Jump!*" leaping into the air and splashing down into the squishy mud, spraying it everywhere, including their clothing.

"What a silly song! Mom always had the strangest songs. Come on then!" said Kathryn firmly, as the two walked towards town.

Across from the stone bridge arose the enchanting town of Ballyrun; it was a faerytale idyllic Irish town. On the corner was the post office where Mr. and Mrs. O'Keefe engineered the daily ins and outs of the evening post. Letters that arrived via truck bright and early in the morning would be sorted straight away, while Mrs. O'Keefe would go door to door within the town, delivering the mail to each person. If the names weren't written in proper format with your precise name, Mrs. O'Keefe would wait for a signed release order form from the sender even if there was a slight typo. So, any mail that went to Margaret O'Sullivan had to be 'Margaret O'Sullivan,' not her nickname, 'Peg'. Unfortunately, for Mrs. O'Sullivan this made her life a wee bit difficult and many hard words were spoken between Mrs. O'Keefe and Mrs. O' Sullivan on that precise topic. All other letters, outside of the town, were handled by Mr. O'Keefe and his beloved, Jezebel; a sturdy donkey that carried the letters up and down the nearby hills of Ballyrun to any inhabitants on the outskirts of town.

Next door to the post office was the bookstore, Crawely's it was named, a Mr. Sodge Crawley was the proprietor. He was known, of course, for being the only person in town who hadn't cracked a smile since 1968 and that was because Mr. Hennessey, the butcher, had accidentally set fire to his beard one night after drinking a few too many nips of whiskey with his cider.

Next door to Crawley's was Hennessey's butcher's shop, where the whole town would get their fill of chops, bacon, mutton, and any makings for a delectable Ballyrun stew. Only a few families knew the true recipe, which had won many blue ribbons at the annual festivals west of the Shannon.

Then there's the Dimmler's General Store where Mr. and Mrs. Dimmler, along with their daughter, Mary, always have grand smiles on their faces with a chipper 'good morning to you,' when a patron walks through the door.

Their neighbor was the barber, Micky Cavanaugh, or as some people called him, 'Nicky' Cavanaugh. He was a good enough barber, as decent as a man could be. He had learned his trade very well, but he began to lose his edge when he began to frequent Finnegan's Wake a few too many times in the course of the week. This in turn, caused his hand to shake and after a few sporadic wayward cuts of his scissor's blade upon his patrons' head, he earned the nickname, Nicky.

Further on down the main road was St. John's Church whose steeple could be seen from five miles away (Only if it was a very clear day and you were standing on a very tall building, on the highest part of the roof with very powerful binoculars, and you squinted quite hard, you could see the teeny-tiny upper most part of the steeple. Of course, then again, you might not see it at all, but eyes of a hawk we all do not have). Now, St. John's Parish was the pride and joy of Ballyrun and most importantly there was the very small alabaster cup that Fr. O'Toole cared for every day and was believed to be the Holy Grail itself. Though no pilgrims ever visited Fr. O' Toole's cup and no miracles were ever performed, though he tried many, many, many times! Did I say many times? Indeed I did, many times!

Next to St. John's was Ballyrun's school, a place of learning, creativity, and play. Many clever minds came out of Ballyrun's school: the Browne family, known best for their quick-witted political debates; as well as the McSweeneys, also a very articulate family. Cesar McSweeney, himself, went on to be a very notable and distinguished barrister in Dublin, fighting for the good of children's welfare. The Buckley's, too, are a very renowned entrepreneurial family, opening up over a dozen pubs around Ireland. And how can I forget the noble Lott family that came here from Belfast a few years back? Their children currently attend the Ballyrun School as well.

Now back in Ballyrun, staring aimlessly into Crawley's store front, Kathryn smushed her lips to the side, quietly contemplating the stellar books laid out before her; William Butler Yeats, George Bernard Shaw, Samuel Beckett, and Seamus Heaney. Suddenly, *Bam!* Kathryn crashed forward into the display window at Crawley's, nearly chipping her tooth against the glass.

"Whoa there buddy! Take it easy! You almost made me drop the precious whole milk!" she said sarcastically, clenching a plastic bag with the green lettering *'Dimmler's'* splashed across it. "Meet up with you in ten?"

"Deal," replied Billy promptly and darted down the road.

Kathryn gently turned the doorknob and entered the shadowy bookstore. The smell of musty papers filled the air and her heart sang with each sniff she breathed in. On the inside of the Crawley's however, the books were definitely not as organized as the store front window had displayed them to be. In fact, it was quite the opposite; books were carelessly piled up on the floor alongside the bookshelves and sloppily placed on their side so no one could read the titles. Kathryn grazed past the bookshelves as puffs of dust danced in the streaming light from the tall iron lamps that were situated randomly throughout the store. Fat and thin books were glued together, appearing as one, as her eyes hunted the bookshelves, trying to figure out what book area she was in. Seeing no soul in sight, she slipped closer toward the back and snooped around a stack of old warped books, silently lifting the top one off its home. Brazenly, she blew a pile of dust off the cover and ran her fingers over the title.

"The Lost," she whispered, "Treasure of the Knights T...," Kathryn licked her forefinger and began to smear away the years of filth.

"May I be of service?" said a dull voice ringing out from amongst the books. Kathryn froze in place, feeling as if the principal was summoning her into his office.

"Ummm, yeah," she uttered, covertly placing the book down back to its home. "Sure, I was looking for a..." gradually she turned around to see a pale, lanky man. It was Sodge Crawley, the mind-numbing, feeble proprietor of Crawley's bookstore. *Oh no, not Sodge*, she thought to herself. "Yeah, a book."

"A book?" he said harshly. "How very original."

"Yes," she said moving forward. "A book on... ummm... on Arthur's Seat?"

"Arthur's Seat?" he said stiffly and walked back to the counter.

Kathryn followed, "Yeah, or ummm... maybe something on.... red-winged ravens?"

Then, out of the corner of her eyes, she spied a tiny yellow book with the emblem of a seal sitting on top. In the blink of an eye she snatched it up, shook off the dust and then wiped the cover discreetly.

"Young lass," he said sternly, propping his glasses further up on the bony bridge of his nose, "that's very expensive."

She placed the yellow book back on the shelf. "Oh! Or perhaps Aählyéé?" she asked.

"Rubbish!" he replied severely, shaking his head so hard his stringy combed back hair fell down to his lips. "Young lady this is a proper bookstore! Not a bookstore on silly myths and legends." He slid his hair back over his bald spot and leaned forward with his lips quivering. "We deal with facts young lady, just facts!"

"But, don't you have books on folklore?" questioned Kathryn.

"No!" he said curtly, setting himself back down in his sturdy chair. "Though, you may want to try Mrs. Flannery's on the corner." He pulled his jacket taut. "Yes well, she deals with less meaningful things."

"Great!" she said excitedly and exited through the door. "Thanks, later!"

"Later?" he said, perturbed while huffing, "Americans!"

Kathryn ran four stores down and across the street to one of the local pubs. A charming dark wood exterior framed the premises; a large burgundy painted plank of wood framed the top. In gold painted letters it read: FLANNERY'S.

Kathryn pushed the front door open, to her right a plaque read: *Flannery's: Where Great Minds Come to Meet.*

A wee bell jingled as Kathryn entered the darkened pub. To her left ran a long dark bar with a petite, golden haired woman standing behind it, gabbing about the day's stories with a few of her prized patrons.

Now, Flannery's was not your traditional publick house. No, Flannery's was a bit eccentric as compared to the more proper Finnegan's Wake, which was just right up the road. It was Fiona Flannery who made Flannery's the exceptional publick house that it was, with all of her oddball paraphernalia that she had collected throughout the years. The timber beam ceiling at Flannery's was crammed with all of Fiona's unconventional knick knacks, such as her obscure Irish scenery photos with sheep's backsides grazing in the lush Irish fields along stone fences; wee hairy highland cows posing for pictures with straws of grass dangling from their mouths surrounded by large stone circles; old newspaper clippings from the 1930's with long bearded explorers holding up unusual round disks as they posed with grins on their faces and large amounts of mismatched books lining the walls. Even stranger objects, such as a child's stool; a 1930's maroon typewriter with five missing keys; a black metal oil lamp with its handle torn off; a small, hundred year old iron rusted through; a 1920's camera with no lenses; crusty old jugs of whiskey; a beautiful vintage violin; a damaged accordion; a bodhrán that the old minstrels would play on; some scruffy old boxes of luggage with stickers that read: 'Lisbon,' 'Cairo,' 'New York,' 'Belfast,' 'Florence,' 'Rio,' and 'Dublin'; a clunky old radio receiver; a broken golden compass missing its magnetic needle; copper and colored glass bottles; and nailed to one of the highest beams were seven silver keys arranged in size order from largest to the smallest. Indeed, Flannery's was a unique publick house and its proprietor Fiona was even more unique, for she was the town's local news or as some say, gossip.

To Kathryn's right, a warm fire burned brightly and an elderly man who had seen many years of tilling this grand earth of ours sat quietly in the corner drinking his afternoon tea. A splendid assortment of papers and books lay scattered in disarray over the table where he sat. A hefty, robust, dark haired sort of a man sat somberly at the bar with a fresh pint securely grasped in his hands, his cherry red face growing darker with each sip.

Mrs. Flannery was busy cleaning glasses behind the bar and called out, "Another spot of tea for you, Mr. Hewson?"

Mr. Hewson, surrounded by a mound of bizarre papers and books, swirled his cup around and slurped up the remnants of his lovely tea. A rogue drip of tea trickled down his chin. As he used his napkin to wipe it clean, placing his cup back down he said, "Aye! Another would be lovely, Fiona."

Kathryn pensively approached this dapper old man whose hands were riddled with time. His gentle eyes sparked her curiosity as she hovered over the scattered papers and Mr. Hewson's eyes caught hers. He leaned toward her and said charmingly, "How powerful it is to have your words written down," his cracked fingertip pointing down at his papers. "Generation upon generation will read your thoughts and your ideas." Shifting back into his seat, he smiled and then winked at Kathryn. "'Tis a powerful thing, is it not?"

Now Kathryn, awed with his presence, did not know what to say, so she just smiled serenely and nodded her head up and down.

Scooping his pen up with his right hand he said insightfully, "What a pen and ink and a few strokes of the hand will impact upon generations. Children and adults will hear you in their minds forever! Long after you are just a song whispering in the night's wind."

Kathryn's eyes enlarged with alarm and she began to pull away.

"You see," he said eagerly. "I could write incredible things, romantic words, and a poetic sonnet perhaps, stories of horror and ghouls and many will read my words," he shifted his body forward and firmly stated, "but, it takes the wisest and strongest writer to write passages that will change a man, touch a soul, and enrapture a heart for good. · YES! It could be anyone's destiny to write well, to inspire the spirit. That, my lady is a true legacy! So, choose your path wisely and seek it well, for many have a path to choose; for it is the path of a wise man that is never seen, until his journey has ended. As my father's father's father would say, anybody can make history, but only a great man can write it!"

"Do know anything of Arthur's Seat or of Aählyneé?" she asked hesitantly. "Or the Fire Crystal?"

"Ahhh... Yes, it is the jewel that can't be got that is the most beautiful!" he chuckled. "My dear, I have an inkling that you believe in these stories of far off worlds of great mountains, wide valleys, and mystical powers, don't you? They are stories handed down through generation to generation by word of mouth, by great bards who tell of these tales during wartime and of course, they are also told by the Seanachaí, the lone Irish storyteller who will travel from cottage to cottage to tell them to the younger generations. But no, I'm afraid they are just myths and legends; they are not real. Look, a man can have his fill of drink and traveling home that night in the dark with only the moon to light his way, he sees a shadow, hears a noise, then suddenly it was a faery he saw! A giant! A banshee! I'm a folklorist love, and I know many stories, myths, and legends. I have not seen one yet to be true, but I'd be an unemployed folklorist if I didn't encourage my tales and stories. Besides, they're just plain old fun! Life would be boring if you didn't believe in dreams."

Mrs. Flannery approached the table and picked up Mr. Hewson's cracked tea kettle and teacup, replacing it with new ones, and leaving a sweet bowl of sugar on the table as well, smiling warmly as usual.

"Here's your tea, Mr. Hewson," then, turning to Kathryn, she said cordially, "Mornin' love! And what can I help you with?" She wandered back to her bar, picking up some wet glasses which she had cleaned earlier and with a bleached white towel began to dry them.

"Uhhh..." she said timidly. "Do you have any books on... ummm... uhhh... The Legend of Arthur's Seat?"

Fiona placed her glass down and leaned against the bar. "Oh!" she said beguiled, "The Legend of Arthur's Seat, hmmm... Well, I know we had one but, no, no, I'm afraid I just sold the last one about a week ago. Interested in the Legends of Arthur's Seat are you now dear?"

"A bit."

"Me son Ian, he's a very special boy, used to love those stories his father told him, about Aählyneé and Koréna, even tried to climb it once," she said amusingly.

The large red-faced man at the bar turned his head toward Kathryn, grunting, "That legend, 'tis nothin' but rubbish!" he said to her disdainfully, taking a mouthful of his pint. His cheeks were now an exceptional shade of tomato red.

"Climbed it?" Kathryn asked Mrs. Flannery.

"Arthur's Seat dear," she said, placing a glass down and picking up another.

Meanwhile, the bell on Flannery's front door chimed once more and in walked Billy Murphy, rubbing his hands fervently up and down his chubby arms, as his teeth chattered from the cold damp air.

"It's *fah'reeezzzing* out there!" he cried, making his way to the warm roaring fire.

Mr. Hewson sat up straight away upon Billy's presence by the fire; discreetly he turned to Billy and with a wily whispering voice said, "I heard there's a road of two rivers that leads right up the Mountain."

Billy moved his bum closer to the hot peat fire. Bewildered he asked, "A road where?"

Leaning into Billy, Mr. Hewson shoved his papers aside saying excitedly, "Arthur's Seat me boy!"

Billy sharply turned to Kathryn and said exuberantly, "You're gonna climb Arthur's Seat? Sign me up!"

"The weather will be good tomorrow for ya lad, only a slight chance of rain," noted Mr. Hewson.

"Did ya hear that Kat?" called Billy.

"You're both bloody bonkers if you think you can climb that Mountain," grunted the man at the bar who was now a deep strawberry color. "There's a Fomorian that guards it you know?"

"A what?" whimpered Kathryn.

"A GIANT!" he said loudly, pointing up towards the Mountain, "He took a bite out of that stone fort on the lower hill. You can still see that mammoth bite from here!"

"There's no Fomorians up on that Mountain, Mr. Kennedy! And I thought you said you didn't believe in all this rubbish?" interjected Fiona.

Mr. Kennedy made a bitter face and stared into his pint.

"Now Kathryn, I'll tell ya, me son, Ian. He climbed all the way straight up to the northern cliffs, camped there into the wee hours of the morning and was woken up by this horrible howling noise. A massive beast chased him all the way down the Mountain, until he hit your farm."

A snicker bellowed from the red-faced man as he spitted into his pint, "And now he's a fruitcake!"

Then off from the overly cluttered wall, a dark fly landed upon Mr. Hewson's sweet sugar bowl right next to his teacup. Both Billy and Mr. Hewson glared at this wee fly and then caught one another's eye.

"Did you know flies find sugar with their feet?" said Billy informatively.

"Really?" replied Mr. Hewson.

"Yeah... The housefly's feet are ten million times more sensitive than a human's tongue."

"You're a bug man aren't cha?" said Mr. Hewson.

Billy guardedly opened his burly jacket to show tiny pockets filled with an assortment of jars and crawly things squirming inside them.

A sharp creak echoed from the back door of Flannery's, turning the patron's heads. A hefty strawberry blonde man with squirrelly eyes entered the publick house. He had a face on him only a mother could love.

"Ian, me boy!" cried Fiona wholeheartedly, running to the back of the pub to see her son.

"What happened to special?" snorted Mr. Kennedy into his pint.

"We were just talking about Arthur's Seat and when you

went up there dear," said Fiona.

Ian's eyes swirled around the room; his left eye lingered for a moment on Mr. Hewson, while the other one looked straight ahead. "Aye," he said dizzily, with spit spewing out as he spoke. "Twas a fierce beast I'z seen... A huge white dragon with no wings." Ian's eyes landed on Kathryn while he leaned in to stare at her miss-buttoned sweater.

Kathryn promptly pulled away, to avoid the extra spray from his mouth. "Dragon?" she said curiously.

"Aye! A dragon with..." he said spluttering into her face, the spit landing just an inch from her eye.

She rolled her jacket cuff up and wiped the salvia from her face.

Silently, Ian looked into space while the words missed his mouth, "A dragon with..."

Fiona stepped in closer and said inquisitively, "With what dear?"

"With what Ian?" stirred Mr. Hewson.

"With...." he replied.

"Awww.... for Pete's sake.... come on, out with it man!!" cried Mr. Kennedy rudely.

"With," he whispered absentmindedly. "Fluff!"

"Told ya, he was a fruitcake! And you've got a head on ya like a bag of spuds!" snickered Mr. Kennedy.

Being Ian's mother and all, Mrs. Flannery immediately shot Mr. Kennedy a fearful look, to which any reasonable person would not cross, so he carried on sipping his pint, turning redder and redder.

The front door of Flannery's chimed once more in the hush. This time a middle-aged man with blonde shabby hair hauling a shiny black guitar over his right shoulder stylishly sauntered into the pub.

"Seamus!" shouted Mr. Hewson joyfully.

"Seamus!" called Fiona.

"Hey, it's good to see ya my friends!" replied Seamus.

"Now, what can I get for you, Mr. O'Sullivan?" asked Fiona, skirting back behind the bar, picking up a pint glass.

"Kathryn and Billy Murphy! How 'da hell are ya!" said Seamus O'Sullivan gregariously.

"Hi!" said Kathryn.

"Hi? Hi? Is that all I get?" said Seamus perplexed.

"Hey, Mr. O'Sullivan," said Billy pulling away from the fire.

"Well now, 'hey' that's a bit of a modification from 'hi' and

I suppose it's a step up. So I will accept the elusive 'hey' as opposed to the 'hi!'" He rebutted cheerfully. "The usual Fiona, you know me I'm not that picky!" patting his hands on both of their backs. "And what of the two of you, here at Flannery's? Peg and the crew have been asking for you all day!"

"We're just talking about Aählynéé!" said Billy merrily.

"Here you go, Seamus," said Fiona placing a pint of sweet dark beer in front of Seamus.

"Aye, Seamus! Some serious conversations are being had here in this pub with these two!" declared Mr. Hewson.

"You don't say?" said Seamus, sitting down at the bar and cuffing his pint. "You're talking about the Otherworld, I bet!"

"'Da faery folk, they don't like to be spoken 'bout!" said Ian fearfully as he coward into the corner of the darkened room, his eyes wild with fear. "They hear you speakin' of them and then... they start searchin' for the ones that have been talkin' 'bout them you see... They'll find you and taunt you... over and over again, 'til they take you into their world. They'll make you their slave and in their world, of no time, you slowly forget who you are. In the realm of the faeries, you'll remain enslaved by them as they laugh at you, poke you 'til you beg for mercy, and make you do funny dances and sing their songs."

"IAN!!!" yelled Fiona. "That will be enough from you!"

"Told ya he was bonkers!" sneered Mr. Kennedy.

"And you too!" said Fiona severely. "Or you won't be gettin' another pint, ever!"

"Well," interjected Mr. Hewson, "he does have some of it correct."

"Really?" questioned Kathryn as she sat down next to Mr. Hewson by the warm fire. "How's that?"

"Paul, I don't think it's a good idea to talk to them about the Otherworld or Aählynéé!" said Fiona anxiously.

"Come on, Fiona," said Seamus. "It's just harmless folklore and it's always a good bit of *craic* to talk about it!"

"But," she retorted.

"But what?" he questioned. "Come on, let's see there Paul, I know that Aählynéé is said to be the Celtic version of heaven, where the dead in this world go to live."

"Aye! Seamus," he replied. "Aählynéé is a wonderful world hidden by mortal eyes. Some say, one can enter it through hidden portals that one moment are there and by night, or by the way of the moon, they are gone, vanished by the finder!"

"Vanished?" cried Billy. "Like into thin air?"

"Vanished!" replied Mr. Hewson, "like into thin air, wisped away into the night as if it never were."

"Some have called it Tír na nÓg, the land of eternal youth," interjected Seamus, "and time stands still for all who enter it! One never ages."

"And some even say special people gain powers being there," added Paul, "but that's just the Irish version of the Aählynéé, the Welsh version is called Annwn."

"Which was ruled by Arawn the Great," said Seamus.

"How do you know so much about Aählynéé?" asked Kathryn.

"Poppycock!" shouted Mr. Kennedy. "And it's all linked to Arthurian legend and the Holy Grail and perhaps Queen Maeve lives there too, along with the acclaimed Santa Claus to boot! You stupid girl, you'd believe anything they told you and it's all a load of bollocks!"

"It's folklore handed down through stories, word of mouth, it's all part of our Celtic heritage and it's not a load of bollocks," replied Paul. "Your mother knew Kathryn."

"*Silence!*" cried Fiona. "That will be enough from the three of you!"

Ian stood up, lingering over to the foggy window and said, "I'z can still hear its cry when 'da moon comes!"

"Right, Ian," said Seamus.

"Well, thank you!" said Kathryn kindly, heading for the door. "Thank you very much for all the information. I truly appreciate it."

"Kathryn! Billy!" cried Fiona. "Isn't it the two of yas birthday?

"Uh-huh," said Kathryn.

"Yep! Sure is," said Billy blissfully. "Well, today is hers and tomorrow's mine! We're only ten minutes apart though, but born on different days! Pretty weird, huh?"

"Definitely!" remarked Seamus.

"Well, then I must insist on a photo," said Fiona, reaching behind the bar for her camera, "just a quick photo of you and your brother on your birthday!"

Billy jumped next to Kathryn with a huge grin covering his face, holding up a small jar of forewing beetles, as Kathryn managed to coil a thin closed mouth grin. A bright flash of light blinded their eyes. "Perfect picture and you two look just lovely," said Fiona.

Billy quickly ran back to the table where Mr. Hewson was seated. Mr. Hewson leaned into Billy and whispered, "You know son, there are some interesting bugs up on that Mountain. Some that may astonish you!"

"Really?" Billy replied inquisitively.

"Ever hear of the pearl-bordered fritillary or the white fire dwarf?" he whispered.

Billy nodded his head yes as his eyes bulged like a frog ready to croak.

"Billy!" called Kathryn. "Come on, we need to go!"

Billy winked at Mr. Hewson and said, "Thanks!"

"Kathryn, Peg, and the crew will be expecting you! Won't you two stop in for a bit?" said Seamus. "I'm sure your Grandfather wouldn't mind!"

Kathryn opened the front door. "I'll try," she said.

The two walked out the door into the rainy day, the bell chimed again as the door closed.

"Those poor children!" whimpered Mrs. Flannery.

"Americans!" mumbled Mr. Kennedy.

"Their poor mother died on the way over here to meet their Grandfather. It's such a tragedy," cried Fiona. "No mother, no father..."

"They're holding up just fine Fiona," said Seamus.

Ian crossed the bar, staring out of the frosty window, and pressed his fat lips against the glass moving his mouth up and down like a crying beast.

"Who's the Grandfather?" asked Mr. Kennedy, his pint now empty.

"Old man Murphy," replied Fiona somberly.

"Old man Murphy, the recluse?" chortled Mr. Kennedy. "He's been old since I was a kid! Aye... That is a shame!"

The four members of the bar watched Ian as he grinded his teeth against the window.

Whack! Mrs. Flannery whipped her twisted bar towel on his buttock.

"Owww!!" he howled, jumping into the air, rubbing his backside furiously.

Mrs. Flannery, of course, turned around with a whimsical smile on her face as if nothing was wrong to face her patrons.

Mr. Kennedy shook his head and mumbled, "Told you, he was a fruitcake!"

CHAPTER FOUR
A KNIGHT'S TALE

Later on that day, it continued to be a strong, hard pour of rain, with pellets as sharp as knives spraying down across Kathryn's face. Her eyes, mostly water logged now, could scarcely see, nevertheless split apart to peer through the rain as it bled down from her forehead. Darting forward through the massive deluge of water, she finally caught up to Billy, who had taken it upon himself to lead the way. The soaked pair waddled themselves straight up the heavy, mud-covered terrain, to a crooked road, which coiled itself around an old stone barn and nestled snuggly between two smaller houses. To the left was a modest thatched cottage adorned with the loveliest of rose gardens; its prize roses from around the world garnished its beautiful perimeter with shades of lavender, pinks, and reds. While the other cottage had a particular scorching hot pink color painted quite heavily across its frame along with a bright green door and shutters to boot. Kathryn and Billy scuttled close together, while blurry dark shadows began to peer out from the old barn's murky covered windows. Kathryn out stretched her hand towards the wet doorknob on the barn's red front door, but before her hand could reach it, *swoosh*, the door flew wide open.

"Kat'ryn," cried a curly blonde haired man with glasses as thick as ice cubes that gingerly hung off his crooked nose. His head tilted downward and to the right and he wore a big fat red helmet on top. His arms warmly jolted forward out to grab hold of his beloved friend.

"*Whoaaa!* Well, hello to you too, George!" said Kathryn.

George shuffled himself slowly into Kathryn, flinging his warm arms around her tightly and tossing her body back as he hugged her.

At precisely the same moment, a soft fuzzy haired man, wearing a brown cap with its earflaps rolled up, ran towards Billy. His smile shined brightly as the morning sun, while his false teeth popped out from his upper palate as he began to clap repeatedly. His short stature was one of a large child. Even his blue eyes, which slanted upward, were even childlike. Yes, everything about Eddie was of pure, unaltered innocence, for he, along with George, was as some would say, truly special.

"Eddie!" said Billy happily, softly waving his hand from left to right, signaling a 'hi' sign.

Eddie beamed a denture filled grin and sweetly waved his hand left to right. In his other hand, he held an old mutilated coloring book with the pages falling out.

"What's that Eddie?" asked Billy, pointing to the book.

Eddie opened it up, exposing crayon colored pictures of knights and dragons.

"Did 'ya see me new bike Kathryn, did ya see it?" spluttered out George, lowering his head down, rocking his weight back and forth on his gaited knees, his hands wringing back and forth with anticipation.

"Did you get a new bike, George?' asked Kathryn.

"Aye, I did," said George tilting his head up, showing his sweet coffee eyes through his chunky glasses. His hands flopped downward as he grabbed Kathryn's forearm and he whisked her away from the doorway towards a dark curly haired woman sitting quietly at a large table, covered with paints and papers.

The room was vibrant and alive with colorful crafts and drawings, which decorated every wall; in one particular corner, upon an ever so teeny tiny table sat a larger than life paper maché of Arthur's Seat, with all its dark green crags glued on with soft moss. Next to it were other substantial drawings and sketchings of Arthur's Seat, a massive black stone fortress, the Stone of Destiny, and a collage of different characters adorned the posters.

"Oh, 'fer heaven's sake! Now, he won't let you go until you've seen his new bike," barked the dark haired woman with her fists resting firmly on her hips. "And it serves you right not coming for a whole bleedin' week!"

"I'm sorry Peg," replied Kathryn, shuffling across the floor with George.

"Sorry?" she replied disapprovingly, and sat back down at the oak table. "You'll be real sorry when he pulls you out into the bleedin' pourin' rain! That's when you'll be real sorry! Isn't that right, Marie?"

A gentle, elf-like girl dripped paper maché on top of a miniature fat, lazy dragon. Slowly, she raised her oversized bald head up, her fragile body aged to that of a seventy-year-old woman. "I think she'll enjoy it! She did just come in from the rain!" replied Marie with a sweet smile. "Perhaps, it's magical rain?"

"What?" cried Peg defensively. "Magic rain? There's no such thing as magic rain!"

"Yes, there is Mum! You even said so yourself!" said Marie turning to Kathryn. "Do you like my dragon?"

"It's very nice Marie," replied Kathryn, stroking her bald pink head.

"It's for my pen-pal John in England. He's turning twelve next month!"

"Magic rain!" huffed Peg. "There may not be any at this moment, but I suppose when the Nights of the Faeries comes this week, perhaps that rain will be magical. Better, Marie?"

"Yes! Much better, Mum!" replied Marie courteously.

"Aye!" said George. "Wh-wh-what stories d-do you have for us? Kat'ryn did ya - did ya see me drawings, Kat? Did ya? Did ya?"

"I thought I was going to see a bike?" questioned Kathryn.

"Oh, George made a lovely picture of knights riding white stallions today," said Peg. "Didn't ya now, George?"

"Ah, yes! Where's me picture Peg?" cried George as he shuffled to the back of the room. "Where'z me picture? I want ta show it ta Kat'ryn!" George snatched up a large drawing and raised it over his head and hurried back with his masterpiece. "Here!"

Kathryn studied the stick figure drawing of George, Eddie, Kathryn, Billy, and Marie who were drawn, sitting gracefully upon five white stallions dressed up like knights in regal armor.

"Wow! This is absolutely amazing, George," remarked Kathryn delightfully. "Good work!"

Billy stood over Kathryn's shoulder with Eddie lingering over her arm. "True excellence, George!" exclaimed Billy.

"I like how he made the tail of the stallion from chunks of lint from Eddie's furry hat," giggled Marie, while she drizzled a dark purple color upon her dragon, never allowing the paint to spill onto the table.

"And Eddie made one as well!" said Peg handing Eddie his picture.

Eddie smiled from ear to ear, losing the grip of his dentures only once as he grinned. Eddie waved his hands in to the air; he flopped his arms up and down like a bird and then pretended he had imaginary reins in his hands. And before you knew it, he was a knight riding a dragonfly, just like in his picture.

"Splendid work, Eddie!" cried Billy.

"Very nice and look, you even have long hair!" said Kathryn pointing to the fuzzy bits of Eddie's hat that were glued on to his head.

"*Yup!*" mouthed Eddie softly, as he shoved his hands into his pocket and teetered back onto his heels and then on to his toes.

"Y-you see Kat, w-we're knights j-just like King Arthur," exclaimed George pointing to Peg studying his picture. "Just like King Arthur she said."

"Yes, George," said Peg sweetly.

"Peg, you said they could be knights?" asked Billy perplexed.

"Peg?" questioned Kathryn.

"Well, you see..." said Peg sighing, holding up Eddie's picture, and examining it once more. "For some crazy reason," she paused, "I always had it in me head that people with disabilities, such as George, Eddie, and Marie..."

"I don't have a disability Mum!" exclaimed Marie. "I'm perfect the way I am!"

"That you are love, that you are!" replied Peg lovingly, hugging Marie snugly in her arms. "But, I've always had it in me head, maybe deep in my heart. You know, that place that tells you something's true. You know that place deep inside of you? Well, I just always believed that people like them, people with special needs, must have somehow lived or are to live this fabulous life."

"Like real knights!" exclaimed George.

Eddie threw his arms up in the air just missing his hearing aids and flexed his biceps tightly, mouthing with his lips, "muscles!"

"Did I ever tell you about my Grandma?"

"No," replied Kathryn inquisitively, "not that I recall."

Peg took a deep sigh and said softly, "Years ago, when I was just a small lass. Me Grandma used to tell all me brothers and sisters a story of a very special boy she met when she was just a wee child herself. Now, this was back in the day when tinkers traveled these rural country towns, in their wagons. These poor souls were in search of work, a place to lay their weary heads, and for a better life. It just so happened, that one day, a tinker family came riding into

Ballyrun on their raggedly old wagon pulled by a scruffy haired donkey.

"The whole town had come out to watch the new comers journey into town, their bodies' frail, almost skeleton-like, their clothing layered with mud from the road; the scraggly family, a father, a mother, and a young boy, like George and Eddie was truly special. My Grandmother described him to be around age fourteen, slim, tall, and more hair on his head than a hairy highland cow. His hands curled in like a claw and his legs were as crooked as a creek. He was most definitely slower than the boys his age and he was undoubtedly restless in his own skin. His mind may have been feeble, but his body was bursting with energy.

"They traveled through town wearily and made their way up towards Arthur's Seat. There, on the steep crags of the Mountain, they planted themselves and made a home there.

"My Grandma used to tell me as a child, she and her friends used to climb up Arthur's Seat towards the ruins of the old stone fort on the left bank. There they would spend their days exploring its crumbled walls and even found a dark tunnel underneath it that burrowed straight into the Mountain.

"The years had passed and soon the town's folk had all but forgotten about the lone tinker family that lived up on Arthur's Seat. So much so, that even when the parish priest was making his rounds for the Bishop's pledge, he'd even forget to ask them for a donation.

"Well, Grandma was as daring as ever when she made her way up to that fort with her friends one fine day. But, her friends being older and all, had more chores to do back home and left her up on that Mountain, all by herself.

"She said there was something in the air that day, something right, something that pulled her away. The sun was warm and bright, the air was crisp and fresh, and she decided to walk along the sharp crags on the southwestern side of the Mountain. It was a new adventure for her, she said. Going where she had never been, it was quiet and still, almost dreamlike. The only sound she heard was the rustling of a feisty fox, which was down at the base of the crag and she on the top. He was prancing back to his burrow with a limp mouse clenched tightly in his jaw.

"She stepped closer to the sharp edge of the crag, ever so carefully, watching the fox briskly cut through the high grass. She remembered hearing the pebbles cascading down the crag, startling the fox. Then before she knew it, her foot gave way, and she tumbled down the cliff. She recalls only bits and pieces of the fall, for she had hit her head pretty badly and she was in and out of consciousness all night. Her body was banged up gruesomely, bruised and bloodied with lacerations, her right leg was broken in two spots, and her left wrist was crushed from the fall.

"Unable to move at all, the darkness of the night soon came and the temperature plummeted. Her body shivered in the chill of the damp air, her fingers grew numb, and then it began to rain. Her skin began to turn blue and hypothermia was beginning to set in. She thought this was the end and death was near. No one would find her. No one knew she wasn't at the fort and that she had made her way to the rocky crags. This was it, there was no one out there, so she began to pray, and she prayed as loud as she could so that God himself would hear her.

"Hours passed, and night was leaving, her prayers rumbled louder and louder, and a fine soft mist rolled in with the dawn. Her eyes played tricks on her with shadows and light flickering off the dewy mist. She thought she had seen an angel's wings hovering over her through the mist, but it was just her mind playing tricks on her. Soon, her eyes grew heavy and began to flutter close, her voice softened to that of a whisper.

"Then suddenly, out of nowhere, a mysterious rider burst through the frosty morning clouds. He was a knight, with a sturdy sword, and shield to boot. The knight was dressed in a long white robe with a deep red cross on his chest. He scooped up my Grandma up and before she knew it, she was in a strange bed. Her wounds were tended to, her leg set in a cast along with her wrist. The strange knight sat patiently at her bed, waiting for her to awaken. When she did, he approached her; his face she knew in an instant, for it was that same tinker boy that lived up on Arthur's Seat. His legs were now lean and strong, his hands, no longer turned in like a claw and he was renewed. When she came off the Mountain, no one believed her, though she had the wounds and the casts to show for her fall, but, for a special boy like that, to be changed, like that? Well, it made no sense to any of the Ballyrun folk. They had all heard a million other silly stories about that Mountain and what it can do. They shunned her for few years, because she believed a special boy like that could be transformed into a knight. She left for University and traveled the world a bit, after a few years when she came back, it was as if they had all forgotten her story, and life went on as it always did.

"No one ever did see that tinker family again. I suppose they made their way into the Mountain, or perhaps they just rode over it, straight to the other side. It is but a shame that we don't know. God forbid if they died up there, all alone.

"And I have to tell you, to this day, me Grandma swears that tinker boy, all dressed up as a knight and such, rescued her. Though, she was probably delusional from the fall and all, and of course from the hypothermia, but it's a nice knight's tale to tell. Don't you think so?"

"Splendid, indeed!" replied Kathryn enthusiastically.

"So, we decided," said Marie, "that George and Eddie are to be knights because that's what they want to be and I am..."

"A princess," replied Peg, as she gently stroked Marie's cheek.

"No, Mum!" Marie replied curtly. "I am a warrior princess!!"

"Of course you are!" replied Peg.

"A warrior princess who rides through the night saving innocent people from the evil ones who search the lands to pillage and plunder!" said Marie passionately.

Eddie leaped up to his feet pointing to himself and mouthing the words with a slight murmur in his voice, "Me too!"

George's body began to rock back and forth harder and harder in his chair. "I'm a knight Kat'ryn," his voice quickened with every movement as he uttered, "I'm a knight, I'm a knight Kat'ryn... did ya hear that? I'm a knight, a knight, Kat'ryn. Yes, a real knight, just - just like d'ose stories you told us! I'm – I'm like d'em like d'em, Kat'ryn."

"You are, George. You are a real knight," replied Kathryn.

"Very chivalrous, George. A man to be reckoned with," remarked Billy.

"Oh, truly he is! With his grand steed, what a powerful horse to ride on," said Peg encouragingly.

"Very noble George. What do you think we should call you?" asked Kathryn.

"Oooo... I don't, I don't know?" replied George.

"George the magnificent?" shouted Peg.

"Nooo..." replied George.

"George the Great!" exclaimed Kathryn.

"George the Dark Knight?" cried Billy.

"George the Dragon Slayer!!!" exclaimed Kathryn out loud.

"Nooo..." replied George, "I-I like 'dem dragons. I do – I do..."

"George the dragon tamer," murmured Marie.

"Ohhh... I like d'at one! I like it! I like it a lot! I like it! The Dragon Tamer... I do!" said George excitedly.

"Then that will be it George! All hail George the Dragon Tamer!" proclaimed Peg.

"All Hail, George! *The Dragon Tamer!*" cried the group.

Eddie covertly made a gesture with his head towards the oversized dresser bursting with sticky glue, crinkled papers, and splattered paints. Peg gracefully nodded, letting Eddie know it was all right to proceed on. He slid the drawer open and pulled out two presents. The first was a slender box covered with vibrant prickly leaves; it seemed to have every leaf from the forest. The other one was a shiny red rectangular box that weighed at least a full stone.

"What's that, Eddie? What's that you have?" questioned George.

"It's Billy and Kathryn's presents, George," answered Peg.

"Aye! Yes," laughed George, with a sweet note in his voice, "Yes, d'at's right! We g-gotcha a present, Kat! I-I-I think you're gonna like it!

"You think I'm gonna like the present? Do ya, George?" repeated Kathryn.

"Yes, uhhh... yes – yes, I dooo!!! I think you're gonna like it!" said George.

"What about me?" cried Billy. "What am I chopped liver? Did you get me one?"

"Yes, uh-huh, yes, we did, Billy – we gotcha one as well! We did - we did."

"Good! I was startin' to feel a bit left out!" said Billy.

Eddie heaved the red box into George's hands and then handed the crispy foliage present to Billy.

Now, Billy, who has the patience of a Saint, did the complete opposite and ripped off the leaves off his present, in a matter of a nanosecond.

"Wh-what is it, Billy?" asked George.

And with a flick of his finger, he popped the lid on the box and pulled out a Swiss army knife.

"Hey! It's a nifty Swiss army knife!" he said cheerily, holding the sleek metallic knife up for all to see. "Swell!"

"*Yup,*" mouthed Eddie, teetering back and forth on his heels with his hands in his pockets.

"It's a Swiss army knife! Oooh... a Swiss army knife!" said George elatedly.

"George! You know perfectly well what we got him!" said Peg earnestly.

"Nooo..." shrilled George as he coward down lower in his chair, rubbing his eyes wearily with his right hand. "No – no, I-I don't."

"Yes! Yes, you do, George. You helped me to pick it out remember?" stated Peg.

"Ohhh nooo..." said George confused.

Peg raised her voice to be clearer, "You don't remember going into Dimmler's with Seamus on Thursday last and ordering the Swiss army knife?"

"Oh, yes!" exclaimed George merrily, sitting up straighter in his chair. "Yes! Yes, I do, I dooo... Peg, I do remember that!"

"Well, thank you, George," uttered Billy, "Eddie, Peg, and Marie."

"*Rule Number One!*" said Marie pointing to the Swiss army knife. "*Rule Number One!*"

"Aye! *Rule Number One!*" repeated George eagerly.

Eddie raised his pointer finger to Billy and Kathryn, mouthing, "*Number One,*" with a cheery smile.

"You're right!" Billy chuckled. "I almost forgot!"

"*Always be prepared!*" remarked Marie. "That's *Rule Number One*, isn't that right Kathryn? Be prepared?"

"Absolutely!" replied Kathryn firmly to Marie, "always be prepared!"

"Ohhh... Yes! We - we got him one, we did," said George, "We got Billy one! Seamus and me, they told us it was part of rule one. Aye, Seamus told me, yes, be-be prepared. He said, he did."

"I wanted to get you a fedora and a whip, Billy," said Marie. "But Dad says this was more practical."

"There's something else in the box," noted Peg.

Billy scurried through the box and pulled out five large pink packages.

"Double trouble bubble gum!" exclaimed Billy. "No way!!!

That's my favorite!"

"Now, they don't call it trouble bubbles for nothing, Billy. Just be careful! You don't want to come close to what happened last time!" said Kathryn wittily.

"What happened last time?" questioned Marie.

"Don't get me started!" said Kathryn comically. "But, one time when we were living in Brooklyn, Billy swallowed two *whole* packs of double trouble bubble gum!"

"What?" rebutted Billy. "Don't start, Kat!"

"Why not? You did swallow two whole packs!"

"Just - just open your present," remarked Billy trying to change the topic. "George is dying for you to open it, aren't you George?"

"Yes-yes, Kat, I've got - I've got your present!" said George, shoving the red present before Kathryn's face. Her finger wrapped around the box and slid along its smooth borders and then she pulled the package away from George. *Thud!* It crashed down to the table.

"Whoa!" she said startled, picking the package up from the table. "Wow, it's-it's really heavy."

"Very!" said Marie, imploring Kathryn. "Come on, open it up!"

Kathryn ripped the wrapping paper into the air, exposing a cracked leather book. Kathryn took her fingers and traced them across the decompressed gold lettering, which cut deep into the aged cover.

"*The Legends of Arthur's Seat* by Peoke Thumbdill," said Kathryn astonished.

"Peoke?" questioned Billy

"It's not exactly the standard edition of *A History of Celtic Myths and Legends*, or *The Mystical Magic of Celtic Legends*, or even the classic *Memoirs of a Banshee*, but it was your mother's favorite book about Arthur's Seat," said Peg, as she brushed Kathryn's hair. "She used to take it everywhere with her when we were children; seems like she believed its contents to be very factual. Personally, I think she liked the pictures and I think it will definitely help you with the Ballyrun Celtic Folklore Competition. Open it up and take a look."

"Open it!" exclaimed George.

"Hurry up and open it!" cried Marie.

"*Open,*" mouthed Eddie with his eyes beaming.

Kathryn's hands gently ran across the coarse bindings, which clamped the dusty pages together. "*The Legends of*

Arthur's Seat," she whispered and with a soft crackling of the rigid cover, she opened the book, letting out a dusty aspiration of air.

Crack! A bolt of lightning tore through the soggy sky and an earsplitting clap of thunder rattled the barn's walls, while the interior lights spookily flickered off and then on again. A wave of silence echoed throughout the room as all eyes expanded to full moons as they looked at one another.

Peg jumped to her feet and hurried over to the window. "That was just a wee too close for me," she said frightened and clenched her thick cardigan tightly together to her chest, her eyes looked out the window into the dark rain.

"Whoa..." murmured Billy and then exclaimed, "That was *AWESOME!!!* Hurry up turn to the next page!"

Kathryn flipped her fingers through the brittle pages, opening it to a page with glistening swords filled with diamonds, radiant emeralds, and sapphires, deep and blue as an evening's star. While great floating orbs of velvety blue, ruby red, and forest green hovered above; below each was the name of a province of Aählynéé.

Billy leaned in. "What does it say?" he asked.

"I-I w-want ta see Kat'ryn!" said George curiously, closing in to a small huddle.

"Well, it says, there are seven provinces of the great land of Aählynéé, each one controlled by a magic orb and sword. Hmmm..." Kathryn read aloud.

Her finger lifted up one of the tattered pages, and as she turned it, a grand picture of a magnificent snow palace appeared with crystal turrets, frozen moats, and icicles dangling in the windows. There, in the center, was the most beautiful woman they had ever seen. Strangely enough, she had light blue skin and jet-black hair. Sitting next to her was a large sapphire blue orb, a fluffy white animal with the head of a bear and the body of a horse, and in her hand was a sparkling diamond sword.

Billy pointed to the blue skinned woman and exclaimed, "Who's that? Nice outfit!"

"Tirana, the ruler of Snowden who guards and protects the orb of questions," said Kathryn.

Kathryn leisurely turned the page again, this time to an emerald green forest. A longhaired wizard made of cracked wood sat among tiny green colored newts and woodland faeries with an emerald orb suspended above him. He held on to an emerald sword in his hand. Kathryn continued,

"This is Nyaïn, the wizard of the Forest of No Return, who guards and protects the orb of fortune."

"So... like there's more than just the one story?" questioned Billy. "You know like there's more than just Koréna trapped in that Mountain and the red-winged ravens?"

"Wow!" cried Marie. "There's so much to Aählynéé!"

"Aye!" said George.

"Check that out!" said Billy pointing to a scaly black dragon with two horns perched on top of Nyaïn's shoulder. "He's got his own pet dragon! Can you believe it?"

Eddie flashed a bright smile to Billy and wiggled two fingers over his head like horns, imitating the creature's features. Billy chuckled and Kathryn turned to the next mysterious page. A quiet echo then hushed over the room as Kathryn gently broke apart two pages that were stuck together. The group marveled undoubtedly as strange markings began to appear before their eyes on the left page; images of wavy lines, swoops, and loops with strange dots and slashes were marked across the page. Images appeared of wee little creatures with enormously large ears and tusks shooting out of their mouths worked diligently inside and outside tiny houses of twisted wood, tree leaves, stones, and shady moss. The wee little folk worked heartily on their gardens of herbs, flowers, and saplings; while others were busy sewing patches on leathery vests, ripped shirts, and holey boots. Puffs of smoke wisped out of little chimneys where these wee little folks labored over their evening's tea.

"Look! Mum! They look like me!" giggled Marie, "But they're really – really tiny!"

"Yes, Marie!" replied Peg, "you'd be a giant there!"

"Me, a giant!" chuckled Marie, in her tiny frame.

"Wh-Wh-What's that Kat?" questioned George pointing to multiple sets of impish eyes looming through trees.

"Huh?" said Kathryn.

"Yeah, check it out there's like a bunch of fiendish eyes hovering all over those trees," said Billy worriedly. "Watching those little things! Is there a name for what they are? I've never seen anything like them before!"

"No, no, I don't see anything except all the weird writings on the other page. That probably tells you what they are!" replied Kathryn informatively.

"Well then what on earth are those evil demon like things staring at them?"

"Don't know," said Kathryn, "but they're seriously creepy!"

"Seriously," replied Billy.

Abruptly, a gale of howling wind blasted through the barn's front door, tossing leaves, twigs, and branches into the tidy room causing a great havoc. An indistinguishable figure emerged before the ghostly bunch, which had clutched together for comfort.

"Whew! There's a real squall out there today!" said the darkened figure.

"Seamus! Geezzz... you had scared us half ta death!" groaned Peg.

"Da!" exclaimed Marie, running into the arms of her father.

"My wee, Marie!" cried Seamus swooping his daughter up into his arms, while his soggy coat dripped on her pretty pink dress.

"Guess what?" said Marie excitedly.

"What?" asked Seamus.

"I'm a giant!" declared Marie.

"Really, are you now, love," said Seamus, kissing her forehead. "Aren't cha now?"

"Yup!" replied Marie.

"Big enough to terrify even the smallest unsuspecting colony of ants now that you are!" chuckled Seamus.

"No!" stated Marie, "I'm big enough to squash some wee little folks in Aählyéé that are smaller than me!"

"What's that?" said Seamus curiously.

"Come here now, love," said Peg, pulling Marie from Seamus, and then tipping her head to the side. "Go on... Have a look!"

"A look at what I'd might ask?" asked Seamus.

"K-Kat'ryn's book! See Seamus, look 'dere!" said George impatiently as he pointed at the leather bound book open on Kathryn's lap.

Seamus crossed the room, gazing down at Kathryn's book, confused. He said, "What's this you have?"

"It's called *The Legends of Arthur's Seat* Dad!" said Marie.

"Peg gave it to me for my Birthday!" said Kathryn with enthusiasm.

"You don't say?" replied Seamus. "Peg?"

"It used to be..." said Peg.

"Our, Moms," said Billy solemnly.

"Your, Mums?" repeated Seamus.

"Yes! Our Mums!" replied Kathryn.

"Well, let's have a look now!" said Seamus, as he nestled his way next to Kathryn. "So, show me whatcha got, but make it fast. Colin is stopping by to jam a few chords before we open for the Céilí Wednesday Night."

"Oooh.... I love 'da Céilí!" uttered George rocking back and forth in his chair, "I do... I do... I love 'da Céilí!"

"Show him the strange creatures, Kathryn!" said Billy.

"Well, we found these small creatures on this page," said Kathryn, turning to the picture of the wee little folk. "They're living in these fat and knobby trees and then there's these evil glowing eyes peering out from the dark woods behind them! Seriously *creepy!!!*"

"Let's have a see!" said Seamus, picking up the book and examining the page carefully. "Hmmm... Oh yes, funny little buggers aren't they?"

"And look here, there's some weird writing on this page," pointed out Billy. Seriously, *creepy!!!*"

"Yes! I see that!" replied Seamus.

"What do you think it is?" asked Kathryn.

"It's a bit of a mess isn't it?" said Seamus. "This writing?"

"Why do you think that?" asked Kathryn.

"Well, it's got all these spaces, ya see," said Seamus pointing to a few areas where there was no writing. "And I'm not sure 'bout you, but we in the western world try to write on the lines. There's no consistency with these scribblings at all. Can I call them scribbles?"

"Sure... I guess so," said Kathryn perplexed.

"There's absolutely no order to these scribblings and the spaces," declared Seamus.

"It is pretty messy, the writing!" said Billy leaning in closer.

"Maybe they're not words at all?" said Kathryn, still baffled.

"Maybe," said Seamus. "I bet you once you figure out what the scribblings actually are, the spaces will make more sense to you!"

"Great!" said Billy exhausted. "That's all we need now, another mystery!"

"Just a second now. Look here, in the corner..." Seamus pointed to three circles intertwined together. "I believe I've seen that Celtic symbol before, but I'm not sure where."

With that, the front door swung open fiercely and a dark haired man with glasses and a vanilla hued guitar strapped upon his back entered the barn.

"Cheers! God Bless all here!" he said poetically.

"Colin, me boy!" said Seamus exuberantly, slamming the book shut, leaping to his feet to greet his friend.

"'Tis a fierce one out there today, Seamus!" said Colin, shaking off the wetness.

"Colin get in here and sit for tea!" said Peg, taking Colin's jacket from him.

"Hi, Colin!" said Billy.

"Hi, Colin!" said Kathryn.

"Oh well, hello there, you two! And look who else we have here today, the beautiful Marie, the charming Eddie, and the resolute George!"

"Aye! Colin, hellooo!" replied George. "Wh-what does res-res..."

"Resolute?" repeated Colin.

"Aye," replied George. "Wh-what d-d-does 'dat mean?"

"Aye, George! Resolute means you are determined and unyielding man. Someone who is unwavering and by the way I see it, to be reckoned with!" replied Colin.

"It's a good thing, George," remarked Kathryn.

"Aye!" replied George, nodding his head.

"Well!" exclaimed Colin. "Shall we begin our session?"

"We should be heading back now," said Kathryn, standing up and grasping her new book securely to her chest.

"No! No!" exclaimed Seamus. "Sit and listen to us!"

"Just one song?" cried Billy.

"No, I think we'll be on our way!" said Kathryn.

Kathryn and Billy darted out once again on the lonely road down towards the village and still the rain sprayed down hard as if slivers of ice dusted across their faces. In the distance, three figures walked along the far road headed out of the town. Kathryn and Billy's eyes squinted to see the three indistinguishable figures more clearly, but the rain interrupted their view.

♦ CHAPTER FIVE ♦
A FINE POURIN' HAND

From the blackness of the night, a soft glow emerged slowly from within the wee cottage beneath the great Mountain. Peering through one of its cracked windows, one could see a big, fat waxy candle dripping onto a fluffy white cake covered in coconut. Sheba hovered next to it trying not to trickle any saliva from her unbridled snout. She snorted and then shook her mane wildly to shake off the pink and white polka-dot party hat that was placed haphazardly upon her head. Perhaps done, as what some of us might refer to as, a joke.

"Now Billy, go and get 'dat last light, 'dere in 'da corner," commanded Grandpa.

Billy limboed under Sheba's moistened lips, which smelled of the day's dirt and hay, then blew out the oil lamp.

Grandpa with a crystal glass of whiskey in his hand, raised it up high, and began to recite to Kathryn, "'Ta Kathryn, may you always have work 'fer your hands 'ta do, may your pockets hold always a coin or two, may 'da sun shine bright on your window pane, may 'da rainbow be certain 'ta follow each rain, may 'da hand of a friend always be near you, and may God fill your heart with gladness 'ta cheer you!! *Lá breithe mhaith agat sláinte,* Kathryn!"

Kathryn smiled and said coyly, "What does, *La-bree... mha...* mean?"

"It means happy birthday 'ta you... cheers!" he said delightfully, holding up his nip of whiskey and then slamming it down on the table next to a thimble sized glass of the amber liquid.

"Oh, ok," she said lamely, "and why is there a second glass of whiskey on the table?"

"Whiskey?" said Grandpa, taken aback from Kathryn's question. "Ahhh... Uisce Beatha!"

"Uisce Beatha?"

"Whiskey! It is the water of life!" stated Grandpa, waving his flabby finger at the small caramel colored glass of whiskey on the table. "And *that* is the Angel's share!"

"Gotcha," said Kathryn with a wink and then with the breath of a thousand winds she blew out the candles from her fluffy white cake.

Grandpa took a small gulp of his whiskey as Billy relit the oil lamp. Sheba wrestled uneasily at all the commotion, stomping her hind legs against the stone floor, nearly tossing her party hat off her head onto the cottony white cake.

"Ahhh," Grandpa sighed pulling out an old crusty pocket watch made of silver. "Just a sec 'dere now, Billy." Billy struck a match and re-illuminated the candles once again. "'Aw right now, get 'da lights out and come on back!" Billy once again slithered under Sheba's drooling mouth and snubbed out the oil lamp and then returned quickly to the table.

"Ummm," said Kathryn curiously, "aren't we going to eat it?"

Grandpa refilled his glass of whiskey from the dusty, black glass bottle and raised it once again, "We will - we will! Hold on 'ta ya 'orses!" he said, glancing at his ticking, rusty pocket watch once again. "Right, 'tis twelve now, now it's Billy's birthday!" And with that, he raised his glass up high. "'Ta Billy, may you have love 'dat never ends, loads of money, and lots of friends, health be yours, whatever you do, and may God send many blessings 'ta you! *Lá breithe mhaith agat sláinte,* Billy!"

Billy pumped his lungs deep like a bullfrog and blew out the candles with a fierce croak.

Grandpa gulped down his glass of whiskey again, his eyes now glazing over.

"Why do I feel gypped?" said Kathryn heatedly.

"'Tis best we share in 'da festivities," remarked Grandpa as he refilled his glass once more. "No need 'ta be havin' two cakes now!"

Billy began to slice up the frosty white cake, placing an extra hefty piece on his cracked plate.

"What's the big deal?" said Billy, his mouth jam-packed with cake.

"You know in Brooklyn it's still my birthday!" she retorted shoveling a plump piece of cake on to her fork.

"Well, you're not in Brooklyn anymore! Best be gettin' use 'ta 'dat idea lass!" grumbled Grandpa as he began to shuffle through the drawers under his bed. He reached deep underneath the headboard area and pulled out two small objects, wrapped in old newspapers. "Right!" he said as he rose to his feet, his face now red like a rose. "This one's 'fer you, me lady." He handed one of the gifts to Kathryn. "This one's 'fer you, Billy, me boy!" handing Billy his gift.

"Whatcha get, Kat?" asked Billy, watching her open her gift.

"A brush," she said disappointingly, holding up a wooden block with some stiff black bristles poking out of it.

"Now, that's not just any 'ol brush that you have!" slurred Grandpa as he swished another whiskey down. "'Dat 'dere is a fine 'orses brush! 'Da finest in all of Ireland it is – it is! You can use it on all sorts of 'tings! Like removin' 'dat caked on muck from your coats, its good 'fer your hair and 'fer scrubbin' down, Sheba." Grandpa settled down at the table and said to Billy firmly, "Here me boy," pointing to the bottle of whiskey.

Billy picked up the bottle and began to pour it for his Grandfather.

"You have a nice fine pourin' hand, me boy! Keep it comin' - keep it comin' 'tis a celebration 'taday! 'Da two of you growin' up before me eyes! I could barely keep up with ya! Now, your twelves!"

"Billy, what did you get?" asked Kathryn.

Billy ripped open his gift and said gleefully, "Hey, it's a horseshoe!"

"'Dat's right! 'Da best 'orseshoe in all of Ireland! It will bring 'ya much luck me boy! It will - it will!"

"Thanks, Grandpa!" said Billy appreciatively. "I'll put it on my bedroom door!"

"You're quite welcome! Splendid idea!" replied Grandpa.

"Yes, thank you for the brush as well!" said Kathryn glumly.

"Oh, we should show you the new book Kathryn got!" exclaimed Billy.

"Book?" said Grandpa strangely, as he sipped his whiskey generously.

"It's called *The Legends of Arthur's Seat*," said Kathryn mysteriously.

"'Da Legends of Arthur's Seat?" snickered Grandpa. "Oh, 'dat 'ting! 'Dat's just a load of bollocks! Why don't 'cha get a real one?"

"A real what?" questioned Billy.

"A real book boy!" exclaimed Grandpa. "Like, *'Da Mysteries of 'da Sidhe Revealed*. Now, 'dat 'dere is 'da best book in all of Ireland. 'Dat will tell you 'bout 'da faery folk!"

"Really?" said Kathryn hopefully, "that would definitely help with my report for the Ballyrun Celtic Folklore Competition! Where can I get one?"

"Geezzz.... girl! I don't know! It was destroyed years ago... as I recall! No way of knowin' what was in it!" said Grandpa dismissively.

"That's a shame," replied Billy.

"Well, I do know 'bout Danú," said Grandpa retrospectively.

"Who's Danú?" questioned Kathryn.

"Danú!" he said with a twinkle in his already glassy eyes. "Ahhh... yes, Danú! She's called 'da Queen of 'da Sidhe."

"I thought Kendryck was the King?" questioned Kathryn.

"No! No! Don't ya pay attention, girl?" snapped Grandpa.

"I'm so confused now," said Billy as he licked the crumbs off his plate.

"No, Kendryck was 'da King of Aählynéé! Danú is 'da Mother or Queen of 'da Sidhe! 'Da Sidhe is everything! All magic! Aählynéé is just a wee part of 'da Sidhe! Didn't I tells ya 'dat already?" wheezed Grandpa.

"No," replied Kathryn.

"Nope, don't remember that story!" said Billy, slicing an even larger piece of cake then plopping it on his plate.

"Oh?" said Grandpa humbly, as he wiped his nose with his finger, and took a deep breath. "Well, in 'dat case, I suppose I would be obliged 'ta tell ya something of, Danú? Danú is said 'ta be 'da oldest Celtic Goddess, she's 'da mother of all magic. Her magic extends far out beyond Ireland and 'da British Isles. All 'dose who followed her were called 'da Tuatha Dé Danann, 'da children of Danú. When she left our mortal realm all 'dose years ago, all of 'da children of Danú followed her into 'da mystical hills of Ireland and they too became immortal. And now, 'dey are called 'da Sidhe or 'da faery folk. Her rule over 'da Otherworld can never be defeated by any man, woman, or child. Hers is 'da legend 'dat continues on and on, hers is 'da magic 'dat one might see in 'da mist of 'da evening twilight. Hers is 'da presence of fertility and goodness throughout the land."

"Wow!" replied Kathryn, "I wonder if Peoke Thumbdill has anything in his book about Danú?"

"Peoke?" said Grandpa inquisitively, "Thumbdill, you say.... never heard of him!"

"I don't think many people have," said Billy stretching his arms over head and yawning, "with a name like Thumbdill."

Grandpa stretched his arms outwardly as well with the yawn of a lion. His eyes were heavy with sleep as he stood up and stumbled across the floor over to his bed, heaving deep into his thick covers. A mumble arose from his lips, "'Ta bed," and with that, he was fast asleep and snoring like a wart hog.

"Billy," whispered Kathryn, "come up to my room, I have to give you your present."

Billy and Kathryn *'shhhed'* Sheba not to make a sound, and then began to climb the wobbly ladder up to Kathryn's room and closed the door behind them.

"Whatcha get me?" asked Billy, plopping down next to the book on Kathryn's springy bed.

"Hold on!" she said edgily, cracking open the paint chipped cupboard's door in the wall, "it's in here somewhere!"

"*Da Legends.... of Arthur's Seat!*" said Billy in his best Grandpa impersonation and rested the weighty book on his wide lap. His ears perked up listening to Grandpa, who was beginning to mumble in his sleep, snorting, "Send 'em 'ta 'da dungeon!"

Billy smiled amiably, "He's got good dreams," and began to flip randomly through the pages, probing through its dark secrets.

Kathryn looked back at Billy, "Don't mess with that! I've found some great stuff in there about Aählyneé and I'm making a whole story board of what really is going on the other side of Arthur's Seat."

Billy's fingers carefully split apart two sticky pages, a picturesque woman wearing inky black feathers in her hair, was wearing the citrine necklace. The same seven-tiered citrine necklace, which Grandpa had hidden behind the portrait of his grandmother in the wall, below it read:

The way to the Raven's Gate is found by the departed,
Who search for their way home above the moors,
And for those who search for it may become broken hearted,
Those who are called to it will see its doors,
And by the birds of the sky, they shall lead you there in time,
For upon the rising of the Hawkmoon seven times,
The gate will open with the rap of three.

"Whoa... Kat!" roared Billy as softly as possible, "take a look at this! It's the necklace that Grandma's wearing. The one we saw earlier and what looks like a clue on how to find the Raven's Gate!"

Kathryn was on the floor deep into her cubbyhole of a closet throwing boxes of debris on to her floor, "What???" she mumbled.

"Hmmm," he said flipping a few more pages. "What's this?"

"Found it!" she called out from the cubbyhole and began to wiggle out.

Billy skimmed the pages of what appeared to be scratchy lines up and down Arthur's Seat. His eyes danced along with the words that seemed incomprehensible, but in his mind they made sense.

> *Where there is no sea in sight,*
> *One can see the wind of light,*
> *Let no man fall asunder,*
> *Go to the gap of wonder.*

"Here ya go!" said Kathryn holding a clear box filled with sandy soil.

"What is it?" inquired Billy.

"It's a doodlebug," replied Kathryn as she held up a jar of ants, "and plenty of ants to feed them for a month!"

"No way!" exclaimed Billy.

"*Shhh...* keep your voice down. Grandpa will hear you," she said scolding him.

Grandpa just turned over and garbled, "wretched little beasts... stealin'..."

"Nah! He can't hear nothin'," stated Billy. "I can go down there now and play a trombone and he wouldn't hear a thing!" Billy smirked and then winked. "I have a fine, strong pourin' hand!"

"Stealin'... I found you now..." snorted Grandpa.

"See, can't hear a darn thing! I feel bad, I don't have anything for you," said Billy sadly.

"Oh?" sighed Kathryn.

"Well, I was going to get you a fedora just like Indiana Jones wears, but – but, it was on back order," said Billy sadly.

"It's ok, Billy," she replied. "I'm used to being let down by you. It comes with the territory!"

"Awww... Come on, now!" he said loudly. "I don't always let you down?"

"Grab 'em - grab 'em!" grunted Grandpa, waking Sheba from her sleep. "Wretched little beasts... I have you!"

"Wow, he can sleep through anything can't he?" she said astonished. "What about on the boat trip over here?"

"Come on," said Billy, "that's ancient history! Listen, I promise I'll order you that fedora!"

"Even though it's on back order?" said Kathryn.

"Yup! I promise!" answered Billy.

"I think I've heard that before too!" replied Kathryn.

"I'll make it up to you, Kat! I promise!" said Billy with a wink. "And you can take that to the bank!"

◆ CHAPTER SIX ◆
MISS SHELIZA LOTT

Morning cracked into the dim cottage through a small jagged hole in the shutter. The morning's light pierced the silence in the home, all except for Grandpa who slumbered on. Kathryn and Billy now began to stir into their daily regime as Grandpa tossed and turned in his dreams with a few more grumps and snorts, snuggling deeper under his squishy duvet.

"Should we wake him?" inquired Kathryn as she cut a thick piece of bread and slid it into her mouth.

"Nah!" said Billy, holding Sheba's reins and escorting her out the door. "Last night was the most excitement he's had in a long time. Let him sleep off the whiskey!"

And before you knew it, the two of them were off, down the road and heading to school.

Kathryn and Billy took their seats on the cold, wooden desks in the back of the bleak classroom as the bell tolled for the last time. The teacher Mrs. Mackenzie was already at the blackboard writing down the day's work.

A quirky, short neck boy sat down next to Billy, his hair clumped down with grease and dirt, a slight foul stench emanated from his clothing, if one, of course, were to ever get a little too close.

"*Psst!*" called the smelly boy to Billy.

"Yeah, Mugs?" replied Billy softly.

"Hi, Mugs!" said Kathryn good-naturedly.

Mugs rolled his eyes over Kathryn's misaligned buttons, which caused her sweater to be off center and then glanced down at Kathryn's mismatched brown and black shoes. "Nice shoes! I 'ave a pair just like 'da brown one," he said, and then turned to Billy. "Are ya goin' to be enterin' into the competition 'fer Wednesday?"

"No," replied Billy.

"No?" he question, "why 'da bloody hell not? It's just 'da most important contest this town has seen!"

"Well, I'm not!" replied Billy. "But Kat will be entering it!"

Kathryn grinned at Mugs.

"But she's just a bleedin' girl!" replied Mugs snidely, "What can she do?"

Mrs. Mackenzie turned around from the blackboard and began clearing her throat stridently, signally Mugs to sit up straight and to face the front of the classroom. It was that or be given detention with Fr. O'Toole where he was surely to be bored to tears hearing all the stories of his wee alabaster cup, also known as the 'Holy Grail' of Ballyrun.

Just then, the classroom door opened and in sauntered a regal, hoity-toity kind of woman with short, blunt black hair, her chin held up high; though upon further inspection no neck was to be seen lifting it up. Behind her was a young lass, her hair spun like fine gold, her eyes pools of crystal blue; she was perfection in every way. The young lass sat down in the front of the class, making eye contact with Kathryn with a cruel look in her eye.

Mrs. Mackenzie announced to the class, "Class we have a visitor today, Mrs. Enda Duffy. Now, Mrs. Duffy, as you all know is putting together the Ballyrun Celtic Folklore Competition, which is this Wednesday to commemorate the beginning of the Nights of the Faeries and she is going to fill us in on what to expect for the competition, Mrs. Duffy!"

Kathryn sat up straight in her seat as if she had swallowed a crowbar and with great zeal, she listened to Mrs. Duffy.

Well, when Mrs. Duffy opened her mouth and began to speak she showed the overbite that even a rabbit would be jealous of. "Good morning, class!" she said pleasantly.

"Good morning, Miss!" said the class in unison.

"Well," she said disappointingly, stepping in front of Mrs. Mackenzie and leaning on her desk. "I've heard better welcomes than that before, but it will have to do for now. Next time, let's hear a sort of joy to your, *good morning*, shall we? Now, this Wednesday, I am proud to be running the Ballyrun Celtic Folklore Competition, which will be held here at the Ballyrun School in the cafeteria at precisely nine o'clock in the morning on Wednesday. All students are welcome to enter into the competition. The winner will be judged on creativity, eloquence, and presentation of their personal interpretation of local Celtic folklore. Now, mind you students that just because we live in the shadow of one of Ireland's most infamous folklores does not mean you should only choose that legend. There are many other myths, legends, and folklores to choose from! Isn't that correct, Miss Lott?"

The golden haired girl smiled sweetly. "Yes, Mrs. Duffy!"

she said enthusiastically.

"Good Sheliza! Now, students that's the way you answer a teacher like myself!" said Mrs. Duffy as she scanned her trolling eyes around the room and pursed her lips like a button. "Right! So, judging will be done by myself, a Mr. Sodge Crawley, of Crawley's bookstore in town, and Mr. Paul Hewson, our local historian and folklorists. Top prize is one hundred pounds and a special field trip up Arthur's Seat, to what Mr. Hewson believes to be, the Stone of Destiny, and finally a lovely plaque and ribbon to commemorate your first place award! So, now children... any questions?"

A frail little girl with dirty blonde hair wearing a knitted cap threw her hand up into the air immediately.

"Yes!" said Mrs. Duffy pointing to the little girl.

"Yes, Mrs. Duffy are we expected to have poster boards and pictures?" she said softly.

"Honey, if you have visuals, you're more likely to win aren't you?" answered Mrs. Edna Duffy. "But it's whatever you want it to be."

Kathryn threw her hand up rapidly into the air.

"Yes, young lady!" said Mrs. Duffy.

"Will there be any points on the accuracy of the legend at all?" asked Kathryn.

"No," said Mrs. Duffy firmly. "Were you *not* paying attention young lady? Miss Lott can you please tell this young lady what you will be judged on!"

Sheliza turned around and with a spiteful grin on her face, said condescendingly, "My pleasure, Mrs. Duffy. Kathryn, Mrs. Duffy said the winner would be judged on creativity, eloquence, and presentation of their personal interpretation of local Celtic folklore, not on accuracy!"

"But shouldn't there be points on whether or not the folklore is accurate?" said Kathryn humbly.

"Young lady, how do you know? They are just folklores; it's not a competition on history with facts and figures, dates, and people who have recorded them through time. These are myths and legends! Things that are not real, how would you prove your folklore if it's not real?"

"By," said Kathryn softly.

"By what?" questioned Mrs. Duffy.

"By research, by researching it in different books and by stories handed down from generation to generation," replied Kathryn.

"You seem to think that the people who wrote these books and told these stories actually saw firsthand these stories come to life?"

"Well, how would they have created them if they didn't see them?"

"They made them up!" retorted Mrs. Duffy, "and if I were to say to you that banshees liked to eat Cadbury chocolates covered with caramel for breakfast and tend to sleep until noon. You would agree with me? Or trust that it was the truth?"

"Well, I'd research what others may have said about banshees and see if there were any consistency to your story with other stories and see if you were a valid writer with other stories you told."

Mrs. Duffy's face turned sour and her upper lip sneered. "Class!" said Mrs. Duffy boisterously, looking away from Kathryn, "the competition will be this Wednesday. You will be judged on your creativity, eloquence, and presentation. All other facts will be ignored! Thank you Mrs. Mackenzie and class have a good day!"

"Geezzz... Kat, you really pissed her off!" whispered Billy.

"I didn't mean to..." she said. "Really, I didn't mean to offend anyone. I was just making a point."

"Unfortunately, your point was made to one of the judges."

"Great..."

"Well, there are two other judges, Mr. Hewson likes you and then there's Sodge..."

"Sodge? He hates folklore, myths, and legends, especially about Arthur's Seat. I'm going to have to give this my all if I'm going to win!"

"You will, no worries," said Billy.

The bell tolled once again, a flood of children filled the hallways. Posters of faeries with wings, hairy pookas, and shrieking banshees, were pasted against the cement walls. One poster read:

Nights of the Faeries Céilí, Wednesday at 7 p.m.

Come for the craic,
Come for the joy,
Come for the music,
Come for the boy,
Come for the dancing,
Come for the merries,

Come for the singing,
But most of all come for the Faeries...

Special appearances by:
Seamus O'Sullivan and Colin Hennessey.
Formerly of 'The Red Doctors.'

"That should be good fun!" said a scrawny little red haired boy.

"It should, shouldn't it," said Sheliza as she licked on a cherry lollipop, turning to Kathryn. "Are you and your intellectually dysfunctional friends going, Kat?"

Kathryn stood quiet, her anger keeping her silent.

"Listen Lott, you can have issues with us, but don't be rude!" replied Billy heatedly.

"Always fighting your sister's battles? Huh, doughboy!" giggled Sheliza.

The frail little girl with the knitted cap squeezed in between the group. "Are they going to have food there?" she asked.

"I think so, Mary," replied Kathryn.

"Oh good, I'd rather eat there than at home," she said. "Mum makes us eat livers and onions on Wednesday nights. She says it keeps the pookas away!"

"Along with the werewolves right, Mary?" snickered Sheliza.

"Nothing wrong with preventing werewolf attacks!" said a prissy little boy in pleated slacks.

"Sure Quinn there are loads of werewolves in Ireland!" said Sheliza mockingly. "Along with little green men from Mars!"

Mary cowed her head down and sulked away.

"Did you see Mary's cap?" said Sheliza to Quinn, insultingly. "It looks like our Granny's!"

"It does, doesn't it?" he sniggered back with a snort. "Maybe, she borrowed it from her?"

"Hey! Lay off of Mary!" said Billy defensively.

"Why? Are you the comedy police?" remarked Sheliza.

"No," said Billy hotly. "Just leave her alone!"

"What about her?" said Sheliza coldly, gesturing to Kathryn. "Is she ever going to say anything? Or is she going to stick to saying nothing, like she always does?"

"I say stuff!" blurted out Kathryn.

"Oh, it speaks!" said Quinn cruelly. "Thought the *cat* got

your tongue, again!"

"Well, Kat's going to win the folklore competition on Wednesday," said Billy informatively.

"Really?" laughed Sheliza. "I'm sure she'll have *lots* to say!"

"She's got the best book ever to do her research on!"

"What's that?" asked Sheliza.

"*The Legends of Arthur's Seat,*" replied Billy proudly, "by Peoke Thumbdill."

"Hmmm... Never heard of it!" said Sheliza pushing her way past Kathryn. "Next time Kat, try washing your face, it does wonders! Oh, and by the way, nice shoes!"

"Talk to ya later, Kat!" laughed Quinn as they both walked away.

"Kat!" cried Billy, "why do you just freeze up like that?"

"I... I... don't know?" replied Kathryn.

"Geezzz... Kat, you better win that competition!" said Billy. "Top prize is a hundred pounds! You can buy all the items on the true Indiana Jones apprentice list! For both of us!"

"We could really go up Arthur's Seat! Once and for all!" she said optimistically.

"Well, we could always go up there without the gear," Billy suggested. "And without anyone taking us!"

"I do have that flashlight," remarked Kathryn.

"The one we found down by the river?" asked Billy.

"Yup!" replied Kathryn.

"You got that grimy thing working?" asked Billy.

"Of course, Seamus cleaned it up and then replaced the batteries," she replied. "Funny, he said he never saw a flashlight like that before. What do you think that means?"

"I guess it means he's never seen one like that before!"

"You're a real comedian! *Soooo...*hilarious!"

"Well, I don't want to be stuck with a flashlight that even Seamus hasn't seen before! We need to get you setup so you can win this thing and that means no horsing around!" said Billy determinedly.

"I need cardboard and flour to make more paper maché and maybe some more sparkly stuff!" replied Kathryn.

"Sure!" replied Billy. "You know, Kat, Sheliza's like your Koréna, ya know?"

"Hmmm... Maybe I can stuff her in a Mountain too! And be gone with her forever!!" she said humorously.

♦ CHAPTER SEVEN ♦
BALLYRUN CELTIC FOLKLORE COMPETITION

It was Tuesday night, the night before the Ballyrun Celtic Folklore Competition. A soft rapping noise came from Kathryn's bedroom door.

"Yeah?" she called out.

The door creaked opened slowly. Billy moseyed into her wee bedroom, which was now covered wall to floor with shredded papers, paints from every color of the rainbow, paper maché models of goblins, knights, and faeries, along with bits of sticky glue.

"What a mess!" he said blatantly.

"There's too much information in this book!" she huffed. "I can't tell them everything! I haven't even read it all! Just a few pages."

"You don't have to tell them everything," said Billy calmingly as he sat beside her on the floor, pushing aside some disfigured paper dolls, shaped like portly faeries, "what have you got so far?"

"Well, you just sat on my woodland faeries!" she bleated out, picking up a crushed faery with its arms dangling off.

"Oh, sorry about that!" he said remorsefully, brushing off the pieces of paper on his derriere, "anything else?"

"I've got this collage of the seven provinces of Aählynéé," she said, holding up a poster board filled with bright vivid colors with seven different sections, separated by some yarn. "See," she said excitedly, pointing to a shimmering orb made of Styrofoam and sparkles, which looked similar to a mirrored disco ball and a drawing of many Silver Lakes with a smooth slick river gushing out. "These are the Silver Lakes." She pointed to a dark blue marble, glued above a drawing of a pale blue-faced woman with silky black hair, "This is Tirana, from Snowden. Here are the Knights from the Black Hills with their ebony orb, and here is the Golden Tree, and the Forest of No Return with some Newts, and Llangdon, and Lourtima, and here is my report and..."

"What about the Raven's Gate?" interrupted Billy.

"I don't have time to do that too!" whined Kathryn.

"If you did, you'd surely win!" he stated standing up, nearly knocking over a rusty tin can full of paintbrushes.

She sighed tiredly, "Don't you think this is enough to win?"

Billy picked up, *The Legends of Arthur's Seat* and opened it, placing it down on the bed and he said confidently, "Look," pulling out the seven-tiered citrine necklace from his pocket, "use this as your prop!"

"Where'd you get that?" she said intriguingly, taking the necklace from his hand. "You didn't?"

Billy smirked.

"Billy, if Grandpa finds out, we're gonna get reamed for this!" she said fiercely.

"Kat! This is the key to the Raven's Gate, read this!" he said boldly, placing his finger on the caption below the woman's picture.

The way to the Raven's Gate is found by the departed,
Who search for their way home above the moors,
And for those who search for it may become broken hearted,
Those who are called to it, will see its doors,
And by the birds of the sky, they shall lead you there in time,
For upon the rising of the Hawkmoon seven times,
The gate will open with the rap of three.

Now, Billy wasn't much of a thief by far, but he knew deep down inside that there was a reason for them to see Grandpa holding up that necklace the other night and there certainly was a reason for him to see that picture with his Grandmother's necklace in that book. No, by far, Billy was not a thief at all, he was a bug man, and he was his sister's only best friend. It is written down in the great books of our time that a man is nowhere without a woman by his side, but in Billy's case, it was his sister.

Morning came and the house bustled once more.

"And don't forget the paper maché figurines I made in that shoebox!" yelled Kathryn anxiously, waiting impatiently by the open cottage door.

The rain, which had thrashed down incessantly the night before on the cottage's shutters, had finally ceased.

"I'm just trying to cover it up with something!" cried Billy, his pudgy fingers sloppily fastening a large paper bag around a miniscule shoebox.

"Come on!" she cried again, tightening her grip on a rolled up white poster board in her hands, "I bet we can make it there before the rain starts again."

"Done!" yelled Billy, pulling out his pack of double trouble bubble gum, unwrapping a plump piece and tossing it in his mouth while he dashed out the door.

The morning turned out to be very dirty indeed, but country people in Ireland don't mind the rain too much. So, Kathryn and Billy hopped down the puddle-ridden road and headed towards Ballyrun. They had a spring in their step and a jolt in their heels, laughing happily on what they had discovered and the hopeful joy of winning the competition!

A hard growling noise came up from behind as they walked in the road. A large silver box shaped car speed swiftly up on their left.

"Kat! *Move!*" cried Billy frightfully, lurching his sister to the side of the muddy road.

The car swerved to the right and then straight into a deep pothole. *Splash,* the most disgusting filthy rain water drenched the two of them from head to foot. Even a pig would have been offended if he was that dirty.

"Ahhh..." screamed Kathryn, "*Sugar Booger*!!!" Dripping in stinky sludge water, her hands were white knuckled around her poster board, which was now covered in mud as well.

Laughter began to resonate in her ears as she looked up through her grimy eyelids and watched Sheliza and Quinn's faces pressed to the car's back window, amused at her misfortune.

"Sugar booger, is right! Are – are you ok, Kat?" asked Billy, after ingesting a piece of his gum. He too was covered in mud water as well, but for him it seemed very natural.

"My poster is ruined!" she sighed, slopping off chunks of mud off her hands.

"Well?" asked Billy, looking dismally into the destroyed shoebox.

"Well, what?" she said jaded, angrily marching down the road, "there goes my high marks for presentation!"

Billy brushed off a handful of muck off his coat and followed Kathryn, "Watch your step!" he said cautiously.

Kathryn turned around, drew her eyebrows up, squishing her forehead, and scowled at him.

"You know, you still have the necklace, you can't really ruin that!" he declared, pulling out another piece of double trouble bubble gum and popped it into his mouth.

Kathryn sighed, "I suppose so," brushing off the filthy wetness from her own coat. "That girl has absolutely no heart! You know they could've stopped to help! But, *nooo!* She cruises by and destroys my work and – and – and - laughs about it! No feelings, whatsoever!"

"Come on, Kat! We'll show them!" said Billy encouragingly, wiping a glob of soil from her face. "There, everything is perfect now!" Billy took a deep breath and blew a baseball size bubble and then, *pop!*

"Sometimes, I wonder if you're an asset or label?" suggested Kathryn.

"You mean, liability," added Billy.

"Yeah, that's what I meant, liability," answered Kathryn, descending down into the waterlogged town.

Energy buzzed throughout the cafeteria, children from all grades were doing the daunting task of setting up and preparing their projects for the Ballyrun Celtic Folklore Competition. Mary Dimmler sat quietly in the corner of the room flipping through each one of her index cards, her eyes now closed, mouthing her words trying to remember her lines. Amazingly enough, each card had a leafless tree, painstakingly hand drawn upon it.

Mugs, on the other hand, was across the room and was busy protecting his entry by covering it up with one of his mother's white linen sheets. There he stood before it, like a soldier standing at attention, scouting the room for enemies as he guarded his secret project.

Then, there was the wee ginger haired boy who had a fascinating larger-than-life paper maché of a great lake. Upon it were four snowy white swans floating leisurely on its surface.

And then, wouldn't ya know, Kathryn and Billy shuffled into the cafeteria dripping mud onto the floor as they walked through the cafeteria. They both looked like they had rolled around in Mr. Hennessey's pig pen.

"Just a second you two!" said Mrs. Duffy ardently, strutting across the room, her thick ankles keeping time with her feet. "Look at the two of you! Covered in mud and gunk! Go to the toilets this instant and clean yourselves up before you set up for the competition! By the way, you're slotted as number four, Kathryn!"

Billy, of course, just smiled and blew another bubble.

"And for you young man! Out with that gum at once!" exclaimed Mrs. Duffy.

In an instant, Billy swallowed his piece of his double trouble bubble gum and smiled at Mrs. Duffy's discerning face and then walked away.

"Unbelievable! They just traipse in here like they own the place! Mister Shea! Mister Shea!" said Mrs. Duffy harshly to Mr. Shea, who was standing awkwardly in the corner. "Come over here and clean this horrible mess up! At once! We cannot have the parents seeing such an atrocious representation of our school! I swear those Murphy kids will be the death of me!"

The eager crowd began to squeeze into children size plastic seats, which were lined up before a teetering wooden table on a low-level platform in the back of the cafeteria. A lively humming noise filled the brightly lit room. Peg and Seamus inched their way to the far back of the room and acquired their seats. Marie, of course was strategically placed on Seamus' thin lap, while George and Eddie wedged themselves in between the two of them.

A horrendous squealing noise echoed through the shoddy speakers, causing the crowd to flinch in pain. Mrs. Duffy then situated herself in front of the microphone on the platform and tapped it twice. The audience cringed again from the mind numbing feedback, which reached a frequency higher than any dog could ever hear. She straightened out her blouse. Above her head was a long black banner strung out, which read:

Ballyrun Celtic Folklore Competition.

"Good morning, ladies and gentlemen," said Mrs. Duffy proudly into the microphone, "it is time to begin our Ballyrun Celtic Folklore Competition the day before the Nights of Faeries three day holiday. To start the competition, I would ask if you would refrain from talking or from making any disrespectful statements to our students. The judging will be done by Mr. Crawley, Mr. Hewson, and myself. Furthermore, the contestants will be judged on creativity, eloquence, and presentation, each will be calculated from a score of one to ten and will be tallied up at the end of the competition to produce our winner. Now, without further ado, here is our first contestant, Mr. Christopher Hennessey."

Christopher's face turned pale white as he lugged his indigo lake and beautifully feathered swans onto the stage and placed them gently on the shaky table. Turning towards the audience he gulped down some air, opened an orange book, and said informatively, "A long time ago, there once lived King Lir, who was said to be one of the Kings of Tuatha Dé Danann, the ancient people of Ireland. King Lir had four beautiful children: Fionnuala, Aodh, Fiachra, and Conn. One day the King's precious wife died and he was very, very sad, so he married his wife's sister, Aoife. In the beginning, Aoife was a good wife and mother to her stepchildren, but soon jealousy began to boil in her blood. Her love soon grew into writhing hatred and a cold bitter heart. So, one day she called upon a magical druid and told him of her four stepchildren who took away the King's love from her and so he gave her magical wand. The following day, she forced her four stepchildren onto a fiery chariot to Lough Derravarragh. There, she commanded the children to swim in the lake. Once all four children swam in the lake, she then pulled out her magical wand, waved it around three times, and turned her stepchildren into swans." Christopher swayed his hand over the four model swans floating on his deep blue lake. He raised his voice louder and said dreadfully, "She cursed them to live as swans for nine hundred years! The first three hundred years would be on Lough Derravaragh, the next three hundred years would be on the Straits of Moyle, and the last three hundred years on the Isle of Inish Glora. It is said to end the spell they would have to hear a bell ring, of the arrival of a new God. However, when Aoife returned home without the children, King Lir became very suspicious and demanded to know where they were! Aoife immediately denied knowing where they were and said she had done no wrong. But, the King knew better and began to search for them, all over his vast kingdom, until he came upon Lough Derravarragh. There he came upon four of the most beautiful swans he had ever laid eyes on, and their song was as beautiful as any bird he had ever heard. The children of course recognized their father immediately and told him what had happened. The King was now enraged by Aoife's actions and banished her to exile, as an evil demon of the air. After nine hundred years, living as swans with the most splendid voices, the curse ended when they heard a holy man's bell toll and the children returned home to their father, King Lir, once again. The end."

The audience clapped exuberantly, Christopher bowed and then gathered his project and stepped off stage.

"Excellent job, Christopher. Next up, Miss Mary

Dimmler," said Mrs. Duffy.

Mary stepped up to the raised stage, holding her preordered index cards tightly.

"Mary, no props?" asked Mr. Hewson inquisitively, from the side of the stage.

"No, Sir, I don't have any," she replied blandly and then stood before the audience. "A long, long, long, time ago, in a land, far – far – far – away, there was a great Kingdom of Elves known as, Nezroth. Once, Nezroth had a Queen Elf, some believe her to be Danú, the goddess of the Tuatha Dé Danann. All of Danú's powers were kept in her loyal pet, a magnificent dragon of fire, but the barbaric Queen Maeve one day murdered her dragon. Its heart was ripped out and broken into pieces, so no one from Nezroth could ever find them and whisked away to another land. The Nezrothians, once the most powerful of all faeries were weakened by their loss. It was then that the Danyär, a group of Holy Elves was created. They swore an oath to recapture the dragon's heart. Their oath entailed destroying Queen Maeve and anyone who came between them and all the pieces of the dragon's heart and bring it back to its land of origin, Nezroth."

The room applauded cheerfully for Mary as she flipped through a few more index cards.

"I'd like to now read you a quote that was said to be written by a changeling," she said notably. "For those of you who do not know, a changeling is an offspring of a faery who is sickly, perhaps from a grotesque troll, a treacherous elf, or a smelly goblin. The faery baby is then is switched with a human baby, unbeknownst to the parents. The faery parents then raise the human child and the human family then raises the changeling, who is really an unhealthy faery. A parent usually can recognize a changeling, by noticing many calamities occurring in their household and also, the changeling will shriek and howl throughout the day, at a frequency that exceeds the limits of human endurance. So, here is a saying that I found written supposedly by a real changeling, which I thought was interesting. I believe it to be in relation to discovering whether or not your child is a faery. The quote is by C.C. Changeling, *'Signs sometimes are never seen, they are always there, but until they are understood, they are never known.'* And so it is with folklore, how do we know what the signs are until they are shown to us in fact? Thank you!"

Applause reverberated throughout the cafeteria as Mrs. Duffy exchanged places with Mary and said warmly, "Thank you Mary that was lovely! Now, our next participant is the," Mrs. Duffy halfheartedly glanced over to see Mugs licking the dirt off his two fingers and run them across his eyebrows, "very posh, Mr. Michael Kennedy, Mugs!"

Mugs hobbled up the steps, carrying his massive project hidden by one of his mother's bed sheets, and gently placed it down on the frail table. He turned his back on the audience and whipped the sheet off his project, revealing its secret: a colossal mountain shaped exactly like Arthur's Seat. In the center, a cascading river trickled down representing Wallace's Way River, the one lone river that flowed from Arthur's Seat into Ballyrun, tiny pebbles assembled on the Mountain formed remnants of an ancient fort. At the base of his masterpiece was a copper clasp holding the project tightly together and at the pinnacle of the Mountain was a wee Castle, made of stones and fastened together with clumps of sticky white glue.

Mugs stood before his attentive audience and upon clearing his voice, he said boisterously, "Back in the days of 'da great High Kings and Queens of Ireland, there lived a beautiful sorceress named Koréna." Mugs took out a figurine of a red haired woman and gently placed her within the Castle. "She was one of 'da nine maidens of 'da Otherworld. One day, this sorceress discovered a horrible truth. Her father Dúcäin, along with Queen Maeve were forming an alliance, scheming against their High King to steal 'da living heart of a dragon which held all the High King's powers. Upon hearing 'da news, she went at once to see 'da King 'ta warn him and to help him! But, it was too late! Queen Maeve and her father had already known of her plans! And they had another idea!" Mugs quickly pressed an ebony button in the back of Mountain. Shockingly, he began to hurl down tiny dynamite snaps at the audience and they yelped with terror! The Mountain started to gurgle at first, but then it vibrated fiercely, and then the Castle spun the doll of Koréna around, like she was in a washing machine. "Queen Maeve and Koréna's father cursed her and forced 'da great Mountain, Arthur's Seat, to swallow her whole!" Koréna's replica and the Castle swirled deeper into the Mountain. "Swallowed her whole, it did, that Mountain! Cast into its belly, for all eternity!" The model Mountain sat bare now, with no Castle or Koréna to be seen. "Koréna's wailings can still be heard 'till this day up on that 'dere Mountain, heard in the howlin' of 'da chillin' wind." Mugs unlocked the clasp to allow his model Mountain to separate. "Here she is," he said audaciously, pointing to Koréna's likeness trapped within the paper Mountain. "Alone, cursed, waitin', searchin' for 'da dragon's heart and to finally free herself from her lonely tomb!" Mugs turned to the audience who had their jaws dropped. "'Da end!"

Thunderous applause echoed loudly through the cafeteria as Mrs. Duffy climbed onto the stage with Mugs and said pleasantly, "Well done - well done, Mugs! Very nice, indeed! Now, for our next competitor," Mrs. Duffy gazed over towards the grubby Kathryn, holding her poster board in hand, which was now bleeding black ink from its pictures. "Our next competitor, newly transplanted here to Ballyrun, all the way from Brooklyn, New York, is Miss Kathryn Murphy!"

The audience clapped uniformly as Kathryn stumbled up the steps to the stage with her report and poster board, Mugs nodded his head cordially. Mrs. Duffy grazed by her and brazenly picked a leaf from her hair, tossing it to the floor, and said snappily, "Hurry on there, Kathryn, plenty more children to go!"

Kathryn stood before the audience wide-eyed, her heart pounding like a bodhrán. Carefully, she unrolled her poster board out; her pictures lay wet and pruned, the yarn dangled off fraying at the ends, and the sparkles dribbled down the board, while bits and pieces of her Styrofoam shapes were crushed.

"Ahem!" she said clearing her throat, "many fallacies have been created throughout the ages about what is truly real in Aählyneé. These fallacies will now be debunked as I explain what is truly occurring in the land of Aählyneé or as some others have reported 'the Sidhe', 'the Otherworld', or even, 'Tír na nÓg."

Kathryn raised her hand firmly, directing her audience to the seven different sections on her poster board, separated by flimsy yarn. "Here are the seven provinces of Aählyneé: Rootunda, Snowden, the Black Hills, Llangdon, the Forest of No Return, and the Silver Lakes." Kathryn looked out into the silence, her throat dry and raw, so she coughed. "Excuse me," she said anxiously, "just a little parched. As you can see, each province is represented by a ruler, a sword, and an orb." The stillness of the audience made her ears ring and her palms sweat. "See here," pointing to a shiny American penny, which was stuck next to some, dried up potato roots, "this is the golden orb for Rootunda, we don't know too much about Rootunda, it's still a mystery, but we know it is considered a bit of an enigma area within Aählynéé."

Mrs. Duffy raised her eyebrows high and peered over to Mr. Hewson. Mr. Hewson, of course ignored the silent message sent by Mrs. Duffy while crossing his legs and passively tapped a finger to his chin.

Little beads of perspiration began to drip down her forehead as she continued on nervously. "And here, here are the Black Hills, they have a sword of onyx and an orb that tells secrets of the past," she said, pointing her finger to crayon drawn Black Hills, while knights in armor guarded a shriveled up woman. "And ummm... here are woodland faeries within the Forest of No Return. They're standing next to a wizard and they are represented by an emerald orb and an emerald sword." Kathryn gazed over at Billy who had his mouth open while shaking his head left to right. "Snowden is represented by Tir – Tir - ummm... Tirana and she's surrounded by these white wolves and owls and there is a blue orb that tells the truth and a ummm... a crystal sword as well." Kathryn glanced at Mrs. Duffy whose her hand was now clasped to her forehead. Kathryn sighed and looked to the back of the room where Peg, Seamus, George, Eddie, and Marie were sitting and she smiled crookedly. "Right, so we have one, two, three, and four done, ummm... provinces done, that is, and we also have the Silver Lakes with a silver sword and their orb is considered to be, ummm... a friend, is that right? Yes, a friend. Not sure what that means?"

Mugs and Mary giggled in their seat.

Kathryn's face heated up to a roaring red and continued her speech, "And then we have Llangdon, which is where Koréna is said to be from, they have the red orb, known for love, and the fire sword. Here, we have Lourtima, which is the city in the clouds and this has the white orb known for peace and the sword of diamonds."

Kathryn looked out into the bored audience. Billy placed his hand over his neck area and pretended to choke a few times. Even Eddie had fallen asleep, his head tilted to the side, his mouth wide open with a trickle of salvia dripping from it.

"Right!" she said brazenly, reaching deep into her pocket and pulled out the citrine necklace, holding it up high before the audience. "Here, is the key to the Raven's Gate!"

The audience members were aghast, but they were also enlivened and filled with awe. Whispers pulsated throughout the crowd and then the whispers grew to into a soft roar.

Kathryn smiled, knowing the audience was finally hers and said bravely, "See," raising the necklace higher into the light, its colorful beads shimmered, "it's some sort of key that will lead you to the Raven's Gate! Where's my book?"

"That will be enough, Miss Murphy," barked Mrs. Duffy, ushering Kathryn off the stage.

"But – but, it is!" she exclaimed, Mrs. Duffy clenched her arm tightly. "I swear it is! I saw it in the book! It's real!"

"There will be none of that! Now, kindly leave the stage so the next participant can come up!" said Mrs. Duffy unsympathetically.

"I don't understand!" she cried. "What did I do wrong?"

"Go sit down Kathryn and be quiet for once!" reprimanded Mrs. Duffy pushing her towards the audience to take a seat.

"Kathryn!" cried Seamus, waving his hands in the air for her to sit next to him.

"Here, Kathryn!" called Peg cordially, "sit here!"

Kathryn slumped her shoulders, dropped her head, and took a seat next to the O'Sullivan clan.

"Kathryn, you did nothing wrong," whispered Peg, rubbing her back, "it's just that."

"Ladies and gentlemen, we're now ready for our next participant!" said Mrs. Duffy merrily.

Sheliza Lott stood charmingly by the stage, like a garden flower with her golden daffodil hair.

"It's just what?" said Kathryn innocently.

"I'm happy to introduce our final contestant for the competition, Miss Sheliza Lott!" announced Mrs. Duffy.

"It's just that," Peg whispered back, "that necklace was your Grandmother's and the whole town knows it."

"So?" questioned Kathryn.

"Well, it's said to be cursed!" said Peg uneasily.

"What?" remarked Kathryn, "cursed? Why?"

Sheliza stepped onto the stage with a grand smile on her face. She boldly snapped her fingers. Suddenly, the back doors swung open and a swarm of workers buzzed into the cafeteria carrying in a sleek, top of the line modern television set, along with hi-fi stereo speakers. The band of drone workers quickly assembled the equipment in record time, while the audience looked on dumbfounded by all the glossy hi-tech gear.

Sheliza, of course, took her spot on stage before her grand audience and called out, "Lights!" The cafeteria was now pitch-black. Sheliza called out once more, *"roll it!"*

Lights twinkled, like a starry night, filling the darkened cafeteria with speckles and the monstrous television turned on. Scenic pictures, taken from a helicopter, displayed picturesque views of Ireland: rolling emerald green hills checkered with lines of ancient stone walls, crashing cliffs, crystal waterfalls pouring into pools of water, and then a panoramic shot of the great Arthur's Seat.

"Some say, Arthur's Seat is a gateway to Aählynéé," said Sheliza extravagantly, "which holds the five lands within Aählynéé!"

"That's not true!" whispered Kathryn to Peg. "It's seven provinces! Not, five lands!"

Mrs. Duffy glowered at Kathryn.

Pictures of great knights in stylish armor along with powerful warriors appeared on the screen, "Even Arthurian legend links King Arthur to Aählynéé!" said Sheliza impressively.

"What?!?!" huffed Kathryn, "You've got to be kidding me!"

"If a Miss Murphy doesn't contain herself, perhaps she should be disqualified?" warned Mrs. Duffy.

"Could Aählynéé be Camelot?" said Sheliza intriguingly, "Or, is it where King Arthur lives now? For the Mountain is called Arthur's Seat!"

"Poppycock!" cried Kathryn assuredly.

"Disqualification it is then," asserted Mrs. Duffy.

"But!" cried Kathryn.

"Shhh," hushed Peg, "better let her have her win now, Kathryn."

"One of the most intriguing parts of Arthur's Seat sits on its western crag and that is the Stone of Destiny," remarked Sheliza. "Stones, in mythical folklore are said to absorb people's emotions and energies which become stored in the stone forever. It is said, that if one were to touch the Stone of Destiny, he or she would one day understand all the mysteries of Aählynéé and be crowned the ruling sovereign. Now, this Stone of Destiny, which has been elusive to the public for many years, was just rediscovered on Arthur's Seat by our own local historian and folklorist, Mr. Hewson. What is not known of this Stone of Destiny, which is also known as Lia Fáil, is that it is magical! When the rightful High King of Ireland places his feet upon this stone, the stone should roar with joy! It just so happens that the Stone of Destiny throughout Celtic folklore has also been known to have the ability to rejuvenate the King's kin and to bless his family with a long reign. It is also said that the Stone of Destiny contains the soul of Rav'ailín an Tulloch, a banshee expelled from Aählyneé who roams the forbidding cliffs and crags of Arthur's Seat, wailing night after night, in search of her long lost love. Many fear the mourning cry of the banshee, for she is a messenger of the Otherworld, a fallen angel," Sheliza's television's colors flickered and began to show a single cloaked woman roaming the cliffs of Arthur's Seat, "For it is said that the howling cry of the banshee forewarns an unavoidable death in one's family. The night you hear the shrilling, skin-crawling wail of a banshee, within the next few days, someone you love will die." Suddenly, the cloaked woman on the television set morphed her form into a screaming, bawling banshee; her hair was wild in the wind, while her eyes began to bleed with tears. "She who cries into the silent night, who gives her victims an awful fright, lonely and cold she sits all alone, preparing to make her scary moan, angels of death riding from on high, come charging in, and won't pass you by, she is the banshee that wails for you, cause this day will be the last for you!"

Kathryn's eyes popped open like a full moon, as did everyone else's in the cafeteria, even Mrs. Duffy was as scared as a chicken in a fox hole.

The television screen began to show pictures of a woman changing from a young attractive woman into an ordinary matron and then into a bloodcurdling old hag. Sheliza continued, "Now the banshee can appear in many ways to her victim. Sometimes, she's a young beautiful woman at other times she's a matronly more innocent woman. But, she can also appear as an old twisted, spine-chilling hag. From history, all three of these disguises can come to represent the Celtic goddess of war and death. The banshee usually appears cloaked in a glowing long shriveled robe. And in the night, when the moon is full, and you hear her wailing song off in the distance, calling you from the

Otherworld, and then a soft rapping sound taps on your door... it's best not to answer it, for it may be the call of the banshee. Even now, as I speak, telling you the secrets of the banshee, my own life is in danger, for one will seek me and my own family out, to tell me of my misfortunes." Sheliza stood in the darkness and said, "Thank you."

A deafening clamor erupted from the hushed audience. Sheliza curtsied, while Mrs. Duffy stepped onto the stage expressing her abundant joy for her prodigy and said exuberantly, "Brilliant Sheliza, just absolutely brilliant! Ladies and gentlemen we're going to tally up the votes and announce the winner, please have some refreshments as Mr. Hewson, Mr. Crawley, and myself determine the lucky winner!"

Peg leaped from her chair and approached Mrs. Duffy, "Mrs. Duffy," she called thoughtfully, "Mrs. Duffy, you should rethink disqualifying Kathryn. She didn't intentionally mean to disrupt Sheliza's speech and the girl never had a chance to finish her own project."

"Mrs. O'Sullivan, I understand your concerns, but we mustn't have pupils disrupting others and allowing them to get away with it!" replied Mrs. Duffy candidly, walking past Peg.

Marie's short stature stepped in front of Mrs. Duffy. "Please Mrs. Duffy, give Kat another chance!" said Marie imploringly, startling Mrs. Duffy.

"I think you're being extremely unfair, Mrs. Duffy!" proclaimed Peg.

"Who? *What?*" said Mrs. Duffy frazzled, her eyes focused on Marie's tiny frame and wrinkled skin. "What are you?"

Peg picked up Marie and said, "This is my daughter, Mrs. Duffy."

"She's - she's like a living, breathing changeling!" said Mrs. Duffy crazily.

"A changeling?" repeated Marie.

"She's a little girl, with Progeria, she's not a changeling Mrs. Duffy!" said Peg strongly.

"She's so," mumbled Mrs. Duffy.

"So?" replied Peg.

"So," paused Mrs. Duffy, "I'm sorry Mrs. O'Sullivan, but Kathryn showed a spiteful lack of respect to her fellow students and definitely does not know when to keep silent! I must tally the votes now."

Mr. Hewson and Mr. Crawley handed their paper tallies

to Mrs. Duffy, as she approached the stage. Scattered strands of hair now fell out haphazardly over her face from her once smoothed out bun. "Ladies and gentlemen," she said self-righteously. "I have the winner of the Ballyrun Celtic Folklore Competition! The winner of the Ballyrun Celtic Folklore Competition will receive the glorious top prize of one hundred pounds, a very special field trip up Arthur's Seat, to what Mr. Hewson believes to be the Stone of Destiny, and finally this magnificent plaque!"

The audience's chatter softened into a quiet hush, Kathryn sat somberly in the back of the cafeteria next to Billy who was blowing his double trouble bubble gum.

"And the winner of this year's Ballyrun Celtic Folklore Competition is," pronounced Mrs. Duffy, "Miss Sheliza Lott!"

A howl bellowed from the audience, Sheliza stepped onto the stage next to Mrs. Duffy.

"Here you are my dear," said Mrs. Duffy proudly, handing Sheliza a shiny gold plaque and a blue ribbon.

"Thank you so much, Mrs. Duffy!" replied Sheliza arrogantly. "I can't believe I won! What an honor!"

Kathryn pursed her lips, while rolling her eyes back into her head, "You've got to be kidding me!" she muttered.

"Now Sheliza will also be taking a field trip up to Arthur's Seat, to see the Stone of Destiny, which how ironically is what part of your report was on!"

"Yes, it was!" exclaimed Sheliza.

"Let's all give a hand to all our participants and for all their creative efforts!" proclaimed Mrs. Duffy. "Thank you all for coming to our Ballyrun Celtic Folklore Competition."

Kathryn stood up and approached Mrs. Duffy.

"Mrs. Duffy!" said Kathryn.

"Yes?" replied Mrs. Duffy irately, flipping through some papers.

"I was wondering if I wasn't disqualified... If-if I would have won?" asked Kathryn.

Sheliza glided over to Mrs. Duffy; Mr. and Mrs. Lott followed with Quinn.

"No," replied Mrs. Duffy annoyed.

"Kathryn, have you seen my plaque?" giggled Sheliza, unwrapping a red lollipop and then shoving it in her mouth.

"No?" questioned Kathryn to Mrs. Duffy. "Why not? Everything I reported on is true! They are facts that I read in a book! I have references and everything!"

"Not very good ones I might say!" said Mrs. Duffy snippily, turning her back on Kathryn to face the Lotts.

"Not very good ones," chuckled Sheliza to Quinn. "She said not very good ones!"

"What?" exclaimed Kathryn.

"Child, do you really believe that there is a sorceress in that Mountain? And there's this whole Otherworld full of magic?" said Mrs. Duffy rudely, packing her papers into her over sized chocolate purse.

"Yes," replied Kathryn happily. "Yes, I do!"

"She believes in faery tales!" laughed Sheliza to Quinn and her parents.

"What a dodo bird!" snickered Quinn.

"Why?" questioned Mrs. Duffy bluntly, "you've never seen anything. You've never been there, how would you know?"

"My life would be pretty boring if I didn't believe," remarked Kathryn.

"Oh, it's already boring Kat!" chortled Sheliza.

"Foolish girl!" scoffed Mrs. Lott.

"You don't know fact from fiction! What is truly fact and what is fiction eludes you with all these myths and legends!" declared Mrs. Duffy.

"But, don't you want to know? Don't you want to know if it is real? Don't you want to know who created Aählynéé and why? Don't you want to know who lives there? What they're like?" retorted Kathryn.

"You pose too many questions with no answers," spurred Mrs. Duffy.

"Well, no one really has the answers," said Kathryn reflectively, tapping her finger to her lips. "You'd have to actually go to this world to find out what is real and what isn't!"

"Stupid girl! *Wake up!*" yelled Mrs. Duffy angrily. "There are no such things as faeries! This is all done in jest! It's part of our culture, our heritage. The Irish have been passing down stories for thousands of years from generation to generation! But, to believe in them without proof, without true insight, it's - it's just, tom-foolery!"

"Whatever!" said Kathryn rolling her eyes.

"Young lady, do not roll your eyes at me!" demanded Mrs. Duffy.

"Uh-oh," harped Sheliza snidely, elbowing Quinn in the ribs, "she's going to get it now!"

"Kat, come here!" called Peg earnestly, as she approached

the group with Marie.

"But!" cried Kathryn perplexed.

"You!" said Mrs. Duffy madly, her face burning with anger. "You are a.... self indulgent, childish fool that is what you are!"

"Me?" question Kathryn horrified. "Self indulgent with what?"

"With your curiosity!" snapped Mrs. Duffy heatedly.

"Tsk-tsk!" whispered Quinn, shaking his head side to side, waving his finger back and forth.

"Stop this!" cried Peg provoked, "this instant!! Bloody insanity! What is wrong with you?"

"I didn't start it!" remarked Kathryn.

"Stupid little girl, you are so dimwitted and naïve! Uttering your featherbrained ideas around like.... like anyone here truly cares, you are overly indulgent in allowing her to be so impudent!" declared Mrs. Duffy hastily.

"And you Mam are overly compensating with your stupidity!" announced Peg.

"I beg your pardon!" spluttered Mrs. Duffy.

"No need to beg!" countered Peg irritated, "because you won't be gettin' it! Come now, we must leave!"

"Please do!" stated Mrs. Duffy, turning to the Lott's again. "Well, now we can certainly understand why people may say they are changelings!"

"Did - did she just insult us?" remarked Peg to Seamus.

"Well, ummm..... yeah!" replied Billy fearfully, gulping down another piece of double trouble bubble gum.

"Don't do anything Peg!" begged Seamus.

"I'm going to give that woman a piece of my mind!" said Peg irritated.

"It's not worth it Peg!" said Seamus and then sighed. "That poor woman is doomed now."

"You! You... think you can just say rude things to us because no one will say anything to you... don't you?" argued Peg. "Well, I'm here to tell you, you're wrong! They are beautiful human beings! Not changelings! They have more heart, more soul, and more life than a pathetic old bag like yourself! You think only the beautiful and powerful have a right to exist! You are a shame to your profession and you are a shame to the whole human race. All of you are!"

"Come now, Peg, we have to go now!" said Seamus.

"Let's face it Kat!" remarked Sheliza pulling out her ruby red sucker, "you're nothing! You own nothing! You say nothing! What, what was that? Oh yeah, that's right you say nothing!"

Marie shrieked in high pitch voice just like a banshee.

"Well, that would explain a lot about your daughter!" roared Mrs. Duffy, "Hmphh... a changeling if I ever saw one!"

"How dare you Mrs. Duffy! Let me tell you something, in life when you have the choice to be kind or cruel, always choose kindness! Come now children! I've finally realized what being a special education teacher means," said Peg ushering Marie, Eddie, and George to the door.

"Less of a salary," commented Mrs. Duffy to Mrs. Quinn.

"No! It's so I don't have to work with pompous old crones like yourself!" spattered Peg as she walked away with her family.

"They're not all pompous!" suggested Kathryn.

"Kathryn, one day you'll learn that it's how you exit the stage that truly makes you a star! Let's go now! Come now, my precious Marie," said Peg as they left the cafeteria.

Chapter Eight
Nights of the Faeries Céili

It was a grand group that had joined together for the Nights of the Faeries Céili, down in the basement beneath St. John's Church. Each one of the Kennedy's, including Mr. and Mrs. Kennedy had made a night of it. All nine kids had come out to enjoy the festivities and a glorious night of good 'ol Irish *craic*. Now, for those of you who may not know, craic is what the Irish deem as merriment, fun, light-heartedness, and having a bit of a go!

Of the Kennedy's nine children, there was Patrick, the proud eldest, who could do no wrong in his mother's eye. William was the second son and was a bit of a hermit; he liked to sit in the corner and read books on Saints, while the others danced it up. Annie, the third child was a statuesque beauty with long jet-black hair. The fourth and fifth children were fraternal twin girls, Nancy and Megan. Nancy was a bouncy, curly blonde with her hair tied up in a loose bun, ready to kick it up with her Irish step. Megan was a wavy red head whose dress was always too big, due to the fact that it was a hand me down from her elder sister Annie. Then there was Liam, the sixth child, who was sitting in the corner, already in trouble for taking wee sips of alcoholic drinks. The seventh child was Robert; he was the handsomest of all the boys and always seemed to be fighting off Mary Dimmler as she followed him around like a sweet puppy waiting for a dance. Then, there was the eighth child, Michael, or as his friends called him, Mugs. He was busy in the back room playing a simple game of dice with Paul O'Keefe. Kaitlin, the youngest practiced diligently with Megan and Nancy to see who could kick the highest, by kicking a tin can off a barstool. Then, there was the beautiful Mrs. Kennedy who was still as lovely as the day she was married; not a crease, furrow, or crinkle soiled her face, while Mr. Kennedy's face was still as red as a rose from his earlier visit to Flannery's.

Mrs. Fiona Flannery was also there for the festivities, along with her somewhat unique son Ian. They were seated with Ethel Crawley, who is, simply, the most forbidding woman to those who do not know her. But once she knows you well, you might actually see her crack a smile every fortnight, if the moon is full, her husband Sodge is out of town, a glass of sweet wine is in her hand, and the stars are in proper alignment. Then of course, there was Joan Crawley, Ethel and Sodge Crawley's daughter, a flawless creature that had ever graced the land and with more charm than Casanova himself. Mr. Hennessey on the other hand, sat far away from his shop neighbor, Sodge Crawley.

With all due respect, it was an actual mandate from the Bishop himself. Fr. O'Toole had written to the bishop about their ever so fearful feuding. Especially about the time when Mr. Hennessey ran out of newspapers to wrap up his fine chops and decided to use Sodge Crawley's world famous encyclopedia collection on extinct swans and their mating rituals to finish wrapping them. Sodge Crawley was absolutely furious with Mr. Hennessey and even Fiona Flannery stated that she saw Sodge Crawley's head turn every shade of the rainbow and actual steam come out of his ears. To retaliate, Sodge Crawley snuck into Mr. Hennessey's butcher shop and removed all the eggs from the shelves and shoved them into the meat freezer. When Mr. Hennessey found them the next day, he had a good laugh at Sodge Crawley's expense by telling the local town's folk about his prank; for most of the town's people knew that eggs couldn't be frozen in their shells. Mr. Sodge Crawley was again, shown in a not so commendable light and this fueled their never ending feud between the two.

So, the Bishop ordered that whenever there was a town function, Mr. Sodge Crawley and Mr. Hennessey had to sit on opposite sides of the room at all times, and that was that. If one were to get up to speak to a friend, the other had to mirror him and stay completely on the adjacent side of the room. Mr. Hennessey had been known, on a few occasions, to pull Sodge Crawley's chain by standing opposite a group of teenage girls, just to have a bit of a laugh at Sodge's expense. And because of the mandate, Sodge would have to sit for hours with a bunch of chatty girls, talking about bubble gum and hair products, no doubt. Sodge Crawley on the other hand, had also won the right to drink at Finnegan's Wake. Where as Mr. Hennessey was only welcome to part take at the fine establishment known as Flannery's.

Now across the room sat Peg O'Sullivan chatting it up with Fiona Flannery and Ethel Crawley. Eddie was busy playing drums on the table, whistling a soundless ditty through his fleshy gums, while George hung on every word that Seamus said. Marie was dolled up with silver faery wings that would twinkle like a thousand stars when the light struck them just right.

Amongst the deafening hubbub of the room, the basement door swiftly crashed open and Kathryn and Billy strolled into the grand faery wonderland that Mrs. Flannery and Fr. O'Toole had decorated so diligently the days prior to the Céilí. Whimsical faery wings flew along the ceiling, while wee furry, orange-haired leprechaun cutouts danced around the outer walls.

Mr. Dimmler approached the two, grinning a grand smile and said the traditional Irish blessing, "*Rath dé ort.*"

"Hey!" said Seamus, jumping out of his seat and bustling towards Kathryn and Billy.

The two transplants moved about the room in wonder, listening to the grand fiddles strumming in the Céilí band, the tin whistles that sang high with every note, and the party-goer's feet as they thrashed about in glorious dance, while the bodhrán's drummed fiercely to the throbbing beat. The whole room was charged up with electrifying energy and the crowd took to merriment like ducks to water.

"Good 'ta see ya!" cheered Seamus, hugging Kathryn and Billy. "Good 'ta see yas! Now, we're all the way across the room there!"

Seamus waved to Peg and she reciprocated, along with Marie who was now on her high tippy-toes, waving her glittery wand on strangers' heads.

"Cool," replied Billy, blowing an enormous pink bubble.

"Where's your man?" asked Mr. Dimmler, walking back to his seat with a fresh pint of Guinness.

"Should be along, shortly!" replied Seamus.

"Where's – where's your man Seamus?" asked Billy confused.

"Colin," replied Seamus. "He's asking when Colin's comin'."

"Wow! You guys definitely speak differently than us," chortled Billy.

"Now, whatcha think he asked?" said Seamus.

"Hmmm... not quite sure," answered Billy.

"Ah... You two... Now, do you know where faeries come from?" asked Mr. Dimmler taking a sip of his foamy beer, leaving a thin, milky mustache on his upper lip.

"Ahhh... I hear a story comin' from your mouth, Michael!" said Seamus gleefully.

"Ummm... no?" replied Billy.

"Where do they come from Mr. Dimmler?" asked Kathryn curiously.

Michael Dimmler took a long sweet sip from his pint, wetting his whistle, and then cleared his throat. "Long, long ago, before you and I were born, before the fox ran across the green grasses and the birds built nests in men's beards. Before ever there was an Ireland... there was God and his angels. And on one particular day, there was a great uprising in Heaven when Lucifer the archangel decided he would not follow God's laws anymore. So, God kicked him out by opening the grand pearly gates of Heaven. But, then a horrible thing happened: Unbeknownst to God, all the angels began to fall out! Down... down... down they all fell, down to the Earth below. Now, the archangel Michael looked around Heaven and was gob-smacked. For there were hardly any angels left in Heaven anymore. He said frightfully to God, 'God, what in Heaven are you doing? All the angels are falling out of Heaven! We have to close the gates or there won't be any angels left in Heaven and we'll be left here all alone!' So, God saw the wisdom in that and closed those pearly gates of Heaven before all the angels fell out to the Earth below. Now, the angels who fell to Hell with Lucifer, who is now called the devil, you see, stayed there in Hell. They are now the dark angels and demons, which prowl around whispering in your ear to do bad things and trying to ruin your soul. The angels who landed on the Earth stayed there and they are the faeries we now see, who are always testing our faith sneaking about and hiding in the great faery mounds. The angels that landed in the sea became the sea faeries, who are known to protect sailors and ships, so they don't get swallowed up by the great sea meeting their doom and of course, so they can watch over all the sea creatures. The angels that landed in the air are the air faeries, which fly around looking over your shoulder, making sure you do right.

"Now, that is where faeries come from! They are always a part of us, and watching over us, you don't have to believe in them, but they certainly do believe in you!"

Well, they were all in good humor now.

"Michael, what a smashing story!" laughed Seamus with an approving thump on Michael's back. "You'll come by and say hello to Peg and the gang won't you?"

"The devil himself couldn't stop me Seamus. But perhaps a lovely banshee may!" laughed Michael as he skipped his way back into the Céilí.

Fiona Flannery, Ethel Crawley, and Peg O'Sullivan huddled together intensely at the far end of the table. Mrs. Flannery seemed to be ablaze with worry as Kathryn and Billy approached silently.

"'Tis was the strangest looking person I'd had ever laid me eyes on," remarked Ethel oddly, sipping her icy glass of Irish cream.

"It didn't have a face," said Fiona shockingly. "I saw him, or it, or whatever it was walking through town, cloaked in a dark robe, which only the angel of death would wear!"

"Fiona, how could it not have a face now?" questioned Peg holding her rich amber glass of whiskey, "did it not have a head on it, to steer its body in the right direction?"

"I couldn't see the face neither when he came into the shop, but for a second, I could see a tattoo over its left eye," whispered Ethel leaning in towards the two women. "A shadow was cast over his face from the hood he wore and it was too dark to see any more of its face!"

"You're having me on!" remarked Peg.

"He even dared to ride into town on a horse!" said Fiona, picking up a bag of crisps and ripping them open.

"Is it a fact, Fiona?" asked Peg puzzled. "Who rides in on a horse? It wasn't Jezebel was it now?"

"Definitely, not Jezebel!" said Fiona frantically, popping a crisp in her mouth. "It almost felt like...like..."

"Like what?" asked Peg.

"Like, it was not of this world," said Ethel.

"A faery?" cried Peg.

"*Shhh,*" hushed Ethel.

"Perhaps, he just did not seem human," declared Peg.

"No, no," said Fiona. "He didn't seem like he was from around here at all!"

"More like... from the Otherworld," noted Ethel.

Peg's mouth dropped open. "You don't say?" she gasped.

"And he asked me an awful lot of questions," said Fiona.

"Me too... Fiona," replied Ethel.

"Well, what type of questions?" asked Peg.

Ethel leaned in and whispered, "Questions about..."

Fiona looked up and observing that Kathryn and Billy were approaching the cluttered table, kicked Ethel's shin.

Ethel yelped in pain.

"I'd rather not say right now," said Fiona apprehensively, cocking her head towards the two youngins.

"Good to see ya!" said Ethel, rubbing her shin vigorously in pain.

Kathryn and Billy smiled as they sat down at the table with the gang.

"Good 'ta see you two!" cried Peg as she sat up straight flashing Fiona a concerned look.

It was then that Mr. Kennedy came crashing into the room, his face as white as a ghost!

"I think – I think, I done seen a pooka!" he cried horrified.

"A pooka?" said Seamus. "Man, look at you! You're as white as the moon!"

"You're having us on!" said Sodge Crawley.

"I swear, I seen it with me own eyes!" rattled off Mr. Kennedy, panting heavily. "I saw a set of glowing eyes in the bushes, just out back!"

"You're sippin' on the whiskey too hard there!" said Mr. Michael Dimmler.

"I told ya, I done seen one!" replied Mr. Kennedy emphatically.

"Let's go and have a look," said Mr. Paul Hewson intrigued.

The four men wandered out back, and let their eyes adjust to the darkness. A rattling noise came from behind one of the bushes, startling them.

"Hear that?" said Mr. Kennedy flustered.

"I do," replied Mr. Paul Hewson, moving ever so close to the jiggling bush.

The thorny bush shook and then shivered, it became still, and then it shuddered a few times.

"Be careful now," said Mr. Michael Dimmler fearfully.

"Stand back now faery!" cried Mr. Kennedy, holding a stick and waving it at the trembling bush.

Mr. Paul Hewson outstretched his aged, withered hand, reaching slowly behind the twisted bush. The men fell silent as the grave as his hand and then his arm disappeared into the bristly leaves. Mr. Paul Hewson's eye lurched outward as he sucked in a deep stream of night air. His mouth dropped open and he screamed, "You fool!" Clenching his hand on a rope, he pulled out a scrawny donkey, "It's just, Jezebel!"

The men laughed whole heartedly.

"You need to cut back on that whiskey, Mr. Kennedy," said Mr. Paul Hewson.

The gentlemen made their way back into the Céilí, all with a good laugh in their belly, all except for Mr. Kennedy, whose face was now bleach white. Mr. Kennedy's sour face soon changed after he grabbed himself a pint and began to roam aimlessly around the Céilí.

"Now, is your Grandfather not coming?" asked Peg to Kathryn.

"No," said Kathryn, sitting next to George who was dressed up like a faery, all glittery and shimmering with wings mounted on his back.

"Ol' man Murphy hasn't been seen in town since the time of the flood," said Mr. Kennedy after over hearing Peg's question.

"Yeah, he's too busy looking for leprechaun's than to come down here! Now, where's the grub?" said Billy hungrily.

"Over there by the wall, there are some lovely stews, bangers and mash, and some fish and chips for you," replied Peg.

Colin Hennessey made his way over to the table, his haired slicked back to contain all his bouncy curls. "Come on, Seamus!" he said smoothly, gazing over to the lovely Joan Crawley, whom was sitting next to her father Sodge Crawley. "'Tis time to have the women swoon over us!"

"Oh, I already have my women here, Colin," remarked Seamus, placing his hands tenderly on Marie and Peg.

"Aye," remarked Ian stepping in between Seamus and Colin. "She's a dreamy lass that she is, oh, but I'd be keepin' me eye on 'dat one 'dere, before the faeries come prowling to take her in the night, to be one of them!" And then he staggered away.

"He's daft that fella now, isn't he?" declared Colin, strapping his guitar over his shoulder and walking on to the stage with Seamus. The crowd cheered eagerly.

"Don't kid yourself! If you don't think he'd give you a run for the money for Joan," whispered Seamus to Colin and then flipped on the microphone and began to speak into it. "We'd like 'ta thank all of you for comin' out this fine night and helping us celebrate the Nights of the Faeries. Tomorrow is the official beginnings at sunset. So, be careful to protect yourselves against those wee little faeries or they'll come and snatch you right up! Though, there are a few folks here in town that not many of us would mind if they were taken away! Am I right there, Colin?" chuckled Seamus.

"Some could go... and some could stay!" said Colin amusingly, staring at Joan.

"Now, then a toast to the Nights of the Faeries, *sláinte!*" said Seamus, raising his frothy glass up high.

"*Sláinte!*" roared the room.

"A one, a two, a one, two, three, four!" sung Colin as he began strumming on his fine-looking guitar.

What do you do with a screamin' Banshee?
What do you do with a screamin' Banshee?
What do you do with a screamin' Banshee?
Early in the evenin'?
Wey-hey up she wailing,
Wey-hey up she wailing,
Wey-hey up she wailing,
Early in the evenin',
Duck out of the way of the silver comb,
Duck out of the way of the silver comb,
Duck out of the way of the silver comb,
Early in the evenin',

Eddie dressed up as a leprechaun with his tweed trousers and hardened leather boots, leapt on to the table and began to tap his feet to the music, and then ducked down low as he could as if the banshee was throwing her silver comb at his head.

Wey-hey up she wailing,
Wey-hey up she wailing,
Wey-hey up she wailing,
Early in the evenin',
Give 'er dose of salt and water,
Give 'er dose of salt and water,
Give 'er dose of salt and water,

George picked up the saltshaker and sprinkled a dusting over Marie's head, while Marie dipped her fingers into water glasses and splashed water droplets on George's bulky glasses.

Early in the evenin',
Wey-hey up she wailing,
Wey-hey up she wailing,
Wey-hey up she wailing,
Early in the evenin',
What do you do with a screamin' Banshee?

What do you do with a screamin' Banshee?
What do you do with a screamin' Banshee?
Early in the evenin',
Wey-hey up she wailing,
Wey-hey up she wailing,
Wey-hey up she wailing,
Early in the evenin',
Pull 'er eyelashes out and make 'er cry,
Pull 'er eyelashes out and make 'er cry,
Pull 'er eyelashes out and make 'er cry,

And when you are not supposed to laugh, it is the very devil himself to keep it in. Little Marie then tried to pull out Billy's eyelashes, while he pretended to cry like a wailing banshee. Kathryn was beside herself with laughter as they horsed around the table. It was then that the entire Lott family entered the cafeteria with Mrs. Duffy.

Early in the evenin',
Wey-hey up she wailing,
Wey-hey up she wailing,
Wey-hey up she wailing,
Early in the evenin',
Make 'er kiss the drunken sailor,
Make 'er kiss the drunken sailor,
Make 'er kiss the drunken sailor,

Marie started then dancing around all the men and kissed them on their rosy cheeks. I believe Mr. Kennedy especially received more than one, while Sheliza strolled over towards their table with Quinn.

Early in the evenin',
Wey-hey up she wailing,
Wey-hey up she wailing,
Wey-hey up she wailing,
Early in the evenin',
What do you do with a screamin' Banshee?
What do you do with a screamin' Banshee?
What do you do with a screamin' Banshee?
Early in the evenin',
Wey-hey up she wailing,
Wey-hey up she wailing,
Wey-hey up she wailing,
Early in the evenin',
Stick your fingers in your ear,
Stick your fingers in your ear,
Stick your fingers in your ear,

The ladies at the table clapped happily along with the pounding beat of the band, while Marie began to poke her fingers into George's ears and then surprisingly enough, it was Billy's turn. Sheliza approached the table observing Eddie wiggling his wide butt around with the points of his fingers sticking into his floppy ears.

Early in the evenin',
Wey-hey up she wailing,
Wey-hey up she wailing,
Wey-hey up she wailing,
Early in the evenin',

The crowd clapped wildly in their seats when Seamus and Colin finished their set.

"Oh look Quinn, it's the retard family," said Sheliza scathingly to Quinn, staring at Marie who was still dancing around in her feathery faery costume, "with their pet changeling!"

"Mind your manners young lady!" said Peg, disgusted, her chest flaring about.

"By the way Kat, your shirt is inside out," laughed Sheliza taking a seat at a nearby table.

"Am I a changeling Mum?" asked Marie, "because then I would be a real faery!"

"No, dear," said Peg her eyes fixed on Sheliza. "You're my beautiful sweet little girl."

Sheliza raised her voice for Kathryn and her companions to hear, "So, Dad is it true that we own the Murphy's land and they may lose their home?"

"What is she talking about Kat?" asked Billy puzzled.

"No clue..." said Kathryn.

"Some say 'da Lotts own your land. Way before your Grandfather came. 'Da Lotts own half 'ev 'da Mountain, but I say 'da faeries own it! See, only a few years ago I found the secret," said Ian bizarrely.

"What secret?" asked Sheliza inquisitively, towering over the table.

"Can't you mind your own business, Sheliza?" barked Billy, crossing his legs on the empty seat next to him.

"Wh-wh-wh secret," chanted George, rocking back and forth in his faery outfit, his wings flittering.

"'Da secret way to get into Aählyéé, I'z found it!" said Ian scratching his neck.

Now, it just so happened that Mr. Hennessey had just crossed the room which allowed Sodge Crawley to make his way over to the table to visit his wife and daughter.

"The only way into Aählyéé is through the Raven's Gate, Ian," said Kathryn informatively.

"'Tis a lie!" cried Ian. "Those faeries can pop out anywhere, so why would there be only one way in and one way out?"

"Because, that's what the legend says," urged Kathryn, "that's why!"

"I tells ya, there's more than one ways in!" said Ian irritated.

"You're all a bunch of fools, if you ask me!" said Sodge as he walked by. "If you can't see it, or touch it, or hear it... It's not real! All you youngins' dream your life away on these myths and legend! It's just an absolute waste of time if you ask me!"

"Yeah, you're a bit crazy, Ian!" said Billy.

"I'm not crazy! I know... I have been there!" said Ian passionately, throwing his napkin on the table and marching away.

Oddly enough Sheliza followed him as he walked away.

Father O' Toole approached the table, his face round like a bouncy ball with two thick eyebrows hanging over his eyes. "Are you havin' a good bit of craic now?" he said kindly, sinking into the seat next to Kathryn.

"Brilliant craic, Father," said Fiona jovially, "just brilliant!"

"Father, can I ask you? How does a Priest have a Nights of the Faeries Céilí in a Church's basement?" asked Kathryn, with a note of confusion in her voice.

"Oh, it's all in good fun!" said Father O'Toole, "but, it's a very good question dear. It goes way back to when Ireland was a pagan land, filled with Celts and their beliefs in faeries. The Christian monks came across the great big sea to spread the good word. When the monks came, they found it difficult to change the old ways of the people. So, they embraced the local traditions and sort of intertwined Christianity with their pagan practices."

"I don't understand."

"Well, take St. Brigid for example," said Fr. O'Toole. "There was a pagan goddess named Brigid, did you know that?"

Kathryn shook her head in reply.

"Well, back in the day, the monks took this influential pagan goddess and her feast day and made it Saint Brigid's feast day, a Christian holiday. This helped them create a connection and they incorporated certain customs, like walking around St. Brigid's well barefoot into our Christian Saint Brigid's feast day. They understood this and liked the practice of this ceremony. So now, where there was something pagan now has become a Christian ritual to a Christian Saint. And they did all these little changes in order to convert the Celts to Christianity, so they would understand Christianity better."

"Oh wow!" said Kathryn, taking a bite of her crunchy salt and vinegar crisp. "So, what does that have to do with the Nights of the Faeries?"

"It's all about embracing what was and knowing what is, that's all," answered Fr. O'Toole.

"So, do you believe in faeries, Father?" asked Kathryn.

"I, my child, believe in God and that's all I need to believe in," replied Fr. O'Toole serenely.

"Excuse me! Excuse me just for a second," said Seamus into the microphone. "We have a wonderful surprise! Michael Dimmler here is going to tell us a story, just like the old Seanachai's did back in the day."

"I'll be seeing you at Mass this Sunday, won't I?" asked Father O'Toole to Kathryn.

"Yes, Father," said Kathryn respectfully.

"Here he is," said Seamus blissfully.

Michael Dimmler placed a tweed cap on his head and slid down into a hard wooden chair. A blazing peat fire was behind him, filled with cast iron pots and pans. He cleared his throat and began, "Now, where would a storyteller be without his hat and sittin' by a beautiful roaring fire? Now, you've all heard of the stories of Queen Maeve and all about her grand fight in the story of the Cattle Raid of Cooley with the brown bull of Ulster and the white horned bull of Connaught. Queen Maeve herself had untamed hair like a lioness and dressed in wild animal skin along with soft thick animal fur. No mortal man would dare to fight her, none that would want to live to see another day that is. Well, what you don't know about is when Queen Maeve crossed over to the other side, into the realm of faeries, yes, the Otherworld as some call it, or as we say, into the world of Aählyéé!

"Well, when Queen Maeve arrived in Aählyéé, all the faeries did not bow down to her. For they said amongst themselves, *"Who is she? She is but a mere mortal Queen and we faeries already have many of our own Queens! Why should we bow down to this one?"* Well, that sent Queen Maeve into a tizzy. She tried to recruit the smaller faeries, the weaker ones, but they just danced around her and put flowers in her hair. *"Well, no faery will rule over me!"* she declared. So, then she went in search for her long lost bull, the white horned bull of Connaught and when she found him, she brought him back to Aählyéé and paraded him around in front of all the faeries. The faeries said amusingly enough, *"Who is this Queen of Bull?"* and laughed at her.

"So, Queen Maeve set out on a long journey, to find the most beloved treasures in all of Ireland. When she returned, some of the faeries were impressed with all her jewels of power, crowns of Kings, goblets of youth, with all the tasty luster of gold and the rarest most brilliant gems. But, then the faery folk said to her, *"Of all the jewels in the entire world, none has such beauty and power as the Fire Crystal. You show us that and we shall bow down to you and give you allegiance."* Well, Queen Maeve set out on a quest to find the one true Fire Crystal. But, what she did not know was that it lived inside a monstrous dragon. She searched through every valley, under each rock, swam through all the lakes and rivers, and climbed every mountain. Until one day she found her dragon, but unbeknownst to her, someone else had already found him. The dragon lay dead and its heart was already ripped out and Queen Maeve was left with nothing. And to this very day, the faeries bow to no mortal Queen and Queen Maeve searches endlessly for the Fire Crystal."

The crowd burst into applause and Michael tipped his hat.

"Tell us about Seamus' relations!" cried Colin from across the room slowly sneaking closer and closer to a Miss Joan Crawley, whose eyes batted every time he breathed.

"Seamus?" asked Michael.

"Awww... Go on now," said Seamus.

"Alright then," said Michael, sitting up in his seat. "Let me bring you back to a time when Ireland was full of the faery folk. The Tuatha Dé Danann were known as the ancient people, who were living amongst us mortals. So, it was a time of magic, people, and faeries co-existing together in this land, while we mortal people would fear the night. For all sorts of creatures and fearsome faeries wandered theses lands, seeking to grab hold of you and take ya away, down deep into the depths of the faery mounds, never to be seen or heard from again! It was on one dark and dreadful night, just near twelve o'clock, the witching hour, when Finn O'Sullivan, the local musician, was sittin' in his wee cottage when a terrible rainstorm blew in from the sea. He tried his best to keep himself warm and dry as the crazed winds howled and moaned outside his door, but then, in the thick of it all. Finn heard three raps at the door, ~*thump, ~thump, ~thump*, it went.

"'Who is it?' he called, but no man answered. Then, he heard it again! Three more raps at his door, ~*thump, ~thump, ~thump*, it went. "Who is it, I say?" asked Finn, but still not a sound.

"So, Finn got up from his warm chair by the fire and walked straight away to the door. He feared the faeries were playing with him. So, he called out again, "I heard you knock," he cried. "Will you not answer me?" And then it knocked three more times, ~*thump, ~thump, ~thump*, it went.

"Finn thought to himself, "What if it is the beautiful Kathleen O'Brien, traveling back from her father's house to town, exhausted from her weary travels, and I, the only one who could save her from this dreadful night?" Finn gained the strength of a hundred men and opened the door to see if it was indeed the lovely Kathleen. And do you know what he saw? 'Twas seven faeries just about the size of his thumb, which knocked on his door, soaked to the bone, they were. Finn stared at these wee folk, not sure what to do, so he did the unthinkable and asked them to come in. Well, the faeries made not a sound and waltzed right into his living room and sat down by the fire. At first, Finn couldn't keep his eyes off of them, fixed on their large glowing eyes and knobby ears. Their skin was like the color of dirt and their eyes were as yellow as the sun. Finn of course, being a hospitable host, made them a fine cup a tea along with some biscuits. And after they were all warm and feed, they took out their wee instruments and began to play for Finn. Well, it was the most joyous music that he had ever heard in his life and he couldn't help himself from jumping to his feet and dancing up a storm. Finn laughed, danced, and sang all night with the faeries. As dawn grew near and the storm died, Finn did a bold thing; he opened his mouth and said, "I wish I could play like you!" And then, *poof,* the faeries were gone. They disappeared, right before his eyes.

"Finn found himself back in his warm bed, waking up to the sound of chirping birds. At first, Finn thought of it as only a dream. He went to town and told the locals of his extraordinary dream. They told him, "The faeries had either cursed him or blessed him and the only way to know is to play!" So, Finn took up his fiddle and began to play. And do you know what happened? All the towns' people began to dance around as jolly as they could be, including the lovely Kathleen. For it was the most beautiful music they had ever heard before in their lives. And to this day Finn is known as the best musician in all of Ireland. And so, he married the beautiful Kathleen and all their children to this day are blessed with faery music pulsing through their blood. And Seamus here is one of the descendants of Finn and Kathleen. That is why we all jump to our feet when he begins to play. Will you have a go?"

"I will!" said Seamus happily, cradling his silky fiddle under his chin and began to play like a musical faery.

Colin grabbed a goat skinned bodhrán, while Mr. Hennessey picked up his ten-key accordion and began tinkling his fingers merrily over the ivory keys. The joyous crowd leapt to their feet and then each couple tightly held one another around the waist. Boys and girls began to twirl and spin around the room to the steady beat of the thumping bodhrán with their feet keeping time to the music, knocking heavily on the flagged floor, while shadows, cast by the glow of the fire, began to dance against the walls.

It was then the Kennedy girls, all dolled up in their Sunday's best of gold and emerald green embroidered dresses came stomping out doing their best Irish step. It was, right foot *~tap, ~toe,* left foot *~tap, ~toe, ~knee kick up, ~back, ~toe, ~toe, ~kick,* around and around they danced, *~toe, ~tap, ~knee kick up, ~toe, ~tap, ~kick.* Their bodies jumped high in the air with their soft curls bouncing around like a football in a tournament. The crowd laughed and sang all through the night, and if ever there were a faery out tonight, they just might as well have joined in on all the festivities.

♦ CHAPTER NINE ♦
The Golden Stag

The next day, in the damp misty afternoon air, a hush echoed throughout the school as Kathryn and Billy made their way down the frigid hallway. It was so cold, they could see their breath turn into tiny, misty ice particles before their eyes. The two of them walked as swiftly as they could, hoping to exit the school before they saw the infamous Lotts. Unfortunately, Kathryn and Billy nearly hopped out of their skin when Sheliza and Quinn appeared out of nowhere and stood before them with an annoying smirk on their faces. It was just then that Kathryn became as silent as the grave, holding her head down to the floor as she walked by the snickering duo. They had just reached the door when Sheliza started to do what she does best.

"Great job on your report, Kathryn," said Sheliza snidely, holding up her newly awarded plaque. "Too bad it was drowned in road water! Whatever could've happened to your poor project?"

"Maybe a faery sprayed her with some faery water!!" laughed Quinn.

"Your presentation probably wasn't too bad, if it had survived the splash," remarked Sheliza, buffing her plaque to a shiny high finish, "but your delivery!"

"Heinous!!" said Quinn cruelly. "Two syllables, *bor-ing*!"

"She sounded like a zombie on Ritalin!" snorted Sheliza.

"Will you two cut it out!" said Billy heatedly, pushing past them. "So, you won, Sheliza! *Congrat-you-freakin' lations!*"

"Yes, I did!" smirked Sheliza, "easily too."

"Oh, I wouldn't say that!" commented Billy.

"No?" said Sheliza smugly. "Let see, who's going to see the Stone of Destiny tomorrow?"

Billy rolled his eyes, grabbed Kathryn's arm and said firmly, "Come on, Kat, let's head home. No need to be listening to all this bollocks!"

"Remember, tonight at sunset is the beginning of the Nights of the Faeries!" yelled Sheliza. "Don't be scared when they come knocking on your door, to steal your precious book!"

"Or that cursed necklace!" shouted Quinn.

Billy zipped up his dirty jacket and flipped his hood over his head, while Kathryn remained silent, shivering in the dewy air. A stiff breeze began to blow.

"You've got a real problem with conflict, Kat!" said Billy bitterly, walking down towards the Post Office. "What the hell? Why can't you say anything to her?"

"I-I-I," babbled Kathryn, buttoning her jacket up unevenly, again. "Ugh! I just don't know, I just..."

"Just what?" replied Billy, "you're chicken!"

"No!" exclaimed Kathryn, "I'm not!"

"Seems like it to me," noted Billy. "You just can't seem to open your mouth when someone eggs you on, or does something wrong! Face it, Kat, you don't like any friction, which means, by default, you're chicken!"

"Shut up!" said Kathryn angrily. "I am not! I yell at you all the time!"

"That's because you've known me forever," said Billy. "I can fight with you, but you - you can never stand up for yourself! Ever! You see how snide she is and you just... Well, you just stand there like a pin cushion being poked by needle after needle!"

"I'm not a pin cushion!" said Kathryn furiously as they crossed the stone bridge.

"Yeah, you are!" remarked Billy. "I call them like I see them!"

Kathryn stopped at the edge of the bridge; her face filled with hurt and pain. Her eyes glanced into the raging river water and then she began to walk north along the river, towards the island.

"Where are you going?" screamed Billy, standing alone on the road. "We're supposed to go this way!"

Kathryn remained silent, listening to thunderous river pounding on the stones beneath its murky riverbed. The damp day softened the air like a mushy pillow on Kathryn's pale face as she hiked her way along the river's sunken path, her mismatched shoes squished into the soft mud. Gnarling bushes scratched at her clothing as she progressed further up the overgrown path, while shooting branches, which seemed to jump out in front of her, pricked in her face.

Soon, she was by herself, no one in sight. She was at one with the river, it rumbled and thrashed itself about her. The island's solitude called to her. Standing before it, her eyes squinted through the thick air, she caught a glimpse of a fallen deer, stuck deep in the sandy island, its body covered in sweaty dirt.

"Oh my!" she cried, moving closer to where the deer lay as its hind legs shot down into the moistened sand. "It's stuck!" she said. A furious rush of blood flooded her body as she thought, *Rule Number Four: It's okay, to make a plan as you go!!! It is... the Indiana Jones way! Go For It!*

Kathryn bravely scoured the shoreline, searching for a way to cross over. With her wits about her, she began to search underneath the twisted thorny bushes and piles of mud soaked leaves. There, at the bottom of all the gunk and grime, she found a warped wooden board covered with rusty old nails, which were as sharp as wolves teethes and were as filthy as a pigpen.

Gently, she clasped her hands around the weathered board, hauling it over to where the river narrowed between the land and the island. She lowered the board down and the cold river water rushed over her hands, which quickly wrinkled like a raisin as the furious river surged down upon her. Carefully, she placed the board upon the larger rocks that broke the chasm between her and the island. The river continued to crash down upon her bridge. Stepping back, she slowly peeled off her jacket, removed her discolored shoes along with her patched up socks, and then rolled her pant legs up one at a time. Lifting one foot up, she softly placed it on the rotted board; chills tingled up her spine from the rushing ice water dancing around her bare feet. The cold went deep into the marrow of her bones as she murmured, *"Cold, cold water...* Yeah, that's all I need!"

Wobbling across the wafer-thin-board, she rapidly made her way to the other side of the island and began to sing, as she shivered, "Take me to the river... drop me in the water..." Chills bubbled through her as she pushed her way through the sharp thistle flowers towards the lame deer. The wounded deer jolted with fear as Kathryn hovered in closer.

"It's ok, I'm not going to hurt you!" she whispered, walking behind the animal, as it flinched upward away from her presence.

Kathryn caught a glimpse of its back left leg, which was bloodied and broken.

"You poor thing!" she said moving closer. The deer struggled in pain, trying to escape from her. "Oh no! I'm just making this worse aren't I? I'm sorry." The deer floundered again trying to flee free from her. "I-I was just trying to help.... Oh, no," the deer yelped, "I'm sorry... I'm just causing you more pain."

Kathryn slunk her head down, dawdling back to the crooked bridge. "There's nothing I can do for him," she said sorrowfully. Stepping onto the unsteady bridge, her bare foot scrapped against one of the rusty nails, slicing it open.

"Owww!" she screamed, squirming in pain, hopping back to shore on one foot. "*Sugar booger*! That hurt!" Writhing in pain, she picked up the board and spun it quickly around, clipping a tree. The board propelled back towards her, gashing a large wound on her calf. "*Sugar Booger*!" she yelped in distress and dropped the board. Grabbing hold of her bloody leg, she cried, "This is just not cool!" Kathryn bent down, cupped some water from the river and washed her oozing wound. "Grandpa is going to kill me!" she said nervously, rolling down her pant leg and slipping back into her socks and shoes.

It was just about twilight when Kathryn stumbled home from her brazen adventure. Grandpa was outside with Billy, lighting miniature cottages with mini oil lamps within them. For some reason, he believed it would ward off tourists if they thought there were leprechauns living in the houses.

"There now, that will be 'da last of 'em," said Grandpa contently, standing up over a wee cottage, which glowed brightly as if someone was truly living inside it!

"Gramps..." stated Billy, "I-I don't know how to break it to you, but, tourists love leprechauns. They're - they're not scared of them at all!"

"Of course they are!" said Grandpa, squishing his fat lips together. "Those leprechauns are scary, fierce, evil little buggers! They'd be running far, far, away if they knew 'dat they lived here!"

"Ummm... Well, no, sorry, but..." replied Billy cautiously, he looked up to see Kathryn limping on the road. "Hey, it's, Kat!"

"Finally, that girl's back! I've got a few fine words for her!" mumbled Grandpa, adjusting the crooked shingle on one of the cottages.

"People like leprechauns, Grandpa." repeated Billy. "Tourists think if they find one, there's a pot of gold he's stashing away somewhere! So, no, they're not scared of leprechauns, at all, I promise you!"

"What? What! They aren't scared? No, I don't believe it! I tell you! They're fierce critters those leprechauns," grunted Grandpa.

"But, they like them!" said Billy earnestly. Billy's eyes gravitated towards Kathryn's gashed and bloody leg. "What the heck happened to you?"

"I found an injured deer on the island. It was stuck in the sand and I was trying to help it!" she said panting heavily, and then lifted her gooey pant leg up, "and I cut myself, real bad on a rusty nail."

"What? Awww.... Geezzz! What have you done to yourself, girl?" scolded Grandpa, examining her gooey leg. "Look at ya! I am at a loss for ya, girl! Actin' like your Mother, you are! Well, there be none of 'dat! I told yas 'ta come home, straight away, and this - this is what 'ya come back as?"

"I'm ok, I'm fine, really," said Kathryn. "It's just a small itty-bitty flesh wound. I can barely feel it at all!"

Grandpa threw two fingers into his mouth and whistled like a bullhorn. Sheba sluggishly trotted over to him.

"Now, get yourself on Sheba and she'll getcha fixed up!" ordered Grandpa.

"But!" cried Kathryn hesitantly.

"No buts!" snapped Grandpa, smacking Sheba's wide rump. "Billy, help her get up on Sheba!"

Billy held onto Kathryn as she wiggled up on to Sheba's bare back with her leg still dripping blood.

"Gramps!" said Billy. "We can look at her gash and clean it up, ourselves!"

"No! No! She's got a rusty nail cut into her leg and 'da closest good doctor is a three hour drive, with Doctor Cavanaugh out of town and all! Now, off ya go! The devil fly away with you, Kathryn," said Grandpa brashly, whacking Sheba's backside with his weathered cane. The horse began to trot rapidly, up past the old great white oak tree.

Kathryn's eyes squinted in bewilderment as she saw small grayish creatures the size of her hand wiggling their puny wrinkled bodies up the tree's bark; their eyes were burning a deep midnight blue. She rubbed her own eyes in astonishment as she observed these peculiar creatures, which were pouring out of the oak's trunk.

Sheba let out a high pitched *'neigh'* and bolted up Arthur's Seat with Kathryn on her back. Kathryn hung on for dear life as Sheba pranced along the rocky path, flailing her body about like a wee rag doll. Kathryn's head began to whirl. *But, Sheba is so weak. How is she carrying me?* She thought.

Higher and higher they rose up the Mountain, passing steep crags that shot up and down all around them. Hoof by hoof they climbed high into the towering ridges filled with flowering purple heather, handsome pennywort, wild thyme, and brilliant red flowers.

Sheba approached a small causeway, lined with rich emerald green leaves creating a deep tunnel, with a long dark path before her. On the left, a stark tree ravaged with age stood upright, marking its entrance. Sheba made her way through the sea of green; at the end of the passage appeared a small decaying shack. More than just one hole ravaged its roof while the windows appeared glassless and the shutters were held up with one nail which fell haphazardly from the shack.

Sheba stepped onto the dilapidated front porch, stopped, stomped her hoof three times before the warped gray door, and then let out a boisterous, *'neigh!'* The door cracked open and Sheba stomped inside the bewildering, darkened shack.

Kathryn's eyes were heavy from the trip and her body weakened by her open wound. Gurgling and clicking sounds pecked into her ears; her eyes were still shrouded in darkness. Sheba bent her front leg and knelt down and then Kathryn slid off Sheba's back and onto a bed made of dried grass.

A cloaked figure emerged from the back of the shack and Sheba withdrew knowingly. The dark presence drew closer to Kathryn, wheezing deeply as it moved toward her. Kathryn's head turned and watched as a horrifying crinkly white hand rolled up her trousers. Her eyes blurred with tears, but she still was able to see part of this ominous creature's gray face. Where there should have been a nose and lips, there was none; scar tissue pulled straight down to its upper lip as it gave a ghastly snort. The pungent stench of fermenting skin repulsed Kathryn as a deep feminine voice snorted, *"Leighaes cneá."* A piercing torment crippled her body; her leg throbbed in bewildering agony, followed by a soft cooling sensation and calmness. The veiled stranger patted Sheba on her rump and in a stern voice said, *"Téigh."*

Flashes of light pulsated in and out of her eyes as her body was once again thrashed down the mountain upon

Sheba's back. The sounds of crows cawing banged on her eardrums until she was sound asleep.

When she awoke, all her cuts and lacerations were covered in white goo. Looking down, she could see her leg was bound tightly in earthly colored bandages. *How did I get back here? And what the heck was that thing on that Mountain?* she thought.

The wind whipped the leaves around outside her window and then a voice began to bellow from her rusty tin can. "Kat!" it cried, "Kat! Are you up yet?"

Groggily, she searched for her tin voice-box invention.

"Yeah," she grunted, pressing the cold can around her mouth.

"Kat! Kat! You're up!" cried Billy's voice happily from the tin can. "Where have you been?"

"Long story..." said Kathryn as she began to explain her journey up the Mountain and her interlude with the old hag.

"You're not going to believe this one!" blurted out Billy.

Kathryn watched her window's shutters grumble fiercely from the cold wailing winds outside, *~thump, ~thump, ~thump,* it went.

"Believe what?" she asked mildly into the tin contraption.

"What I saw!" rumbled her vibrating gizmo.

Kathryn rolled around onto her stomach, flinching in pain, then cracked her door open and peered out across the living room to meet Billy's crystal blue eyes.

"What?" she said lazily into her doohickey.

"I went back to the island! You know, where you saw the deer, stuck in the dirt!" said Billy cautiously, gazing down at a comatose Grandpa, sleeping heavily in his submerged bed.

"You went back?" questioned Kathryn surprisingly.

"I did, Kat, and - and I saw that same deer! And I tried to save it too," whispered Billy. Kathryn flashed him a fearful look. "I went back! And - and it was magical! It began to change colors and glow like the sun! At first, it was just a blah, boring brown and then it – it began to glitter and pulse with this bright white light and before I knew what was happening, before my very eyes, it changed to *gold!* And it lifted up out of the mud and ran straight up the Mountain! No kidding!"

"It did *what?*" exclaimed Kathryn, causing Grandpa to moan, shifting his weight heavily about in his mushy bed.

"It turned to a brilliant gold and it – it ran up the Mountain! No lie!" declared Billy, with his eyes bulging and his mouth wide open.

Kathryn shook her head in disbelief. Then, a shivering breeze crossed Kathryn's room from a small crack in her window and slammed her bedroom door shut. Kathryn turned on to her back and rolled her eyes muttering, "Boys!"

Kathryn tossed her body weight around forcefully on her bed positioning herself on her right side. Ever so carefully, she slid her hand under her lumpy mattress, pulling out the infamous citrine necklace that had once belonged to her Grandmother, the same exact one which was said to be cursed and had caused such a stir at the Ballyrun Celtic Folklore Competition. She raised the crystal beads up into the dismal light emitting from the cracked oil lamp, perched awkwardly on a rickety stool just beneath her window. The howling wind streamed through the tiny cracks of her weathered shutters, hinged together with a measly strip of wood. Soon, the shutters rattled from the baying winds, drumming uncontrollably against her window, *~thump, ~thump, ~thump*, it went.

She clenched her pillow tightly against her chest as the wind knocked tirelessly against the barred portal. Suddenly, the strip of wood gave way, blasting the shutters open into a spine-tingling boom! Kathryn leapt to her feet and ran quickly to the window; stillness enshrouded her as Arthur's Seat, proudly sat in the distance. Her eyes scouted the hillside searching for life, but none was found. *This place gets weirder and weirder by the minute,* she thought. Holding her necklace up, she twirled it around against the night's sky. *Perhaps you are cursed?* she thought.

Kathryn closed the shutters, placing the broken wood strap between its hinges.

A lone wailing cry from a woman howled outside her window as she turned back to her bed. Every hair on her body stood up at attention as the wailing screech echoed loudly through the night. *What the heck is that?* she thought.

Kathryn sat on her bed, her pillow now glued firmly to her chest as she sat back and took a gulp of frosty air. "What? What was that?" she said fearfully aloud.

The wind knock harder upon her shutters, *~thump, ~thump, ~thump*, it went. Then, another shrieking sound bellowed loudly from the lonely night, like a thunderous bodhrán pounding away at her window, it grew louder and louder after each strike. Her heart seemed to keep the same beat with the wind as she listened to them both. She did not know which one was louder, the wind or her heart.

Another ear-piercing moan jolted her up to her feet, standing upright on her bed. The wee strap of wood began to bend with the brute force of the thrashing wind, *~thump, ~thump, ~thump*, it went.

Crack! The wood strap gave way and the howling wind roared throughout her room, knocking Kathryn back down onto her bed.

Then there, right outside her window, against the blackened night sky, arose an ominous gray woman with milky hair that floated like a feather upon the wind. Her robe was illuminated brightly from the moonlight and she was swaying freely with the moaning of the wind. Slowly, her bony white hand reached out and snatched a silver comb from her unbridled locks. Then, once more, she gave a shivering wailing cry, hurling the silver comb at Kathryn. Kathryn crashed down to the floor.

Thud! The shutters slammed closed. Grandpa pulled out a thicker strap of wood and hammered it into the hinge with his cane. He then inserted a long finger-like purple flower on top of the hinge, turning to Kathryn, he said, "That'll be enough 'ev that tonight!" And then left her room.

*She who cries into the silent night,
Who gives her victims an awful fright,
Lonely and cold she sits all alone,
Preparing to make her scary moan,
Angels of death riding from on high,
Come charging in and won't pass you by,
She is the banshee that wails for you,
Cause this day will be the last for you!*

♦ CHAPTER TEN ♦
The Stone of Destiny

It was another fine brisk morning in Ballyrun when the children entered the wee frigid classroom at the Ballyrun School. Mrs. Mackenzie was busy doing her best brushing away the powdery chalk from the blackboard, but instead she was disastrously causing large amounts of white smoke to puff into the air, causing her to cough incessantly and her eyes to well up like a soggy bog.

Kathryn nestled into her chilly chair and leaning forward she whispered into Billy's ear, "She floated on the wind, I tell you!"

"Awesome!" he replied.

"Class take your seats!" ordered Mrs. Mackenzie with the sound of the bell ringing.

Sheliza Lott swooped into the classroom a few minutes late, smiling grandly at the humble class and then of course at Mrs. Mackenzie, like she was a Queen.

"Thank you for making us a priority, Miss Lott," said Mrs. Mackenzie as she began to write diligently on the slate blackboard. "Don't forget, you'll be leaving early today to meet up with Mrs. Duffy and Mr. Hewson."

Sheliza smirked and then shot Kathryn a cheeky look.

Kathryn just turned away and listened to Mrs. Mackenzie speaking about what was on the agenda for the day.

"Now, here is the pop quiz that I've been alluding to over the week!" said Mrs. Mackenzie while the class groaned. "Take one and pass it back," she said, passing out warm ink covered papers to each of the students in the front row.

"You never told us 'dere was going to be a quiz, Miss!" complained Mugs, smearing the silky ink on his fingers.

"I know, Mugs," she replied strictly, walking back to her spick and span desk, "that is why they are called pop quizzes! Now, no more talking!"

Kathryn took out her clumpy blue pen, signed her name and the date at the top of the bleach white paper, and began to read her quiz.

Kathryn Murphy
October 31st, 1992

1. Neolithic is defined by:
A) Domestication of livestock.
B) Domestication of harvested plants, such as, wheat.
C) Settled communities.
D) Pottery used for storage and cooking.
E) All of the above.

2. What is the name of the Neolithic site, which was discovered in the late 17th century?
A) Stonehenge.
B) Skara Brae.
C) Hill of Tara.
D) Newgrange.

3. Check all that apply:
Which of the following are considered, 'passage tombs'?
A) Newgrange.
B) Knowth.
C) Rúaidhri De Valera.
D) Dowth.

4. Known as, *Árd Rí na hÉireann,* the Hill of Tara was considered to be:
A) Seat of the High King of Ireland.
B) An Iron Age burial site.
C) Where the Stone of Destiny exists.
D) A sacral site associated with Indo-European Kingship rituals.

There was a pounding knock on Mrs. Mackenzie's classroom door, which made the children jolt upright in their seats. Mrs. Mackenzie looked through the door's etched window and saw it was Mrs. Duffy, her face pruned up like a raisin and the austere Fr. O'Toole.

"Class, continue on. I'll be right outside the door," said Mrs. Mackenzie abruptly, before stepping out into the hallway.

Many of the student's eyes glared around the room suspiciously, noting the absence of Mrs. Mackenzie and listening to the animated voices arguing outside the classroom's door. Kathryn braced her hand snugly onto her forehead and continued reading the question.

5. In what year was Skara Brae discovered?
A) 3100-2500 B.C.
B) 3000 B.C.
C) 1928.
D) 1850.

    Biting her fleshy lip, she circled answer D. on the paper. A peculiar rustling sound pricked at her ear. Looking sideways, she saw Sheliza discreetly slide out her European History book and quietly opened it. Kathryn poked Billy's right shoulder with her leaky pen; leaving a thick mass of blue ink on his plaid shirt. He turned around guardedly. Kathryn joggled her head to the side in the direction of Sheliza. Disgusted, they both watched Sheliza flip through her book. The voices outside the door finally quieted down. The doorknob turned. Quickly, Sheliza positioned her book under her seat and remained motionless. Billy and Kathryn rolled their eyes and shook their heads.
    "Mr. and Mrs. Murphy! Are you two cheating?" cried Mrs. Mackenzie rashly, standing in the doorway.
    "No! No, Miss!" they both cried.
    "Well, you better not be or I'll have you both down to see the principal!" said Mrs. Mackenzie walking back to her tidy desk.
    Kathryn tapped her finger repeatedly against her bottom lip as she read the last question on the quiz.

10. Stone Circles are considered to be from the:
A) Neolithic.
B) Late Neolithic/Early Stone Age.
C) Bronze Age.
D) Don't know.

    "Times up, class! Please pass your papers to the front!" said Mrs. Mackenzie, with a hint of annoyance in her voice. A few greenish veins had popped out on her face, creating a roadmap across her once smooth forehead.
    Kathryn quickly circled answer B. and handed her paper to Billy.
    "Right! I also have news about today's dismissal," announced Mrs. Mackenzie reluctantly, collecting the

papers from each student at the front of the row. "Since today is Friday and we're celebrating the Three Nights of the Faeries, I have been instructed that class will be dismissed early today."

Cheers roared throughout the classroom.

"So, Miss Sheliza, you and Quinn will be going up the Mountain when we all get out at noon."

At precisely twelve, the bell tolled which erupted the class into a speedy dash towards the door. Mrs. Duffy and Mr. Hewson had arrived at Mrs. Mackenzie's door spot on, as a swarm of children whipped around them.

"Are ya comin' out tonight, Bill?" asked Mugs.

"What's tonight?" inquired Kathryn.

"It's just 'da best night for 'da Nights of the Faeries! We all dress up like faeries, leprechauns, banshees, and pookas. We carry torches and then go and try to spook as many people as possible. Me Mum dresses up like a wailing banshee every year! And one year, she got me Dad so scared, he puked himself! It was brilliant!" said Mugs with a boastful laugh.

"Ewww... he got sick?" questioned Kathryn.

"It was a good laugh! No one gets hurt! So, are 'yas comin'?" asked Mugs.

"Sure!" answered Billy, waving at Mugs while he shimmied past Mrs. Duffy who still blocked the doorway.

Billy turned to Kathryn and said, "See, it was probably Mug's Mom that was wailing at your window last night!"

"She was floating!" remarked Kathryn. "And she was not human'ish! Is that a word? Anyway, I'm telling you something is going on with this, Nights of the Faeries! Real faeries are coming out! I saw those little ghoulish gray creatures on the oak tree, there was that stag which turned to gold and ran up the Mountain, and then, on top of all that, there was a banshee wailing and banging at my window last night!"

"Cool! Maybe we can break Koréna out of the belly of Arthur's Seat too! Bring her to Ballyrun and show her off like show and tell!" said Billy sarcastically.

Kathryn laughed, "You know, I still don't quite understand how Grandpa climbed my ladder and swooped in there so fast."

"Don't know," shrugged Billy.

Sheliza once again made a majestic exit from the classroom, swaying her golden locks as she followed Mr.

Hewson and Mrs. Duffy down the hall with Quinn trailing behind.

"Check it out!" remarked Kathryn. "They're leaving! Who was talking about the Stone of Destiny having a banshee in it?"

"That would be, Sheliza," answered Billy.

Kathryn beamed, while Billy arched his fuzzy caterpillar eyebrows.

"Are you thinking what I'm thinking?" asked Billy deviously.

"Let's follow them!" replied Kathryn adventurously.

"Deal!"

It was a bright and dry day as Kathryn and Billy trekked up the Mountain, keeping a large enough distance away from Sheliza and her entourage so they wouldn't be noticed.

Billy, who always had a whale of an appetite, reached down into his backpack and pulled out an enormous sandwich and proceeded to gobble it down as the two of them huffed and puffed up the Mountain.

"Whatcha got there?" inquired Kathryn.

"A good 'ol cabbage sandwich!" mumbled Billy, as tiny bits of bread spattered out of his mouth and onto his shirt.

"Really? Didn't you have beans and toast for breakfast?" questioned Kathryn.

"Yup!" replied Billy happily, wiping his sleeve across his mouth. "Tis good!"

"Well, good luck with that!" said Kathryn, as they came to a smooth level area on the Mountain, where a substantial embankment rose behind it.

"Wait!" cried Kathryn, holding Billy back and pointing to her stalking victims. "There they are!"

"And look, there's the Stone of Destiny!" said Billy elatedly, waving his chubby finger at an oblong stone jutting out of the Mountain which was surrounded by a black iron fence.

"Yes! There it is! Don't suppose, if we touch it, it would *roar?*" said Kathryn jokingly.

"Either that or a banshee will come out!" chuckled Billy as his stomach grumbled. "Ohhh, I'm thinkin' that cabbage sandwich was a little too much for me!"

"Come on! Let's get closer and listen," said Kathryn cunningly as she climbed through a prickly bush and slipped behind a well-worn boulder. Billy's stomach gurgled again as the two cocked their ears to listen to Mr. Hewson speaking near the Stone of Destiny.

"Once again, this monolithic stone, called Lia Fáil in Irish or the Stone of Destiny, is perceived to be at the Hill of Tara in County Meath, but here," said Mr. Hewson eloquently, gesturing to the solitary stone, entombed by a cast iron fence, "we have what I believe to be the true Stone of Destiny!"

"How's that?" inquired Quinn.

"Well the stone, which is said to have been brought here by the Tuatha Dé Danann," said Mr. Hewson.

"The ancient people of Ireland," added Sheliza presumptuously.

"Yes, Sheliza, the Tuatha Dé Danann erected the Stone of Destiny on top of the King's Seat on the Hill of Tara. But, it was moved in 1798 after the battle of Tara to mark the graves of 400 men who died there. Now, the Tuatha Dé Danann, the ancient people, would not have liked their treasure moved. So, I believe they placed a counterfeit stone at the Hill of Tara in its place."

"Well, why would you believe this one be the true Stone of Destiny and not the one at the Hill of Tara?" asked Sheliza plainly.

"Excellent question Sheliza! Spot on, girl!" remarked Mrs. Duffy overconfidently.

"Well, what many lay people do not know is that the Stone of Destiny does not only roar for the true King, but whoever touches it will have their destiny revealed to them in exactly seven years! And also, the difference between this stone before us, and the one on the Hill of Tara are the markings of the Tuatha Dé Danann shown here at the base of the stone, as you can see," said Mr. Hewson informatively, directing the group to the faded circular etchings on the stone on the lower left hand side. "See, down here are three circles intertwined. These are the markings of the Tuatha Dé Danann."

"Isn't the Hill of Tara supposed to be a portal to the Otherworld?" asked Sheliza confidently.

"Fine, fine questions Sheliza, keep 'em up!" harped in Mrs. Duffy.

"Yes, yes it is, but we too have our legends here as well, such as Arthur's Seat having its own gateway, portal, or what have you," said Mr. Hewson.

"The Raven's Gate!" shouted Quinn.

"Yes, the Raven's Gate! Another gateway into the realm of

the faeries," suggested Mr. Hewson. "So, it would make sense that the Tuatha Dé Danann would move it over here!"

"Well, how did they do it? The Hill of Tara has got to be close to 300 kilometers away!" questioned Sheliza brashly.

"It's all done through the mists, swirls, and the mystery of magic," said Mr. Hewson harmoniously.

"Well, what do those circles really mean?" asked Quinn.

"Now, you're asking the good questions me boy!" said Mr. Hewson enthusiastically.

Sheliza let out a loud huff and crossed her arms across her chest.

"See, how the three circles are linked together? This is what is known as the Celtic knot, which can represent a variety of things in our world. The knot can represent the mortal world, the Otherworld, and the celestial world, sort of like, Earth, Purgatory, Heaven and Hell. It can represent the family; father, mother, and the child. Or even God, as we Irish Christians describe it with the shamrock leaf, the Father, the Son, and the Holy Spirit. Even with time, there is always a past, a present, and a future. And then moving forward to the human existence there is the mind, the body, and the Spirit; all connecting, all dependent upon the other and needing one another to exist, all of them alluding to a beginning or an end. It's a cycle of birth and rebirth in our world, and in the ethereal realms.

"Ether - Ethereal realms?" questioned Quinn.

"The Otherworld, boy! The faery realm! Aählynéé! You see, the Celtic knot shows how one circle is dependent on another and in turn when unified together, make it complete. Without one of the three circles, it would all fall apart! Don't you see that?" said Mr. Hewson.

Sheliza and Quinn stared blankly and then blinked at Mr. Hewson, like someone opened the windows in their ears to let in some fresh air, only there was nothing to refresh.

"Now, come along this way! There are some very interesting ruins of an ancient fort over this mound that I'd like to show you," said Mr. Hewson, walking up the high embankment with Mrs. Duffy, Sheliza, and Quinn following behind, doe-eyed.

"Come on, let's check it out!" said Billy impatiently, leaping to his doughy feet as a thunderous rumble rose from his lower belly.

"Are you, ok?" asked Kathryn, as they moseyed over to the Stone of Destiny. Billy just shrugged his shoulders and was tight lipped as he slowly turned pink. "Look Billy, the three circles, that's the mark of the Tuatha Dé Danann. That's in *The Legends of Arthur's Seat!*"

"But, what does it really mean, besides three things dependent on one another?"

"I don't know, but I want to touch it! See if it *roars*!" she said animatedly, holding her hands up like a lion.

Kathryn's muddied shoe stepped upon the fence's iron frame. She lunged with her right arm out towards the stone, as far as she could possibly go. Her fingers dangled in the cool air, she was ever so close to the magnificent stone.

"I - I think, I can reach it!" she said wishfully, straining her arm towards the stone.

"Not unless you grow another two feet!" said Billy cynically.

Kathryn heaved a woeful sigh and stepped down from the fence. "Maybe, I can if..." she said hopefully, flopping back down to the ground. She untied one of her brown shoes and then peeled off her sock. Leading with her stubby big toe, her bare foot slid through the fence, and then her leg followed through the posts, her toes just barely touching the frigid, silent Stone of Destiny. "I think - I think - I think I can make it!" she cried, pressing her body harder against the iron fence.

Lingering voices arose from the other side of the embankment, stopping Kathryn in her tracks.

"Kat!! They're coming!" cried Billy nervously.

Kathryn pushed away harder from the fence, causing her big fat toe to spring outward farther just scrapping the stone's surface. A brilliant flash of light flickered from the Stone of Destiny.

"What was that?" questioned Billy suspiciously, grabbing hold of Kathryn's sweaty armpits and forcefully heaving her away from the stone.

"I don't know. Strange, I just felt an electric shock," replied Kathryn frazzled, promptly grabbing her mucky shoe and sock.

The voices from the other side of the embankment grew louder.

"Come on, hurry up!" cried Billy impatiently. As the two darted behind the boulder, they could hear the sweet, charming sound of Mr. Hewson's voice rising up off of the Mountain.

"Long, long ago before you and I were born, when the

swallow's built their wee nests in old men's beards, when the faery folk walked in and out of our mortal realm, as indeed they do to this very day, there lived a great chieftain on the other side of the Mountain, near Loch Dorcha. One day, he was snatched away by the faery folk. Sometimes in the morning amongst the fresh dew and mist upon the lake this great chieftain will suddenly appear on the glassy waters of Loch Dorcha, which is on the other side of Arthur's Seat!"

"Really?" asked Quinn.

Billy barreled over on to his back, tightly clenching his fat belly and rolling in unbearable pain behind the boulder, as his stomach gurgled louder and louder.

"*Shhh...*" hushed Kathryn, watching Billy's face turn a bright pink and then to a scorching red.

"I've–I've–I've got gas," he whimpered, holding his stomach, *"bad!!!"*

"Well, keep it silent!" whispered Kathryn, peering out from the boulder.

"The legend of O'Donoghue is said to have taken place on Loch Killarney, but we have had many sightings on Loch Dorcha of O'Donoghue, where he is seen as a ghostly rider, high up on a fantastic white steed accompanied by exquisite maidens riding along side of him, gliding on the surface of the Loch. Perhaps he appears because we are so close to Arthur's Seat?"

"Well, what's the legend?" asked Sheliza.

"Ugh!!" whimpered Billy tearfully. "I-I can't take it anymore!"

"*Shhh...*" whispered Kathryn, turning around to see Billy. Her eyes widened as she watched the back of his jeans begin to swell up, like a hot air balloon.

"What are you doing?" she hissed.

"I'm–I'm trying to – to let one go, *but*," gasped Billy.

"The legend goes, O'Donoghue laid out a grand feast for all his friends and family," said Mr. Hewson impressively.

"It's–it's not comin' out!" huffed Billy, while his jeans began to inflate like a puffed up American soccer ball.

"And then, sitting at the feast's table, he fell into a deep trance and made extraordinary predictions of the grand future of Ireland," continued Mr. Hewson.

"How many double trouble bubble gums did you swallow?" asked Kathryn repulsively, gawking at Billy's enlarging, bulbous seat.

"Then, he stood up!" said Mr. Hewson prideful, his voice carrying down the Mountain.

"I-I don't know," whimpered Billy, "a lot?"

"Billy!" scolded Kathryn, "this is exactly what happened in Brooklyn! What were you thinking?"

"And he stepped out on to the mirror like surface of the Loch, proudly he turned around to his mesmerized guests, and said," said Mr. Hewson.

Pop! A deafening noise exploded from behind the boulder that would've awoken even the dead.

"What? What on earth was that?" exclaimed Mrs. Duffy, thwarting over to the boulder.

"Mr. and Miss Murphy! Are you two spying on us?" yelled Mrs. Duffy irately.

Billy now grasped on to his derriere, which was now stuck to his tender skin and whimpered, "Ummm... No, Miss?"

"This is absolutely deplorable! Spying on us! This is Sheliza's special outing and you two ruined it for her!" hollered Mrs. Duffy.

"Yes, I'm quite disgusted Mrs. Duffy," chimed in Sheliza. "Especially, after all that hard work I did on my project!"

"Now, now ladies! No harm, no foul, they're allowed to climb the Mountain if they want to," remarked Mr. Hewson.

"Mind you two! Your Grandfather will hear about this!" barked Mrs. Duffy.

Kathryn sat zipped mouth, as Mrs. Duffy turned angrily away and began marching down the Mountain.

"Cat still got your tongue?" snickered Sheliza. "I guess we can, officially call you now, Billy *bubble butt*!"

Quinn howled with laughter along with a few snotty snorts.

"I guess you won't be *sticking* around here any longer?" giggled Sheliza, turning away and following Mrs. Duffy down the Mountain.

CHAPTER ELEVEN
THE RAVEN'S GATE

A dense, swirling mist crept its way ever so slowly off Arthur's Seat, causing a thick, heavy haze to blanket all of Ballyrun. No one in the town could see more than just a few feet in front of themselves; even the O'Keefe's stopped serving the post for the day. The chilly and eerie fog had more than half of the town's folks staying securely behind closed doors. At least, that's what they told their neighbors. It was most definitely not because they feared any faeries roaming about in that mischievous mist. Surely that was not the reason why they closed their shutters, locked their doors, and hid in their cupboards!

It just so happened that the white mist traveled down the Mountain when Mr. Hewson escorted Kathryn and Billy bubble butt Murphy into Flannery's. Mrs. Flannery was too busy chatting away with Mr. Kennedy at the bar when the bell clanged three times. Mr. Hewson escorted Billy and Kathryn through the door. Kathryn, of course, was covered head to toe with mucky dirt, while Billy, whom was also filthy, had the extra pleasure of bubble gum goo oozing out of his trousers.

"Fiona, could you help these two clean up?" asked Mr. Hewson, taking off his hat and collapsing on a stiff barstool.

Fiona laid eyes on the dirty crew, stood straight up, placed her hands securely on her hips, and said harshly, "Now, what happened to the two of you?"

Billy squeamishly hid his derriere and mumbled, "Ummm..."

"Seems, these two youngins decided to follow myself, Mrs. Duffy, and Mr. and Miss Lott up the Mountain today, to steal a peek at the Stone of Destiny."

Kathryn and Billy's faces flushed red-hot as they lowered their heads down to the dusty floor, just in time to watch a shiny beetle scurry across it.

"Oh, did you now?" scorned Fiona. "Off, on another one of your adventures, were you now, hmmm? While your poor Grandfather is up in that cottage, all alone! He can barely keep up with the two of you! Come on now, back behind the bar. There are some wet towels and the sink is there as well."

"Sorry, Fiona," said Kathryn softly, shuffling behind the mahogany bar, laden with cloudy pint glasses, chipped china plates, crinkled packages of crisps, and tons of dusty brown liquor bottles.

"Yeah, sorry Fiona," said Billy gloomily, following Kathryn behind the bar.

"May I?" asked Paul courteously, gesturing to the tap of dark porter that sat before him.

"Just a moment, Paul," replied Fiona, running the hot and cold water on a few white towels and wringing them out. "I've got to get these two pig pens squared away!"

"Oy... Would ya look there? Is that your man now?" belched Mr. Kennedy, staring out of Flannery's front door.

"Who's that now?" asked Fiona, leaning over the bar and out the door's window.

"Your dark stranger, I see there across 'da street!" mumbled Mr. Kennedy.

Mr. Hewson leaned backwards on his barstool. Suddenly, a dark stranger wearing a long billowy robe, his face covered by a concealing hood broke through the dense fog and glided, as if on air, up to Flannery's front door.

A spine-tingling chill crawled up Fiona's back and then she said commandingly, "Get on the floor, now!" to Kathryn and Billy.

"What?" questioned Kathryn.

Fiona pushed them both down to the slimy mats covered in stinky beer, "Down!! Get under the shelf, and not a word!" said Fiona demandingly.

The wee golden bell over the door distinctly fell silent as the mysterious cloaked stranger pushed the heavy door open into Flannery's. A soft wisp of damp air filled the room as the stranger made his way in.

Kathryn and Billy squished themselves under the chipped wood shelves, which still smelled of cheap whiskey beneath Fiona's bar. Promptly, the two of them became as still as statues. Kathryn fixed her eye through a tiny teardrop hole cut through the wood bar. Her gaze landed on the stranger's dark cloth boots strapped in leather and adorned with wee crimson crystals, which flickered as if they were alive. Kathryn heard Fiona's shoes squeak away from the two of them, back to the oversized bar taps of harps and dragons.

The clink of a glass hit the bar and then she heard the soft sound of dark porter being poured into the pint glass.

"May I be of service to you, Sir?" asked Fiona directly to the stranger.

A high pitched, somewhat feminine voice spoke gently, "I search for Laurel Murphy's children."

Foam spewed out from the overflowing pint glass, spilling down to the counter and onto Fiona's white shirt. "Oh, dear! What – What a mess!" she cried nervously, flipping the tap off and flicking the foamy beer off her shirt. She walked over to grab a wet towel from above Billy's head.

"Laurel? Children?" she remarked ambiguously, rubbing the dark beer from her shirt.

"Yes," said the stranger persistently.

"Did Laurel have children?" questioned Paul.

"A boy and a girl," answered the beguiling stranger.

"Yes – Yes, Laurel went to America, a long time ago," remarked Fiona accurately.

"She returned," replied the determined stranger.

"Well, she did - did she?" replied Fiona. "But, well no, actually she never did make it back to Ballyrun. Don't know what ever happened to her."

"Thank you," replied the stranger and then exited the bar.

"*Quick!* Lock the door!" cried Fiona frantically to Paul.

"Did 'yas see his eyes? They were as blue as the morning sky," muttered Mr. Kennedy into his pint. "Just, simply beautiful! Hmphh... They remind me of..."

Billy's head popped out from under the bar, along with Kathryn and said excitedly, "I don't believe what just happened! I can't believe Fiona lied! Wow!"

"So, what did he look like?" asked Kathryn, peeling off some remnant pieces of paper now stuck to her knees.

"Oh, dear! This – this is not good!" said Fiona frightfully.

"Fiona?" said Paul anxiously.

"Well, who was he?" asked Billy.

"I'll tell you, who he was," said Mr. Kennedy confidently. "He was a Danyär, *that's* who he was!"

"Mr. Kennedy," said Fiona edgily.

"I know - I know! You all think of me as the town drunk," said Mr. Kennedy, looking down into his dwindling frothy glass. "A man washed away in his drink, a man not smart enough to know the difference between a faery and that smelly old donkey. But, I tell you, I've seen things and maybe I know a bit too much. Perhaps that's why I've made friends with the bottle, for the bottle never doubts me, she's always listens."

"I'd say we all like it a bit too much," said Paul jokingly.

"Go on Mr. Kennedy," said Kathryn encouragingly.

"Yes, I've seen things which would make a grown man, even at my age, cry," said Mr. Kennedy guardedly. "Me mother, she used to tell us tales, when we were just wee lads. Tales about Tír na nÓg and the Otherworld, tales about what really happened when Danú took the Tuatha Dé Danann out of this mortal world and into the Otherworld."

"You mean, Aählynéé," said Billy informatively.

"No, no man, Aählynéé wasn't created yet!" said Mr. Kennedy agitated. "Don't you see... Aählynéé is a world between worlds. It is the world between the Otherworld and the mortal world, a place where man and faery can co-exist, filled from the magic from the teine criostal, the heart of a double red-winged dragon. It is that teine criostal that the Danyär seek!"

"You mean, the Fire Crystal?" said Billy.

"Only a lay man would say, the Fire Crystal. It is the teine criostal, in *Irish*!"

"Who are they?" asked Kathryn, "the Danyär?"

"The Danyär, they are Holy Elves," answered Mr. Kennedy, swirling around the last drops of froth in his pint.

"Holy Elves?" repeated Kathryn.

"Elves, who have taken an oath to find the teine criostal, they will stop for no one; they kill *all* in their path, for they fear no man and no faery. They are ruthless," said Mr. Kennedy forebodingly. "When I was a child, I had gone up Arthur's Seat, like we always did when we were kids, with me brothers. They'd dared me to go up farther, to disappear, to play that game called hide and go seek. So, I hid, I hid very well, not a soul could find me and then, I seen them unholy creatures."

"The Danyär?" asked Billy.

"The Danyär, they captured me, said they were looking for a young woman and a man," said Mr. Kennedy, his eyes glossing over as he gulped down the last of his warm porter. "They hauled me off to a secret campsite, tortured me over and over again, asking me questions about the man and the woman. When the night came, I got me wits about me again and when they weren't looking, I escaped! Never went up that Mountain again! So, it's best if you stay away too!"

"Danyär... in Ballyrun?" said Fiona dreadfully, watching the dense, spiraling mist creep out of town. "Mr. Kennedy shame on you! All these years, you demeaning Ian and all these years, you actually believed in the faeries! Paul, watch the bar," said Fiona shortly, turning to the two misfits, while veins like textured roads began to appear all over her face. "You two are coming with me!"

A frigid chill surrounded the wee cottage's living area. Kathryn and Billy were sitting on two icy, rigid carriage chairs with their shoulders slumped over. Looking up at their Grandfather, their eyes ticked back and forth as they watched him pace back and forth. It was just now, when his knobby cane began to be used as a tool, to display his anger rather than a crutch, and he shook it wildly above his head.

"I don't believe 'da two of 'yas!" he said enraged. "First off, a Mrs. Duffy stopped by 'da cottage with 'da most annoying two little snotty nosed children I 'ave ever seen. She told me 'dat 'yas decided 'ta go and follow them up 'da Mountain 'ta see 'da Stone of Destiny, when 'yas were fully aware 'dat it was not your prize and 'ya took it away from that bratty Sheliza. Then I'm told 'dat at 'da pop quiz today in your class, you were both cheatin'. Now, Fiona brings 'ya on home... with you, Billy, covered all up in this mush that's stuck 'ta your buttocks!" ranted Grandpa, directing his warbled cane towards Billy's bum. "I just don't know what 'ta do with 'da both of 'yas! I tell 'ya this, you're both now grounded, and 'yas can't leave this property, at all for 'da whole weekend! Can't be goin' 'ta town or prancing up 'dat Mountain, ya hear? Now, off 'ta bed with 'yas now!"

"But – but, it's still daylight outside Gramps!" argued Billy.

Grandpa pursed his fleshy red lips, pausing for just a moment and said, "You'll stay there 'til mornin'! Now, up 'yas go!"

Kathryn and Billy both parted ways. Wearily, step-by-step, they climbed up their crooked, old ladders. Kathryn's pant leg tugged against the knobby ladder, revealing her bandaged calf, snugly bound in cloth.

"Oh, and don't think, I forgot about your crazy shenanigans 'da other night with 'dat deer! I didn't be forgettin' 'dat as well! Awww... Geezzz.... What am I gonna do now? I know - I know, I'll go tend 'ta Sheba, sweet 'orse!" said Grandpa, sliding into an aged cloak and cracking open the weathered front door. "Sheba doesn't go off on crazy adventures! Unlike, 'da two of you do! No, she's always 'dere for me!"

Kathryn collapsed on to her bed, her head spinning around wondering what everything meant: the deer, the peculiar crinkly creatures on the oak tree, the banshee, the Stone of Destiny, the old hag with no face, the stranger in town, or should she say, the Danyär in town? *Did these things really happen?* she thought. *Strange how all these odd occurrences began with the Nights of the Faeries.*

Kathryn positioned, *The Legends of Arthur's Seat* on her lap and began flipping through the pages. So many pages, so many pictures of eccentric faeries, sharp elven faces, banshees with wild locks, decaying, skeleton goblin-like figures, half sized hairy men with wart covered noses, medieval knights in black armor, warriors wearing tartan kilts, and peculiar writings, which made no real sense to her, and there wasn't even an index to guide her. She slammed the book shut and bronzed dust spewed out from the closed pages, causing her eyes to blur. She twisted around on the bed, wiggling her hand underneath her mattress, and pulled out the cursed, citrine necklace. Draping her fingers through the shimmering strands, she held the necklace up to the light. The crystals flickered in the warm glow of the oil lamp, like stars dancing in the night's sky. Gradually, her watery eyes began to focus on some anomalies in the coloring of the citrine beads. Some were just a wee bit darker than the others.

Her ears perked up as a strong wind drummed at the shutters, banging once again, as it did the night before, *~thump, ~thump, ~thump*, it went. *That better not be that banshee again!* she thought.

Kathryn took a deep breath, walked to the window and pulled out the purple sprig of flowers and the wood strip. The shutters popped open, allowing the silky warm breeze to caress her face. Peering out the window, a ghostly white horse trotted away in the moonlight, up towards Arthur's Seat. *Is that Sheba?* she wondered.

The ghostly figure was then quickly consumed by the looming darkness of the night. Kathryn raised her hand adorned with her citrine necklace into the moonlight. The crystals reflected its radiance. She didn't know what to make of it. The necklace's shape shifted in her hands and now mirrored the silhouette of the great Arthur's Seat in the distance. A light bulb slowly began to illuminate in her head as her eyes concentrated on the darker crystals. Soon, a sequence of crystals began to mark a path up the Mountain. Each darkened crystal, lead to another one and then to another one, until the last one was darkest of them all.

A smile inched across her face and in a flash, she ran to her bedroom door. Kathryn creaked open the door and surveyed the living room for Grandpa, but he was not to be found. She darted across the icy stone floor and shimmied up Billy's ladder. She began to bang fiercely against Billy's door until it groaned open and Billy's fat head emerged.

Kathryn eagerly blurted out, "I figured it out! I know how to get to the Raven's Gate! Be ready before sunrise!"

"We're grounded," replied Billy groggily, "remember?"

"If we don't go now, the Raven's Gate will close! Tomorrow is the last day of the Nights of the Faeries," cried Kathryn. "Be ready before dawn!"

I'd say it wasn't the brightest thing they ever did, but they did it, nonetheless. Upon the break of dawn, Kathryn and Billy assembled their backpacks filling them with thick ropes, portable flashlights, cheese sandwiches, water bottles, bags of crisps, and the cursed citrine necklace that Billy nicked from the compartment behind the portrait. The two of them always stuck to the rules of being a *true* Indiana Jones apprentice and today, for the first time, they had more reason to be extra prepared!

The air was silent, for no birds had awoken yet when they stepped out of the cottage before dawn.

"Now, the first rule of being a good apprentice is?" asked Kathryn.

"Always," said Billy, striding up the road with his sister.

"Be," added Kathryn.

"Prepared!" said Billy, throwing both of his arms up over his head into the dusky morning sky.

"Flashlight?" cried Kathryn, pulling out her shiny silver flashlight.

"Check!" said Billy, lugging out a heavy, bright yellow flashlight.

"Rope?" asked Kathryn.

"Check!" replied Billy confidently.

"Check, myself!" added Kathryn. "Food?"

"Check!" answered Billy decisively.

"Water?" asked Kathryn.

"Check!" said Billy with certainty.

"Swiss army knife?" asked Kathryn.

"Check!" said Billy, flicking out the shiny blade on his knife.

"Magnifying glass?" asked Kathryn.

"Ummm..." said Billy hesitantly. "Yes! I mean... check!"

"Did you leave a note?" asked Kathryn.

"Check!" answered Billy.

"Ready?" asked Kathryn.

"Check!" said Billy, throwing his backpack over his shoulder, causing one of its flimsy straps to tear apart. A glass jar filled with black beetles dropped out of his backpack, shattering against a nearby rock. Hundreds of squiggling, slick black beetles scurried all over the dirt path. Billy squatted down without hesitation and simply scooped up as many as he could and put them into another jar.

The first appearance of morning's light, steadily burst over the crags of Arthur's Seat as the two youngins made their way up the dirt road. To what, they did not know.

"I think I figured out the necklace!" said Kathryn sluggishly, hiking up the first level of the lush, green hills of Arthur's Seat, splattered with soft, violet heather bushes.

"How's that?" puffed Billy, his face now as red as a turkey's neck.

Kathryn acquired the necklace from her lint filled pocket and laced it between her fingers and then raised it up into the new day's light.

"It's a map!" she said assuredly. "See how it takes the shape of the Mountain?"

"Ummm... Sure, ok," said Billy, pausing for a moment to catch his breath, which had run away from him already.

"See these darker crystals, it seems like it's making a path up the Mountain. And here, here is the last one, the darkest and largest one of all! That must be where the Raven's Gate is!"

"So, what do the smaller darker ones mean?" asked Billy.

Kathryn scanned the horizon. Rising up from out of the Mountain like a torched chimney, black as coal, was a single twisted tree, leafless, lifeless, and by all means, it stuck out like a sore thumb.

"I've seen a tree similar to that one up there," she said vaguely, wiggling her finger towards the dark barren tree. "When Sheba took me up to that shack, there was one just like it," she paused again for a moment, the light bulb in her head was now fully lit. "That's it! The dead trees are the markers! It has to be!"

"You're pretty smart," said Billy wearily, and then took a swig of water from a bottle, missing his mouth partially, causing it to gush out onto his shirt.

"Thanks!" said Kathryn with a squeamish smile.

"Except, for those shoes," said Billy, directing her eyes down to the mismatched pair of shoes; she was wearing, one black, one brown.

"Ooops, maybe I should change them?"

"Forget it! We're already up this high and Gramps is probably pulling his hair out," said Billy. "Come on, we're burning daylight!"

"OK, whatever you say, bubble butt Billy," snorted Kathryn.

The two climbed higher and higher up the great Arthur's Seat. They came to the first coiling, lifeless tree, its arms grasping out for life, but somehow it was frozen in a void, ever so silent, ever so still. Beyond the next soaring hill, they could see the second ominous, dark, and creepy tree. The path to the tree was a difficult rocky road, obstructed by sharp stones and wayward pebbles. After ascending upward, they could see a third haunting tree, curling its misshapen branches up over the horizon.

"See!" said Kathryn animatedly, "I told you they're markers! We're so close!"

Billy huffed and puffed, "Can we take a break?"

"Sure."

"So, that's the third tree?" asked Billy. "How many dark crystals are there?"

"Seven," she replied informatively.

"Seven trees?" gasped Billy. "Lovely, just lovely!"

They continued on to the third distorted tree; their path carried them along a steep, sharp crag over looking Ballyrun. Even from this far away, they could see the steeple at St. John's Church in the quiet town of Ballyrun. Below them, in the high tall grass, was a curled up fox sleeping his day away in a silent meadow on the Mountain. Overhead, a dark lingering shadow of a large bird blocked the sun's rays. Lethargically, they made their way to the third forbidding marker. Before them stood a larger than life decrepit tree, to the left was a small causeway streamed-lined in rich emerald green leaves, creating a deep, long tunnel.

"I remember this place," whispered Kathryn watchfully. "This is where Sheba took me and where I saw the old hag that bandaged me up."

"Oh! We, *soooo* have to go!" said Billy eagerly, heading down the lush green tunnel.

Kathryn paused, took a deep breath, and then followed. Soon, they came to the rotted, lonely shack. For, not even the devil himself would live in a place like that! But still, the two made their way towards the gray, weathered beaten door.

"Should we knock?" said Billy lightly, rapping on the door. Before Kathryn could reply, it slowly creaked open.

Kathryn gulped, and they walked into the dusty, gloomy room, covered in wispy cobwebs. The stench of sulphur and rotting flesh tickled their noses, mechanical clocks ticked back and forth, but yet never moving forward in time. Along the wall were books named; *The Year of the Golden Dragon Eye*, *A Dwarf's Journey with the King*, *Forces of Nature: And How to Make Them Work*, *The Lost History of Newts*, *Cauldrons of Fire*, *The Cry of the Banshee and its Healing Properties*, and *Powers of the Rising Hawkmoon*.

In the center of the next room was a dark cauldron bubbling up with smoke. Along the walls were shiny jars filled with two headed chittering beetles, purple caterpillars with one eye, hairy spiders with glowing red eyes, slugs as large as footballs were shoved into a barrel on the grimy floor, and double red-winged dragonflies flittered in another jar next to golden bugs that looked similar to cockroaches.

"Is it he, who sent you?" croaked a hooded figure, resting in a ripped, dusty chair in the corner.

Kathryn and Billy shivered down to the very marrow of their bones.

"No..." quivered Kathryn, "we came alone."

The stranger's voice wheezed as she spoke again in a sing-songy voice, "You must be careful, in the dead of night, when all the birds take no flight, and when no man roams the night, for the banshee will set you a fright." The cloaked woman raised her white, bony hand. Her sharp black nails waved at them. "You must not stay long... But first, you must be told a story..."

"What story?" asked Billy, trying to see the woman's face.

Her cold, ivory hand, gestured at the black cauldron behind them, it bubbled and gurgled. A fine, steamy mist hovered above it and she began to speak in a raspy voice.

"It is the story of Aählynéé," she said wheezing. "Once, the great sea covered this land called Aählynéé. A young boy set adrift on the vast ocean and landed on a magical island of great beauty. Inside the isle breathed a great double red-winged dragon. The dragon soon gave birth to a wee egg. The young lad sneaked into the dragon's lair and snatched its only egg. Enraged by her loss, the double red-winged dragon searched endlessly, breathing its fire into the roaring sea. The sea arose as vapors into the misty sky. Finally, the broken hearted dragon found the young boy and enveloped him in a wall of fire. Trapped, the boy gave the sea the dragon's egg to save his life. The sea swallowed the flames, but it transformed into a thick mist and the sky swallowed the sea and the land rose up beneath it, saving the boy's life.

"Heartbroken, the dragon landed on a lone, deserted island, which shot out from beneath what was left of the sea and died from the heartbreak of losing her child. The dragon's egg cracked open and the most beautiful girl the boy had ever seen appeared, with hair of fire and emerald eyes. The young boy then climbed up to where the dragon lay and with a fierce blade, cut the dragon's heart out, which is the teine criostal. The boy and girl then married and created the land of Aählynéé."

"That's the story of Aählynéé?" said Kathryn beguiled.

"That's the coolest story I've heard so far!" said Billy.

"You must leave now," said the shrouded woman, glancing at the clock, "for I must rest."

They left the shack about noon, still climbing up the Mountain ever so high and the journey, ever so long. Upon reaching the fourth daunting tree, Billy's weariness grew stronger.

"Do we have to go all the way to the seventh tree?" he said panting.

"Yeah, we do!" replied Kathryn ardently. "It's the last day of the three Nights of the Faeries. If we can't make it to the Raven's Gate, we'll have to wait seven more years to see if it opens!"

"Ugh! Alright!" he moaned.

Further up, the road grew darker as the thick trees created a canopy blocking out the sun's light. Soon, they passed the fifth tree; its shape was low to the ground as it reached outward to the other trees filled with life. Their eyes now played tricks on them with the rustling of the trees' leaves flickering in and out of sunlight. Ghoulish, shadowy images stirred in and out of the shadows, haunting every step they took.

"We're getting closer!" said Kathryn, approaching the edge of the forest.

"Yippee!" grunted Billy sarcastically.

Onward they climbed up the steep Mountain. A mist of white puffy clouds floated over the road, breaking through as they moved closer to the sixth haunting tree. Finally, a small clearing appeared in a field to their left; in the center was the sixth tree, tall and thin, it shot up through the Mountain like a sword.

Billy spied an assortment of dragonflies flittering around the abundant field of flowers and darted off.

Kathryn roamed the field, hunting the Mountain for the last and final marker, the final tree to mark the entrance to the Raven's Gate. Next to the field was a small, rocky path coiling itself up a sharp incline. High above it was a lone, twisted tree suspended on its own hill, away from the Mountain.

"There – there it is," she said amazed, her slender finger waving at the steep vertical climb before them.

"Wow!" said Billy amazed.

"I know," replied Kathryn, awe-struck.

"Look, at all these dragonflies! Maybe I'll find that white-fire dwarf that Mr. Hewson told me about! Look!" exclaimed Billy, holding up a dragonfly fluttering in his hand. "What a good find, right?"

"Billy!" yelled Kathryn, "we're about to discover a magical world, a legend, a real myth, and you're picking up grubs?"

"I like my grubs," said Billy, grinding his teeth.

"Don't you believe me, when I say this is the way?"

"But, Kat! I can't make it up there!" said Billy exhausted. Shattered, he collapsed on the dewy ground, his shirt drenched in sweat. "I'm tired and I just want to find bugs!"

"But, this is the last day we can go!" she said anxiously.

"Kat, really? It's late and we've been walking for hours! I'm tired and starving!"

"Billy, it's right there!" she exclaimed.

"Yeah, up an insane cliff! *Hello???* Seriously, it's just a bunch of stories."

"I knew it – I knew it! You don't believe in it, do you? You don't believe in Aählynéé! You don't think it's real!"

"Kat, we're in Ireland!" ranted Billy sarcastically. "Where everything is a story, a myth, and get this, *a legend!* Let's be a bit more realistic now. Why aren't there more people who have actually been there? Why is it all just stories from locals that almost made it up? Or heard about it from so and so? Huh? Maybe it's just like Mr. Kennedy stumbling home from the bar late at night and then he hears a sound and sees something moving in the dark bush... and then ooohhh... ooohhh... all of a sudden, it's a faery! I've seen a faery - I've seen a faery! Really? Has he now, in all his drunkenness? And then, he has this amazing story to tell his neighbors; cause there's not a whole lot to do here in Ireland, except tell stories! And then, they add on, and on! Soon, it's a leprechaun with three heads, one with a white beard, the other with yellow beard, and the third one has a bright orange beard, chewing tobacco by 'ol man McGarvey's farm! And then - then it's a banshee wailing down by the edge of town, crying in the dark of night, into the wee hours of the morning. Until Mr. Dimmler realizes one of his sheep has died and it must've been the banshee! It must've been and it goes on, and on, forever! I tell you! They're just stories! Just like Mr. Hewson said, he loves them but doesn't believe in them!"

"But – but, I saw the banshee last night!" she said, disappointed.

"It's just the stories getting into your head! It was probably Mrs. Kennedy and Mugs having a laugh!" he replied.

"What about the deer? You saw it turn to gold!" she added to her argument.

"It was dusk. It was a play of the light on my eyes. The deer finally pulled itself out of its hole all covered in wet sand, the light hit it, and it glistened gold and then it ran home, up the Mountain!"

"What about the scary cloaked woman we just saw?" she reminded him.

"She's just an old crazy lady living on a Mountain, telling stories. Just like everyone else here in Ireland does! And she does it, very, very well!"

"But, what if it is real, Billy?" she asked hopefully. "I need to find out!"

"Listen, I'm gonna do what I want to do! You go on! If you really believe in it, who am I to stop you?"

So, the two parted ways; Billy settled into the high grassy field filled with flowers of every color, while Kathryn began the journey up the steep path.

It most certainly was a very hard climb up the last leg of Arthur's Seat, for it was filled with jagged boulders, sheer unending drops, accompanied along with teeny tiny rocks that made scaling that hill even more difficult. If you didn't keep your wits about you when placed your foot down, you'd slide down ten feet. The sun of course, didn't make her climb any easier, for it was high in the sky poking down on her like a burning stoker. The beads of sweat drizzled down her face as she looked up to finally see that last lone, dead tree.

It was just before her, high up on its own one tree hill, silently sitting there, waiting for someone to visit. The hill indeed was at least thirty feet straight up, mind you. It was impossible to climb, but Kathryn reached out her hand on a protruding rock, then jammed one of her mismatched shoes into a crevice, and lifted herself up. Higher and higher she reached, wiggling, grasping, and scaling her way up the steep incline. When there were no more rocks to be seen, she reached for a piece of dried up root, just to her left. Immediately, it gave way, and she slid down the hill, eating a good mouthful of dirt as a shower of red dirt sprayed out from underneath her.

"Gross!" she said, spitting out the scarlet dirt and starting to ascend back up the hill.

Kathryn knew that holding on to dirt and rocks were not going to help her make it to the top. It was then that she saw a sturdy tree root, jutting out from the side of the hill.

It was stronger than the last and most definitely, it was thicker and denser. *Now, that would hold me,* she thought. Kathryn lifted herself up once again and shuffled herself over to the left, wiggling her fingers up high grasping for the root. It was ever so close and yet with all her strength, it still eluded her. She scrapped up the hill advancing her body, scuffing it up against the stiff stones and loose dirt.

"So close," she said, dangling her fingers out, just barely touching the root.

She inched up just a little more, while an avalanche of dirt spewed out from below her. Then, with every ounce of energy she had in her body, she lurched forward and clasped tightly on to the root.

"Gotcha!" she said, pulling herself over to the other side of the hill. She shimmied over and raised her body up. Then, as quickly as she made her way over, the root gave out and she fell down into a massive gorge on the other side of the hill, landing hard on her buttocks.

Kathryn stood up and dusted the filth off her body. Looking up she could see she fell about twenty feet into a deep gorge below. It was just then that the dead, crooked tree branches began to rattle and whisper in the soft wind.

"You got to be kidding me!" she said aggravated, pulling out her thick rope from her backpack. Tying a sturdy knot, she whirled it above her head, and lassoed it around the tree's trunk. It was then, after brushing off another layer of dirt that the magic began to happen. For a single shadow of a bird cast down upon her mismatched shoes. When she looked up, she saw a red-winged raven land on one of those crooked branches. She was amazed, delighted, and filled with awe. Its body was as dark and deep as coal with the sheen of midnight blue and its glorious crimson wings blazed red. She couldn't help herself from saying, "One for sorrow!" with wonder in her eyes.

But, still another landed higher up on the tree, its eyes piercing down below at her, as if the bird was trying to speak.

"Two for joy!" she said blissfully.

Kathryn began to giggle inside, for she could not believe it was real and yet two more red-winged ravens landed on the bewitching tree.

"Three for marriage! Four for boy!" she said anxiously. "Could it be? Are they really there?"

But, it was just the beginning of it all, you see, for a fifth one landed gracefully on another warped branch.

"Five for silver!" she said beaming.

Kathryn's heart drummed inside her chest, for still a sixth one landed on a lower deformed branch, its head cocked to the side as it spied on her.

"Six for gold!"

Oh, glory be! For, she was not imagining it, in fact, she even pinched herself more than once, just to make sure she wasn't dreaming it! And that's when the seventh red-winged raven landed on the tree! All the way at the tippy-top!

"And, seven for the secret that's never been told!" she said filled with amazement.

And that's when one of the ravens rapped three times. A rumbling sound grinded behind her and when she turned around, seven stones that were forged together began to twist and flare away from each other, like a flower opening up in the sun's ray after the rains had come and gone.

"The Raven's Gate," she said filled with wonder. Marveling at the gateway, she stepped inside, and ever so slowly, the Raven's Gate closed behind her.

Chapter Twelve
Into the Belly of Arthur's Seat

The door grinded shut behind her, enshrouding her in a pitch-black cavern, no light to be seen, and no noise to be heard. Kathryn stretched her arm deep into her backpack, her hand groped about clumsily. Finally, she pulled out the smooth silver flashlight and with a flick of a switch, a brilliant beam of light cut through the darkness.

Cautiously, she advanced deeper into the chilling, wet labyrinth; its cold walls were damp and slimy to the touch, while her feet fumbled about on the uneven ground below her. Up ahead appeared a spiraling staircase made of thick stones ascending upwards, to her right was a tunnel descending down into the mountain. She turned to her right and after taking only a few steps, a blast of arctic air swept through her hair. Her body shivered in the soggy, bitter air, while goose bumps decided to pop out and make themselves at home permanently on her freckled skin. She was now happy to have worn her thick woolen drawers that day, for at least, one part of her was somewhat warm.

Kathryn's eyes slowly adjusted to her flashlight's brightness dancing off the cavernous walls. She was not far along in the tunnel when she came across a few strange cave drawings. Her wand of light danced before a few sketchings. One was a King who sat on his golden throne; beside him were his guardsmen, and a brilliant blood red crystal that hovered over a powerful fountain.

"It can't be!" she said in disbelief, placing her hand on the painting. "It - it can't be real!"

Bewildered, she moved on to the next painting along the tunnel. The image was of a larger than life, dark haired female warrior adorned in woven tartan, animal fur, a broad sword, and the skull of a tiger on her head. She stood fiercely before the Hawkmoon.

"Wow!" sighed Kathryn. "Who is that?" Kathryn made her way to the next painting. Nine women were robed in different colors, each with fiery hair. In the background was a thin wiry fellow, dressed in dark robes holding a large staff. Next to it were drawings of strange creatures with glowing eyes, haunting images of fat little people, misshapen ghouls with long arms, and mutilated giants with one eye.

A whispering breeze blew across her neck making her hair stand at attention. She turned back to the tunnel and moved forward, her feet wobbling on the rocky path. A moving shadow caught her eye and then her flashlight beamed on two albino spiders the size of grapefruits scattering into narrow crevices deep in the walls of the labyrinth.

"Ewww... I'll have to make sure I stay away from those creepy-crawly, scary things!" said Kathryn disgustedly, wiping away a few spun cobwebs that blocked her path.

Deeper and deeper she traveled into the dreary cavern, while drippings of water rippled softly down the cave's wall. Kathryn's rusty flashlight batteries clinked together as she toddled through the cave, causing an echo to return from the snaking tunnel.

Kathryn's heart fluttered for a moment when she heard a low moan. *What.... What was that?* she thought. The agonizing moan grew louder and louder as she made her way further down the tunnel. A soft golden light from another cavern illuminated the burrow before her. The subtle agony of a man in pain echoed from the cavern.

Guarded, she moved ahead to the cavern's doorway and then peered into the room. It was an agonizing and dreadful place, filled with vile torture devices. She took a deep breath and stealthfully entered the room. It was filled with the utmost, heinous devices known to man. There was a wicked wooden rack with five-barrel wheels, rotating on a board with rusty nail spikes protruding out at the top. Then, there was an iron lever attached to rope, which led to hand and foot cuffs. Along the walls, rusty iron shackles hung down where the prisoner would be chained to and suspended in the air, while iron spikes shot out from the ground below. Along the walls that surrounded the room were more chains.

In the corner, in the back, was a dark silhouette of a man, his right arm chained up to the wall as his body slumped to the floor where he sat. Kathryn moved in carefully, trying not to disturb all the strange devices that caused such misery. Her shirt ripped when she caught it on one of the spikes, jutting out from another contraption. The prisoner, lying in his own soiled clothing, grumbled from the noise. He was faceless, drowned in a coat of hair that grew down to the floor and his body was frail and covered in grime. Her heart filled with compassion as she knelt down beside him and pulled out a canteen of water.

"Here!" she said softly to the weakened man. "Drink this."

The weary prisoner lifted his head. His sky blue eyes were glazed and vacant, but they still met Kathryn's eyes. She lifted the steel mouthpiece of the canteen to his cracked lips, while he raised his other arm to help balance the water, now gushing down his soiled face. He coughed and then choked for a moment on the cool water. She dug deep into her backpack pulling out a sandwich and broke off a wee morsel, then raised it to his mouth.

"Here, eat this," she said kindly, wiping away his grungy black hair. Gazing up, she could see the crusty iron chain that latched around his withered wrist.

"Tha... tha... thank.... you," wheezed the prisoner.

Kathryn's hands reached up, rattling on the locks.

"Who did this to you?" she said, trying to loosen his chains. "Who locked you in here?'

The prisoner chewed on his food and then gestured for the water. Kathryn raised the canteen to his mouth, trickles of water dribbled into his mouth and down his chin.

Taking another deep breath, he whispered, "Sh...she did."

"She did, you mean Koréna?" said Kathryn shockingly. "Well, what's your name?"

The prisoner paused for a moment and groaned from the food he had just eaten.

"Wil...William," he said, grunting in pain.

"My name is Kathryn, but you can call me Kat, for short," she said gently, as footsteps echoed behind her. "Well, at least, that's what my brother Billy calls me! Do you want some more bread, William?"

William squirmed in his seat and turned to Kathryn, his jet-black hair hanging partially over his eyes now, he heaved a few words, "K-K-Kat, *run!*"

Perplexed, Kathryn pulled back scrutinizing the prisoner's eyes and then did the unthinkable, she looked over her shoulder.

"Run!!" he gasped.

Kathryn, almost literally hopped out of her skin, while jumping to her feet at the same time. Spinning around she saw two hairy half-men with prickly twigs snagged in their body hair, oblong noses, and spiky ears, heading towards her. They were the most disgusting things that she ever laid eyes on. Thick coarse red hair covered their entire bodies, all the way down to their big fat feet with bits of dried up mud and pebbles stuck between their matted toes. Kathryn darted behind one the horrifying rack devices to create a barrier between her and these ugly fur balls.

"Me thinks," said the taller hairy half-man, in a deep guttural voice as he lifted up his bulbous finger, "she'z going to run from us!"

"Me thinks, you're right brother!" said the chubbier one as he moved towards the other side of the rack.

"Run!" moaned the prisoner.

The two flea ridden creatures vigilantly inched their way towards Kathryn.

"Go! Now!" cried the prisoner and then his head fell limp.

A jolt of energy surged through Kathryn's blood as she grabbed the wooden frame of one the strange devices and with the strength of a hundred men, she lifted the rack up, and threw it on the two diabolical half-men. Kathryn sped down the twisting tunnels within the belly of Arthur's Seat like a bat out of hell, until the tunnel split in two.

Now, she had to make a decision; before her was a massive crystal stalagmite shooting up from the frigid floor, twinkling in the light of her flashlight. She hesitated for a moment, not knowing which way to run, and then in a blink of an eye, she took off running through the tunnel on her left.

It seemed as if she ran for miles, sweat poured down from her face, her heart pounding harder and harder in her chest, while her breath was becoming shallower. Flashes of light bounced up and down the barren cave walls from her flashlight, causing her to lose focus of where she was running. Before her was only complete blackness until the light stopped bouncing off the walls. Something in her head told her to stop, just in time too! Dirt rained down from her feet into an abyss of darkness.

Kathryn swiftly flashed her light down to her feet, her toes dangled over a sheer drop. Looking back over her shoulder, she heard only silence, her heart throbbed uncontrollably in her chest. Bending down, she picked up a pebble and threw it off into the void. She stood silent for a few seconds, straining to hear the faint splash of the wee pebble when it hit the deep water below.

Now, not many souls knew what lurked deep down in the depths of the dark Loch below her. Some say it was a plesiosaur, like Nessie at Loch Ness, others say, it was an evil water horse gone awry, or a giant killer eel, but faeries knew it to be a peist. A peist is an Irish lake-dwelling sea dragon with a thick, coiled body like a snake and a head like a brooding bull. Known for their keen sense of sonar in the water and their powerful jaws which could snap a man in two. Peists only dwelled in the darkest lakes and the deepest waters, always guarding a hidden treasure.

Taking a deep breath, Kathryn inhaled the cool air into her lungs, and then gulped it down. She hesitated for a second, turning her flashlight off and then she turned back towards the entrance. Placing her hand on the damp wall as a brace, she slowly and ever so quietly made her way back down the tunnel. The silence was deafening, the only sound she heard was from her feet wobbling along the jagged stones and her panting breath. But, then a wheezing laugh crept into her ear from nowhere and a blinding light lit up her whole body. Her hands shielded her eyes from the intense light.

"Me thinks, we have herself m'lady!" grunted a coarse froggy voice from behind the light.

A shadowy feminine silhouette arose behind the radiant light.

"Release the rocks!" said the mysterious silhouette.

Now, in that moment, Kathryn's instincts kicked in and her heart sank down to her belly. While she watched, a shaggy fat hand reach up to a slimy knotted rope, which hung down from a hefty burlap sack suspended over her head. Kathryn then began to run like the wind down the tunnel, back towards the dark water and the impending sheer drop below.

A thunderous roar of boulders, heavy rocks, and spewing dirt crashed down to the floor below. Gushing rapidly down the tunnel, the avalanche of debris swallowed the passageway, consuming every inch of space in its path. Kathryn's body rushed through the dark and murky tunnel. Taking a deep breath and a leap of faith, Kathryn catapulted out of the tunnel and dove downwards into the murky, black water below. Her body pierced the ice-cold water, breaking the motionless Loch below. Swimming downward, she could hear the deafening sound of the rocks rupturing the water's surface.

Now, with her eyes open below the water, she spied a burning red-hue glowing below her and then her feet kicked to the surface above. Gasping for air, she scouted the Loch's surface.

No hairy little bugger dudes to be seen. What the heck were those things? she wondered.

Kathryn's heart grew warm and peaceful, for a moment she forgot she was being chased. Then, she remembered the fiery object she saw below. Taking a deep breath again, she submerged her body into the water. Her eyes scanned the gloomy water until... there it was!

She swam as deep as she could down into the cool water. Her hand reached out and clenched the fiery crystal. A gentle warmth filled her body as she placed the crystal into her pocket and began to swim to the surface. It was just about at that moment, when one of her mismatched shoes, I believe it was the brown one, suddenly hit against a solid object as she kicked her way back up to the water's surface. Her heart drummed faster, speeding up towards the fresh air. Kathryn broke out of the water, coughing violently and began to suck down as much air as possible. *What the heck was that?* she thought.

White ripples broke the Loch's surface. While Kathryn watched, a torpedo-like object head straight for her, in a continuous churning wake of water. Quickly, she reached for her flashlight, her fingers fumbling with it, trying to pull it out of her belt. Losing her grasp on it, it fell into the inky water below. The fierce creature charged her like a bull, seeing its matador before him. She took a deep breath and dove straight down into the deep water, while her hands waved around aimlessly for her trusted flashlight.

An eerie, screeching sound hummed through her eardrums as the creature descended down into the water after her.

The fiery crystal in her pocket began to glow, illuminating the water. There was the flashlight: deeper and deeper into the shadowy water she swam down into the grimy Loch. The cool water began to quake as the creature began to gnaw on Kathryn's shoes. Her hand reached out once more and seized the flashlight and then she lifted her legs up and repelled off the creatures head. Shooting up to the surface again, she swiftly turned her flashlight on. To her right, she saw dry land about twenty feet away from her.

Swimming as fast as she could, she made her way toward her sanctuary. Behind her, she could hear the creature coming back around for another strike. Her arms crashed down into the water as her feet and legs kicked furiously. Her ears perked up as the shrieking noise grew louder. She was still ten feet away from the dry patch of land. Kathryn stopped swimming and blasted a blinding ray of light straight at her demon. The ball of light lit up the creature's head, sharp arrow-like teeth glistened from the flashlight's searing light. Its face was stern like a bull as it throttled forward, it suddenly opened its inky black eyes. Squealing in pain, it dove deep down into the dingy water.

Kathryn then pulled herself out from the Loch and crawled onto the dry land as her body crashed down upon the ledge, a high pitch shriek reverberated through the cavern. Around her were brilliant crystal stalagmites shooting out of the ground, while stalactites hung down from the ceiling, like diamond chandeliers. Kathryn focused her flashlight on the waves rippling through the water.

Voices echoed in the distance. Without delay, she gathered herself together and began moving down one of the many darkened corridors before her. There, Kathryn stuck to the cavern's wall like a spider as she finally got her first glimpse of Koréna herself.

Oh, Koréna was as pale as a fish's belly, but her lips were blood red and it was true, her hair rose like tongues of flames from her head. Kathryn became as quiet as a mouse and as still as a statue. The two hairy half-men carried torches as they made their way closer to her. They were the most putrid, vile things she ever saw with their thick red matted hair, large flaring nostrils, and eyes the color of piss. They moved ever so slowly towards where she was standing, sniffing the air for a scent of her. The closer they got, the more she caught the scent of curdling, soured cream.

They were grogochs, half sized furry men that lived and lurked in caves, working for their master and the only pay they asked for in return was cream, which they loved ever so much, even more than their master. Now, everyone knows that every faery has at least one magical gift and for grogochs, it was the gift of invisibility. They could disappear in a blink of an eye and never be seen again, unless they wanted you to see them. But, their downfall was their love for dairy cream, and because they love it so much, they will even begin to smell like it.

Now, the shorter heftier grogoch with legs like a pool table and a belly like a cauldron was Earh. The taller, yet nastier one, who had a wooly patch of hair on his long chin, was named, Aldo.

It was then Aldo and Earh both paused, sniffing the cold air with their bulging nostrils and they both raised their bushy arms and waved their fiery torches down Kathryn's cavern.

Earh said, "There, she is!"

"Get her!" cried Koréna commandingly, *"now!"*

It was a sight to be seen, when Aldo leapt on to one of the stalactites before Kathryn, his mouth dripping with saliva. He growled and hissed a few times. He then soared into the air, landing on the ground before her, Earh following right behind him. Their hairy elongated arms stretched out towards Kathryn's waist. She backed away from them and then threw two of her fingers up in the air, making a peace sign.

"I come in peace!" she cried, waving her two fingers in front them. "Peace, I said! Peace!"

Their yellow eyes widened as they inched closer and closer towards her. Then, it just so happened that Kathryn whipped out her flashlight and flipped it on, blinding the two fiendish creatures. They howled in excruciating pain, covering their eyes. Kathryn shifted around them and darted down one of the dark, stagnant corridors. Her feet thrashed down upon the lumpy stones, drips of sweat bled down her forehead as she ran pointlessly through the pitch-black tunnels.

A feminine voice arose from the darkness, "This will illuminate your way! *Soilsigh!*"

Kathryn's feet moved as fast as she could as she raced through the Mountain's labyrinth with a blazing row of flames plummeting down on her. She looked over her shoulder to see the scorching flames pursuing her. Her mind became blank with fear and before she knew it, her shoe tripped on one of the uneven stones. Kathryn smashed down to the stone ground, while the fiery wave of flames drove past her. She clambered to her feet. Then, unexpectedly, a pale arm reached out from behind her and with a frosty hand covered her mouth, pulling her out of the treacherous passageway.

"Shhh..." whispered the voice, "don't scream, or they'll find you, follow me!"

Kathryn bolted down the labyrinth, her hand being pulled by what appeared to be a thin-framed man. Flashes of light and darkness danced in and out of the shadows. She could hear the voices of the grogochs slowly fading. They continued on through the puzzling maze, zigzagging down different menacing corridors. Finally, the stranger stopped abruptly. Kathryn panted heavily, when she finally looked around, she realized she was now back at the Raven's Gate.

"Quickly! You must leave before Koréna finds you and the crystal," urged the stranger, pulling on a twisted dried up tree root three times. "Our fate lies with you!"

Soon, blinding daylight flooded the cavern as the Raven's Gate's entrance twisted open and a howling wind of flames grew closer from behind her.

"The Raven's Gate will take you back to your world and to safety," said the stranger trustingly, his sullen face covered with an overgrown, peppered beard.

"She's down this way m'lady!" shouted Aldo. "I can smell her!"

A row of fiery flames glowed from the tunnels.

"Go, *now!*" cried the stranger unwaveringly.

Kathryn stepped through the gateway, turning around she asked, "What's your name?"

The fiery flames cast its glowing light upon the grungy stranger's face and then the seven stones began to grind close.

"Raedan, and you are Laurel's daughter," said the stranger and then he quickly ducked down out of the flames' path.

Thud! The Raven's Gate closed. A single flame escaped through and hovered before Kathryn's face. Koréna's eyes appeared before her in the scorching flame, they seemed to peer through the fire as if they could see her standing there. That was until a single raindrop dropped from the gray sky, dissolving the flame, and it was no more.

Turning to the hill behind her, Kathryn clamped on to the mangy rope. Gripping the tethered rope with her blistered hands, she hoisted herself up the one tree hill. Her clothing, still drenched from the murky lake, started to collect a thick, muddy crust. Coiling up the rope before the lifeless tree, Kathryn tumbled down the hill, along with pieces of soft grass, loose dirt, and worn pebbles.

She stumbled down the path, her clothing shredded, her body bloody and bruised. Covered in mud, she continued on as long as she could. Raindrops began to plunge down from the cloudy gray sky, and she fell to her knees.

She watched a mysterious figure emerge from the rocky path below. *Billy?* she thought. She then crashed down to the dirty trail. Tiredly, she began to flutter her eyes open. Before her, on a nearby patch of green, she saw a single red-winged raven land and begin pecking into the ground for worms.

"One, for sorrow," she whispered to herself and all went black.

Voices grumbled in Kathryn's head. Her eyes fluttered open to a blurry view of her room. Her ears pounded with the sound of Grandpa's agitated voice reverberating in her head.

"I tell 'ya, that girl will be 'da death of me!" griped Grandpa. "Off gallivanting up 'dat Mountain! When I specifically said not 'ta go!"

"You can't control everything!" said Fiona worriedly. "The girl needs a mother!"

"Yes, she does," replied Grandpa agreeing. "Den it's settled! It is - it is!"

The ladder outside Kathryn's bedroom began to rattle and creak, the door squeaked open. Fiona walked in. Kathryn's leg ached in pain as she sat down on the edge of her bed.

"Feeling better, Missy?" said Fiona sweetly, brushing her fingers across her forehead. Kathryn groaned in pain, "it's been two weeks now."

Kathryn's eyes were so glassy; she could just barely make out Fiona's face.

"Where's Billy?" she asked sluggishly.

"Yes," replied Fiona, picking up a wet cloth. "See, now dear. I do have some not so happy news."

"What?" mumbled Kathryn, as Fiona wiped her face with the cloth. "Wh-where is he? Did he make it off the Mountain?"

"Kathryn," said Fiona softly.

"He's going to kill me... bubble butt," chuckled Kathryn.

"Kathryn, *stop!*" said Fiona hastily. "Kathryn, he's been missing for two weeks now and – and we all *fear* the worst!"

"What?" said Kathryn.

"Billy, Billy's gone!"

♦ CHAPTER THIRTEEN ♦
The Selkies

It was a sunny fall day when a rusty, dark blue sedan drove up to the wee cottage at the bottom of Arthur's Seat and honked its horn twice. No good folk in their right mind would have guessed what was going to happen, not after the loss of Billy. But sometimes, people do, only what seems to be, the right thing to do, at that time. And for poor Kathryn, no one would have known her Grandfather would do what he did. The cab's horn honked again.

"Fiona!" called Grandpa, standing at the ladder's base to Kathryn's room, "cabs here!"

Fiona zipped up the olive green duffle bag on Kathryn's bed and said, "Now, you mustn't worry about a thing! Just listen to the Sisters and they will set you in the right direction."

Kathryn picked up her copy of *The Legends of Arthur's Seat*.

"No!" said Fiona firmly, pushing the book down. "You won't be needin' that now, dear."

Kathryn's eyes streamed with tears.

"I know how it is love when you believe in something so much and you want it to be real. You'd give anything for it to be, but soon enough you grow up and you find out that these things aren't real." Fiona brushed her hair back from her face. "They're just silly stories," she said adamantly. "Silly stories told to children, that's all."

"But," she sputtered out, "some stories - some stories have truths to them."

"I'm afraid not, Kathryn. It's all just in your head."

The impatient cabby honked his horn once more. Kathryn stepped out the front door carrying her duffle bag along with her muddy backpack. Her face was still bruised and bloodied; above her left eye, a butterfly bandage covered her split eyebrow.

"Aye, Miss, let me take that from ya now!" said the statuesque golden haired man. "I'll just throw it in 'da boot for ya!"

Kathryn stood outside her home watching Grandpa drop his eyes down to his red muddied boots; her heart bled with pain. *How could he send me away like this?* she thought.

Kathryn turned to Fiona and pleaded, "Do I have to go?"

"Now, now dear," Fiona said, wrapping her arm around her shoulders and walking her to the cab. "It's in your best interest dear."

"But!" she whimpered, gazing at Grandpa, "I don't want to go! I-I didn't mean for him to get lost! Or..."

"We know, dear," said Fiona, opening the cab door. "It's for the best."

"Please, Grandpa!" she begged. Fiona closed the cab's door. "Don't do this!" She rolled down the cab's window. "I promise I won't get into anymore trouble.... *please!!!*"

Grandpa walked over to the cab. His glassy eyes were turning red, he bobbed his head a few times, pursed his plump lips, and said, "Off to 'da nunnery with 'yas!" And then he walked away.

The cab driver turned the key, stepped on the gas, revved the engine, and drove down the muddy road. The poor girl quickly turned around and watched the wee cottage she had once called home now turn into a distant memory, along with her brother, Billy. Fiona sweetly waved goodbye, while Grandpa moved over to Sheba; her mane had somehow been braided, mysteriously in the night.

Shocked and baffled, Kathryn sat quietly in the backseat of the cab. She stared out the dingy window, observing waves of green hills, endless stone walls, grazing cattle, and white sheep splattered against the hills of rocks. Soon, the cab turned the corner as they headed east alongside Arthur's Seat, its grand crags and cliffs seemed to go on forever.

Kathryn's mind flashed back to her adventure up the Mountain with Billy. Her thoughts were still cloudy; there were birds, a hill... a hill with a tree. She closed her eyes once again, trying to desperately to remember what had happened, but only fuzzy pictures appeared in her thoughts. Flashes of crimson lights littered her head with strange images; a man, a bull, water...? She shook her head quickly, clearing away her thoughts. She simply could not remember what had happened. *Where is Billy? Why are they sending me away?* she thought.

"It's a nice day for a drive eh?" said the curious cab driver, peering into the rearview mirror to get a better view of Kathryn.

"I suppose," muttered Kathryn, picking at the scab on her hand and then staring aimlessly off into the rolling hills.

"Ahhh... The great Arthur's Seat! It's beautiful when it's sunny out eh?"

Kathryn sat silent in her daze, she looked dreamily at swans floating on a lake and in the distance she saw sheep, cows, sheep, a goat, some more lethargic sheep grazing on high grass, tranquil rocks, another cemetery sleeping underneath a round tower, some more grazing sheep, and a couple of blasé cows chewing on cud. *Why is this guy talking to me? Just leave me alone. Oh, look more sheep,* she thought.

"My name's Pete, by the way," said the smiling cab driver into the rear view mirror. "You know my niece, she used to believe in all those stories they told her about the great Arthur's Seat. You've probably have heard them eh?" Pete peered back again at Kathryn in the mirror and then his eyes were back on the road before him.

"A portal into the Otherworld, right? Oh, wait you westerners call it Aählynéé, right? Or, so you say," chuckled Pete.

Kathryn rolled her eyes and continued to ignore Pete, the overly talkative cab driver. Her eyes continued gawking out the window; sheep, cows, stone wall, sheep, big rock, hay, and some more sheep with pink butts.

"She was so determined to see a faery, she actually camped out one night with a friend on that Mountain. Well, they said they had heard an animal howling and shrieking in the night. They got so frightened, they ran straight down the Mountain screamin' bloody murder right in the middle of the night! Left all their gear and never returned!"

Kathryn wrapped her hand around the cuff of her sleeve and rubbed the dirty window to look out at a herd of sheared sheep, golden fields, bushy sheep leaping around in a field, stone ruins of a fallen tower, a scruffy black and white dog barking, puffy white sheep, and some more sheep with blue butts.

"But me, I don't believe a word of all that rubbish! Tales, that's all!"

Pete slowed the cab down and made a left hand turn, heading north up a stone lined road. More rolling green hills littered the valley; rows and rows of stoned walls jailing them in to their owner's field. Kathryn slid over to the left seat, so she could gaze out mindlessly at Arthur's Seat for a while. It seemed so still and lonely, kind of like how she was feeling now.

"There's nothing on the other side," said Pete, pointing at the back of Arthur's Seat. "See, it's just bog land and Loch Dorcha. No faeries, no magical land, no Otherworld, and certainly no Aählyéé, and there's nothing inside either, and that's a fact!"

Pete's words stung her ears. *No Aählyéé, no faeries, no Otherworld? Why talk about such things, if they aren't real?* she thought.

"I heard you hit your head real bad coming down off that Mountain. I once hit me head playing Rugby once. The other bloke had the ball. I went in to tackle him just as my other teammate was doing the same thing and then, *BAM!* Clobbered! I woke up in hospital, had funny dreams while I was there too!"

Pete's eyes squinted into the rearview mirror. Kathryn tried to catch his eyes, but he kept narrowing them as to see something behind him. Curiously, she whipped around in her seat, to see what the talkative cab driver was straining to see. Astonishingly, she had to squint too, for what she saw seemed surreal and quite unusual. Her eyes focused harder as the cab twisted down the long country road. There, in the distance, just past a herd of feeding cattle, she could make out a shadowy rider, galloping fiercely behind them. *Who rides a horse like that on a country road?* she thought.

"Say," said Pete, refocusing his eyes back on the road. "You wouldn't happen to have any friends that would want to make sure you're ok now?"

"Maybe?" she answered lamely, watching the rider loose distance as the cab sped up. "Why?"

"Ahhh... 'tis nothing!" said Pete dismissively. "So, I woke up in hospital. Me head throbbed so much, it felt like they used it to play football with. But, they said I was talking in circles for a few days, thought I was King of England or something, but it all passes in time. So, you're heading up to St. Bernadette's eh?"

Kathryn shrugged her shoulders as she watched hot pink colored sheep gnawing on the tall, green grass. *More pink sheep,* she thought.

"It's beautiful up there, long drive, but you'll have to take the ferry to get there, ya know?"

"Ferry?" she asked frightened. A cold chill ran up her spine. It had been over a year since she was last on a boat, which was when she came over from New York and that's when she lost her mother. *A mother and a brother gone and a grandfather who wants nothing to do with me. I'm batting a thousand,* she thought.

"It leaves once a week," said Pete, stretching his neck out to look at the sky; dark clouds began to blow in from the north. "And, we should make it up there in time. Just hope this weather doesn't go sour though!"

Now, not many good folk ever made their way as far up north to the slumbering town of Mulleam. But, the ones that did were either the fishermen folk, off to fish in the abundance of the great Atlantic Sea or the lassies of St. Bernadette's. Who had to take the ferry from the mainland to Inishmara.

Now, Inishmara was a bizarre, strange island off the northwestern coast of Ireland. And no man in his right mind ever made his way there, for they knew better than to be cursed by the dark faeries that dwelled there. It was many, many years back when the inhabitants of these parts discovered this lone island, which appeared suddenly out of the depths of the Atlantic. Soon, they found out that it was full of life, but strangely enough it was split in two; a massive crack was forged straight down the middle, creating a treacherous narrow ravine, which no man would ever cross.

At first, the island seemed like a blessing, full of fruit and fertile land. Everyday a few of the inhabitants traveled across the wild bitter sea, just to take food from this plentiful island, until one day they never returned. Confused and worried, the remaining souls set out to find what had happened and traveled across the great roaring sea. Tossed up and down in their wee boats on the raging waters, they made their way to Inishmara. Now, what they saw there, on Inishmara, scared them so bitterly, deep down to the very marrow of their bones that they leapt back into their boats as fast as they could. With sturdy hands and great power, they rowed back to Mulleam as fast as they could. Never ever looking back at the island, and never to return, to Inishmara again!

It was about a hundred years ago when a rich fellow from Scotland, whom had made his money in steel, brought his new bride to Inishmara. They had both heard about its great tales of faeries, magic, and mystery when they were just wee children. They both wondered if these great tales of Inishmara were true or not. So, being blessed with a bountiful amount of wealth, they made their way to Inishmara. Upon arriving on the island, the woman fell deeply in love with the land that the man had bought as a gift to his new bride. The wealthy Scotsman built a grand Castle for his bride to live there. But, dark secrets lurked on that island that should never be revealed to us mortal folks. (*For it is a day with the devil that makes a man go mad!*)

Unbeknownst to poor Kathryn, her life was still in for a few more trials and tribulations, which would lead her back into the realm of the faeries, for they were not done with her as of yet.

The corroded sedan choked a few times pulling into the roundabout outside Mulleam's Ferry Crossing. It abruptly stopped next to an iron cast cannon with black cannon balls piled up high, like a pyramid, sitting beside it.

The metal rope flagpole outside of the Mulleam's Ferry Crossing clanked constantly as the brazen wind whipped the green, white, and orange flag on its post. The windows of Mulleam's Ferry Crossing's waiting room had a thin layer of slime that had built up over the years. Looking inside, the patrons appeared as faint ghostly shadows haunting its space. And as the dark clouds blew in from the north, soon the day would turn to night.

"Right!" said Pete, pulling the brake up, "here we are! Best be careful, love. The wind is blowing fiercely out there! I'll grab your bag."

Kathryn clung to her backpack as the wind blew open the cab's door. Stepping out, Kathryn's hair flapped in the wind and then in her face. She pulled the hair out of her mouth, slammed the rusty door shut, and then sprinted towards Mulleam's Ferry Crossing.

Pete pulled out the oversized duffle bag from the boot. A piece of sand flew into his eye, causing it to tear. He rubbed his eye furiously. Now, all bleary eyed, he looked up to see a pulsating steed as dark as coal galloping down the lane. He rubbed harder to check if what he was seeing was real and watched as the rider grew closer.

Inside the waiting room, the glass door flew open, blowing in some dry leaves. Turning around, Kathryn grabbed the door's handle.

A squeaky little voice from behind her said, "Close the door, dear!"

Kathryn braced herself against the door and pushed it shut with all her might.

A fragile pale woman stood before her and said benevolently, "You must be, Kathryn." She was dressed in a navy blue habit and a bleach white collar. "Is that correct, dear?"

"Yes," she replied, observing the nun's clear mustache over her slender lips.

"I'm Sister Mary Margaret. I'll be taking you over to St. Bernadette's," she said touching Kathryn's shoulder with her pasty hand. "Now, where is Seaneen? He should be letting us know when we depart."

The front door of the waiting room opened once again, while a whirlwind of papers flew about like seagulls searching for a place to land.

"Here ya go, love," said Pete, his hair ratted up like a bird's nest as he placed her duffle bag on the floor and then smoothed his hair back.

"Oh, thank you, son!" said Sister Mary Margaret. "That was kind of you to bring her bag in."

"There's a fierce wind out there now, Sister!" said Pete anxiously. "But, I'll take me leave now. There's a storm comin'!"

"Oh, thank you kindly, sir," she repeated, watching the blustery wind whip through the waiting room as Pete left.

A regal man clothed in a tight turtleneck and a dark pea coat brushed by Pete as he exited the waiting room. Kathryn was captured by the man's stern presence and his distinguished beard and mustache.

Captain Seaneen was a man's man and feared no faeries. It was only he that would sail the young students from St. Bernadette's back and forth from Mulleam to Inishmara. He joked about the town, telling the locals of his trips back and forth to the island. *'Those faeries still haven't gotten me yet!'* He'd say to the locals, chewing down their dark brown ales. *'No faery will keep me from sailing to that island. Unless a beautiful selkie were to cast her spell on me – I'll keep doing, what I do.'* The locals smiled and laughed at his stories, but always kept in the back of their minds that they knew better than to make their way near that cursed island. And, a man who is not afraid of the sea will soon be drowned! And even so, for that matter, a man, who is not afraid of the faeries, will soon be cursed by them!

"Tis a fierce one out there," said Captain Seaneen curtly, making his way into Mulleam's Ferry Crossing's waiting room. "Don't think it's a good idea to be leaving in this kind of weather now."

"But, Captain," said Sister Mary Margaret imploringly. "The girls have to be back in class by tomorrow. What will Mother Superior say?"

"Well, Mother Superior?" said the Captain, throwing his shoulders back and flaring his chest out. "Give me a moment and I'll see what I can do, to leave straight away!"

"Thank you, Captain," she said relieved. Sister Mary Margaret clasped on to Kathryn and turned her around to face a group of four girls, dressed in their kick-pleated navy plaid skirts, and their white peter-pan blouses, buttoned tightly up to their collars. "Girls, this is Kathryn Murphy. She'll be starting St. Bernadette's with us tomorrow."

Kathryn was tight lipped as she turned around to see three older girls who were 'chatting it up' like seagulls waiting to swoop down on their prey. The other young lass sat quietly at the end, kicking her feet as the older girls ignored her.

"It's a bit late to be starting school isn't it?" said the frizzy brown haired girl with freckles splattered across her face.

"I'll say!" said the tall girl with the big hazel eyes.

"Well, Oona and Carmel," said Sister Mary Margaret. "We made a special arrangement for Kathryn. Now, Kathryn why don't you have a seat until we board?"

It wasn't so much of a particular look, or a raised eyebrow that the older girls gave her. It was the air about them and it told Kathryn to stay away from them, very far away.

Already bruised, battered, abandoned, and now rejected, Kathryn sat next to the wee little girl with curly jet-black hair. Her eyes were glazed with in boredom, while her legs swung restlessly back and forth.

"Did you have a bad fall?" asked the wee girl, looking up with her baby blue eyes.

"Huh?" said Kathryn, raising her hand to the bandage over her eye. "Oh this? Yes - yes, I did."

"Looks pretty nasty, I'm Maryanne," she said politely, reaching into her pocket, she pulled out a few colorful round gumballs with lint on them, "gumball?"

"No, thanks!" replied Kathryn.

Kathryn's ears perked up as she began to eavesdrop on the older girls as they chatted away.

"I heard from me Mum that there are actual goblins on the other side of the bridge," said Oona, huddling in closer to the other two girls.

"Goblins?" questioned Carmel.

"Big, dark, mean, nasty ones," whispered Oona, as she peeked her head up out of the huddle to see Sister Mary Margaret humming to herself and then back down again. "She snuck out one night with her friend and found the chapel in the cave."

"The one the monks used?" asked a pudgy blonde haired girl, whisking her hair off her shoulder.

"Yeah, Leesa," said Oona. "The one the old monks used on the other side of the Devil's Bridge."

"Wow!" said Carmel, "really?"

"Did she say goblins?" asked Kathryn to Maryanne.

"I guess so, they're always telling ghost stories," replied Maryanne, rubbing the gumball stains from her hand onto her skirt, "trying to scare each other. Are you scared?"

"About ghost stories?" questioned Kathryn.

"Yeah," answered Maryanne.

"No," said Kathryn uncomfortably.

"You seem scared," said Maryanne curiously.

"I just don't like boats," said Kathryn uneasily.

"Why?"

"My Mom," said Kathryn reluctantly, "fell overboard when we were coming to Ireland and drowned. It was a bad storm."

"Oh no! How horrible!" gasped Maryanne.

"She always said, if you don't take from the sea, it won't take from you!" chuckled Kathryn awkwardly.

"Well, it seems you gave a lot to the sea," said Maryanne.

"Maryanne!" called Carmel. "Here, pass me a gumball!"

"I want one too!" shouted Oona.

"Me too!" added Leesa.

Maryanne reached deep into her pocket filled with fuzzy lint balls, stray spitballs, and sticky gumballs and pulled out three. "Here!" she said.

Oona grabbed a blue gumball and popped it in her mouth nearly chipping her tooth and said to Kathryn, "Now, why are you here?"

"Ummm..." said Kathryn hesitatingly. "I'm not quite sure myself."

"Come on, now," said Leesa, "there's always a good reason someone is starting almost halfway through the second quarter!"

"Did you get kicked out of school?" asked Carmel.

"You were truant, right?" guessed Oona.

"No, no," said Kathryn, shaking her head side to side, "I went to school."

"So, why in bloody hell did they send you here?" asked Oona.

"I lost my brother," answered Kathryn honestly.

The three girls burst out laughing.

"You lost your brother? Geezzz!" commented Carmel. "If I lost my sister, it'd be the death of me!"

"How does one lose a brother?" asked Leesa. "Where is he?"

"I don't know," she said shrugging her shoulders. "We went to find the Raven's Gate and we separated and I remember finding my way in... and I was there in a cave... I remember running... and I hit my head. When I woke up, they told me he was gone!"

"She's crazy!" said Oona.

"What if he's dead?" asked Leesa.

"He's not dead!" argued Kathryn. "He's gone..."

"Gosh, how long has it been?" asked Carmel.

"He's been gone two weeks and a day," replied Kathryn.

"Up on a mountain for two weeks?" said Oona. "He's toast!"

"He's dead!" added Leesa.

"Yeah, that doesn't sound too good," commented Carmel.

The howling wind roared into the waiting room as Captain Seaneen reentered the room.

"There's dirty weather coming 'bout, best be leaving now!" said the Captain, taking hold of a few bags, which lay on the floor.

Sister Mary Margaret stood up and clapped her hands two times and said, "OK girls, time to leave! Chop-chop!"

Kathryn gripped her burly duffle bag and threw her weighty backpack over her shoulder. As she marched, her feet kept time with the older girls as they gossiped their way down the weathered dock. Maryanne walked alongside her as she waddled past the rusty boats anchored along the dock. The pungent scent of seaweed ripped through her nostrils as she watched the seagulls squawking over their heads fighting over some leftover fish skeletons.

"You think you'll ever find him?" asked Maryanne, trying to keep pace with Kathryn.

"Billy?" questioned Kathryn. "I sure hope so! He's not just my brother. He's my best friend."

"While he's away... Could I be yours?" asked Maryanne thoughtfully.

"Sure!" said Kathryn smiling.

Sister Mary Margaret stood at the weather-beaten, wooden ramp leading up to the wee ferry. "Hurry along girls," she said as they piled onto Captain Seaneen's ferry.

The older girls immediately made their way down below, so they could get the best seats.

Now, Kathryn wasn't quite sure what made her turn around at that precise moment, but what she saw made her change her opinion about the fragile Sister Mary Margaret. It seemed to be in utter slow motion, when that dark, cloaked rider rode up along the dock just as the girls boarded the ferry. His horse galloped on top of the warbled dock, its hooves clanking down on the rotting boards. The rider's face was shrouded, his body long and lean, dressed in a long flowing black robe, and his boot's heel flashed a bright crimson light. Dismounting from his steed in one quick swoop, he marched towards the boat, and raised his boot up to step on the plank.

It was just at that moment that Sister Mary Margaret looked dead-on into the stranger's eyes, without hesitation and without reserve, she whipped the plank away from beneath his foot, leaving him stranded on the dock. Yes, Sister Mary Margaret knew what she was doing, leaving the stranger high and dry on the dock. Captain Seaneen fired up the engines of the ferry and it chugged away from him.

The only thing left was the smell of sticky tar, stinky fish, squishy seaweed, and the obnoxious gasoline vapors from motor of the ferry filling the air. Kathryn leaned over the steel rail to get a better view. The stranger was nowhere to be seen; he had vanished into thin air. She walked back along the rail, grazing her fingers on the smooth red and white circular life preservers, which lined the upper deck of the old rusty ferry. Along the upper left side of the ferry was red lettering, which spelled out, 'The Crone'. Kathryn gazed up at the three masts that rose from the ferry's belly and then carefully stepped over some waterlogged rope which was entangled in knots along the deck.

"Kathryn, go down below and take a seat," directed Sister Mary Margaret.

Kathryn walked down the stairs, bracing herself along the banister, while the boat began to rock back and forth.

"You can sit with me, Kathryn," said Maryanne, sitting down on a molded plastic seat next to the older girls.

Kathryn smiled and slunk down into the cool seat.

"Girls!" said Sister Mary Margaret, handing out electric orange plastic bags, "it's going to be a rough journey. Take one of these."

"Ewww... Puke bags!" cried Oona. *"Gross!!!"*

"Here, Kathryn," said Maryanne, passing her a bag.

The boat began to rock as they journeyed further away from Mulleam.

"Thanks," said Kathryn.

Pop, went the engine as it revved up faster, their bodies bobbing along with the sway of the swelling waves. Looking around, Kathryn could see Oona beginning to turn a few different shades of green along with Leesa.

"Now, girls," said Sister Mary Margaret. "Please use the bags if you need to! No need to feel ashamed!"

Kathryn turned to Maryanne and said, "My Mom always said, it was better to be on top of the boat when on rough seas. Breathe the fresh air in and all!" Kathryn stood up, her legs wobbling as she walked towards the staircase.

"Wh-where is she going?" questioned Leesa queasily, holding her head over a bag.

"Kathryn, come back!" cried Maryanne.

"Kathryn, please sit!" said Sister Mary Margaret. "You shouldn't be going on top!"

"Don't worry 'bout me!" replied Kathryn, swaying side to side up the stairs. "I'll be fine!"

Kathryn stepped onto the deck. The crashing sound of the sea batted down fiercely on the ferry as it putted towards the northwest. The fresh sea air whisked through her hair, her face now sprayed with the mist from the salty sea as she stumbled over towards the Captain's helm.

"Come up to see the selkies have you?" asked Captain Seaneen, holding on to a knobby wheel.

"The selkies?" asked Kathryn, grabbing on to a steel rail, spreading her feet wide as their bodies swayed with the ocean.

"Might want to put two hands on there!" warned Captain Seaneen. The little ferry dove down into a deep swell spraying the helm's window. "The selkies, they are considered half mortal man and half faery creature, a seal that turns into a human. Many fisher folk 'bout these parts have been lured by such creatures into rocks as they drag them down deep into the cold sea. Yes, many seamen have fallen prey to these treacherous creatures. They say they sunbathe on these dark rocks around us, shedding their hides and turning into the most beautiful woman a man will ever lay his eyes on."

The simple boat chugged away through the rough seas.

"Look!" said the Captain eagerly, pointing into the roaring sea. "See there, there's a seal. Its head poppin' out above the waves to watch us!"

Kathryn stared into the gray ocean searching for the seal and asked, "where is it?'

"There!" he said, pulling back on a large black knob slowing the boat down, "right there!"

The boat's engine clanked ferociously and then it began to spit water in and out. After that, it started to choke on the water, then it cut out, and died completely. Captain Seaneen raised the black knob higher, turning a small key on the mantle clockwise. The engine was silent. The only sound was from the waves thumping on the bow, tossing the wee ferry about in the frigid sea. The mists of sea spray soon began to mix with rain.

"Engine's flooded!" he said, stepping out of the helm, he turned to Kathryn. "You stay put! I'll go see what's the problem."

Kathryn gazed around the dashboard, the big black knob glided up and down a gold sleeve on a half circle. The dashboard was littered with black round circles and a radio that kept clicking on and off. A loud noise exploded from the engine. Kathryn jumped back with fright, but soon she could hear the engine's chugging hum once again. Captain Seaneen stepped back into his helm, drenched in seawater and pushed the black knob forward. The wee ship tossed and turned as she headed deeper into the night. Pellets of rain clinked down harder on the helm's windows, the wind shifted, and the waves began to rock diagonally against the ferry.

"Wind's changin'," said Captain Seaneen apprehensively, turning the helms' wheel to the far right. "It's going to be hell's fury if we get stuck in this storm!"

"How far until we make it to St. Bernadette's?" asked Kathryn.

"She mustn't be too far away now," said the Captain. "Aye! See there, in the far distance, those lights. Can you see it from here?"

"Yes – Yes! I see it!" exclaimed Kathryn.

"That's where we're headed. That's the light from the old bell tower 'ya see there?"

Now, it was just at that moment that a monstrous wave lifted the wee ferry up high, smacking it back down into the cruel sea. Kathryn's body thrashed down as icy water entered the Captain's helm.

"Get out! Get out!!!" cried the Captain sternly, bashing his foot into one of the windows, shattering the glass into the sea. "Go on! *Get out!*"

Kathryn dove down into the water, swimming through the hallowed window. Breaking the water's surface her head emerged in darkness. Gasping for air, she bobbed up and down to the rhythm of the icy sea. In the distance, she heard the older girls crying out.

"Maryanne!!!" cried Carmel, hanging from a life preserver.

"She's still in there!" answered Leesa, clenching on to a wooden box.

Kathryn looked at the boat floating on its side, bobbing in the water. She could hear a buoy's bell clanging with the shifting water. *They're too far away,* she thought.

Kathryn swam closer to the broken boat; one of the masts was split in two above her head, part of it jutting down into the water. Kathryn took a deep breath and dove deep into the dark sea. Her eyes could see no light, just blackness as she felt her way through the stairway, her body shivering in the freezing water. Further into the boat she swam until she was in the sitting room. Kathryn swam to the top into a small air pocket and gasped. There she was, Maryanne, floating in the water before her like a ragdoll. Kathryn took hold of her torso and began to swim back through the stairway and back out to the sea.

Maryanne's body was limp and cold, but there was life in her as Kathryn pulled her out.

"Maryanne!" cried Carmel frantically.

"She's here!" cried Kathryn, choking for air as she snatched a life preserver drifting nearby and placed her on it. "She's over here!"

"The girl's got her!" cried Captain Seaneen.

"Over there!" cried Oona.

"Good heavens! There she is!" said Sister Mary Margaret. "Is she alive?"

"Maryanne!" called Carmel, swimming fiercely through the current.

Kathryn swam towards the group now huddling around a life raft. Then suddenly, out of nowhere a massive wave crashed into the boat and the broken mast slammed down into the water, clunking Kathryn on the head.

The noise from the thunderous storm above now became soft and faded away; her body fell lifeless, down into the bitter sea. Her eyes half open, she could only see the gray sea swirling around and around, bubbles drifted away from her, while the salty tears of the sea filled her mouth. Her lungs began to weigh down like an anchor cast down to the sea's floor. Her energy gone, she slipped deeper and deeper into the abyss. Her eyes grew heavy with sleep and then her body became still, and moved no more.

Now, no one quite sure knows what happened next, except for Kathryn herself, but out of the dull, dreary abyss of that dark sea, as fast as a bullet from a gun, came a fish-like body pushing her up from the depths below. Her hands could feel a cold, sleek creature pushing her up towards the surface of the sea. A rush of air blew into her lungs. She was once again in the mortal realm of the living.

"There she is!" cried Captain Seaneen, grabbing hold of Kathryn's limp body.

♦ CHAPTER FOURTEEN ♦
ST. BERNADETTE'S

A sugary sweet voice tapped softly in Kathryn's ears, "Now, now there, dear. You best be at rest, no one's going to harm you here."

Kathryn's eyes cracked open to a vibrant array of lights, like a kaleidoscope. An image of a soft rosy-cheeked woman over her head spiraled into hundreds. Taking the shallowest of breaths, her chest heaved with the sea. She cocked her head to her side to see Maryanne lying still in the bed next to her.

"Oh, good dear, you've awakened now!" said the rosy-cheeked nun. "I'll let Mother know you've come about."

The wooden door slowly creaked open and Carmel slithered out from behind it. "Is she any better yet, Sister Joan?" asked Carmel.

"Well, this one is," said Sister Joan, rising up from Kathryn's bed and then sitting down on Maryanne's bed, whose face was as pale as the moon. "But, dear Maryanne is not doing well. She's still has a high fever."

"Is there anything I can do?" asked Carmel.

"You can let Mother Superior know Kathryn has awoken," she said, picking up a wet towel and dabbing Maryanne's face.

Carmel turned towards Kathryn, her face stung with fear.

"You saved my sister," said Carmel humbly.

"I-I," mumbled Kathryn groggily.

"I'm sorry, if we were rude to you before. It won't happen again," she said and then walked out the door.

Kathryn's eyes glided around the simple room, a single crucifix hung over a submerged closet. The walls were split in two, the lower part made of dark wood, the upper area painted bleach white. Only two solid iron beds and a sturdy dresser decorated the barren room.

"Now dear, there's something I need to tell you. Since the boat capsized, all your belongings and possessions are now part of the North Atlantic. So, we've collected some old clothing that a few of the girls don't wear anymore and some of the Sister's old habits as well," said Sister Joan, handing Kathryn a postulate's black jumper along with a white peter-pan blouse. "For now, you can wear this, until your uniform arrives."

Oona and Leesa burst through the squeaky door and stumbled into Kathryn's room.

"Mother Superior wants to see Kathryn in her office," said Oona fervently, *"now!"*

Sister Joan took a deep breath and said dryly, "Best not keep Mother waiting or she'll take a ruler to us all."

Kathryn pulled her arm through the crisp white blouse and buttoned the clear buttons up to her neck. Her skin itched and felt smothered in a pile of dried up wool. Sister Joan placed the black jumper over her head and zipped it up in the back.

"Now, let us go see Mother!" said Sister Joan.

It seemed as if Kathryn and Sister Joan walked for hours and hours down that long corridor. To her left and right were other shady, wooden doors, aligned parallel to one another. Shadows filtered through the dimly lit beveled windows as they meandered towards a beautiful statue of a woman at the end of the corridor.

From afar, Kathryn knew straight away it was a statue of the Blessed Mother, just like the one they had in their cramped apartment in Brooklyn. This statue in particular was of course larger and more life-like than the tiny one they had sitting on their television set. Her face was soft and sweet, she was clothed in an iridescent sapphire robe that draped over her open arms. The sweet scent of tiny rosebuds around her feet filled the air. Sister Joan bowed before the statue, making the sign of the cross, and Kathryn quickly did the same. They turned the corner and began ascending up a narrow staircase.

"Best get in the habit of making the sign of the cross dear," said Sister Joan, striding through a carved stone archway, filled with stone rosebuds and Celtic knots, that were in the shape of three circles intertwined together. "You'll need it here."

Through the ornamental archway, they walked into a grand cloister filled with other lesser archways, opening to a courtyard. Stained glass windows filled with the most glorious colors of the rainbow painted the stone corridor with a light from heaven. Cream-colored statues of men and women lined the hallway and courtyard that Kathryn and Sister Joan walked through; men with funny hats holding sturdy books, metal keys, and grandiose staffs. The female statues were of women holding crucifixes, budding roses, thick books, and golden medallions. And as they walked through the courtyard, Kathryn couldn't help but hear what sounded to her like a choir of angels.

At the very end of the corridor was a golden orb with the rays of the sun coming out of it and on the inside was a small piece of wood sitting in its center.

"Sister," asked Kathryn, amazed by the beauty of the golden orb, "what is that?"

"That my dear, is a piece of the True Cross," said Sister Joan. "The Cross of Christ and it is also our order's namesake, the Sisters of the True Cross. It is there to remind us that we all must bear our own crosses in life. But, the greatest one of all is to give of oneself wholly, by loving one another and to show kindness, mercy, and compassion to all of God's children. That is what Christ teaches us and that is why we are here."

Sister Joan stopped outside an oak door carved with creeping vines and opened it. A rush of wintry air seeped out of the room as they stepped inside. Another crucifix was nailed into the wall above a long mahogany desk. Mother Superior sat austerely behind the desk. Along with her bits of bright red hair poking through her wimple, her face looked as though an iron had flattened it. Around her neck hung a wooden crucifix which fell around her bosom, above it a spectacular emerald Celtic Cross, encapsulated by three circles. In the corner stood Sister Mary Margaret and another sister whose pruned face scared Kathryn to death just from looking at her.

Now, there are many stories told about Mother Superior, stories of how she once lived abroad in Spain in a convent with no electricity and no running water. She spent the day walking barefoot on wobbled stone floors of the Abbey and tended to her chickens and cows that lived in a nearby field. At night, her only bed was a single sheet laid upon a pile of stiff hay that poked at her all night long as she slept.

Supposedly, one day she had had enough of a particular bull that charged brazenly at her chickens all day, filling them with fear and causing them to stop laying eggs all together. Even the eggs that got laid turned rotten and spoiled. So, one day Mother Superior awoke again to the sound of her chickens clucking loudly in the wee hours of the morning. Furious, she leapt out of bed, nightgown and all, and walked straight up to this brash black bull. She looked him straight into his marble black eyes, her nostrils flaring, her eyes squinting, until he ran away from her and out of her field, never to return again!

Now, that's how stern Mother Superior is; she even got a wild bull to run away from her without even speaking a word! All she had to do was to look deep into his eyes and he ran away from her, just like the chickens he was charging.

"Miss Murphy!" commanded Mother Superior.

"Yes," replied Kathryn.

Mother Superior lifted up her eyes filled with no emotion and gave her the edge of her tongue, "I did not ask you to speak, Miss Murphy."

Kathryn froze in fear and swallowed any remaining salt water in her mouth.

"It seems that you have made a major mark on our school, before you have even arrived. Sister Mary Margaret informed me that you were told to stay below with the other students. And because you left, Miss Maryanne decided to get up and meet you when the accident occurred. Is that correct?"

Kathryn looked at Sister Mary Margaret, whose face was colorless and her hands wringed together.

"Is that correct, Miss Murphy?" demanded Mother Superior.

"I-I," mumbled Kathryn, "I just didn't want to get sick."

"So, you left the group? So, you could go gallivanting up top!" argued Mother Superior.

"I-I."

"She's just like her mother!" growled the prune faced Sister. "Has no respect for her superiors! We'd be better off without her!"

"Very well, Miss Murphy - you will be punished appropriately," barked Mother Superior.

"Mother Superior may I?" interrupted Sister Mary Margaret, her head cowered down like a dog to its master. "Kathryn saved little Maryanne, if it wasn't for her, Maryanne would be lost to us."

"Sister, I understand your concerns, but am I supposed to give leniency to insubordination just because by some chance, a miracle occurred and that little girl is still alive?"

"No Mother," said Sister Mary Margaret sadly.

"Then, you will be punished, Kathryn!" said Mother Superior. "You will no longer be welcomed at St. Bernadette's and will return home."

"If I may, Mother," asked Sister Joan. "Perhaps, we should think of this differently? If Maryanne did not get up at that time and was sitting in her seat, perhaps, she would have been killed instantly? Perhaps we are assuming things would have turned out differently for the better, when they may have turned out for the worse?"

Mother Superior sat silently at her desk, her foreboding eyes as still as a mountain.

The door handle jiggled and then it clanked. All the Sisters turned their heads to the door.

"It's Sister Gwen!" laughed Sister Joan.

A withered old woman, wrapped in her habit, shaking a crooked wooden cane crept into the room. In her crinkled hand was a crumpled-up envelope.

"Sister, come in!" said Sister Joan, placing her hand tenderly upon her back.

"This - this is for Mother," said Sister Gwen, holding up the weathered envelope, handing it to Sister Joan. "It is for her eyes only."

Sister Gwen looked at Kathryn with a kind smile on her face and with a true happiness to see her.

Mother Superior cautiously took the envelope from Sister Joan and picking up a steel dagger, she ripped it open. A shiny silver coin fell out of the letter and onto her broad lap. Her eyes ticked back and forth as she read the letter that was entrusted to her and her alone.

"It's good to see you, Sister Gwen!" giggled Sister Mary Margaret. "It's been ages!"

Mother Superior placed the letter down on her desk, her hand rubbing her left cheek and her chin. Finally, after a few seconds, she stood up and said, "It seems, Kathryn, that God wants you to stay here with us at St. Bernadette's. This is a letter from your Grandfather. Due to insufficient funds, he has only one silver coin to spare to cover your tuition," Mother Superior raised one of her skinny eyebrows high into her flat forehead. "Due to the fact, he says, a crazed leprechaun has stolen his purse. It is with the lack of funds that he cannot afford your tuition here at St. Bernadette's and has given full guardianship of you to Sister Gwen for the time being. Since, we Sister's of the True Cross have chosen a life of poverty and Sister Gwen has no money to pay for your tuition, room, board, or any return trip home, you will have to work it off by working in the laundry with Sister Mary Elizabeth. You will work six days a week, resting on our Lord's Day, beginning at 5 a.m. until breakfast is served at 8:30 a.m."

"The laundry?" questioned Kathryn.

"You will start tomorrow morning. Sister Mary Martha, please read her the rules of St. Bernadette's," said Mother Superior. Opening her desk's drawer, she dropped the envelope inside, and then locked it with a brass key.

"Gladly, Mother!" said Sister Mary Martha, pursing her thin shriveled lips. "*Rule Number One*: All students will obey the Sister's of the True Cross's orders. No exceptions! *Rule Number Two*: Lights out at exactly 9 p.m. and all students in bed. *Rule Number Three*: No students are allowed in the attic or bell tower, *ever! Rule Number Four:* No student is allowed to tell tales of ghosts or to speak of faeries. *Rule Number Five*: No student is allowed to cross The Bridge of Diabhal, *ever!* Any student who breaks these rules will be punished severely. All punishments are determined and given out by Mother Superior."

"Come now, child," said Sister Gwen. "Let me walk you back to your room."

Sister Gwen slouched over, gripping Kathryn's hand and led her out of Mother Superior's office.

"Don't worry about Mother. Her bark is worse than her bite!" chortled Sister Gwen, positioning her weight heavily on her cane as she wobbled alongside, Kathryn. Her head barely reached up to Kathryn's shoulder. "Your Grandfather and I are rather close. Don't worry about his purse; I'm sure he'll find that feral leprechaun again!"

"Am I, ever going to leave?" asked Kathryn.

"Not 'til you graduate. A little over five years until then," replied Sister Gwen.

"Five years!" replied Kathryn in shock, "but, what about Eddie, George, Marie, and Billy?"

Sister Gwen stopped short at a large square doorway leading into a gymnasium.

"All in good time child, all in good time," said Sister Gwen. "There's someone I'd like you to meet!"

A robust nun with flushed cheeks jogged up to Sister Gwen and Kathryn; her fleshy arms jiggled like jello as she approached.

"Sister Gwen!" said the burly nun, wiping the sweat off her brow. "Good to see you out and about! It's been too long since you've come to see us!"

"Sister Martin Marie this is, Kathryn Murphy," said Sister Gwen. "I will be her guardian for the next five years!"

"Oh you will! Will you?" laughed Sister Martin Marie. "She's a scrawny one now, isn't she? Arms like toothpicks, eh?" she said, grabbing hold of Kathryn's arms and squeezing them tightly.

"I was hoping you could help her with your - what do you call it?" hesitated Sister Gwen.

"My warrior training class, Sister Gwen?" laughed Sister Martin Marie. "Is that what you're asking? You want her to train with the big girls, is that right? Well, she better be prepared to sweat with the rigorous drills I'll make her do! Would you like that dear? Would you like to train with the big girls and me? Make you a warrior to be reckoned with?"

Kathryn stared into Sister Martin Marie's bulging eyes, trying desperately not to look at her stained armpits.

"That would be wonderful Sister," replied Sister Gwen. "When's practice?"

"Every Tuesday and Thursday after classes," she said. "Child, don't you say anything? Or did the devil steal your tongue?"

Kathryn gazed at the enormity of Sister Martin Marie, her body casting down a large shadow on her.

"You're as big as a football player," blurted out Kathryn.

Sister Martin Marie threw her head back, roaring with laughter, then shimmied her hands down her hips and thighs and said proudly, "Well, I'll take that as a compliment, since those football players are just scrawny little lads running around all day!"

"Come now, dear," said Sister Gwen, guiding Kathryn away from the gymnasium.

"I meant an American football player," whispered Kathryn to Sister Gwen.

"Tis best if you don't let her know the difference," replied Sister Gwen. "You know, your mother stayed in the same room that you're in now."

"I didn't know she went to school here," said Kathryn baffled.

"She did indeed child. She learned a lot too. She was my favorite girl, had a wonderful spirit and a wild fire about her. Always getting into mischief, mind you, and reading.

Always having her books about her, she'd guard them with her life," said Sister Gwen.

"What books?" questioned Kathryn.

"The one I gave her and her notes too!"

"Sister Gwen what book did you give her?"

"Do I really have to tell you child? I'm sure you've read it too, seeing how much your mother adored it. She used to sing a song too as she walked down these corridors. How'd it go again? *Two feet Susie, three feet Willy, four feet early, JUMP!*" said Sister Gwen playfully.

"I remember that too! What a silly song," said Kathryn, stopping before her aged bedroom door.

"I suppose so, dear. Here you are! You best be getting to bed so you can be up before 5 a.m.," said Sister Gwen.

"How am I ever going to get up? And find the laundry Sister?" asked Kathryn apprehensively.

"Don't worry child. I'll send someone to wake you up and take you over," she said and then turned away, hobbling down the narrow hallway.

Kathryn tiptoed into the room, slowly disrobing, while she watched Maryanne breath shallowly as she slept.

Gazing around the dimly lit room, she noticed some scratchings carved into the wood framing the wall. With her barefeet, she hopped across the frigid floor and placed her finger on the etched mark, which spelled out *South*.

♦ CHAPTER FIFTEEN ♦
CYRIL'S LAUNDRY SERVICE

Kathryn's body tossed and turned on the spongy mat, which the Sister's of the True Cross called a mattress. Her eyeballs danced around in her head, while her weary eyelids remained closed. Her mind raced with visions of a shadowy labyrinth deep within Arthur's Seat. Faces of hairy creatures with glowing eyes, wayward prisoners chained to walls, a serpent-like monster with the face of a bull charging at her in dark, dreary waters, a brilliant crystal of crimson flashed before her, and then eyes of fire that followed her like a fuse burning, and lastly, the shadow of a stranger approaching her as she laid weakened on the Mountainside.

A warm hand cradled her leg and shook it, three times. Jolting upright, she screamed, "Billy!"

An older nun that she had never seen before placed her pudgy finger to her bleached lips, just missing a few of the discolored, hairy moles that protruded from her crinkled upper lip. The nun handed her some clean clothing and waved her chubby arm, gesturing her to follow.

Kathryn stepped out of her room into the dusk of the morning's twilight, catching a glimpse of a waxy candle hovering in the hallway. Soon, it began to bob up and down, slowly moving further and further away. A soft grunt echoed from the quiet nun and Kathryn followed. Her hand cradled the steel railing as they stepped down the stairs through another deserted hallway, into the stagnant kitchen, and out the back door.

A blast of cold, wet morning air splashed her chilled body as they walked out of St. Bernadette's, down a lengthy winding road of stone and gravel, to a small sterile building. Silence whispered in her ears, not even the birds were awake. When they grew closer, she began to hear the chugging sound of a washing machine.

The timid nun's hand trembled as she opened the heavy, metal door and wiggled her stout body through it. Hot steam filled the air, like puffs of smoke, blurring her vision as she traveled through the misty room. Large, menacing green pressing machines lined one of the stale walls, while running along the other wall were crisp white sinks with steel washer boards poking out of them and dry cardboard boxes sat lazily on the shelves above them. In the center of the room, sturdy tables ran parallel with cushioned ironing boards, while flat, metal irons with thick black snake-like wires steamed sizzling hot air as they waited to be used.

A greasy black haired boy with ears pointed out like an elf stood in the middle of the table folding fluffy white cotton towels and placing them perfectly into the weaved baskets on the floor. The silent nun pointed towards the boy and grunted ever so gently once again. Kathryn approached the yellowish boy, noticing his hands were pointy and slightly smaller than other boys she had met.

The peculiar boy smiled as she approached.

"Welcome to Cyril's laundry service!" he said jubilantly, gazing up at Kathryn with his black pupil-less eyes. "I see Sister Liz brought you down, right on time! Here," passing her a pile of clean laundry and she began folding, "dig in! There's always something to wash here, down at Cyril's laundry. You've got your cotton sheets, absorbent towels, cooking aprons, school uniforms, holey socks, and dirty under-things. The nuns have too much time on their hands, so they tend to change all of them, at least once a day."

"They do?" she asked curiously, folding up a torn apron with only one string.

"Which is great for me, it keeps me busy all day long! You can put that in the basket over there, labeled kitchen," said Cyril, holding a newly folded sheet. "But, it's quiet down her. Sr. Liz sleeps all morning until they wake her for vespers! We've loads of cool stuff here! We have a wash-washing machine and over there is a dryer. You take the green boxes from above the wash-washing machine. I always have a hard time saying that! The green boxes are the detergent that you use in the wash-washing machine. Fascinating stuff!" chuckled Cyril. "And here," placing his hand on a giant, metallic green iron press, "this is Felix!"

"Felix?"

"Yes, Felix! I like to name my machinery. Over there is Rose, Bubble, Hick, and Darth!"

"You name your machines?"

"You see, Rose works beautifully, everything comes out smelling like a rose when you use her! Bubble tends to get a little too many."

"Bubbles?"

"Right! See, you're catching on!" said Cyril excitedly. "So, what does Hick do?"

"Ummm... Hick? Let's see," said Kathryn, pondering for a moment. "Hick, hics every now and then?"

"Ha! You're right!" cried Cyril. "And Darth?"

"Darth? Ummm... Darth, makes everything dark?"

"Good try! But, no! I just thought it was a cool name!" said Cyril merrily, handing her a basket of towels. "Fold!"

"Can I ask, that is," questioned Kathryn. "how do you work in a laundry on an island with an all girls boarding school and you're a boy?"

"Well, me Dad is the groundskeeper," stated Cyril. "Me Mum used to work in the laundry, but she's gone now."

"Oh, I'm sorry."

"Did they give you the rules of St. Bernadette yet?"

"Oh, yeah!"

"You know, technically you're not in St. Bernadette's now. You're in a separate building."

"Why, are you going to start telling me ghost stories?" laughed Kathryn.

"Well, I'll tell you what you need to know and what the nuns don't want you to find out! Like the Devil's Bridge."

"You mean the Bridge of Di... Di... Diabhal? That's what it means? The Devil's Bridge?" said Kathryn alarmingly, raising her voice slightly.

"Shhh... You'll wake Sr. Liz. The nuns named it that because it crosses this great ravine that plummets down into a dark, treacherous abyss of sharp rocks. But, I'll tell you this, when you cross it, you're no longer in our realm."

"Our realm?"

"The mortal realm of man, silly! You cross over into the realm of the faeries. Long ago, a monk crossed the Devil's Bridge. He climbed up the steep, jagged slopes of the island and made a stone honeycomb hermitage for himself, where he was to devote his life to God until the day he died. But, one tormenting year, he came out of his hermitage, his beard longer than his arms, his eyes crazed with fear, and he crossed the Devil's Bridge, and walked right up to the Mother Superior of that time. He whispered in her ear and handed her that emerald Celtic Cross that Mother Superior wears around her neck now. And then, he sailed away from the island on a small wooden boat, off into the great sea, never to return again.

"Some say he went mad, but others say they've heard the nun's story of what really happened. The hermit had made his way into the realm of the faeries. When he crossed over, he fought them off as they were trying to make their way into our mortal realm, to take over! He fought them off with his faith and whatever is in that emerald Celtic Cross that Mother Superior wears. It's what keeps them at bay and keeps the faeries from crossing over the Devil's Bridge."

Sister Liz snorted in her intoxicated state of sleep, frightening the two.

"Where is it?" whispered Kathryn.

"It's just down the lane. They also say ghosts and faeries haunt that side of the island."

Sister Liz awoke to a wee chiming bell, signaling to her it was time to leave and with a wave of her hand and a grumbling grunt, they were off, back up the road to St. Bernadette's.

Now the girls of St. Bernadette's sat like perfect statues, lined up on thick oak picnic tables for breakfast, which turned out to be a measly bowl of lumpy porridge and some dry toast, if you were lucky enough get a slice before they were all gone. Of course, Oona and Leesa seemed to have a plan that gave them a few extra pieces of toast. First off, Leesa would step in front of Sr. Mary Margaret when she was stepping out of the kitchen with the toast tray. Distracting her about nonsense, such as, when did she decide that she had the calling to be a nun? Or, when did she think the previous owners decided to donate the Castle to the Sisters of the True Cross? Or, where did she get her hair done? Oona then would sneak up behind her and snatch up a few good slices, leaving the burnt ones behind for the rest of the not so savvy girls. Stealthfully, she'd slide the toast into her skirt pocket before anyone else caught on.

Along the opposite wall, the nuns sat silently behind a latticed room divider as they ate their fill of porridge and dry, burnt toast. Kathryn filled her stomach up with chunky porridge, grabbed her books, and then jetted off to her first class of the day.

Sitting in an icebox of a room, a chilling draft crawled up Kathryn's arms and legs, covering her thick in goose bumps. No matter how hard she rubbed her hands up and down her arms, she never ever got warm. Looking around the dull classroom, she observed the other girls dressed in their clean peter-pan collared shirts chattering away as if she wasn't in the room. A clink at the door jolted the girls to clasp their hands on the desk and throw their shoulders back, sitting up pin straight and becoming frozen as ice sculptures.

Now, the first of Kathryn's classes was English, with none other than Mother Superior herself. Her face was stern and cold as she walked into the icy classroom, observing all the girls sitting properly at attention, except for Kathryn who shoulders slumped down, her hands now tucked under her butt to keep them warm. A *whack* of a ruler on her sloping wood desk shook Kathryn up to attention as Mother Superior began her class. Her deep, monotone voice began to put Kathryn to sleep many times, but Mother Superior always had a way of waking her up! The ruler was the traditional way for a good burst of awareness, but other times, she made her hold her hands above her head to keep her from dozing off. Another time, when Kathryn was having difficulties with her new vocabulary words, Mother Superior made her stand on top of her desk in front of the classroom and spell out each word, define them, and use them each in a sentence. Oh yes, Mother Superior was the hardest English teacher she had ever had, no doubt about that.

After her demeaning English class with Mother Superior, Kathryn reported to her History class with Sister Joan, which was the complete opposite of English. Sister Joan's classroom was located along the south wall of St. Bernadette's, allowing a brilliant light to warm up the room, where as with Mother Superior the room was due west and had no sunlight whatsoever until the late afternoon. Sister Joan entered the classroom with her flushed red cheeks and kind eyes. The class sat up properly, but were much more relaxed and at ease than with Mother Superior. Her teaching approach was very unique. She would have the class place their desks in a huge circle and they would discuss things like the Norman Conquest over Ireland and the Great Potato Famine from 1845-1849, which left millions of Irish dying from hunger, starving to death. Kathryn was disgusted to hear such a cruel thing could ever happen to anyone.

Sister Joan talked about so many important, interesting things and she never raised her voice to the girls, treating them all as equals. If one of them didn't understand a topic, she'd start from the beginning, explaining everything over again in great details without a twinge of harshness.

Next up was Math class with Sister Liz. Her short round body would roll in just as the bell tolled. She pulled up a chair to the chalkboard, stepped on it, and started to scribble out equations until it filled the entire board. The girls took out their notebooks and began to work them out while Sister Liz would sit back down in her chair and take a catnap until class was over. It was the quietest class she never heard. No one dared to make a peep, for many stories were told about a young girl named Colleen who once asked a question while Sister Liz slept. Some said that the girl had to leave the school immediately and return home because Sister Liz scared her so much. The poor girl wouldn't stop hiccupping and her left eye began to twitch uncontrollably as if she had some crazy wild disease.

After morning classes, Kathryn sat down in the cafeteria on her bench. This time soup was served, but not just any soup, it was a creamy potato soup with leeks and chives, served with hot homemade bread. It was the most delightful thing she had ever tasted.

Maybe, this isn't so bad, she thought, slurping down the remnants of her bowl.

After lunch, Kathryn found herself in Irish class with Sister Mary Martha. Her classroom was also facing due south, but by this time of the day, it was well over ninety degrees. Kathryn began to sweat profusely as Sister Mary Martha entered the classroom with her lips puckered as if she had just eaten a lemon. The first thing she did was to make every girl stand up and tuck in her stiff, white shirt, brush their hair back, tie their shoes again, pull up their knee highs to exactly one inch below their kneecaps, and wash their hands removing all the dirt from underneath their nails.

"Don't know how many germs are crawling all over your dirty hands, 'specially feeding your face in that dirty trough," she'd say everyday when they returned from the cafeteria.

Next thing she would do was to take attendance and re-arrange the seating in the classroom. One day, it would be alphabetical A-Z's, the next day it would be Z-A's, some days she'd do it by hair color or by eye color, on occasion by height or by girth, which was a bit difficult, but every day she'd get the girls up and *'sort them out,'* as she would say.

After all the sorting, Sister Mary Martha would have the girls take out a piece of paper, filling out their full first name, middle name, confirmation name, and finally their last name in the upper left hand corner. After that, they filled out the day, month, and year in the upper right hand corner. Upon finishing that, they had to begin a new paragraph to the left with Sister Mary Martha's full name, the name of the school, the school address, the class year, and the subject matter of the day; but, taking all that time sorting, cleaning, and writing, only left about ten full minutes for her to teach. Upon which, Sister Mary Martha would squiggle the dusty, white chalk on the slate blackboard with strange words like: *Tine, Aer, Ithir, Cloch,* and *Uisce.*

Kathryn would scribble them down onto her stiff parchment paper, writing out the definitions she gave for each of them. *Tine* is Irish for fire; *Aer* is Irish for air; *Ithir* is Irish for earth, *Cloch* is Irish for stone, and *Uisce* is Irish for water. After giving her obedient class the five new Irish words she said unsympathetically, "Now, write that down one hundred times each, until you've memorized it!"

Every day, it was another set of five words with the exact same homework, over and over again. The class reminded her of a hamster rotating around and around within a wheel. *Is this really teaching us anything at all?* she wondered.

When Kathryn entered Sister Mary Margaret's Science class, she was happy to find the temperature comfortable, but the foul-smelling stench when she entered the classroom almost knocked her to the floor. Jars of marinating grasshoppers, pickled worms, and jellied beetles lined the walls, while crystal vials bubbled in the center islands. Sister Mary Margaret hovered over each of the students as they poured different fizzy brews into glass flasks, shaking uncontrollably, expecting something to go wrong. It wasn't until a freckled face girl with pigtails emptied the pink fizzy into the blue fizzy when an actual explosion erupted. Sister Mary Margaret then decided it was best to teach from the farthest corner of the room, hiding behind a clunky, old filing cabinet. From there, she gave instructions as the girls poured, brewed, mixed, cut, sliced, opened, and dissected all their science projects.

The cast metal bell from the bell tower tolled and it was off to gym class with Sister Martin Marie. Now, even though

Sister Martin Marie looked like an American football player, she had a clever sense of humor, which made Kathryn laugh when she got her going. When the class finally entered the clammy gymnasium, they found it was lined with hanging knotted ropes, blue spongy pads, orange cones, dimpled red balls, and quite frankly, the most peculiar display of slim, silver swords, black netted masks, long white gloves, and padded vests. In the center was Sister Martin Marie, standing at attention dressed in a white body suit, padded vest, facemask, gloves, and a thin silvery sword to her side.

"Murphy! You're up first!" said Sister Martin Marie in a husky voice. "Get suited up! Let's see, whatcha got!"

Kathryn fumbled about when she was placing the black padded vest around her chest; it seemed to have a mind of its own, shifting around in all the wrong places. Next, she placed the netted facemask over her head. The gym grew dark and all she could see were tiny little dots creating a picture of Sister Martin Marie before her.

"Come on, now!" she said zealously, whipping her sword up in front of her, swirling it around in the air. "Pick up that foil."

"What do - I do with it?" she asked, clumsily picking up a slender sword in her hand.

"Don't, get hit!" ~*swish*... "En garde!!" she said brazenly, lunging forward and striking Kathryn in the center of her vest. "Now, now Kathryn is that any way to defend yourself?" asked Sister Martin Marie, "You didn't even lift your foil up to defend yourself."

"Sorry," she said timidly, her eyes squinting through her pin-cushioned mask, watching Leesa and Oona covering their mouths as they giggled at her.

"No, sorry!" boomed Sister Martin Marie. "Defend! Again!" ~*swish*... ~*swish*...

Sister Martin Marie thrust her body forward with her silver foil in hand, ~*swish*...~*swish*... while Kathryn jumped back to avoid her attack. In fact, she kept jumping back with every advance, ~*swish*... ~*swish*... until she was off the mat, her back pressed against the wall and Sister Marin Marie's foil was pushed against her chest.

"You can run all you want Kathryn, but you'll never get away from a sword coming after you! You must stand your ground! Defend yourself! Now, again! I want you to move your sword and use your sword to protect yourself. This time, I'll go slowly. Take your stance! Ready! Fence!" ~*swish*... ~*swish*...

Sister advanced her front foot forward thrusting her silver foil sword towards Kathryn's chest, ~*swish*... ~*swish*.... She could hear her heart drumming louder and louder through her vest as she watched the blade spring at her, ~*swish*... ~*swish*.... Her mind told her to run, but she stood still, the blade inches away, ~*swish*...~*swish*... Suddenly, it was cut down to her side by her very own foil.

Sister Martin Marie gave out an exuberant laugh, "Good! At least, you're not running anymore! You'll need practice though girl, lots and lots of practice."

Oona watched from the side all suited up in her fencing uniform and said, "Sister Martin Marie is the best fencer in all of Ireland. Maybe, in all of Europe!"

"Oh, come on now! Maybe not all of Europe, but definitely the top three! OK girls, time to line up on the mats," said Sister Martin Marie.

Sister Martin Marie taught the girls lunges, strikes, counter attacks, how to engage their opponent, how to thrust the sword just right, and how to whip it over to break their opponents attack.

"Fencing can only be taught fifty percent, the rest is heart, conviction, instinct, practice, and believing in oneself!" said Sister Martin Marie, sauntering back and forth.

Later on, she had the girls clambering up thick, sweaty ropes to ring a small golden bell at the top of the gymnasium's ceiling. Kathryn unfortunately, only made it about four feet up until she slid down landing on her butt, which caused the rope to burn deep into the palms of her hand and her thighs. At the end of class, Sister Martin Marie paced in front of the girls in her sweaty clothes, encouraging the girls to, "Step up to the plate. Conquer your fears. Be the "Warrior Queen" that you are!" Sister Martin Marie was known to go on incessantly with her speeches, but finally she paused for a moment, stared at the girls and sent them back to their rooms. Of course she ended every class with a, "Job well done, girls! Well done! Go forth and succeed!"

The bedroom door creaked open and Kathryn tiptoed into the silent bedroom, hoping Maryanne would not awaken. Two white envelopes sat on her pillow. Snatching them up, she collapsed down into her squishy mattress, her aching back and joints twitching uncontrollably. She held both envelopes up with her blistered hands; one envelope was smudged with fingerprints and crumpled, while the other was clean and crisp waiting to be opened, she obliged it and tore it open. It read:

Dear Kathryn love,

I am writing to you on behalf of your grandfather and to let you know about his plight. Due to a lack of funds, brought about by unforeseen forces, he is unable to pay for your tuition, room, and board. He asked me to write, to tell you, he is truly sorry for this. We already wrote a letter to Sr. Gwen, who is an old dear friend of your grandfather's, to take care of you, while you are at St. Bernadette's. She is a lovely woman and your grandfather has the utmost respect for her. Please, do as the Sisters say, for we cannot come to see you as well, but I will write as often as possible and as often as your grandfather will allow. I also enclosed a photo of you and Billy. This is the one I took on your birthday and I hope you treasure it, as we will all so dearly miss him.
Sincerely,
Fiona Flannery

"Who is it from?" asked Maryanne.

"It's from Fiona Flannery and my supposed grandfather, who dumped me here," snarled Kathryn. "I can't believe he just abandoned me like this!"

Kathryn threw down the envelope and ripped open the other envelope with the slimy fingerprints on it and began to read:

Dear Kathryn,

How are you? We were all shocked and devastated to learn of Billy and then to hear that you were sent away to boarding school, without even a goodbye or anything! It is just too troubling. I believe I'll have a good row with your grandfather when I see him next and give him a piece of my mind.

Meanwhile, George, Eddie, and Marie are still horribly upset that you and Billy no longer visit. It was the hardest thing I had to do, to tell them about, Billy. I've never seen so many tears pour down Eddie's face. The poor guy never had his heart broken so bitterly with news like that. We cleared a little area at the workshop and put a picture of Billy and all our favorite things that reminded us of him. Marie even drew a picture of him flying on a dragon. Bless her soul! George made a picture with him flying through the air like he had wings, so darling it is.

Also, the town is still bubbling about that dark stranger that's been knocking on everyone's door! The good news is he hasn't been seen in over a week, so hopefully it was just a passing tourist that wanted to stir up trouble here in Ballyrun.

I hope you don't mind me writing to you, I finagled your whereabouts from Fiona. It took me seven jars of homemade jam just to get it out of her, plus a basket of my scones. We miss you terribly, dear Kathryn. Ballyrun is not the same without you. Seamus, George, Eddie, and Marie all send their love!
Love,
Peg, Seamus, George, Eddie, and Marie.

Kathryn choked back her bubbling tears to no avail, her eyes turned into swirling pools as her heart sank.

"Are you ok?" asked Maryanne.

"How could Grandpa have left me to rot in this place?" said Kathryn distraughtly, wiping her nose with her clean crisp sleeve. "Stuck doing laundry all morning, eating stale porridge, stuck in classes that are way over my head, nuns that have absolutely no heart and no compassion."

"Sister Joan is sweet, she gave this stuffed bear to keep me warm," said Maryanne, hugging her fluffy white bear.

"Don't you get it? Everyone hates me here! I have no friends!" bawled Kathryn.

"I'm your friend!" replied Maryanne.

"I know! I'll sneak out! Go back to Ballyrun and I'll stay with Peg and Seamus. And I'll get Billy back! I'll find him. Its just... this all seems like some crazy dream," said Kathryn. "All I wanted was to find out if it was real or not."

"What was real or not?" asked Maryanne.

"Hey girls!" said Carmel, barging into the room, "just wanted to check on you, Mar."

"If the legend was real or not," whined Kathryn.

"What legend?" asked Maryanne.

"The Legend of Arthur's Seat."

"Oh no, here we go again!" said Carmel, rolling her eyes.

"I can't take this anymore," said Kathryn, plopping her head on her feathered pillow. "I just want to see my friends again and - and that stupid sugar booger, Billy. I need to get out of here!"

"Whoa, did I come at a bad time?" questioned Carmel.

"But, isn't your brother dead?" asked Maryanne.

"I don't know! We had a fight, he went his way and I went mine, all because I figured it out!"

"Figured what out?" said Maryanne.

"I figured out what the necklace was trying to tell me. It showed me the way into the Raven's Gate!"

"It did?" marveled Maryanne.

"Hey, what are these markings here?" asked Carmel, gliding her finger along the wood paneling. "It says north?"

"There's one over there that says south," said Kathryn, pointing to another scratching on the opposite wall.

"Is there an east and a west?" asked Carmel inquisitively.

The girls became like caged animals set free and promptly dove in different directions to see, if there was an east and a west, carved into the walls.

"Yup! There's a west here!" chimed in Carmel.

"Mine says east," said Kathryn.

"Didn't you say your Mum stayed in this room?" asked Maryanne.

"That's what Sister Gwen said, she also used to sing some ridiculous song too. *'Two feet Susie, three feet Willie, four feet early... JUMP!'*"

"What a whacky song!" said Maryanne. "Do you think it means something?"

"It's a code, silly!" said Carmel abruptly.

"Code?" repeated Maryanne.

"Sure, Susie is south, Willie is west, early is east!"

"What's north?" asked Kathryn confused.

"North, is where you start," said Carmel, walking over the scratched area labeled north. "Move to the side and watch! How'd it go again?"

"*Two feet Susie,*" sang Kathryn.

"So, one, two feet back," said Carmel, walking two steps backwards.

"*Three feet Willie,*" sang Kathryn.

"One, two, three feet to the left," said Carmel, stepping three feet to the left.

"*Four feet early,*" sang Kathryn.

"One, two, three, four feet to the right!" said Carmel, stepping four feet to the right.

"*JUMP!*"

Carmel leapt up into the air. When her feet landed on the ground a gnarled strip of floorboard flew up into the air, nearly clocking Kathryn in the nose.

"Here we go!" cried Carmel, lowering herself down to the splintering floor and laid down on her belly. "Have a look!"

Maryanne snaked her hand through the opening, wiggling her fingers about, and pulled out a dusty weathered journal with leather strings binding it together. Maryanne took a deep breath and blew off the dust, exposing the cracked leather.

"I think it's your Mother's," said Maryanne, wiping away the initials on top, LJM.

Now, what the girls had found was not any 'ol book, it was Laurel Murphy's personal journal from her time at St. Bernadette's. Inside were pages and pages of notes and pictures of what she learned when she read *The Legends of Arthur's Seat* by Peoke Thumbdill. There were pages of dragons and myths, leprechauns, banshees, woodland faeries, flower faeries, pookas, peists, fomorians, selkies, grogochs, Danú, Queen Maeve, Elves of the sea, forest, and snow, warriors from long ago, such as, Rob Roy, The Knights Templar, King Arthur, Mordred, William Wallace, Finn MacCool, Tír na nÓg, The Sidhe, Tuatha Dé Danann, the nine maidens of the Otherworld, red-winged ravens, and the cursed necklace. She had translated all the text from *The Legends of Arthur's Seat* that Kathryn and Billy couldn't read into her prized journal.

Maryanne skimmed through the delicate pages as Kathryn and Carmel looked over her shoulder.

"What if Aählynéé is real?" questioned Maryanne, sifting through the notes and drawings.

"Come on, Mar! It's all a bunch of hooey! It's all tales! It's all for fun! We're Irish! We all love a good story. Embellish it a wee bit - and we're drooling."

"It's *real!*" cried Kathryn.

"If it's real, prove it!" snapped Carmel.

"You have my word!" said Kathryn honestly. "I was there!"

"All this work your Mum did, pages and pages of notes and drawings. She really believed in it," said Maryanne. "There's got to be over a thousand pages of notes."

"She did believe in it," said Kathryn.

"Maybe there's a way to find out if Billy's alive?" asked Maryanne eagerly. "Maybe this book can tell us something about where he is?"

"If you find out, let me know, but I'm outta here," said Carmel candidly and then stood up and left the room.

"She doesn't believe me either. It's hopeless!" said Kathryn discouraged. "Might as well pack my things up and head on out! Oh, wait... I have nothing. I almost forgot. I guess I might as well just leave!"

"Well, you'd have to wait for a ferry to come and get you. Since 'The Crone' is now at the bottom of the sea, I doubt that a new one will come anytime soon, but what if this journal can help us?" asked Maryanne, tapping her finger upon the aged leather. "What if Billy is alive? Like you said he is. Don't you want to know?"

"Sure, I do!" answered Kathryn.

"Well, let's find out what's in these pages!" said Maryanne, flipping through the many frayed pages.

"I don't have time!" whined Kathryn, "I've got laundry duty, classes, and now I'm signed up for some warrior training classes, plus homework!"

"Then, I'll gladly do it," said Maryanne cheerfully. "I'll read every page of this journal and we'll find a way together! Deal?"

"Deal!" said Kathryn, finally cracking a small smile on her face.

♦ CHAPTER SIXTEEN ♦
GHOSTS IN THE ATTIC

The lights went out at precisely nine o'clock as Kathryn sank her sleepy head into her squishy pillow, causing the goose feathers to poke out into her left cheek. She was so heavy with sleep, she could hardly keep her eyes open. Her body throbbed with cuts, scrapes, bruises, contusions, and a few paper cuts as well. She was just dozing off into dreamland when a bolt of lightning lit up her room. Kathryn nearly jumped out of her mushy bed and out of her skin. A wee light fluttered in and out of the bedroom, showing a dark, shadowy figure standing over her bed. Kathryn screamed.

"Will you be quiet? It's just me!" whispered Carmel. "Come on... lights out!"

Maryanne slipped into her soft slippers and burly robe and tiptoed towards the door as a crackling roar of thunder boomed from outside the window. Kathryn screamed again.

"You comin'?" whispered Carmel to Kathryn.

"Where?" asked Kathryn, curling underneath her flimsy blanket.

"Just follow me!" said Carmel, waving her flickering candle in the doorway.

She stumbled out of bed. Her eyes began to dance with shadows as the lightning lit the room up.

"Grab Maryanne's hand," directed Carmel, while she latched on to Maryanne's other hand.

The door squeaked like a frightened mouse as it opened. Carmel cautiously let her gaze wander up and down the hallway. She waited for the right moment when she felt not a soul was near and then they crept down the narrow hallway.

Kathryn's eyes swelled. The narrow corridor before them was altogether indiscernible between darkness and the shadows which surrounded them. No light was to be seen at all, except for the bold bursts of lightning, which sporadically lit the way. The only thing she knew was that she was walking up splintered wooden steps into the heights of St. Bernadette's. They then turned a corner and walked down another long, murky corridor. Kathryn's eyes still played tricks on her due to the dimly lit windows that flashed on and off from the storm outside.

Onward they walked until they reached another staircase; this one had icy, cold stones that twisted round and round in a circular motion. Her feet could barely fit into the slender steps as they made their way up. Finally, they entered a larger room and a soft light flashed suddenly on a bearded man's face through a window. Kathryn shrieked in horror.

"What's wrong with you?" said Carmel agitated. "Be quiet! It's just an old statue."

Carmel pulled out her flashlight. The beam of light gleamed against the broken statues, some with missing arms, a few without legs, and some torsos even missing their heads. A deep eerie chill ran up Kathryn's spine as they continued on.

"Where are we?" Kathryn whispered.

"We're in the attic," replied Maryanne.

The three made their way further in, until a sudden pulsing beam of light flashed into their eyes. All three raised their hands, shielding their eyes.

"Password?" said a voice behind the light.

"Will you give me a break!" cried Carmel. "You know there's no password!"

"That is correct!" said the voice, lowering the light down. "Come on in, we're just about to start!"

It was the three rules of St. Bernadette's, number two, three, and four, that seemed to get broken every so often by the girls: *Rule Number Two*: Lights out at exactly 9 p.m. and all students in bed. *Rule Number Three:* No students are allowed in the attic or bell tower, *ever! Rule Number Four:* No student is allowed to tell tales of ghosts or to speak of faeries. These three rules were the easiest to break; *for even a thief would hop into an open window, if he were to pass one by.* For the girls of St. Bernadette's, sneaking into the attic after lights out was an adventure. And to include stories of ghosts and ghouls with their adventures, was surely the whipped cream and cherry on top of their ice cream sundaes!

"OK, are we missing anyone?" said Carmel, glaring around the room.

"Nope! We're all accounted for!" said Oona, flaring her flashlight into Kathryn's black and blue face. "Who said she was invited?"

"I did!" snapped Carmel.

"Since, when do we welcome losers to our ghost stories?" said Oona mockingly.

"Since she saved Mar's life, that's when! So, cool it Oona!" declared Carmel.

Kathryn gazed around the small room, her eyes slowly adjusting to the dim light; she could see a tiny brass bed in the corner, an oak dresser pushed up against the wall, and a wee sink with two faucets garnishing the room.

Oona hastily went around the lonely bedroom, striking matches to light the wicks of thick, white candles, which sat on the floor. The girls took a seat on the cool floor and sat Indian style in a circle, while Leesa set a flashlight down in the middle of the group. Kathryn could see it was just her, Maryanne, Carmel, Oona, Leesa, and two older girls, whom she had never met before. One girl, Brenda, was very sweet and grinned constantly, while the other girl, Karen, was more serious, dark and sat somberly next to Maryanne.

"This is how we play. We spin the flashlight, whoever it lands on has to tell their best ghost story," said Leesa.

"Aren't we forbidden to tell ghost stories? Isn't that one of the rules of St. Bernadette's?" asked Kathryn.

"What the nuns don't know - won't hurt 'em!" said Carmel fearlessly. "Who's up first? I'll spin." Carmel stretched her hand out and spun the flashlight. Around and around it went, landing its beam of light on Leesa.

"Leesa! You're up first!" said Oona.

Leesa picked up the flashlight from the floor and held it under her chin. The artificial light glinted, giving her a ghostly look about her as she began her story.

"It has been said, for a long, long time, there's an invisible line that runs straight down the middle of Inishmara," said Leesa direfully. "On one side, there's dark faeries lurking about and on the other side, is the mortal world of man. All that separates them is one lone bridge, the Devil's Bridge, or as they say in Irish, the Bridge of Diabhal. For most people when they land on Inishmara, they soon realize there's something quite different about this island. It's filled with ghosts."

All the girls yelped in fear.

"Years back; there was once an old minstrel... a warrior bard... who told the tales of ancient wars. One day, he set sail on a golden boat with other brave warriors destined for greatness. When suddenly, a fierce storm from the north blew in, tossing the boat up high and slamming it right back down into the murky waters below, shattering it into bits and pieces; all aboard drowned that day, all except for the lone minstrel who washed ashore on the rocks of Inishmara.

"The nuns found him half dead in the wee hours of the morning, with nothing on him except his clothes and his bagpipe, still clenched in his fists. The Sisters took him in, warming his withered body by hearth. Soon, he awoke, nourished and warmed by the nuns. He told them his stories, of faraway lands and of ancient myths; where great warriors fought for the just, in distant wars. Fascinated, the Sisters themselves began to divulge their own stories of Inishmara.

"Soon, the minstrel became fueled with curiosity about this island and of all the faeries that lived here, especially the ones that lived on the other side of the ravine, across the Devil's Bridge... They warned him not to go across the bridge, for it was full of dark, evil faeries, seeking the ruin of any mortal man who crossed it. Then, one evening at twilight, while he played his bagpipe, he saw his golden boat once again in the harbor. Now, it was just a ghost ship filled with fallen warriors. He dared himself to cross the Devil's Bridge and then began to chase it down.

"They say he crossed the bridge, climbed up to the highest peak and played his bagpipes for his fallen soldiers, one last time. But, he never returned....

"Now, sometimes on cold, crisp evenings at nightfall, some say, you can still hear him playing his bagpipes on the other side of Inishmara. When the moon is resting on the still sea, and no bird is flying in the sky, you can still hear him play, trying to steer his fallen soldier's home."

"Wow! That was a good one, Leesa," said Carmel. "Who's next? Let's spin!"

"Well, did he die?" asked Kathryn.

"He never returned..." answered Leesa spookily.

"So, he could still be alive? Like Billy?" said Kathryn curiously.

"No, he's dead! Just like Billy," said Oona snidely. "Next!"

"Come on, girls! Let's keep this going!" said Carmel, whipping the flashlight around until it landed. "Oona!"

Oona smiled and snatched the flashlight from Leesa. She lowered herself down on to her bony knees and centered the flashlight below her chin.

"Now once, long ago, there lived a man who made his wealth by creating evil weapons that killed and maimed hundreds and thousands of men, women, and children," said Oona creepily. "One day, this man, who had more money than a thousand men could ever spend in a lifetime, saw the most beautiful woman he had ever laid eyes on. With his massive fortune, he wooed her with diamonds, rubies, gold, and more pearls that could ever be found in the ocean. Soon, the man and the woman married and traveled the world on their honeymoon. Until one day, they came to Inishmara. They quickly fell in love with the beauty of the island and built this grand Castle that we live in today. But, little did they know, that this land was cursed!"

The girls hurled back, shivering in fear.

"This island was cursed by the dark faeries and then thrown back into the mortal world. Soon, the couple had a son, who grew up to be a bright young boy, the apple of their eye. But then, the curse of Inishmara happened and the bride became sick with yellow fever and soon died before her time. Consumed with pain for his loss, the man found solace with a maid and soon married her. His new wife bore him another son, who was not as strong as his elder son. Paranoid of losing her fortune to the eldest son, she locked him away in this very room in the attic."

"Wasn't the husband suspicious?" questioned Carmel.

"She told him he was sick and needed to be quarantined. The elder son had no friends, except for his younger brother, who'd sneak out after dinner to play with him. The two boys created a strong and loving bond, but soon the stepmother found out.

"So, one gloomy night, when the moon was dark and no stars shined in the sky, the stepmother snuck into her stepson's bedroom. Then, taking hold of a pillow she placed it over his face as he slept in bed... until he was no more..."

"She killed him?" squealed Leesa.

"She *muuuurdered* him! Right there!" said Oona horrifyingly, pointing to the simple bed in the room. "The younger brother, after finding out his brother had died, came every night to see if he'd come back to play. Then, one night he heard his brother laughing outside this very window. He ran over to the window, excited to see his brother and leaning out, he saw his brother's ghost playing on the grounds down below. When the ghost didn't respond, he leaned out further, calling after him, louder and louder he cried, *'brother... brother... I am here!'* But soon, his foot gave way and he fell from this window, down to the cold, hard ground below."

A soft, howling wind whipped through the room, blowing out all the candles as the girls gasped in horror. Kathryn and Maryanne embraced each other.

"Wh-What was that?" asked Kathryn frightened.

"It was just the wind," said Carmel calmly, striking a match and relighting the candles.

"Now, the two brothers are reunited in death. To this day, you can still hear them roaming and playing in the Castle. Now, that they are free to be together... *forever*!"

"That was a good one Oona! You had me going there for a second! Especially with the wind blowing out all the candles and all! Right! Let's spin!" said Carmel, twirling around the glowing flashlight. Around and around it spun, until it stopped on Kathryn.

"All right, Kat! You're up scare the crap out of us!" said Carmel humorously.

"Well, I don't know any ghost stories," she said lamely.

"Just make one up! Tell us about when you lost your brother. That should be good. Been dying to hear that one," said Carmel.

Kathryn took hold of the flashlight, her heart pounding steadily in her chest. *I don't know any ghost stories. What am I going to say?* she thought. Holding the flashlight up to her fleshy chin, she took a deep breath, closed her eyes, and then took another deep breath and began.

"This is a true story. Long, long ago, there was once a young girl who traveled across the great sea with her brother," said Kathryn effortlessly, as she began to remember. "They traveled one stormy night to a distant country where they knew not a soul. Having been orphaned, they went to live with their crazy grandfather who'd tell them stories of vicious leprechauns who'd sneak up on him, trying to steal his purse. He'd tell them stories of Elven villages on remote islands off the coast with powers greater than any mortal man would understand.

"Stories of pookas, which are a type of shape-shifting faery that are greatly feared, their glowing yellow eyes, would terrify all the farmers. One minute they would be a wild black stallion, the next a goat, or a dog, perhaps even a tiger, but the worst was when they changed into a hungry goblin, which would roam the lands at night, terrifying farm animals and destroying crops. But, the most interesting story he'd tell, was a story about an evil sorceress trapped inside an entombed Castle buried deep beneath the great Mountain, Arthur's Seat.

"So, one day the two children discovered an ancient, cursed necklace, which showed them the way into this Mountain. Defying their grandfather, they both snuck out early in the wee hours of the morning and went in search of the evil sorceress. But, instead of sticking together, they fought bitterly of what to do and parted ways. The girl in possession of the necklace found the hidden entrance, the Raven's Gate. Upon entering, the door slammed shut, trapping her inside. Deeper and deeper she traveled through the cold, wet tunnels of Arthur's Seat. Until, she came into a dungeon just below the Castle. Within the dungeon was a mangled prisoner who hadn't been fed in centuries; he wore ragged dirty clothing, his whole body was covered in hair, and his arm was shackled to a rusty chain, binding him to the wall. The girl took pity on him, she gave him water and tried to free him from his chains, but it was too late, she had been found...

"Two creepy, hairy half-men with fat feet had discovered her. Quickly, she lifted up one of the torture tables to block their attack and she bolted out the door. She ran and ran, through the dark, her breath grew heavier and heavier as she made her way to the end of one of the tunnels; stopping, just in time. Below her... only darkness and a long drop into a gloomy abyss of water. She tried to head back down the tunnel, but one of the foul smelling half-men let go of a bag of rocks and dirt, which caused her to run away and jump straight into a cold, dark lake below.

"At first, she felt safe, far away from her attackers, but then her eyes caught a glimpse of a sparkling crimson crystal. It mesmerized her. So, she dove down into the cold, murky water and she seized the Fire Crystal. But, once she felt safe, there was yet another attack! This time by a long, thick eel-like creature with the face of a bull, and horns like this," she added, raising her index and middle fingers above her head, forming a 'V' shape. "His iridescent eyes focused on her as he made his way closer and closer. Charging forward with his mouth wide open, you could see his sharp, piercing fangs, which were as big as her arms. Immediately, she took out her steel flashlight and clobbered him over his head, knocking the slimy creature unconscious.

"She swam to shore, her body dripping wet, her clothing, now a dark gray, which was covered in a strange inky substance. Then she heard voices and she hid, and just in time to see the sorceress herself. Her eyes were blood red, her hair burned with fire and her skin as pale as a fish's bottom. The sorceress saw her holding the Fire Crystal, the one object she desired most of all. Their eyes met and the girl threw her flashlight with all her might high into the air, breaking a massive stalactite off from the ceiling. It crashed down into the sorceress's long gown, pinning her to the ground and trapping her there. Quickly, she was off and running again, not knowing where to go and unable to see before her, now with her flashlight gone. All she could hear were the writhing screams of the sorceress, vowing eternal revenge. Running, turning, tripping through the dark, she finally made her way back to the Raven's Gate.

"She took hold of a small twig, pulled on it once and the Raven's Gate opened, freeing her from her nemesis. She left the cave, but not before a wave of flames came pummeling down after her. The gateway closed. A single flame stood before her; she could see the sorceress' eyes staring at her. So, she inhaled deeply and blew out that solitary flame. She then made her way back down the Mountain, the Fire Crystal now in her possession.

"Until, a dark, deceitful stranger came from behind her and knocked her on the head. She lay in a deep sleep for months. When she awoke, she was told her brother was gone, missing, lost on the other side of the Mountain. Until this day, she dreams of the sorceress and of her lone brother, who now haunts her dreams... calling for her every night to rescue him."

"Wow!" said Carmel.

"That was awesome, Kathryn!" said Maryanne.

"What a bag of bloody bollocks!" said Leesa scathingly.

"What a liar!" added Oona. "At least, make something up about ghosts! Not about the Legend of Arthur's Seat"

"She's *soooo* lying!" said Oona.

"You said, tell a story," said Kathryn.

"Yeah, but you said it was true!" said Oona heatedly.

Kathryn hesitated, "It is true, mostly..."

"Relax guys," interjected Carmel. "It's just a story!"

"Carmel!" griped Oona. "She said it was true!"

"Well, is it?" asked Carmel.

"Yes..." said Kathryn humbly. "Mostly...Well, I didn't throw the flashlight at the stalactite, and I actually turned my flashlight on to scare the eel thing, but it sounded good! And the sorceress didn't get pinned by the stalactite... And..."

"Awww... Come on now Kat, don't be pulling that one on us!" said Carmel annoyed.

"It is true... mostly true... about 98% true," said Kathryn honestly.

"Well, then where's the Fire Crystal?" asked Oona snootily, placing her fists on her hips.

"I told you. The dark stranger has it," answered Kathryn.

"You know, I don't mind a few scary ghost stories, but don't be comin' in here - telling us a story about sorceresses and Fire Crystals and tellin' us it's true!" said Carmel infuriated. "Or as you say... mostly true. You've got a lot of nerve!"

"And your dead brother, haunting your dreams?" snickered Leesa, "waiting for you to rescue him!"

"I believe her," said Maryanne proudly, standing next to Kathryn.

"Well, go right ahead Mar!" said Carmel hotly, blowing the candles out. "But, I'm not hanging out with Miss Looneytunes anymore!"

Now, it's hard enough to have lost your mother, then your brother, and to top it all off, being abandoned by your only living relative, which sent you to a convent with a bunch of quirky nuns. But, it's when you have no one who believes in you that can cause any heart to break to a place, where no one person could ever gather the pieces, and put them back together. However, Kathryn did have one friend who believed in her, Maryanne. And for the next few weeks, Maryanne read her mother's journal. Right after all her schoolwork was done, she popped open that notebook and read it from flimsy cover to flimsy cover. Then, one day Kathryn entered their bedroom and Maryanne was sitting patiently on her bed, grinning from ear to ear.

"I found a way to find out if Billy's alive!" she said cheerfully, holding the crackled book tightly to her chest.

"You did?" exclaimed Kathryn.

"Yup! There's a way to make," said Maryanne, "get this, a faery door!"

"A what?"

"A faery door!" said Maryanne animatedly. "You gather hawthorn to make the door and place it against a northern wall and ragwort to make a protection circle around the door. You cut a bunch of dandelions to make a bouquet and offer it to the faery, and then at midnight of a full moon. You knock once above the door for north, then to the left of the door, for west, and then to the right, for east and then a faery comes out!"

"A faery?" questioned Kathryn, "a real faery comes out of a door? That you make? How is that possible?"

"I don't know, but it's written down, right here!" said Maryanne, pointing to a drawing within the notebook of a twiggy door with flowers scattered around it in a semi-circle. "If a faery comes out, you can ask him if he's seen Billy and then you'll know!"

"I'll know?" said Kathryn bewildered and then excitedly, *"I'll know!* But, what if the faery isn't helpful or it doesn't know where my brother is?"

"You're forgetting the most important thing!" said Maryanne informatively. "All faeries are magic and they can find out anything. And faeries are obliged to help you, if you ask them. We'll build the door, show him Billy's picture, and ask the faery to find him!"

"And, if we have to... We'll bribe it!" said Kathryn sneakily. "With whatever it wants from our world!"

"Well, it does say to offer it a dandelion," said Maryanne. "Maybe that can be your offering?"

"A real faery!" said Kathryn elatedly, "in our room!"

"I hope it's cute!"

It didn't take long for the girls to gather the items for the faery door. It seems hawthorn trees, ragwort, and dandelions grew all over Inishmara. It took just a few hours to make a decent sized door out of the gray thorny twigs of the hawthorn. The directions stated the height and width of the faery door should be exactly two and a half inches high and two inches wide. Cutting the wood was a bit difficult; Maryanne had to borrow a sharp knife from the kitchen just to cut through the hard wood. They glued the pieces together making a slight arch on top and glued a pearl earring on for the doorknob.

The girls grinned and laughed the whole week as the first full moon was approaching. Even Oona and Leesa didn't seem to bother Kathryn as much.

It was a cold, damp night when the moon finally became full. Kathryn and Maryanne had collected all their materials: a wooden door made out of hawthorn branches, a bushel of ragwort to make a ring around the faery door, and some dandelions tied together to make a bouquet. They spent most of their day after classes, making up a list of questions to ask the faery when it came out like: *Do all faeries do magic? What's it like in Aählynéé? How long does a faery live? What color is a faery's blood? What do faeries eat? Do faeries get sick? What do faeries do for fun?* The questions went on and on. Maryanne especially wanted to know why faeries didn't come into the mortal realm anymore.

It was just about half past nine after the lights went out and Carmel came rapping at the door once again. "Psst! You comin'?" she whispered through the edge of the cracked door.

"No!" replied Maryanne.

"No? What do you mean, no?" said Carmel hotly. "It's time for ghost stories in the attic! Supposedly, Leesa's got a great one tonight!"

"Sorry, I've got plans already," said Maryanne as she flipped through the crinkled, yellow pages of Laurel's journal.

"What?" said Carmel perplexed and stepped into the room. "Come on Mar, stop your horsin' around! We need to get up there, before they start!"

"I told ya!" replied Maryanne, her finger sliding across one particular sentence in the journal, which read: *It is imperative to knock, exactly at midnight!* "I've got plans!"

"What plans?" inquired Carmel.

"We've made a faery door," said Kathryn enthusiastically, holding up her wee mangled hawthorn door. "And at midnight, when we knock, a faery will come out!"

"What?" said Carmel stunned. "You've got to be kiddin' me?"

"No," said Maryanne. "I found it in her Mum's journal."

"Well, hell! I'd rather stay and see a faery than listen to a bunch of bad ghost stories!" said Carmel, closing the door behind her. "Sign me up!"

It was only about twenty minutes later when another rap was heard at the door.

"Hey, where's Carmel?" whispered Oona.

"I'm in here Oona!" replied Carmel.

Oona poked her head through the doorway and said, "Will you hurry up girl? We're all waitin' for ya!"

"Sorry Oona, I'm gonna pass! Mar and Kat seem to have something way more interesting going on!" replied Carmel, holding the faery door, running her fingers around its rigid roots.

"What's that?" asked Oona, opening the door and sliding her head through.

"We're waiting for a faery to come out of this door we made," replied Kathryn.

"A what?" said Oona astoundingly.

"A faery!" declared Maryanne.

"A faery? A *faery*?" said Oona, rolling her eyes. "Man, you are *all* bonkers!" She shut the door, shaking her head left to right repeatedly and strolled down the gloomy hallway with her dripping candle. They could still hear her muttering, "A faery? A *faery*? Bloody bonkers!"

Kathryn and Maryanne took the faery door from Carmel and placed it firmly against the north wall, bracing on the floor. Kathryn sprinkled the ragwort starting at the edge of the wall, all the way around the door, in a half circle and then rested the golden dandelion bouquet in the center.

"Now what?" asked Carmel.

"Now, we wait until midnight and we knock!" said Maryanne.

The girls impatiently waited for midnight to roll around. Carmel took a nap, while Kathryn removed the last of her sticky bandages from her body, and Maryanne continued to read the journal. Then, at midnight they heard faint footsteps coming from down the hallway.

"Who's that?" whispered Maryanne.

"I don't know," said Kathryn, shrugging her shoulders and kneeling before the door.

"Well, don't stop now!" directed Carmel. "In three, two, one! *Knock!*"

Kathryn made a tight fist and rapped once above the top of the faery door, "North!" *~thump*. Then, she knocked to the left, "West!" *~thump*. Their bedroom door creaked and squealed open. She knocked to the right, "East!" *~thump,* it went.

"If it's a faery you're knocking for, you won't be getting one to come out on this side of the island!" giggled a scratchy voice from the bedroom door. The girls turned around and watched Sister Gwen enter their bedroom.

"Sister Gwen! I'm sorry," said Carmel terrified, standing up to her feet. "I-I-I was just leaving!" And snaked past Sister Gwen out the door.

"What do you mean, on this side of the island?" asked Maryanne.

"Seems you're on the wrong side, it won't work," replied Sister Gwen casually. "Maryanne, it just so happens, Cook left out a nice piece of banoffi pie in the fridge. Why don't you go, finish it up?"

"Certainly," said Maryanne, hopping off the bed and darting out the door.

"I'm sorry, Sister Gwen. Did I mess up again?" asked Kathryn.

"You're fine child. You are magic!" said Sister Gwen, glancing down at Laurel's journal. "You are special child!"

"I don't feel so special," sighed Kathryn.

"Let me tell you about your Mother. She used to run amuck up and down these halls," joked Sister Gwen. "Mother Superior at that time was her Irish teacher as well. She would have her red-faced, burning up, rip-roaring mad, every day!"

"Do you believe in faeries, Sister Gwen?" asked Kathryn.

"Of course I do! Faeries are notorious little magical creatures, the little people, and the wee folk. To some, they are a wild leprechaun with a pot of gold or a wailing banshee in the night. But, I believe them to be our angels or our demons. They lure you in with hopes and dreams, or they can poke fun at your faults always testing you," she laughed. "Those little buggers!"

"But, you're a nun! How can you believe in faeries?" questioned Kathryn.

"God makes all of us, correct?" she replied.

"Correct, but if you don't see faeries, how can they be real?" she said curiously.

"Let me, ask you a question dear. Do you go to Mass?" asked Sister Gwen.

"I do," she replied.

"Do you believe in God?"

"Yes, of course I do!" she said baffled.

"Do you believe in the Holy Spirit?" said Sister Gwen, continuing on.

"Yes!"

"Have you ever seen God or the Holy Spirit?" asked Sister Gwen, "or Love?"

"Ummm... No."

"It's the same way, one believes in faeries. Oh, you may see one faery as a monster and I see it as a butterfly fluttering by. But, we both see different things, maybe you call the creature a monster or a faery, perhaps I call it a demon. The butterfly you see may be a winged angel to me, but in your mind, it's a faery. It's all about perception. Don't worry dear, you'll know what to do when the spirit moves you!"

"I will?"

"Just listen to your heart! When the time is right, you'll know. Just let it go and your heart will guide you. Sometimes, each one of us finds what we need when we least expect it. You just have to have faith and trust in the spirit," said Sister Gwen confidently. "I believe it's called inspiration... to be inspired by the spirit and when it does inspire you dear, don't hold back, embrace it. Now, about this faery door you're building? You know, you need to create it on the other side of the bridge don't you?"

"No," replied Kathryn.

"Well, it won't work on this side, that's for sure! Only across the Devil's Bridge. There's an old cave up there where the monks lived that would be your best bet! Place it on the north wall. In the night, at precisely midnight, you knock north, west, and then east, around the door. When the faery appears, you'll need to capture him! So, I'll give you a glass container. So, he won't go running back home, as they usually do when they come into our realm and when he's captured ask him what you like."

♦ Chapter Seventeen ♦
The Devil's Bridge

The moon was full and fat, sitting in the frosty night's sky when they made their way to the Devil's Bridge. The bridge of course, was the connection, the link between our mortal world and to the rougher side of Inishmara, the side that is said to be inhabited by the dark faeries. It didn't take long for Kathryn, Maryanne, and Carmel to sneak out of their rooms, down a few dimly lit stairwells, past a row of Saintly statues and out the back door by the stinky dumpster. A strange rattling noise ruffled through the dumpster, startling the three at first. Quickly they collected themselves and continued down the winding road towards the laundry.

The night air breathed and the three lasses shivered in a huddle waiting behind the laundry.

"Hurry up and make tracks!" said Carmel impatiently, flipping on her flashlight now, out of the view of any nun. "What are we waiting for? Let's go!"

"*Shhh...*" whispered Kathryn, "we're waiting for Cyril."

"Cyril?" questioned Carmel, "why the devil did..."

"Greetings m'ladies!" said a voice from behind.

"Hi Cyril," said Maryanne, "isn't this exciting?"

"Great! Another body!" sighed Carmel. "Now we'll definitely get caught!"

"On the contrary, m'lady!" said Cyril, "For I know the way to the monk's cave."

"That's why I brought him along!" said Kathryn.

"Shall we?" asked Cyril engagingly. He turned around and sauntered away, showing his pointy ears peeking out from behind his gruffy hair.

"And it's a monastery! Not a cave!" called Carmel to Cyril. She then stifled her voice and seized Kathryn's arm, wrenching her backwards. "Are you crazy? Don't you know what Cyril is? He's a faery, Kathryn... a changeling, if I ever saw one! Look at him! His ears... his eyes... the way he smells! *Oh and he smells, alright!*"

"Really?" said Kathryn puzzled. "He does look a little odd but, I just figured, he was, I don't know, he was unique."

"Unique alright, even Mother Theresa wouldn't kiss him, he's a changeling!" declared Carmel. "Now he's gonna take us back to his faery mound and make us all work for the faeries until the day we die! You just wait and see Kat, I'm just saying that's what's going to happen!"

"Carmel, I doubt he's a changeling," said Kathryn calmly. "And he's not going to take us to his faery mound and make us work till we die!"

"Believe you - me! He's a changeling - if I ever saw one! And don't ya think it's a bit odd that your non-faery friend doesn't need a flashlight to find his way around in the dark?"

Kathryn paused for a moment, gazed around at the dusky night's sky and said, "Uh, there's a full moon. Don't worry Carmel, if we get stuck in the Otherworld working for some evil faeries, I'll do half your work, ok?"

"Don't you know that people say Cyril's never left this island? Ever!" said Carmel tensely. "Isn't that a red flag to you?"

"Relax, Carmel," said Kathryn soothingly. "I believe Cyril will not lead us astray, just trust him!"

"I don't know about this," replied Carmel, "But, I've got my eye on this one."

It didn't take long for them to make their way to the Devil's Bridge, though in Carmel's head, it took an eternity. At first, their eyes couldn't make it out, but gradually as they grew closer, the clouds swept past the moon, and it revealed itself. There, suspended over a broad, shadowy ravine was their perilous bridge, standing before them with frayed ropes laced between wooden, warped planks.

"There she is," said Cyril.

"It's so cool!" murmured Maryanne.

"It doesn't look - all that doom and gloom," said Kathryn.

"Wait 'til you get closer," said Carmel out of the side of her mouth.

Upon closer inspection, they saw that the spaces between the planks on the bridge widened further and further apart. Maryanne fearlessly stared at the plummeting drop below and said, "I'll go first!"

Maryanne's hands clenched tightly on the shredded rope as she carefully placed her shoe on the first wooden plank. Her feet grounded firmly on each board, she waddled across the bridge.

"Right behind you, Mar!" called Carmel, lifting her foot up and positioning it down on the rickety bridge. "I'm not looking down! Just don't look down, *don't look down!*"

Carmel's feet were planted firmly on the rotted wood planks as she began to stagger her way haphazardly across. The bridge swayed side to side above the deep ravine, making an eerie creaking noise while she crossed.

"I don't know if it can hold the both of us, Mar!" yelped Carmel, glaring down into the dark abyss below. Her foot slipped into the space between two planks. "Whoa there..." Clasping her fist tighter to the aged rope, she looked down again. "Crap! I looked down!"

"Almost there!" called Maryanne, leaping off the bridge, which buckled and jerked.

Carmel screamed.

"Help!" cried Carmel, her legs dangling between two planks, her arms trying to push her torso up. "I'm gonna fall!"

"Carmel!" cried Maryanne.

Cyril cautiously stepped out onto the Devil's Bridge, trying hard not to disrupt the balance. Lying down on one plank and his feet on another, he reached out his hands to Carmel. "Here!" said Cyril, wiggling his fingers out to Carmel.

"What are you doing?" cried Carmel baffled.

"Give me your arms and lean towards me," said Cyril reassuringly.

Then like an acrobat in a circus, Cyril hooked his pointy fingers under her armpits and hoisted her up, pulling her back towards him. Astonished and blinking incessantly, Carmel looked at him and said, "You're a real clever one, aren't you? Still doesn't change what you are." Then raised her body up, "but, thanks anyway," and wobbled across the bridge.

Cyril moved in the same direction, following her across the bridge, and then finally made it to the other side.

Now, Kathryn's heart began to beat like a thousand drums when she stepped out onto that dilapidated bridge. At first, her legs were steady, but soon her legs began to quiver and her arms began to tremble uncontrollably.

"Stay balanced," yelled Cyril, "center yourself!"

It took all her might to center her body as she stepped across the bridge, one moment she was balanced, but then all of the sudden she'd be leaning heavily to the left, and then tossed to the right. "Stay centered," she whispered to herself, "focus." She slid her hands along the gnarled rope railing with smaller, more refined steps as she finally made her way across.

"It's up this way," said Cyril as he disappeared into the darkness.

Carmel splashed her flashlight on the thousand crooked stone steps curving up the steep incline on the mountainside and followed.

Kathryn paused for a moment, her heart still racing and then her eyes caught a glimpse of a small shadowy figure of a rabbit, jumping behind a thorny bush. Curiously, she approached it and saw two yellow eyes glowing from behind it. Swiftly, the eyes leapt out from behind the bush, turning into a black goat with wild hair. Kathryn blinked a few times. How could her eyes have mistaken a rabbit for a goat? The goat *'bahhhed'* and then jumped onto a large boulder rising above her, changing its shape now into a dark, cunning Celtic tiger perching itself stealthily on the rock. It began to speak in a deep, low growling voice.

Deathly travels do you seek,
Just so you can take a peek,
Unearthly paths mark your way,
As the sun appears this day,
Be forewarned my dear young one,
Some things cannot be undone.

The fierce, wild-haired Celtic tiger was indeed, a pooka. The tiger threw its paws forward, its sharp nails scraping into the solid stone. He stretched and elongated his thick body and then flew off the boulder, transforming before her eyes into a wild black steed galloping off into the mysterious night.

Stunned, Kathryn turned away and hastily sprinted up the vertical steps, soon catching up with the others. The full moon shone through the damp night air, creating swirling mists to appear along their long trek up the thousand stone steps to the old monk's stone monastery.

"It's over this way ladies," said Cyril, striding toward a honeycomb stone building embedded into side of the island.

"Looks like an upside down boat!" remarked Carmel as they bent down and squeezed their way into the one small arched doorway leading into the monastery.

Upon entering, the ceiling shot up as if in a grand Cathedral. The room was broad and wide. Along one wall were shelves filled with clay plates and utensils. A small altar with a stone Celtic Cross sat against the back wall and a raised stone bed was tucked away in the corner, close to a wee hearth.

"Its half past eleven now, all we have to do is set the door up against a wall, facing north," said Kathryn, pulling out the wee faery door from her pocket and placing it against the north wall. "And make a semi-circle with the ragwort around it."

"I've got that!" said Maryanne, sprinkling the golden flowers like a horseshoe around the faery door.

"Now what?" asked Carmel.

"We wait until midnight and then knock," replied Kathryn as she sat on the icy floor.

"North, west, and then east," said Maryanne jubilantly. "And then, the faery comes out! I wonder what it will look like? Probably, teeny-tiny with the size door of the door we made. Maybe, we should have gone bigger?"

"What's that over there?" asked Carmel, pointing to a deep, mysterious tunnel.

"I'll take you if you would like to see it m'lady?" offered Cyril, bowing down to Carmel.

"You're not gonna start that crap again?" jeered Carmel.

"Crap? No crap for you, m'lady!" said Cyril benevolently. "Only the utmost respect!"

"You're a real nincompoop, aren't ya?" asked Carmel sarcastically.

Cyril smiled politely.

"Well, come on then! We've got time to kill," said Carmel, snatching hold of Cyril's arm as they headed down the underground passageway.

Maryanne and Kathryn didn't shiver too long in the darkened cave. They had just finally made themselves at home when they heard alarming shouts echoing through the tunnel calling, "Come here, *quick*!"

The two bolted swiftly through the dreary tunnel into a massive room filled with stalagmites, poking up like fat fingers from the cave's floor, while stalactite's dangled down from the ceiling like razor sharp teeth, ready to chomp down on its next victim. The room was lined with cavernous long shelves and in the center, against the back wall, were two vertical large stones about seven feet apart from each other, with a third one sitting horizontally on top.

"What is it?" asked Maryanne, amazed at the stones' size.

"Beats me!" said Carmel, inching herself closer to it.

"I know what that is!" answered Kathryn.

"You do?" replied Carmel.

"It's a passage tomb. We learned about them in Mrs. Mackenzie's class, back in Ballyrun."

"It's a gateway," said Cyril. He took Carmel's flashlight and beamed it on three circles etched into the bottom of one of the stones. "Don't get too close."

"What do you mean Cyril? Now, you're gonna get in touch with your faery side?" snickered Carmel, moving closer towards the three stones.

"Don't *touch it!*" warned Cyril.

Carmel stopped dead in her tracks.

"See here," said Cyril, walking over to the dark shelves that lined the walls.

Cyril shifted Carmel's flashlight along the dark cavernous shelves, the luminous light flashed on a distorted skull before them. Maryanne and Kathryn squirmed a bit.

"This is an army of faeries, waiting to be called upon!" said Cyril.

"You can't be serious?" exclaimed Carmel, peering in closer to the decaying skeleton. She pulled out another flashlight and ran it up and down its mangled remains. "An army for who? The faery King?"

"Is there a faery King?" asked Maryanne.

"I only know about Koréna and King Kendryck," said Kathryn, "Oh yeah, and Danú and Queen Maeve."

"We should leave here at once! Before we awaken the dead!" said Cyril worryingly, striding back down the tunnel.

"Cyril!" yelled Carmel, watching Cyril leave the cavern. "That's as funny as a burning orphanage! You are so full of it! An army for a dead faery King! It's more like a mausoleum – I mean this was a monastery, right? This is where all the monks lived," Carmel pointed to the three stones. "And that there, is just a head stone for all these poor monks, may they rest in peace! Come on, Mar, time to see if that faery will come out!"

Maryanne reached out to touch one of the decomposing skeletons; its skin was still festering on its bone. "What do you think happens to us when we die?" she said oddly.

"We turn to dust?" said Kathryn.

"Don't you think we go somewhere?" she asked, her fingers hovering over cobwebs. "Like... Heaven?"

"I sure hope so!" said Kathryn, standing next to Maryanne. A chill pricked the back of their necks, as they studied the twisted remains. "These skeletons though, they - they don't look human at all. They have no clothing on them."

"And look," remarked Maryanne. "Their heads look bigger too. Even their eye sockets are like the size of grapefruits! Strange."

"Come on, Mar!" called Carmel impatiently. "Remember, the faery door? The reason we're here!"

"When I die," said Maryanne, "I hope I go to Aählyneé and live with the faeries!"

It had just turned midnight when Kathryn placed the bouquet of flowers in the center of the ragwort circle. She made a fist and knocked with her knuckles, once on top of the door, once to the left of the door, and once to the right of the door. "North, west, and east," she said.

"Now what?" asked Carmel, perched over the door, holding a clear glass container, ready to pounce on the faery at a moment's notice.

"We wait!" replied Maryanne.

"How long?" said Carmel impatiently.

"Until he comes out?" said Maryanne.

A few hours had passed by when Carmel finally said, "I've had enough! There is no faery! It's all a hoax! And we have to get up in the morning for class. Come on, Mar, let's go!"

"But, don't you want to wait and see the faery?" implored Maryanne.

"He should be out soon," said Kathryn. "Maybe, we have to wait until morning?"

"Mar, I love ya! I love ya, like a fat kid loves cake! But, there's no such thing as a faery and this book obviously is just a bunch of stories that people have made up! So, get up and let's get back down before one of the nun's figures out that we're not there!"

"I'll take you back m'lady," said Cyril courteously.

"Whatever!" huffed Carmel and turned to Kathryn. "You comin'?"

"I-I'm going to wait 'til dawn," said Kathryn, clinging tightly now to the domed glass container.

"Suit yourself," said Carmel, and she then squeezed through the slender doorway, along with Maryanne and Cyril.

Now, it wasn't the dark or the frigid temperatures that scared Kathryn the most sitting alone in the monk's cave, in the middle of the night. It was the strange noises she heard once they had left. At one point, she heard a bloodcurdling shrieking sound that soon turned into laughter coming from the tunnel. Then she heard a howling noise coming from outside the cave. She never did tell the others about the peculiar hairy animal with the scary glowing eyes she saw by the bridge. They all would never have believed any animal had gone from a fluffy bunny, to a goat, into an intense Celtic tiger. Especially because it spoke to her in rhymes and then transformed into a wild horse and galloped off into the night.

No, she knew better. Carmel already didn't believe her about the story of her discovering the Fire Crystal. Would she believe her now, about an animal that changes shapes and speaks? And now, the faery didn't come out of the faery door? What was she doing, sitting in a cave by herself, on the other side of the world? She thought about Brooklyn a bit. Billy and her Mom, they had such good times, but now she was here, alone where no one believed her. All she wanted to do was to go back home to Brooklyn, back to when she was happy, back to when she was loved.

Kathryn must've dozed off into a deep slumber, because finally her eyes could see light, coming from the arched doorway. Dawn had finally come and still, no faery.

CHAPTER EIGHTEEN
THE FAERY DOOR

Kathryn snuck into Cyril's laundry still dressed in her grimy clothes, reached for a shirt from a pile of clean clothes from yesterday, and began folding the laundry. Sister Liz moseyed in a few minutes later, looked at Kathryn with curiosity, then slumbered down in her stiff chair and fell fast asleep.

Kathryn progressed with the morning rituals at Cyril's laundry service, shoving all the white aprons, peter-pan shirts, white collars, and undergarments in the washing machine named Rose, pouring in some electric blue powder, and pressing hot. The machines hummed, churned, gurgled, and bubbled up a bit, and then began to swish heavily, but still no Cyril to be seen. *I hope he made it over the bridge all right,* she thought. Kathryn dumped out the contents of the washers, piling them into the dryers.

Her ears pricked up after a few quick snorts and wheezing from Sister Liz. Turning around, she watched her chubby leg jerk a few times in her catnap, while a lone rogue drip of salvia dribbled down her chin. The buzzer went off and she emptied out the hot fresh clothes into a wicker basket and began to sort them out.

Maybe that creature found them and devoured them alive? I knew, I should've warned them about him! she thought, *but, what about if they slipped and fell off the bridge, then no one would know how they died, or where they went, or even why they went there?*

The day's laundry was done. Hoisting up a wicker basket full of laundry; she made her way towards the exit. She was going to have to tell Mother Superior that one of her adventures had now cost three more lives. She was doomed and surely, she'd be kicked out of St. Bernadette's and sent back to Ballyrun. At least she'd see George, Eddie, and Marie again. Kathryn wandered up the hill that led to St. Bernadette's, trying to figure out what her punishment would be. A soft breeze tickled her cheek and a few yellow ragwort flowers waved in the wind. She thought of Maryanne sprinkling them out on the floor, Carmel asking what they were and sniffing them, and Cyril bringing them to the monastery. What was she thinking? Her friends could be dead! She needed to find out where they were and she needed to find out *now!*

Kathryn dropped the laundry off in the kitchen and raced down the elongated corridor filled with rigid statues. She fled further down; passing the courtyard filled with rose bushes and before she even reached the first flight of stairs, there was the unsympathetic Mother Superior before her.

"Looking for your friends?" she inquired stiffly.

"I was wondering where Cyril was?" said Kathryn, breathing heavily. "He wasn't at the laundry all morning and, and I-I was worried."

"Yes–yes, you would be! Well, Cyril is alive and well. He, Miss Maryanne, and Miss Carmel are all in detention right now. Caught sneaking *into* St. Bernadette's, in the wee early hours of the morning. Sister Mary Martha found them re-entering through the back door when she was having a snack in the kitchen. Brought them straight to the library, where they've been all morning. Seems rather odd that you were only looking for Cyril now and not the other two? Seems you four have formed a sort of bond. Nevertheless, they have been reprimanded and must serve detention for a full month. Looks as though you'll be doing the laundry all by yourself this month, Miss Murphy."

"Not a problem, Mother," replied Kathryn politely.

"Good. Be on your way! Breakfast will start soon enough," she added.

"Yes, Mother," replied Kathryn, her rosy lips curling into a soft smile.

"Oh, and Kathryn, you may want to change your clothing," said Mother Superior perceptively. "You're covered in dirt."

"Yes, Mother," said Kathryn.

"You may not have gotten caught this time child, but I have my eyes on you," declared Mother Superior.

"Yes, Mother," answered Kathryn.

A few hours' later Carmel and Maryanne returned to Kathryn's meager room.

"A month's detention! A whole month," cried Carmel slamming down on the springy bed. "I told you guys, I should've scouted the kitchen before we walked in! But, Cyril is as sharp as a beach ball. Sure, he can lead us up a mountain, but ask him to be a bit discreet and everything goes to hell!"

"We're getting way too sloppy with the mission," said Maryanne.

"What *kills* me is that we didn't even get to see a faery!" said Carmel furiously.

"There's got to be a reason," said Kathryn, flipping through her mother's battered journal. "Maybe we missed something?"

"We probably missed some itty-bitty detail and if we could just figure it out, *voila,* the faery will come out!" retorted Maryanne. "But, what could it be?"

"Well, Sister Gwen is the one who told us we had to do it on the other side of the island. In the realm of the faeries. Maybe she'd know?"

"Just give it up!" chimed Carmel. "We're just chasing our tails now, spinning around and around. Besides, we're stuck in detention for an entire month."

"I think you should ask her," said Maryanne.

"I'm asking," replied Kathryn.

Kathryn walked down the long corridor of the nun's quarters; the stained glass windows' colors danced against the white walls. The Sister's rooms were bare and simple, just a small lumpy bed, an oak dresser, an oil lamp sitting on a rickety table, and a crucifix above their bed. Kathryn continued on taking many winding stairways and long, deep hallways to reach Sister Gwen's room. It was located in the farthest stone tower, tucked far away from all the other Sisters. Strangely enough, a low-raised flowerbed made of shiny steel crawled along the corridor, overflowing with wild herbs. Kathryn turned the corner at the end of the passageway and rapped twice on a thick wood door.

"Come in," called Sister Gwen.

Upon entering Sister Gwen's bedroom, Kathryn found it warm, inviting, and filled with rich tapestries hanging from the walls along with steel swords and jeweled daggers. Along the far wall was a golden harp with what appeared to be a winged angel jutting out from the top. Behind it were two thick arched doors, hinged with black iron. For a moment, Kathryn could have sworn she heard someone knocking on the other side of one of the warped doors.

Sister Gwen was seated on an upholstered mahogany chair, writing on some bulky parchment with a red feather pen. Her habit had been removed and folded neatly on her bed. Her soft, silvery hair was exposed and it trickled down her back like a gushing waterfall.

"Sit Kathryn, sit!" she said pleasantly, pointing to a three-legged stool beside her.

"Sister Gwen," said Kathryn, plopping herself down on the stool. She looked into her piercing blue eyes, which were filled with youth. "Sister, I tried the faery door like you said, in the cave, and it didn't work, no faery came out!"

"I see," she said, still scribbling on the old piece of parchment paper.

"Am I missing something?"

She placed her fluffy crimson pen down and said sincerely, "Last night was the first night of the three full moons, dear. You have to go up to the cave each night and knock on the faery door!"

"Each night?" gulped Kathryn.

"Yes, every night precisely at midnight, you must knock north, west, and then east! On the third night, your faery will come out!"

"The third night?" repeated Kathryn.

"Correct," answered Sister Gwen, cocking her head at one of the wooden arched doors, ~thump, ~thump, ~thump, it went.

"But Carmel, Mar, and Cyril all have detention! They got caught last night, sneaking back in!" complained Kathryn, as she watched one of the aged doors begin to rattle.

"Then you, my dear, will have to go alone," said Sister Gwen.

"But Sister Gwen, there's a creature on the other side of the Devil's Bridge!" said Kathryn alarmingly.

"What'd he look like?" asked Sister Gwen.

"Everything!" said Kathryn perplexed, noticing that a fine mist was starting to puff out from underneath the door. "At first, he was this wild, hairy rabbit with glowing eyes like the sun! And then, he turned into a goat and before I knew it, he was this massive dark, smoky tiger with sharp talon-like claws! He spoke to me in some strange rhyme and then, *poof*! He changed into a wild stallion and galloped into the night!"

"Oh, child that's a pooka. If he hasn't killed you yet, then he's a good pooka! It is best to listen to his rhymes, though."

"A *pooka?*" shrieked Kathryn, partially from the name pooka, but mostly because one of the doors began to breathe in and out. Kathryn looked away quickly, in hopes that it would stop or perhaps Sister Gwen would do something to make it stop.

"A faery creature that changes shapes, love," said Sister Gwen nonchalantly, ignoring the breathing door in the back of the room. "They can be many things, a soaring eagle, a mischievous goblin, a cute rabbit, a precocious goat, a fierce Celtic tiger, a wild stallion, or even the boogey man in the form of a shriveled up, decomposing goblin... Was he very hairy?"

"Yes, a bit..." she answered anxiously as the door began to quiver. She could hear some faint tapping on the other side of it, *~thump, ~thump, ~thump,* it went.

"Well dear, it sounds like you made a new friend," said Sister Gwen sweetly, ushering Kathryn to her front door and opening it. "As I said before, if he hasn't killed you yet, then he's a good pooka, best be listening to him." Kathryn stepped outside Sister Gwen's door and returned back to her room. As she walked away, she heard a deathly, shrilling howl coming from Sister Gwen's room. She shook her head and knew it was best to leave it be.

Now, not many people would have traveled out on that murky, soggy evening. Oh, with the wet wind blustering right through you, to the marrow of your bones and to the depths of your being. But, Kathryn needed to knock on the faery door that night and even the next, in order to let a faery into our world. She, of course, had to know if it was real or not. Making her way across the shaky bridge, she saw the lustrous golden eyes of the pooka staring at her from the prickly bush.

"I know who you are," she yelled at the quivering bush. "You're a pooka! Sister Gwen told me and since you haven't killed me, you must somehow be good. I'm just going up to cave again..."

The pooka's eyes blinked a few times as it watched her climb up the slippery wet steps on her way up to the monastery. Out from the hollering winds, Kathryn's ears found peace from the sound of the gusting wind when she entered the cave. Her body shivered from the dampness of the cave. By the hearth, she noticed some crusty old peat, a handful of kindling, a striker, flint, and some cloth. *The pooka must have put it there, to keep me warm,* she thought.

Kathryn pulled out the cloth, picked up the striker, struck the flint against it, caused a spark, the cloth ignited, and then she placed the flame under the dry kindling perched up like a pyramid. She took out the watch Carmel had loaned her; fifteen minutes until midnight.

The sweet smell of peat permeated through the cave as the fire began to ignite. The flame rose high and filled the cave with a glowing light. Her eyes stared hypnotically into the fire. Soon it was ablaze and to her disbelief, she could see some figures stirring around in the body of the fire as if they were putting on a small play. A woman's silhouette lounged on a long chaise, while two furry men lay on the floor with their fat bellies up, staring at what appeared to be dragonflies fluttering about on the vaulted ceiling, and then she began to hear singing voices.

Nine hundred and ninety-nine dragonflies on the wall,
Nine hundred and ninety-nine dragonflies on the waaaa'll,
Take one down 'smush it around,'
And we'll be there to thank ya' all,
Nine hundred and ninety-eight dragonflies on the wall,
Nine hundred and ninety-eight dragonflies on the waaaa'll,
Take one down and 'pass it around,'
And we'll be there to thank ya' all,
Nine hundred and ninety-seven dragonflies on the wall,
Nine hundred and ninety-seven dragonflies on the waaaa'll,
Take one down and 'mash it around,'
And we'll be there to thank ya' all,
Nine hundred and ninety-six dragonflies on the wall,
Nine hundred and ninety-six dragonflies on the waaaa'll,
Take one down and 'bash it around,'
And we'll be there to thank ya' all,

"It's *not* a wall! You, stupid grogochs! It's a ceiling... a ceiling!" said the silhouette irately. Indeed, the silhouette was Koréna, the evil sorceress trapped within Arthur's Seat. "Bring one of those, puffy enclosed things over to me."

"You mean a cocoon, Koréna?" asked Aldo.

"Yes!" said Koréna furiously. "That's what I said, a cocoon!"

Aldo carried over a quivering dragonfly cocoon to her. Her hand slowly waved over the cocoon as she said, *"Éiri mór."*

A full-grown dragonfly cracked out of its slimy cocoon and flew high to the ceiling above it. It flittered about and then its wings abruptly stopped in mid-air and then it suddenly dive-bombed down to the ground.

"Your growth spell is getting better," said Earh reproachfully. "That one actually made it to the ceiling."

"Silence!" demanded Koréna. "Aldo, bring me another."

"What is going on?" said Kathryn perplexed.

"*Who*? Who said that?" said Koréna, bolting up right in her chair and then snapping her fingers. "Someone's watching us!"

Kathryn's view of Koréna disappeared and then unexpectedly, two slanted eyes appeared in the blistering fire. "I see you have returned, child. Please believe me when I say, how much I need that teine criostal. I know you have it and you're the only one who can bring it to me! Long, I have waited to see it joined together. It must be done soon, for the thousandth Hawkmoon approaches. Evil faeries and mortals desire it and will use it for evil, while I will use it for good!"

"You are not good!" screamed Kathryn. She knew in her heart that Koréna somehow had Billy in her clutches, hidden from her somewhere in Aählyéé. "And you're a liar! I know who you are Koréna!"

"Who told you I was evil? For I am not! I know where your brother is. Come, bring me the teine criostal and I will take you to him!"

"Billy?" sighed Kathryn.

"Yes!" exclaimed Koréna's pulsating eyes. "Billy, he is with me! Here, in Aählyéé. Come, join us!"

"No!" said Kathryn heatedly.

"He is here. Come, bring me the teine criostal and you will see your brother again!" said Koréna.

Kathryn scrapped her feet along the dusty floor and sprayed dust over the fire. "*Noooooo!*" she cried.

"Come!" said Koréna, her eyes glistening with the heat of the fire, "and you will see him again!"

"*Liar!* You're a liar!" cried Kathryn. Scooping up handfuls of dirt with the palm of her hands, she poured it on to the fire. "You are evil! And just want the teine criostal." The fire began to disintegrate into ashes, while only warm embers glowed. "I will *not* be fooled!"

The fire burnt out and the ashes lay still in the hearth. Kathryn looked at her watch, it was just about midnight. She knelt down before the door and she began to count down the seconds. Watching the second hand, three, two, and one! She knocked north, ~*thump*, west, ~*thump*, and then east, ~*thump*, it went. Kathryn sat there in silence, knowing that night two was complete. Just one more night and she would know if this worked. *And then what?*

Kathryn met up with Carmel and Maryanne at breakfast that morning. For some particular reason, the Sisters had served scrambled eggs, crisp bacon, sautéed mushrooms in butter, and grilled tomatoes. The toast was still pleasantly burnt as it always was; seems the toaster was a bit quirky.

Kathryn decided to tell them everything that had occurred since they began, 'The Faery Door Project.' Carmel seemed a bit taken back when she told her about the pooka and all the shapes he changed into, but Maryanne on the other hand was very intrigued, indeed. Especially when she heard about the strange visions Kathryn saw in the hearth's fire.

"What's a grogoch?" asked Maryanne, dipping her toast in the golden egg yolk.

"A very hairy, ugly half-man who smells like stinky sour milk!"

"Ewww... I'll take a look in your mother's book to see if she mentions anything about them," said Maryanne logically.

"Well, did you get the knock in?" asked Carmel impatiently. "It is the reason you went up there in the first place!"

"Yes, I did!" answered Kathryn proudly. "I'll sneak out tonight and see what happens!"

"Sneak out where?" asked Oona inquisitively, pulling some extra toast from her pocket.

"Nowhere," replied Kathryn.

"Come on now, you must be sneaking out somewhere?" inquired Oona. "Tell us!"

"Please do," chimed in Leesa.

Kathryn remained as silent as the grave, not knowing what to say. Maryanne on the other hand began to play with her food.

Then Carmel finally said, "None of your darn business, Oona!"

"Excuse me?" retaliated Oona.

"You heard me! It's none of your business," said Carmel powerfully. "The whole world doesn't revolve around you! So, beat it!"

Oona pulled back from the group with a sour look on her face as if she had just sucked on a lemon. "It's not a good idea to make enemies with me, Carmel," snapped Oona, standing up from the bench. "Just remember, I can make your life miserable."

"Yeah, well, if you keep on eating toast like you do, you'll definitely make my life miserable by sitting on me!" snickered Carmel.

Kathryn and Maryanne chuckled uncontrollably.

Oona and Leesa left the table, but not without a good sneering look at the group as they departed.

Tonight was finally the night. Kathryn piled everything she thought she needed into a pillow case; her mother's journal, a wiry notebook, a pen that worked, Billy's picture, a sprig of dandelion, the clear glass container that Sister Gwen had given her, a flashlight, a rope, and some extra food to sustain her for a few hours.

Traveling down to the Devil's Bridge, she felt a twinge of guilt. Carmel, Cyril, and Maryanne had all wanted to go, but now they could never see what she was about to see. *I wish I had a camera*! she thought. Eagerly, she crossed the bridge, her body swooshing side to side. She had actually gotten pretty good at crossing it and could make it across without any sudden jerks from the frayed rope railing. When she reached the cave, she noticed the hearth was clean.

"I betcha that silly pooka set me up," she muttered to herself and began her countdown once again. "This is it!" She placed down a sprig of dandelion and said blissfully, "Three... Two... One!" She knocked once above the faery door, "North!" *~thump*. She knocked to the left of the faery door, "West!" *~thump*. She knocked to the right of the faery door, "East!" *~thump,* it went.

Now, at first the faery door lay silent as it did every night before. Soon, Kathryn began to hear noises behind it. The door shook a few times, rattling like a cage. Her hand seized the glass container and she hovered, like a dangling spider, over the door. The doorknob clinked, and then clanked; there was a quick jingle and a tinkle. Kathryn's heart drummed faster and faster. *Here it comes!* she thought.

The doorknob rattled again and out sauntered a murky, green wee of a man just about three inches tall, whistling his happy tune. It looked as though he had been expecting a different room, because his whistling stopped abruptly and then he looked left, then right, then up. Nothing terrorized him more than seeing Kathryn suspended over him, ready to swoop down on him like a bird preying on a fish of the sea. The little fellow darted back towards the faery door, but Kathryn dropped the clear container around his little body.

First off, this was not your typical faery that looks sweet, fluttering around the air with its wings floating from flower to flower. No! This was a short stocky faery, which had only three hairs sticking out of his bald head, two fanged teeth that shot out like tusks from his lower lip, and a tiny leather tool belt filled with hammers and nails that hung snugly around his beer belly. He dressed in shredded leather clothing sewn together with dried up vines, which also were used to lace up his leather sandals on his big fat feet.

The portly faery rapped on his invisible cell wall, flaring his hands up and down, his mouth opening and closing ferociously as he spattered words in silence. His bulging eyes now began to sprout red rivers through his eyeballs.

At first she thought he'd die of a massive heart attack from his aggressive behavior. "OK! OK! Relax!" she said tranquilly, waving her hand before him.

But the little fellow kept stomping around angrily in a circle, then pausing for a second and waving his fist in the air back at Kathryn.

"Listen, I'm not letting you out until you calm down!" said Kathryn firmly.

The wee creature tilted his head, cupped his hand to his ear, and shrugged his shoulders.

"*I Said, I'm Not Letting You Out Until You Calm Down!!!!*" she yelled as loud as she could.

The three-inch man tapped his hairy feet, rolled his eyes, and pointed his plump finger to his ear.

Kathryn sighed, "This must be what they mean by *Indiana Jones Rule Number Six: Learn a valuable trait by speaking the local language.*" She then pulled out her notebook promptly and wrote down in large letters: *Promise You Won't Run And I'll Let You Out!!!* She ripped out the paper and held it up to the faery, but the little fellow had fallen to his knees, his hands wrapped around his throat, sticking out his purple tongue.

"He's choking!" she gasped.

Speedily, she picked up the container. He began to pant heavily and then took three deep breaths of fresh air through his wide nostrils.

"Sorry," she said softly.

The little bugger's eyes looked up, and faster than you could say *sugar booger*, he bolted towards the now glowing faery door. She grabbed her mother's journal and slid it down in front of the door, blocking his exit.

"*Out!* Out! I need out!" he squealed, running around within the perimeter of the golden ragwort.

Kathryn positioned herself once again over him, swaying the glass container back and forth, ready to swoop down on him, but his little feet moved too fast.

"Will you stand still?" she asked annoyed.

"*Out!* Out! I need out!" he cried in a guttural voice, racing around and around the circle.

Finally, Kathryn got smart and just gave up. She watched him walk up to the ragwort to see if he could cross it and then run back to her mother's leather journal blocking the door. He placed his fat hands on the book and with all his might, he tried to move it, but it didn't budge.

"*Out!* Out! I need out!" he howled over and over again!

Kathryn sat Indian-style and sighed a few more times. After about a half-hour, the wee creature began to slow down, exhausting all his energy, but never once stopped crying, "*Out!* Out! I need out!"

Hungry, Kathryn snatched her pillowcase and pulled out a large scone smothered in sweet butter and raspberry jelly.

The little faery sniffed the air, his nostrils flaring and stopped dead in his tracks. He turned to Kathryn, "Grub! Gah'bun?" he said leering at Kathryn. "You have a gah'bun?"

"What, the scone?" she said baffled.

Smiling brightly he said, *"Gah'bun!!!"*

"Would you like a piece?" she asked kindly.

His little eyes lit up as he nodded yes. She tore off a piece; half his whole body size and handed it to him. He gobbled it right up and the two sat peacefully together eating their gah'buns.

"I'm Kathryn," she said, pointing to herself.

"Glubgrub," he said with a glob of jelly stuck on his tusk.

"Nice to meet you Glubgrub!" said Kathryn, giggling as he stuffed his face with butter and jam.

Grinning from ear to ear, he poked his wee chubby finger into the center of the scone, scrapping out a chunk of sweet butter and popped it into his mouth. It was as if he had never tasted anything more delectable than the creamy taste of butter. Kathryn chuckled again to herself. What happened to the crazed faery she stared at for over a half an hour?

Glubgrub's eyes grew heavy with sleep, his belly round like a ball now. He curled up on the ground falling into a deep slumber. The little tyke slept off the gah'bun and when he awoke, Kathryn was waiting.

"Let me tell you a story," she said, lying down on her belly with her bony elbows bracing her chin up.

"Me, go home!" whimpered Glubgrub.

"Please..." she implored him. "It's very important and when I'm finished, I will bring you as many gah'buns as you want!"

Glubgrub paused for a moment. His belly now full with a glorious gah'bun, but to have more... as much as he could eat? He agreed immediately.

Kathryn began telling him her story of traveling across the great sea to live with her Grandfather. About the stories he'd tell them about Arthur's Seat and its mysteries. The decrepit woman living in the shack on Arthur's Seat and how she had told them how Aählyneé began.

Glubgrub shook his head and said animatedly, "She wrong! Glubgrub has another tale! Glubgrub tell... Once, great sea covered land, young girl floated on ocean in boat, stole egg from dragon. Dragon angered, chased her, breathed fire on sea, sea into mist, mist into thick fog, dragon see no more, landed on mountain, girl watch dragon, sneaks up, and cuts out dragon's heart. Girl evil, Queen Maeve..."

"Queen Maeve? Not Koréna?" she asked perplexed. *Well, which tale was true?* Hers or Glubgrub's and were there any more tales that were different?

Kathryn continued on, telling him of Billy and her fighting, and about her finding her way into the Mountain, meeting Koréna, and the two grogochs.

"Creamers," he said disdainfully when she mentioned the grogochs.

Kathryn went on about falling into the water, finding the Fire Crystal, coming face to face with a peist, and escaping Arthur's Seat with Koréna in pursuit.

"Can you find Billy for me?" she asked wholeheartedly, handing the picture of Billy and her to Glubgrub. "I know he's still alive, but I can't get back into the Raven's Gate,

not for almost another seven years. I'll give you a hundred scones filled with jam and butter... I mean a hundred gah'buns!"

"Gah'buns!" cried Glubgrub, taking the photo from her fingertips. It was twice his size; he leaned back on his feet and wobbled a bit, and then fell to the ground, dropping one of his hammers. He then gestured to the picture with his plump finger, "Billy?"

"Yes! That's him!" she cried.

"Many gah'buns?" he grumbled.

"Will you find him for me? Just, see if he's really there and give him this..." said Kathryn, handing Glubgrub a little envelope.

Glubgrub laid the envelope on the ground, rested the photo on top, and began to roll it up like a cigar. "Glubgrub do job, for many gah'buns!" he said decisively, throwing the coiled up letter and photo under his left arm and shook Kathryn's finger.

"Glubgrub go home now?" he inquired.

"Yes!" she said confidently, lifting up the book. He waddled to the faery door, opened it, and in two shakes of a lamb's tail, he was gone.

"Wait!" she cried, picking up his wee hammer from the floor. "You-you dropped your hammer!"

Now, it just so happened, that when Kathryn finally came down from the monastery, it seemed like a great weight was finally taken off her shoulders. She could finally find out if Billy was alive or not. Well, she also now knew she didn't dream her adventure into the belly of Arthur's Seat and she knew that Koréna was real. But one question puzzled her the most of all, if she did indeed find the Fire Crystal, where was it now? Who was that stranger?

Just like a true Indiana Jones apprentice, she had finally completed the task at hand and just had to wait a few more weeks until the next full moon.

"Did ya see it?" asked Maryanne restlessly. "What'd it look like?"

"He was short, tubby, and grubby looking!" replied Kathryn with a sweet smirk on her face. "He had tusks shooting up out of his lower lip and he was a dirty green color!"

"Come on, I thought faeries were pretty butterfly things that floated around like Tinker Bell?" said Carmel dismissively.

"Nope, he was scruffy and a bit smelly, but he's going to look for Billy and that's all that matters!"

"Why, don't I believe you," said Carmel coldly.

"I believe you, Kat!" said Maryanne sympathetically. "If you say so."

"Thanks, Mar! Carmel you have my word. Is that not good enough?" asked Kathryn.

"If I were mad, it would be! It's as useful as a chocolate teapot!" said Carmel disbelievingly. "Do you have a picture of him or anything?"

"No," answered Kathryn.

"Here we go again!" said Carmel. "How are we supposed to believe you when you have no proof? I'm just supposed to believe you willy-nilly that a real faery came out that door because you said so? I'd be mad to believe you, if you didn't have some solid proof!"

Kathryn reached into her pocket and pulled out a wee hammer smaller than a thumbtack and said, "Is this proof?"

Carmel snatched the copper hammer and held it up to the light and said, "That's proof! When's the next full moon?"

Now, the girls and Cyril were so excited that they had real proof that a faery truly did exist. And a whole other world of magic and mystery was just on the other side of Inishmara and they now had solid proof of it. It didn't take long for all the girls of St. Bernadette's to begin whispering that there was indeed a portal to the Otherworld just beyond the Devil's Bridge.

Pretty soon, the other girls began to smile and wave at Kathryn as she passed through the halls. For, wasn't it just a week ago that she felt like no one liked her and now she was everyone's friend? Girls would stop her in the hall asking to see Glubgrub's hammer. Rumors even flew around the school, saying the hammer had great mystical powers. If you placed it on your forehead while holding your history book; you would somehow mysteriously retain all knowledge of one's homework. Other rumors swirled around, that it could get rid of headaches, toothaches, and any other menacing pains you had. Kathryn decided it was best not to loan out the hammer, though she didn't mind showing it to anyone who asked her.

Even Sister Mary Martha was curious about seeing the mystical hammer. "That's just a doll's toy you have there, nothing special about it at all," she said snidely. "Just plain old rubbish it is!"

Strangely enough, none of the nuns ever did ask her where it came from, except for Sister Gwen.

"What a lovely souvenir you have," said Sister Gwen cheerfully. "Now, if you could just bottle up one of those faeries and bring him to me, it would be such a joy! See, I told you dear, faeries do exist! Isn't it funny, how no one believes you until they can touch something or see if for themselves? We are the ones with better faith and we are blessed to believe without seeing. That's why he came out to you, you know, because you believed in him!"

"Something inside me always knew them to be real. And now that I know, I'm not crazy and others believe me, it's amazing!" said Kathryn.

"Well, if they didn't believe it, would you still believe?" asked Sister Gwen.

"Of course, I would!" answered Kathryn.

"Good girl..." replied Sister Gwen.

"Besides, I have to go back soon after he's found Billy," said Kathryn eagerly.

"Of course child, but you know, you do have awhile to wait now, don't you?" said Sister Gwen.

"Just a few more weeks until the next full moon," said Kathryn.

"Oh, didn't I tell you?" said Sister Gwen mindlessly. "It's not any full moon. It's three nights of a moon being full precisely at midnight and that's not for almost five more years."

"Five more years?" gasped Kathryn.

"And a few months, sometime in June from my calculations," added Sister Gwen. "Right near your graduation."

Kathryn's mouth dropped open and she crashed to the floor. "Five more years? Five more years?" whined Kathryn.

"And, a few months!" said Sister Gwen. "Come along, back to studying! We have many years to get you ready for your return!"

CHAPTER NINETEEN
THE WARRIOR QUEEN

Indeed it was true, for only when the moon is full three days in a row at midnight, then and only then, if one were to knock above a faery door, made from the wood of a hawthorn tree, would a true living faery come out!

"I can't wait five years!" whined Carmel. "I'd have graduated by then! Go figure, my dumb luck!"

Maryanne hugged her sister tightly and said kindly, "Don't worry, Carmel. We'll figure something out."

In the years passing; day into night, night into day, fall into winter and winter into spring, rounding out into the long days of summer. Kathryn spent much of her time over the next few years with Sister Gwen, whom by the way, liked to tell her stories of ancient Ireland, including all the great Warriors and Saints that had come to this land many years ago. Kathryn's mind began to understand how the Irish, in all their great wisdom and understanding, passed down stories to one another, from generation to generation.

"First, it's a story, my dear," said Sister Gwen, roaming through the great arched halls of St. Bernadette's. "Then, the story becomes myth and then the myth becomes legend. What is real and what is not, we do not know. But, it is a choice we are given to believe in one or the other. I choose to believe. What do you choose?"

"I believe too," agreed Kathryn. "Others may not believe me, but I believe…"

"Fine, fine, no one can change what one believes… unless," said Sister Gwen vaguely.

"Unless, what?" asked Kathryn.

"Unless, you begin to believe differently, of course!" laughed Sr. Gwen.

Oh by glory, Sister Gwen filled Kathryn's head with tales of St. Patrick, the great patron Saint of Ireland who drove out all snakes and brought great peace to this land.

"No snakes in Ireland?" said Kathryn bewildered.

"Not a one! Saint Patrick drove them out of Ireland hundreds of years ago!" replied Sister Gwen.

"Good, *Rule Number Five* is taken care of. *"Avoid snakes at all cost!"* said Kathryn relieved.

"Snakes avoided, love," said Sister Gwen.

Yes, Kathryn's head was filled on a daily basis with stories, myths and legends. Some of Christian Saints, such as St. Brendan 'The Navigator,' who is a legendary Saint that had set sail hundreds of years ago, from just around these parts. He went off to spread the word of Christianity. There were also myths of lake dwellers and spirits who lived under the waters along with the precocious selkies.

It was during one of Sister Gwen's stories that she handed Kathryn her first report card.

"Since I'm your guardian, I seem to be receiving these," said Sister Gwen. "I thought you might want to have a look.

Kathryn took the green colored paper and opened it up and began to read:

Saint Bernadette's School
Inishmara, Ireland

Name: Kathryn Murphy	Grade: 6				
	First Quarter	Second Quarter	Third Quarter	Fourth Quarter	Final Grade
ENGLISH: Mother Superior's Comments: Student lacks the ability to stay awake in class and needs to be disciplined regularly. Needs much improvement.	n/a	D	D	C	D
HISTORY: Sr. Joan's Comments: Kathryn is a delight in class and adds a great deal to class discussions.	n/a	B	B	B	B
IRISH: Sr. Mary Martha's Comments: Child is often dirty and needs a haircut. Overall, class participation is adequate.	n/a	C	C	C	C
MATHEMATICS: Sr. Mary Elizabeth's Comments:	B	B	B	B	B
SCIENCE: Sr. Mary Margaret's Comments: Student exhibits a wonderful curiosity in all lab classes.	n/a	B	B	B	B
PHYS. EDUCATION: Sr. Martin Marie's Comments: Kathryn is an exuberant student that needs to build on her self-confidence. Once she begins to believe in herself she will excel.	n/a	C	C	C	C

"Sorry I didn't do better, Sister Gwen," said Kathryn, handing her back the report card.

"Now, now child, if you were perfect you'd only get worse. But, you see, you can only get better and that's all that matters!" she said, passing her two white envelopes. "You also have some mail as well."

Kathryn ripped open the first letter and began to read:

Dear Kathryn,

How are you? Well, another summer has come to Ballyrun. George spent all of his time wearing his apple red helmet, trotting around the town taunting Mr. O'Keefe's donkey Jezebel with the new bell on his bike. Mrs. O'Keefe, of course, says that I had told him to do it after giving me so much grief over the letters that are not labeled correctly with my full name. I, in return, informed her that he is a free spirit and does what he likes. But, I may have mentioned that donkeys can turn into dragons if they hear bells ringing. For that I am guilty, but it was worth it!

Eddie, on the other hand, has formed an attachment to the Kennedy girls and loves doing the Irish jig on the tables as Seamus plays. It's great craic! On a happier note, Seamus and Colin have started to play regularly at Flannery's. The crowd is filled with such joy when they sing! Plus, it gives me an excuse to get out with George, Eddie, and Marie.

And what about our sweet Marie? I am happy to say, she is doing well! We just returned from hospital and she was given good news on her progress with Progeria. The doctors say she's doing well. Her medication had to be adjusted, but no major upsets. We are expected to keep her around for many, many years. Her pen pal John is finally coming over to stay for the Nights of the Faeries festivities in the fall.

I do have some news on Colin, the sly dog finally got up the nerve to ask Joan out! Of course, he did this when Sodge was away visiting his sister. But, he did it and the date is next week. All the ladies around town have been giving him advice! Hopefully, he will choose the one I gave him, which was to cut that shaggy head of his!

We miss you terribly, dear Kathryn. Ballyrun is not the same without you! Seamus, George, Eddie, and Marie all send their love!
Love,
Peg, Seamus, George, Eddie, and Marie.

Kathryn folded up the letter neatly and placed into her side pocket. She then began to read the second letter:

Dear Kathryn love,

Your grandfather has asked me to write to you. He hopes you are enjoying your time at St. Bernadette's and is happy to receive letters from Sister Gwen about how you're progressing. We took up a collection at Flannery's and we were able to pay some of your tuition next year! Because of this, Mother Superior said that you could cut back on your hours working at the laundry. So, you can focus on your schoolwork, which she said, is greatly needed.

Your grandfather, on the other hand, is still talking about the leprechaun that finagled his purse from him. I'm going to have Dr. Cavanaugh have a look at him. Make sure he hasn't bumped his head by accident. As far as Ballyrun goes, it's still the same old town.

I know you probably despise your grandfather for sending you away to boarding school on that awful island! Just remember, that from great hate, follows great love.

Sincerely,
Fiona Flannery

It is said, a long time ago that from the darkest, murkiest depths come the brightest souls. In the case of Kathryn, her trial and error days were a long time coming. And just like lighting a match to kindling, she grew into a wild fire as the years passed.

Saint Bernadette's School
Inishmara, Ireland

Name: Kathryn Murphy	Grade: 7				
	First Quarter	Second Quarter	Third Quarter	Fourth Quarter	Final Grade
ENGLISH: Mother Superior's Comments: Student is now staying awake in class, but her auditory skills and ability to follow directions are very limited.	C	C	C	C	C
HISTORY: Sr. Joan's Comments: Kathryn is an outstanding student. She follows directions and listens very well. Outstanding!	B	B	B	A	B
IRISH: Sr. Mary Martha's Comments: Child is cleaner than usual. Skills are progressing. Still needs a haircut.	C	C	C	B	C
MATHEMATICS: Sr. Mary Elizabeth's Comments:	B	B	B	B	B
SCIENCE: Sr. Mary Margaret's Comments: Student is beginning to excel at a steady pace.	B	B	B	B	B
PHYS. EDUCATION: Sr. Martin Marie's Comments: Kathryn's ability to fence is progressing nicely. She still has difficulty climbing ropes, but is very focused on improving.	B	B	B	B	B

Dear Kathryn,

How are you? Well, it seems as though Colin and Joan Crawley are on the outs now. It's such a shame! He really fell head over heels for her, but Sodge of course, has been pestering her about dating Doctor Cavanaugh. And, as you know, he's been widowed for over twenty-two years now and is thirty years her senior. Poor Colin has been spending his time at Flannery's drinking away his sorrows.

Did I tell you? Marie's pen pal, John, his mother, wrote to us a few weeks ago, to tell us that John has been having some complications to the new medication he's been taking for his Progeria. So, please keep him in your prayers!

By the way, George has had his bell 'officially' revoked when Mr. O'Keefe's donkey tore down the middle of the road with all the mail in his cart, trailing behind him. He leapt into river and destroyed all the mail for the day, which supposedly contained a letter to Sodge. So, he was in an uproar when the incident occurred. Now, without the bell, poor George stopped riding his bicycle and now accompanies Eddie as he follows the Kennedy girls around town. We miss you terribly dear Kathryn. Seamus, George, Eddie, and Marie all send their love!
Love,
Peg, Seamus, George, Eddie, and Marie.

Dear Kathryn love,

I am sorry to write to you about another inconvenience your grandfather is now experiencing. He is having some major difficulties with the Lott family. Supposedly, Mr. Lott has found an old land document claiming that his great, great, great grandfather owned the land that your grandfather lives on. And he is now some sort of squatter and has no right to your house or to your land at all! This has deeply upset him and he is building a great stone fence around your property along with planting some daisies along side of it. I must tell you, your grandfather is a bit bonkers at times. I don't know how a fence and some flowers will change the fact that Mr. Lott has a document, stating that he owns the land, but your grandfather keeps saying, 'Don't worry! It should keep the riff-raff out!' Nonetheless, there's no way of changing his mind once it's set on something.

Have I told you Seamus and Colin are singing at my bar? They do a lovely job, but I'm getting a bit worried about Colin. He seems to be spending more and more time here drinking his pay away than singing. Such a shame and it's all over that Crawley girl, wouldn't you know? She parades around town with the Doctor as if they were teenagers! I don't know why he's so heartbroken, beauty isn't only skin deep, as I say. She obviously,

shows a lack of restraint on her part. Oh, but why am I fussing around about Colin, that fool. Until next time!
Sincerely,
Fiona Flannery

SAINT BERNADETTE'S SCHOOL
INISHMARA, IRELAND

Name: Kathryn Murphy	Grade: 8				
	First Quarter	Second Quarter	Third Quarter	Fourth Quarter	Final Grade
ENGLISH: Mother Superior's Comments: Student is improving slowly, now that she has cut back on her hours at the laundry.	B	B	B	B	B
HISTORY: Sr. Joan's Comments: Absolutely outstanding student!	A	A	A	A	A
IRISH: Sr. Mary Martha's Comments: Child is progressing nicely. Tends to be very neat these days.	B	B	B	A	B
MATHEMATICS: Sr. Mary Elizabeth's Comments:	B	B	B	B	B
SCIENCE: Sr. Mary Margaret's Comments: Exceeds expectations.	A	A	A	A	A
PHYS. EDUCATION: Sr. Martin Marie's Comments: Kathryn is mastering all parts of the 'Heroic Warrior' principals and if she continues to progress at this rate, she will pass with flying colours.	A	A	A	A	A

Dear Kathryn,

It seems as though Colin is still having his heart broken, for Joan has been dating Doctor Cavanaugh since last year. He pretty much mopes around town, even his singing is suffering and Fiona had to let Seamus and Colin go.

George and Eddie also began playing snooker at Flannery's since they installed a snooker table in the back. Seamus is also allowing George and Eddie to have a pint or two while they're playing. Which

George is ecstatic over, but Seamus told me that if you don't watch your pint, George would be the one drinking it! Fiona also installed a wall jukebox after she let Seamus and Colin go. George loves to play music on the jukebox and seems to have settled on his two favourites, Gary Glitter and Queen. Eddie of course, can't hear a dang thing; he just smiles and dances to anything. We miss you terribly dear Kathryn. Seamus, George, Eddie, and Marie all send their love!
Love,
Peg, Seamus, George, Eddie, and Marie.

Dear Kathryn love,
 The town is still in an uproar after I let Seamus and Colin go! I just couldn't continue watching Colin drown his sorrows away every night because of that trollop, something had to be done! I also put in a new jukebox to make up for the lack of music. Seems to be going well! Especially, with all the new snooker players that have been coming in. It's just grand!
 In the meantime, I'm glad to say your grandfather finally produced a paper stating that he indeed owns the land and the Lott's have no rights to it at all. If you ask me, those Lott's just want to stir up trouble! It is beyond me how they are suddenly claiming the rights to your family's land! Your grandfather has been on that land, even when my father was a child. It's just inconceivable how Mr. Lott can justify trying to hijack your grandfather's land like that! It's just deplorable! By the way, your grandfather was able to finish that stone wall around your property, which amazed all the town's people! How a man of his age could even pick up a stone, nevertheless build a wall? But, I am happy to say, it is now complete.
Sincerely,
Fiona Flannery

Saint Bernadette's School
Inishmara, Ireland

Name: Kathryn Murphy	Grade: 9				
	First Quarter	Second Quarter	Third Quarter	Fourth Quarter	Final Grade
ENGLISH: Mother Superior's Comments: Student is beginning to excel.	B	B	A	A	B+
HISTORY: Sr. Joan's Comments: Exceptional student.	A	A	A	A	A
IRISH: Sr. Mary Martha's Comments: Finally, the student is at a normal level.	A	A	A	A	A
MATHEMATICS: Sr. Mary Elizabeth's Comments:	B	B	B	B	B
SCIENCE: Sr. Mary Margaret's Comments: Exceeds expectations.	A	A	A	A	A
PHYS. EDUCATION: Sr. Martin Marie's Comments: Above Average.	A	A	A	A	A

Dear Kathryn,

I have some grave news to report to you! Sweet Marie's friend, John, has passed away from complications to Progeria; his little body couldn't take the illness anymore. Marie has taken it very harshly knowing that John was just a few years older than her. She keeps asking Seamus and me, when she is supposed to die. What do you tell a ten year old? I keep explaining there is no expiration date on her and that she can live as long as she wants. But, she has definitely changed. She doesn't play knights and dragons anymore; she will hear no more stories of Aãhlynéé. What is a mother to do?

On a stranger note that defies all common sense, Sheliza has been spending time with Ian Flannery, which is the most unlikely couple. But nonetheless, they have been seen about town and going up and down Arthur's Seat. We'll see how long that one lasts once her Mother finds out about it! We miss you terribly, dear Kathryn. Seamus, George, Eddie, and Marie all send their love!

Love,

Peg, Seamus, George, Eddie, and Marie.

Dear Kathryn love,

    Well, it turns out that your grandfather's document is not valid. Mr. Lott brought it to a barrister and examined it. It turns out, the signature and the dates don't add up! Your grandfather is furious over the turn of events and he keeps claiming that it is indeed his land. In fact, the whole Mountain is his! He is livid and told Mr. Lott that if he was younger, he'd duel him over the land than to bring it to the courts!

    By the way, I had Doctor Cavanaugh check your grandfather out to make sure he's playing with a full deck. Turns out, your grandfather is as healthy as an ox and is sharp as a tack! Needless to say, Mr. Lott who, I surely believe is in cahoots with the devil, if you ask me, will still be following through with the claim.

    I do have to say, that it has been very peaceful around here since the jukebox has been broken. Turns out, someone was putting in the wrong change and broke the machine! Well, when I find out who did that, I'll give them the sharp edge of my tongue!

    Also, I am very worried about Ian who has been gallivanting off with the devil herself, Miss Sheliza Lott! I told him her family is no good, but he keeps telling me, she loves to listen to his stories of Arthur's Seat! And they often take trips up the Mountain together. I suppose it's nice he finally does have a friend. What is a mother to do?

Sincerely,
Fiona Flannery

Saint Bernadette's School
Inishmara, Ireland

Name: Kathryn Murphy	Grade: 10				
	First Quarter	Second Quarter	Third Quarter	Fourth Quarter	Final Grade
ENGLISH: Mother Superior's Comments: Acceptable.	A	A	A	A	A
HISTORY: Sr. Joan's Comments: Exceptional student.	A	A	A	A	A
IRISH: Sr. Mary Martha's Comments: Good.	A	A	A	A	A
MATHEMATICS: Sr. Mary Elizabeth's Comments:	B	B	B	B	B
SCIENCE: Sr. Mary Margaret's Comments: Exceeds expectations.	A	A	A	A	A
PHYS. EDUCATION: Sr. Martin Marie's Comments: Heroic Warrior material!	A	A	A	A	A

Dear Kathryn,

It's been a rough year since John's death. Marie is still not handling it well at all! And now, on top of that, George and Eddie have also started asking questions about death and their mortality. And that Sheliza Lott even had the audacity to tell them that because they're different they won't live as long as a normal person would. Well, that had George asking all kinds of questions about when he's going to pass over to the other side. I say it's all a bit too much. That Sheliza just likes stirring up trouble, I tell you, just like her father!

I'm sure Fiona has been telling you that Mr. Lott is trying to take your grandfather's land away from him! Just absolutely deplorable, those people are ruthless! He's been on that land since my grandparents were born! Oh, and on top of it all, Sheliza said to George and Eddie, that if they want to live, they need to go to 'Tír na nÓg,' the land of everlasting youth! In other words, she wants them to find a way into Aählynéé, so they can live forever, and to end up like poor, Billy? I think not! Tomorrow, I will walk straight up to her Mother and tell her what she's been doing! The nerve of that girl!

I know... I know... In the past, I had played around with the idea that people with handicaps, like George and Eddie could be changed if they were in the Otherworld. But since what happened to poor Billy, you'd think she'd know better than to egg them on to climb up that Mountain! It is absolutely unacceptable!

Oh Kathryn, we are all looking forward to your return next year! We have so much to catch up on! I'm sure you have turned into a beautiful young woman!! I, on the other hand, am still fighting off the hands of time! Maybe I should move to the land of eternal youth? Though, they should've taken me there about ten years ago! We miss you terribly dear, Kathryn. Seamus, George, Eddie, and Marie all send their love!

Love,
Peg, Seamus, George, Eddie, and Marie.

Dear Kathryn love,

Just a quick note about what is going on with your grandfather. Well, it seems that our Mr. Lott told everyone around town that he has indeed sent a petition into the courts to retrieve the land from your grandfather. Mr. Dimmler told me that it takes years for papers like that to go through the system and not to worry about it! It'll just get stuck in all the red tape. I, on the other hand, told Mr. Lott that he is no longer welcome in Flannery's. To think this man has the audacity to take your grandfather's land and house is certainly unreal!

In the meantime, keep yourself safe and warm while you're at St. Bernadette's. Before you know it you'll be back in good 'ol Ballyrun again! We're all looking forward to your return, especially George, Eddie, and Marie.

Sincerely,
Fiona Flannery

Saint Bernadette's School
Inishmara, Ireland

Name: Kathryn Murphy	Grade: 11				
	First Quarter	Second Quarter	Third Quarter	Fourth Quarter	Final Grade
ENGLISH: Mother Superior's Comments: I am hopeful that her level of achievement will continue through to next year.	A	A	A	A	A
HISTORY: Sr. Joan's Comments: Outstanding as always!	A	A	A	A	A
IRISH: Sr. Mary Martha's Comments: Consistent.	A	A	A	A	A
MATHEMATICS: Sr. Mary Elizabeth's Comments:	B	B	B	B	B
SCIENCE: Sr. Mary Margaret's Comments: Bravo!	A	A	A	A	A
PHYS. EDUCATION: Sr. Martin Marie's Comments: She could definitely give me a run for the money!	A	A	A	A	A

The years at St. Bernadette's had passed like a thief in the night. Every day, it got closer and closer to when the three full moons would once again come about; which would allow Kathryn to knock once more on the faery door and for Glubgrub to come out. It was in these passing years that Kathryn grew like a weed in the sun. Finally, she had aced all her classes, but most importantly, she was now a true warrior as far as Sister Martin Marie was concerned.

"Right, one last time before this last class ends," said Sister Martin Marie to Kathryn, dressed from head to toe with her white breeches, padded vest, wiry mask, and her sword held high, "One, two, three... *En garde!*"

Sister advanced with a lunge, *~swish...~swish...* Kathryn counter attacked, pushing her back, *~swish...~swish...* Sister parried the attack and advanced forward, *~swish... ~swish...* Kathryn's feet danced back a few paces as she evaded the advance... *~swish... ~swish...* She lunged with her right arm forward, striking Sister's sword down... *~swish...*

"You know, I can do this all day," said Sister Martin Marie whimsically, whipping her sword around, ~swish...

"So, can I," smiled Kathryn, ~swish...

"I see you can finally stand your ground," she said, crossing her blade high and advancing, ~swish... ~swish... "And, for that! You get an A!"

"Are you afraid, I may beat you?" countered Kathryn as she cut her sword away and advanced rapidly, ~swish... ~swish...

"Afraid?" cried Sister Martin Marie, astonished, recovering her stance. "Child, I am never afraid!" ~swish...~swish...

Kathryn's feet danced forward and then back again with Sister Martin Marie's. When one would advance an attack, the other would cut her sword down and advance themselves... ~swish... ~swish...

"You are good, I must admit! Never have I had a student, progress so quickly, I must say," said Sister Martin Marie, her breath now slowly getting shallower, ~swish...~swish... "And give me a run for my money or for my habit, for that matter!"

"Go, Kat!" cheered Maryanne, sitting on the sidelines.

"Knock her habit off!" yelled Carmel, sitting beside Maryanne.

"You'd think a teacher's assistant would be on the side of the teacher?" cried Sister Martin Marie as she began to sweat profusely. "Enough! Enough, now... *disengage!*"
Sister bent over, panting heavily. "You..." she said taking a deep breath. "You sure can give an old nun, a run for her habit! Good job!"

It is most certainly not the norm for any Sister to have their own personal graduating ceremony, but Sister Martin Marie did, and she called it *'The Warrior Queen'* ceremony. All girls that have completed a certain level of training were granted, 'Heroic Warrior' status. Now, you ask what one must do to become a "Warrior Queen?" Well, first off one must be able to climb the twenty-foot rope in the gymnasium, three times in a row, up and down, and to ring the great cowbell at the tippy-tippy top. One must be able to run a treacherous obstacle course on Inishmara, which includes climbing up steep cliffs, rock climbing, and swimming across its small bay, while carrying a twenty pound pack on their shoulders. Easy, do you say? Well, try doing it blindfolded! And of course, one must complete this all in less than two hours. Then, to finish it off, one must duel Sister Martin Marie in a fencing match and she must concede in order for you to be considered a "Warrior Queen."

"There you go dear," said Sister Martin Marie, smearing blue war paint under Kathryn's eyes. "There is a warrior's code that you all must abide to ladies! And this is not to be taken lightly!"

"Yes, Sister!" said Kathryn, Oona, Maryanne, and Leesa in unison.

"Like girls before you, such as Carmel here, we warriors take pride in truth, honesty, and upholding all things good."

"Yes, Sister!" replied the group.

"You girls make me proud and when you leave St. Bernadette's, you will stand firm in being truly courageous in times of doubt."

"Yes, Sister!" replied the group of girls, all now smeared with a brilliant blue war paint under each eye.

Well, it just so happened, that the day of the "Warrior Queen" ceremony was the same day Kathryn needed to go back up to the monk's cave, to knock once again on the faery door. Carmel had stayed on as a teacher's assistant, just so she could see the faery door open. And to finally see that darn faery pop out of that door, with her own two bloody eyes! In the meantime, Kathryn was preparing for her return home in over five long years, for she was graduating in just a few days.

The bell tower clanged seven o'clock as Kathryn plopped down next to Carmel and Maryanne in the cafeteria. Cyril was too busy playing with Carmel's soft curly hair to notice Kathryn's presence at all.

"So, nothing really happens the first two days except for knocking," said Kathryn informatively. "You guys stay back and I'll go up alone."

"You're probably right," said Carmel, trying to scratch out some apricot jam that fell on her vest.

"I'm so excited! It seems like forever, since we went up there," said Maryanne, flipping through Laurel's notebook

"That's because it has been," said Carmel, reminding her sister, as a sister does.

"If you like m'lady, I can have that stain out for you in a jiffy!" remarked Cyril.

Carmel looked at him like he had two heads, then rolled her eyes and said, "Oh sure, why the hell not!" She removed her vest and handed it to Cyril. Speedily, he bolted out the door, with a spring in his step.

"Are you sure, you'll be all right? Going up by yourself Kat?" asked Maryanne.

"I'll be fine! It'll just be me, the wind, and that pooka," she laughed.

"It should, but..." said Maryanne hesitantly.

"Did you guys know?" said Carmel, after Cyril left the room, "that Cyril really has never left Inishmara?"

"How's that?" asked Maryanne.

"He told me last week. I mean it was a rumor and all, but for him never to ever leave. That's pretty weird, huh?" said Carmel, fidgeting with her hair.

"Ummm... What were you doing, hanging out with Cyril?" asked Kathryn. "I thought you deplored him? Being a changeling and all."

"Well, he kinda grew on me," said Carmel. "He's not all that bad, after all."

"Oh, really?" smirked Kathryn.

"Yes, really," said Carmel mockingly. "Don't you, like, have some where to go? Like, cross the Devil's Bridge or something?"

The wind that night had been blowing fiercely, like it was trying to break free from Inishmara. The moon hovered silently over Kathryn's head as she traveled across Inishmara. *Is the island really that cursed?* she thought. *Really it just is only that annoying pooka! Cursed? They should try living in Brooklyn. Now, there were some serious characters in Brooklyn! Not just a talking, rhyming pooka! But some seriously interesting characters!!!*

It didn't take long, for her to make her way back across the Devil's Bridge and up the steep steps to the monk's monastery. The small dwelling seemed not to have changed in the last five years. Diligently, she knocked precisely at twelve o'clock, like the good warrior she was.

She remembered the last time she climbed into this cave, how she felt like the whole world was against her and an overwhelming sense of loneliness. Her mind shifted to Grandpa on her way back down the mountainside. All these years, being on her own, did she want to go back at all to Ballyrun? She thought of George and Eddie. She missed them desperately, as well as Peg, Seamus, and Marie. She missed the town, but did the town miss her?

The night turned into day and then day back into night, as she went back up the mountain to the cave and knocked once again at midnight. Heading back down the stone steps, she was curious about the pooka. *Where is he?*

Right then and there is when the sulphurous glowing eyes of the pooka cracked through the darkened landscape and spoke in its growling voice once again.

A warrior's heart, is not free,
When pain and hurt, it does see,
Past and present will collide,
When crossing the other side,
Do not waste time on decay,
Destiny is on its way.

"Thanks, pooka! Not sure what that means, but I'm sure I'll need it later. See ya tomorrow!" said Kathryn and crossed the bridge.

The hairy pooka, in the shape of a Celtic tiger, cocked his head at her response, for his words seemed not to seep into her head.

Night transformed into day, and then the day back into night.

"You can't come!" argued Carmel, packing her backpack with scones, a flashlight, some rope, a compass, and a handful of dandelions.

"Sorry, but the last time I checked, *you* weren't the master and commander of me and Leesa. Whether you like it or not Carmel, we're coming!" said Oona determinedly. "I want to know if they're real or if it's just her over developed imagination! Can you blame us?"

"Suit yourself, but you'll have to take orders from Cyril and Kathryn. Or the bewitched, decomposing goblins, will get you!" said Carmel tauntingly.

"Goblins?" gulped Leesa. "I thought we were just seeing a faery?"

"Goblins are faeries, Leesa. You should know that by now! Goblins, pookas, banshees, leprechauns, elves, pixies, I can go on forever," said Carmel, strolling out the door. "So, are you comin' or what?"

The girls scouted the hallway out before they made their way boldly to the exit, tip-toeing all the way. The Sisters of the True Cross slept quietly in their snug beds as four of their students, one teacher's assistant, and Cyril made their way out of St. Bernadette's down to the Devil's Bridge.

"You go first," said Oona to Leesa.

"Why do I have to go first? You go first!" said Leesa angrily, staring at the dilapidated bridge.

"Hurry up!" called Carmel, from the other side of the deep, narrow ravine. "We haven't got all night!"

Oona and Leesa continued to argue over who was going to cross the bridge first when Carmel turned to Cyril, Kathryn, and Maryanne and said, "They're never gonna get their act together, let's go!" And so, the remaining four made their way up the steep, winding stone steps to the monk's cave.

Upon entering the monastery, they found remnants of the old ragwort from years ago. It was just mere dust now, and the wee faery door was still securely resting against the northern wall.

"Mar, can you sprinkle the fresh ragwort around the door?" asked Kathryn, pulling out her bouquet of dandelions and placing it down before the door.

"You couldn't wait for us?" cried Oona, ducking through the cave's door.

"We both nearly fell off that bridge!" said Leesa, with a hint of sheer panic in her voice.

"It seems ladies, everyone has a difficult time crossing the Devil's Bridge the first time," said Cyril.

"Where's the faery?" said Oona, gazing around the cave.

"You have to wait until midnight Oona," replied Carmel. "Just be patient, will you?"

"What's down there?" said Leesa, beaming her flashlight down the dark, sinister tunnel in the back.

"Just a bunch of dead monks," said Carmel, crossing her legs Indian-style on the cold floor.

"You don't say?" said Leesa intriguingly.

"Actually, it's a passage tomb to the other side, guarded by deformed, rotting goblins," said Cyril looking at his watch. "Just about twelve Kat!"

"Did you say deformed, rotting goblins?" asked Leesa.

"Let's have a look!" said Oona eagerly and then bolted towards the tunnel with Leesa.

"I wouldn't do that if I were you!" called Cyril.

"We're just about to knock! Can't it wait?" yelled Carmel irately.

"We'll be just a second!" said Oona sneaking down the tunnel with Leesa closely behind her.

"Forget them!" said Carmel.

"Are you guys ready?" asked Kathryn. The three nodded their heads up and down, "Mar, why don't you go first?"

"You want her to knock?" asked Carmel.

"Why not?" said Kathryn, shrugging her shoulders.

"OK!" said Maryanne excitedly, leaning over to the faery door. "North," ~*thump*. "West," ~*thump*. "And east," ~*thump*, it went, knocked Maryanne around the twiggy faery door.

At first, the door was as stiff as a corpse, not even a jingle or a jangle came from it. But, soon they began to hear a soft buzzing noise from the other side. The doorknob shook and then it rattled.

"Here it comes!" cried Maryanne.

The pearl doorknob began to twirl and twist around.

"I don't believe it," said Carmel.

"Surely, it is coming now!" said Cyril, as the faery door burst open with a flash of light. A sparkly winged faery came whizzing out the door, zipping around the ragwort perimeter, like a humming bird.

"It's real," said Carmel gob-smacked, her eyes dazzled by the winged faery doing loop-de-loops.

"Kat said it was real and it was!" said Maryanne, observing the faery hovering before her face.

"That's not, Glubgrub!" said Kathryn aggravated, peering through the faery's door. "We need Glubgrub!"

The faery swooped down and picked up the bouquet of dandelions, *"Pre-eety flow-eerz!"* she said, smelling the dandelions. She then began to dance around on her tippy-toes like a ballerina.

"What should we do?" asked Carmel, holding out her hand to touch the dancing faery.

"Well, maybe she knows where Billy is?" said Maryanne and then looked at the green haired faery. "We're looking for a young man, about seventeen who's *not* a faery, but looks like her," pointing to Kathryn. "Have you seen him?"

The wee flower faery fluttered in front of Kathryn, eyeing her up and down. Then, with a whimsical smirk she said, *"Noooo!"* And flew back into the homemade faery door and slammed it shut.

"What was that all about?" asked Carmel.

"Never trust a flower faery," said Cyril. "They're more mischievous than honest."

"What do we do now?" asked Maryanne.

"I don't know," said Kathryn.

"Let's try again," said Carmel and reached over and knocked above the faery door. "North," ~*thump*. "West," ~*thump*. "East," ~*thump,* it went.

"Try again?" asked Kathryn. "How many tries do we get?"

"I don't know, but it can't hurt!" A deep rumbling came from behind the door as the doorknob trembled once again. "I don't believe it!" said Carmel in disbelief. "I think another faery is going to come out." The faery door bulged inward and began to let out a soft, wailing moan.

"What was that?" quivered Maryanne, grabbing hold of Carmel's shirt.

The wailing began to grow louder and louder. And then, the door began to breathe in and out like a lung.

"Whatever it is, I don't like it!" squirmed Carmel.

"Faeries are a serious business," said Cyril, backing away from the now breathing door. "One must be cautious at all times before one embarks on contacting one."

"This isn't good," cried Kathryn as the door burst open and out walked two greasy haired, dirty faeries. Their eyes were half the size of their faces and their noses were just two tiny slits below their eyes. Hunched over, they slithered into the circle, trailing ooze behind them as their marbled eyes spied around the cave. The one who looked like the female of the two, carried a large pair of silver scissors in her back pocket.

"What the heck are those things?" asked Carmel, pointing to the shanty-clothed faeries.

Maryanne picked up Laurel's journal, flipping zealously through the pages and said, "I don't know. I've never seen them before!"

"Hey! Do you guys have a name?" asked Carmel, bending down to the wee little creatures. The male just looked around, snorted, and waved his fat finger at Carmel's shadow on the ground. "They're not much for words are they?"

"I guess not," said Kathryn, studying them. "They're a bit, U-G-L-Y if you ask me."

"Best not to offend any faery!" said Cyril, pointing to the female faery as she began cutting Carmel's shadow from the ground. "Look!"

"What the?" shrieked Carmel, jumping up from the ground. She could only move one leg, for her other leg's shadow was cut away. *"Crap!* Help!" Her leg lay limp and tied to the floor.

At once, Cyril took a handful of ragwort and threw it towards the female faery, causing her to drop her silver scissors. Kathryn recaptured Carmel's shadow and fastened it back to where it should be.

"I'm free," said Carmel gleefully, nearly hopping out of her skin with delight.

"Stay clear," warned Cyril. "Don't let them get a hold of any of your shadows."

"Here it is!" cried Maryanne as she began to read from the journal. "Bog faeries! They steal shadows from the light and are not very nice and quite grumpy!"

"Nasty little buggers!" said Kathryn.

"Great Mar, but how do we get rid of them?" asked Carmel.

"They don't like bright lights like any faery that lives in darkness," answered Maryanne.

"Shine your flashlights in their eyes!" cried Kathryn, flashing a bright beam of light in their faces, causing the bog faeries to shield their eyes and cower away.

"Good idea!" said Carmel, blinding the grumpy faeries with her illumination as well.

Cyril and Maryanne did the same. The light in their eyes was so bright, they quickly slithered back through the faery door leaving a slimy trail of faery goo.

"How come Glubgrub never came out?" asked Kathryn, examining the faery door.

"Faeries are very peculiar beings," said Cyril. "Why don't you knock?"

"I want to see what comes out when Cyril knocks!" said Carmel. "I betcha we'd get a dragon or something. Where are Oona and Leesa? They're missing all of this."

"Here we go!" said Kathryn, reaching towards the faery door. "North," ~*thump.* "West," ~*thump.* "East," ~*thump,* it went. "Come on, Glubgrub!"

"If those girls come back and start complaining there are no faeries, I'm gonna ..." said Carmel frustrated.

The wee faery door began to rustle once more and then it began to rattle. The doorknob clinked and then it clanked a quick jingle and then a tinkle. Oh yes, the wee little murky, green man with tusks sauntered out, one more time into the faery ring.

"*Glubgrub!!!*" cried Kathryn with delight. "Finally, did you find Billy?" Kathryn handed him a super-sized scone with extra apricot jam and sweet butter.

"Gah'bun!" he said blissfully, snatching up the scone and shoving it into his mouth.

"That's Glubgrub?" asked Maryanne. "He's so cute. Can we take him home?"

Glubgrub looked at Maryanne and smiled.

"Glubgrub, did you find Billy? Is he there on the other side with the faeries?" asked Kathryn, once again.

"Glubgrub, not find, Billy. Glubgrub find many other men, but none look like him," he said apologetically, handing Kathryn her old photo of her and Billy.

"No Billy?" said Kathryn deflated.

"He - he really is dead..." whispered Carmel.

Maryanne hugged Kathryn and said, "I'm sorry, Kat..."

Glubgrub licked a hunk of butter and jam from the scone and said, "She knows you lookin'."

"Who's she?" asked Kathryn puzzled.

A loud, shrilling cry rang out from the gloomy tunnel.

"What was that?" cried Carmel, leaping to her feet and darting down the tunnel.

Cyril and Marianne followed her.

Kathryn turned to Glubgrub and said hastily, "I'll be right back!" And then she pursued the other three down the dire tunnel.

When they all entered the black cavern, they saw before their eyes a swirling cloud of lights floating within the passage tomb.

"What did you do?" cried Cyril, clasping on to Oona and Leesa's arms, wrenching them back.

"We - we didn't do anything!" said Oona frightened.

"You must've done something," cried Carmel, clutching hold of an old tree limb.

The mist puffed with shades of royal purple and emerald green, and a growling sound echoed from behind its lair.

"Get back here!" cried Kathryn, seizing hold of a solid stick that could double as a sword.

Then before their eyes, a large woman with a Celtic tiger skull on her head marched through the passage tomb. The decomposing, distorted skeletons began to crackle as they shifted in their beds.

"Who - who is that?" shrieked Leesa, now hiding behind Oona.

"That's Queen Maeve," said Cyril, tightening his grip on his flashlight. "You touched the tomb didn't you? Didn't you?"

"What...?!? That thing?" said Oona, squirming about. "That stone? So what?"

Queen Maeve walked through the passage tomb her body covered in layers of cowhides, fur, and animal skin. Her eyes shifted to the group. She was at least three Sister Martin Marie's put together. She lifted her broad sword up high and slammed it down to the hard stone floor. Waves of electric sparks poured into the crypts. The hideous goblins began to empty out of their tombs. Their faces were steel gray and they were drenched in cobwebs, their arms scrapped the floor as they hunched over, reaching for the girls and Cyril.

"*Ruuuun!*" cried Cyril.

Immediately, they sprinted down the evil tunnel. Beams of light sliced through the darkness, while goblins crawled along the walls and ceiling, chasing them into the monk's cave. Glubgrub turned to see Kathryn barreling down the threatening tunnel. Swiftly, he turned and scampered back into the faery door, slamming it shut. Unfortunately for the group, only one person could leave the cave at a time. Maryanne went first, then Leesa, and then Oona.

The goblins festered around Carmel, Cyril, and Kathryn.

"Get out of here, girls," cried Cyril, whacking a slimy goblin in the head with his flashlight. Its head spun around three times as it landed on the ground. *"Go!"*

Carmel made her way out. Kathryn scuttled through the doorway and then her leg jerked back as a bony hand coiled around her ankle. Oona and Leesa quickly grabbed Kathryn's arms and yanked her out as Maryanne picked up a large rock and smashed it down on the goblin's arm, causing it to wither away.

"Cyril!!" cried Carmel, peering into the cave. She could see he was surrounded; unsavory goblins biting and scrapping at him. "Give me that rock," she demanded and took a firm grip on her branch. "Get down the mountain and don't *stop!*"

Carmel lowered her head and went back into the cave.

Oh, the horrendous amount of shrieking, screams, and cries that bellowed from that cave, which could even be heard all the way to Mulleam's Crossing from of course, the goblins no doubt.

Finally, Carmel and Cyril made their way out, a bit banged up, but both in one piece.

Carmel turned to Maryanne and said, "I thought I told you to go down the mountain? *Go!* Move it!"

Kathryn turned to Oona and said, "Do you believe me now?" Oona shivered a bit in the damp night air and nodded yes. The group began to descend down the stone steps of Inishmara; shadows and wisps of light flashed around them. A large roar echoed from the cave.

They had almost made it to the bottom of the mountain's slope when two goblins tackled Maryanne and Oona to the ground. Kathryn held her branch tightly, thrashing it down on the goblin's back. The creature hissed as it turned its head, its face oozing with slimy decay. She pulled her branch back thrusting it into its chest. A loud high pitch shriek stung her ears as it shriveled to the ground, turning to dust.

"Help!" cried Oona, trying to wrestle the goblin's corroding limbs off her.

Leesa grabbed a rock. "Get off her!" she screamed, bashing it down on top of its head, obliterating it into dust.

A deafening sound battered all their ears as Queen Maeve burst through the stones that created the small doorway into the cave. She stood before the monk's cave, a brown and a white horned bull were beside her, both as large as an elephants. She raised her sword and slammed it down to ground. The putrefying goblins, the powerful bulls, and Queen Maeve all charged forward towards Kathryn and her friends.

The group raced down the stone steps and found themselves engulfed by hissing, foul-smelling goblins; their eyes glowing blood red, their nails as sharp as knives, their teeth as hard as nails. They were trapped.

"Stick together," cried Kathryn, holding up her large branch, her eyes glancing over the hissing goblins.

Suddenly, a mischievous goblin jumped out at Carmel and she smacked it down with her tree branch. "We have to get to the bridge!" she cried.

"We'll never make it!" yelled Oona.

Then out of the dreary night, a grotesque goblin leapt into the air towards Kathryn. She had no time to react as a hairy tiger's body slammed against it, hurling it to the ground. Standing up, it growled at the other goblins.

"It's the pooka!" cried Kathryn. *"Go!* Go to the bridge, *now!"*

The group ran towards the Devil's Bridge, the mighty Celtic tiger pooka wrestled a goblin and then another two to the ground, allowing them to escape.

Maryanne, Leesa, and Oona scurried across the Devil's Bridge.

"Hurry!" cried Cyril to Carmel and Kathryn, still kicking a few angry goblins off them.

Queen Maeve rode her thunderous bulls down to the Devil's Bridge. Then, Kathryn watched Carmel and Cyril sway across the Devil's Bridge before following after them.

It just so happened that the meanest and largest of all the goblins with wretched gray teeth and a gruesome gory face, hopped in front of her as she made her way across the dangerous bridge. Kathryn stopped; the snarling goblin blocked her way. Turning around, she saw Queen Maeve advance forward, ready to cross the bridge. There was no way out!

The goblin snickered and shook the bridge side to side, causing Kathryn to lose her footing. Her feet slid between two planks and she became stuck between the two wooden boards. The hissing goblin's eyes flickered with madness mocking her, inching closer and closer before reaching his warped hand towards her slender neck.

A light then flickered in his eyes. He flinched, and soon his back burned with a searing pain. He howled like a banshee in the night and peered over his shoulder.

And there, at the other end of the Devil's Bridge was Mother Superior, standing there with all the Sisters of the True Cross around her. In her hands she held the vibrant Celtic Cross the monk had given the Sisters years before. Frozen in pain, the fierce goblin looked at Queen Maeve, and then he fixed his eyes on Mother Superior, and then back at Kathryn.

He knew not what to do. His back burning and writhing in pain from the emerald Celtic Cross, he knew only one way to relieve his anguish, so he leapt off the bridge, down to the mysterious ravine below.

Mother Superior steadied her eyes on Queen Maeve with her army of seething goblins and brute bulls, her nostrils flaring and her eyes squinting. I believe it was the harsh look on Mother Superior's face along with the Celtic Cross she held in her hand that made the mighty Queen Maeve, the Warrior Queen, not cross the Devil's Bridge that night. And so, she turned around and rode back up to the monk's cave with her white and brown bull along with her decaying army of goblins.

Was Queen Maeve defeated that cold and bitter night? Absolutely not! But, I do suppose her ego was knocked down a few notches. However, we all have to remember her power is stronger when she is in her own realm, you remember, in the realm of the faeries... or as we like to say, in Aählynéé.

♦ CHAPTER TWENTY ♦
KENDRYCK'S SECRET

Oh it was a sight to be seen, the group standing in Mother Superior's office after that mess. Now, wouldn't you know, she never raised her voice once to the girls or Cyril. She didn't have to, for they knew that they had crossed the line and they were surely done in.

"Miss Murphy, here we meet again..." said Mother Superior sternly, standing austerely behind the emerald Celtic Cross shimmering in her eyes.

"Yes, Mother," replied Kathryn.

"Sister Mary Martha, how many rules of St. Bernadette's did these girls and Cyril break tonight?" asked Mother Superior turning to Sister Mary Martha.

"I imagine all of them!" noted Sister Mary Martha, her lips pursed together like a shriveled up like a raisin.

"How many...?" repeated Mother Superior.

"Four, Mother!" hissed Sister Mary Martha. "If you ask me, the devil had carried them away!"

"Four rules... Miss Murphy... four rules all in one night!" scorned Mother Superior. "Would you care to go up to the bell tower and break all five of them? I believe it would be a new record, indeed, it would. And of course, you'll have another story to tell."

"No, Mother," answered Kathryn.

"It seems like all fun and games to you Miss Murphy, for this world you seek," said Mother Superior as the emerald Celtic Cross dangled around her bosom, a soothing warm halo emanating from inside it. "But do you really want to know the unknown? There is a reason it is hidden away from God's children and I'm afraid once you cross that line you'll never be able to come back, though you'll want to, Miss Murphy. Now, I need you to go up stairs and pack your things. Your time at St. Bernadette's is officially over!"

"What?" cried Kathryn.

"Mother, you are being too harsh," said Sister Joan.

"No ceremony, no graduation. Miss Carmel your position has now been terminated as well," said Mother Superior, picking up a sticky ink blotter and stamping it down a piece of stale parchment. "Oona and Leesa, since this is a first offense for you two, I will deal with you differently. Maryanne you are to leave the school as well and return back to your home. Mr. Crowe, your laundry service will no longer be needed. One of the other Sisters will take on your duties," A few of the Sisters silently backed away from Mother Superior when they heard her say laundry duty. "Captain Seaneen has been contacted and the ferry will be here to take you, Miss Maryanne, and Miss Carmel in the morning."

Indeed, it was a terrible fright that came to Kathryn as she began to pack her things along with Carmel and Maryanne. There was no need in arguing with Mother Superior, even Queen Maeve the fiercest Warrior Queen of all, didn't try to argue with Mother Superior, why would they? It comes to mind now, who truly is a Warrior Queen? Mother Superior or Queen Maeve? Oh, such thoughts are too cumbersome on the mind and must be whisked away!

"Sorry you have to leave school because of me," said Kathryn, tossing in her assortment of clothing she had collected over the last few years.

"Don't be!" said Maryanne, unloading her clothing into a stained suitcase on her bed, "Don't you see, they're real! Faeries are real, Kat! No one believed it, but you did and you proved it to everyone they do exist! So, we have to go back to Drogheda, but to see a faery and to be chased by them! That will last me a lifetime!"

"It seems like the Sisters knew about the faeries," said Kathryn peculiarly.

"I think these nuns know a lot more than they let on," said Carmel, barging through the door once again. "Let's get out of here before I start to cry."

There was a soft wind blowing off the sea the next morning. The three girls stood upon the small creaky dock on Inishmara along with Mother Superior and Sister Gwen. In the distance, a wee white spot emerged on the horizon, which grew closer and closer with each squawk of the gannets as the wind blustered around them.

Kathryn's head lay low to her chin. She felt horrible for what she did, but at the same time, she felt it had to be done. Her ears chimed with the ever so faint sound of bagpipes bellowing from the other side of Inishmara. Her head tilted up and her eyes squinted. She could see the shadowy silhouette of what she assumed to be a warrior bard, playing out his melody from the highest peak, his lonely notes lingering on the soft wind, floating down to her ears.

Sister Gwen cradled her hand on Kathryn's shoulder, "Don't worry child, you will see me again…"

"I do hope so, Sister Gwen," said Kathryn looking into her kind eyes.

"I know so," she replied with jubilance as 'The Crone II' scooted in beside the dock. "Just remember to use your inspiration!"

Captain Seaneen fastened the boat to the dock with hearty ropes and dropped the walkway, "How are you girls?" he asked as Carmel and Maryanne loaded themselves onto the ferry with their heads as low as their knees, Kathryn soon followed on board.

"Just a second, Miss Murphy," said Mother Superior holding a pile of papers. "Here, this is your homework for the last day." Mother Superior then lowered her voice, for only her ears to hear. "We're all on different sacred paths, Miss Murphy, leading us to the same destination. Just make sure you're going in the right direction, child."

Mother Superior then backed away and stood there firmly on the dock, like an anchor on a boat. Sister Gwen waved her tiny, delicate hands back and forth and sent the girls away for their next journey.

'The Crone II' spewed out a few bursts of dark smoke as Captain Seaneen fired up the engines and pulled away from the dock. "Not as good as 'Crone I,' but she'll do!" he said as they chugged away on the high seas.

The girls waved goodbye to the Sisters, while the Captain handed them their orange plastic puke bags for the return trip home.

"Let the spirit inspire you!" called out Sister Gwen as the wee ferry chugged away back to Mulleam's Ferry Crossing.

'The Crone II' jerked and jeered a bit less when the girls sat down below deck. This time, there were long wooden benches lining the lower deck. Carmel's face looked indifferent as she played around with her plastic bag, trying to open it. Maryanne continued to read Laurel's journal and Kathryn closed her eyes replaying Queen Maeve's face in her head.

"I don't know about you," said Carmel putting her bag down. "But, that's was bloody brilliant!"

Maryanne and Kathryn laughed.

Kathryn opened her eyes and said, "It was - wasn't it?"

"Not only did we see three faeries, but Queen Maeve and those wretched snotty goblins!"

"I think they were some sort of pooka possessed by Queen Maeve, to do her bidding," said Maryanne as she flipped to a page in the journal. "Says here," pointing to a picture of pookas, "Pookas not only can take the shape of an eagle, rabbit, goat, Celtic tiger, horse, and goblins, but when provoked can be possessed and the master can control how they shape shift."

"A pooka?" said Kathryn shocked. "But my pooka was good and better looking."

"I think anything is possible in the realm of the faeries. You just don't know what you're ever going to get. That's a bunch you can never let your guard down on, that's for sure," muttered Carmel.

"It says here," said Maryanne turning to another page in the journal. "The Raven's Gate is controlled by the teine criostal ..."

"How?" asked Kathryn.

Maryanne cleared her throat and read out loud, "When one possesses the teine criostal, they possess all of Aählynéé. All ways in, out, and within are controlled by whoever bears the teine criostal."

"Whoa!" said Carmel.

"Really?" asked Kathryn looking at the journal. "I can't believe that..."

"You just saw the scariest looking Warrior Queen escape out of a portal tomb, attack us with decaying and decrepit goblins," said Carmel, looking at Maryanne with a vile look in her eye. "OK! Pookas... goblins... whatever... and you can't believe that the Fire Crystal... I mean the teine criostal which is the sole source of all power in Aählynéé, can control the gateways in and out of its world?"

"Well..." said Kathryn quietly to herself, pausing she fiddled through the papers Mother Superior gave her. "I can believe it, but sometimes, the first time you hear something that defies all rational logic, it throws you off a bit."

"I can see that," replied Carmel.

Kathryn pulled out two cream-colored papers with a golden seal pressed into them. "What's this?" she asked bewildered and examined both pieces of parchment, it read:

St. Bernadette's Diploma of Accomplishment.

"I don't believe it!"

"What's that?" asked Maryanne.

Kathryn held up the papers to Maryanne and Carmel and said, "It's our Diplomas Maryanne!"

"Let me see," said Maryanne stretching over Carmel's lap and pressing her hands on Carmel's thighs. "I always knew Mother Superior was a softy!"

"I'll tell you who's not a softy," grunted Carmel to Maryanne. "You! Get off of my lap! You weigh a ton!"

The ferry chugged closer to the main land, a few feet away from the weathered docks at Mulleam's Ferry Crossing. Maryanne lifted up Laurel's cracked leather journal and handed it to Kathryn. "This is your Mother's," she said kindly. "Thank you for letting me read it, but I have to give it back now."

The ferry jolted as it slid against the dock.

"I'm going to miss you two the most of all!" said Kathryn with tears in her eyes.

"You've been the bestest friend anyone could hope for, Kathryn," said Maryanne, throwing her arms around Kathryn tightly. "And if you want, I'll go help you find, Billy."

"Thanks Mar," replied Kathryn. "But, there are a few things I've got to do when I get home that I need to do by myself."

"You won't forget about me?" asked Maryanne.

"Never," replied Kathryn. "And when I find a way into Aählyéé, I'll make sure I come back and bring you there myself!"

"Well, you're not gonna forget about me too, are ya now?" said Carmel. "I couldn't let the two of you go gallivanting off into Aählyéé without me!"

"I'll come and get you too, Carmel," answered Kathryn.

"Now, that's better!" said Carmel, opening her arms out wide. "Now, come here and give me some love!" Carmel and Kathryn embraced, only to have Maryanne wrap her arms around the both of them.

"Alright, already," sniffed Carmel. "Enough of this lovey-dovey stuff! You've got a Fire Crystal to find, a portal to cross, and a brother to find, who in our hearts isn't dead, just yet! Settle this thing once and for all!"

"I will," said Kathryn hopefully. "I'll find out what became of Billy!"

"And don't be lettin' no Queen Maeve get in your way!" added Carmel.

"Be well, Kathryn," said Maryanne.

"Be the Warrior Queen!" said Carmel, raising her fist up firmly in the air.

"And Indiana Jones Apprentice!" added Maryanne, patting Kathryn lightly on the shoulder.

"I will," answered Kathryn. "Good bye!"

Carmel and Maryanne strolled down the windy dock with their hair flapping in the wind as the squawking seagulls danced overhead. Kathryn was left standing alone. She gazed around Mulleam's Ferry Crossing, watching the metal rope on the flagpole still clanking constantly with the wind, while the iron cannon sat in silence with a pile of cannonballs next to it. She did not know how she was going to return home nor who would come and pick her up.

Then she saw him, and by all means, it wasn't Pete the cab driver that drove Kathryn from Ballyrun. No, it was an older fuzzy bearded, festering sort of fellow who dashed out from a bright yellow sedan, which had round swirls painted on it with every color of the rainbow. Kathryn watched the chubby man wearing a purple headband, a fringed leather vest, and granny glasses trot over to her.

"Are you?" he said, out of the side of his mouth. He then pulled out a piece of paper from his paint-spattered trouser's pocket, opened it up, and said, "Kat'ryn Murphy?"

"Yes," she replied, eyeing his wide belly that stuck out like a water balloon.

"Me name's Dermott," he said, outstretching his hand to shake hers.

"Good to meet you, Dermott," she replied.

"They sent me to take you back to," Dermot paused for a moment reading the little piece of paper in his hand again. His long frizzy hair blew into his eyes along with a few long wiry braids from the back of his head. "Ah, right, Ballyrun! Let me take your bags."

Dermot snatched up Kathryn's new duffle bag and scooted over to his eccentric car. Kathryn slid into the back seat of the car covered in vivid flowers painted on the ceiling. Shiny plastic beads and flowers hung from every known surface of the car. Dermot plopped into the driver's seat and revved the car up.

"Aye... you've been to Inishmara now, haven't ya?" he asked, peering into the rear view window, which had a large silver peace symbol dangling from it.

"Yes, I have," replied Kathryn. She felt a bumpy object underneath her rump, so she reached down and pulled out a pretty blue button that had an orange bear dancing on it, holding a red rose.

"Now do tell me..." said Dermott eagerly. "But, did ya happen to see anything?"

"Perhaps," replied Kathryn, watching the rolling hills splattered with white sheep painted with hot pink butts.

"I's knew it! I's knew it!" he cried with a crooked smile, showing he had three teeth missing. "That island is from the realm of the faeries it is! It is one giant portal into the unknown."

"Perhaps..." she replied, gazing out the clear window.

Dermott made a right and drove down the long and winding country lane that once had a dark lone rider galloping on it. *I wonder who that rider was?* she thought.

"Did ya... did ya go there?" he asked impatiently.

Kathryn cracked a smile. She was happy to watch the grazing cattle and fluffy white sheep with blue butts, the stone lined hills and roads, the random Church with its towering steeple, its yard filled with lonely tombstones, yelping dogs, stone towers, and those sheep with purple butts as well.

"I said," repeated Dermott louder. "Did ya go there?"

"Go where?" asked Kathryn, pulling her away from her daydream.

"Into the realm of the faeries," he said anxiously. "The faeries... into Aählynéé... did ya go there now, love?"

"No," said Kathryn calmly.

"What a crime!" said Dermot, driving past Loch Dorcha. "So close, If I were to go there meself, I'd go and talk to every different type of faery there was now and document it all! Yes, I would now... I would!"

"What if they don't want to talk to you?" asked Kathryn, trying to be the devil's advocate.

"*What?*" he said alarmingly, his eyes bulging out behind his round lavender spectacles, "I'd make 'em talk to me! I would! But you do have to be careful now, I agree, with ya on that one. Faeries have been said to maim men passing in the night. They've said that all right! The faeries, they can curse a man walking down the road in the dead of night they say, make them become twisted, distorted, paralyzed, eyes could go crossed, blind, or even make the poor victim deaf!"

"Why?" she replied bewildered. "Why would a faery do that?"

"Don't know," replied Dermott. "But it's been known to happen."

The psychedelic car made another right and Arthur's Seat was now in view. Kathryn rubbed her eyes in disbelief. It was larger than she had thought it was. Somewhere, somehow she needed to find that Fire Crystal and to make her way through that Mountain once again.

The cab rolled into Ballyrun in front of Flannery's.

"You can stop here," said Kathryn decisively.

"Are you sure Miss?" asked Dermott stopping the car and pulling out the crinkled piece of paper. "It says to take you to the cottage at the bottom of the Mountain."

"This is fine," said Kathryn hopping out of the car. Dermott took out her bags and placed them on the ground. Kathryn outstretched her hand, "It was nice meeting you, Dermott. I'll try and let you know if those faeries are evil like you said, one day!"

"It's been a pleasure," replied Dermott. He hopped back into his sparkly car and sped down the road.

It had seemed like eons ago that Kathryn stood in front of Flannery's, the sign: *Flannery's: Where Great Minds Come to Meet* still hung beside the door. Kathryn pushed through the front door and the wee bell chimed.

"Kathryn! It is you!" said Fiona fiddling around behind the bar. "Welcome back!"

"Ahhh... that's my girl!" said Seamus hugging Kathryn. "Look at you! A grown woman! I'm so happy to see ya!"

Peg stood up from her chair and said, "Come here! It's my turn now!" Peg held Kathryn tightly, almost squeezing the stuffing out of her. "So happy you're home again in good 'ol Ballyrun!"

"Have you seen the new jukebox, Kathryn?" interrupted Fiona as she shined up the colorful jukebox hanging on the back wall. "I told you all about it! Just had it fixed! Seems like someone was putting in one pence coins in it and broke the machine! It's as good as new now!"

"Aye, that was me," said George honestly, hovering over the snooker table eyeing up his next shot.

"George!" said Seamus, laughing uncomfortably. "We don't know if it was you or not."

"Aye! Seamus, it was me," said George his hand trembling as he took a sip of his dark brew. "Aye, I-I likes playing Garry Glitter! I do... I do..."

The back door burst open as Ian and Sheliza strolled into the pub. Sheliza's hair glistened like molten gold down her shoulders, while Ian's face was splattered with bumpy red pimples.

"You?" said Kathryn coldly to Sheliza, "What are you doing at Flannery's?"

"What a nice welcome," replied Sheliza smoothly. "Don't be silly Kathryn. Many things have changed since you left, Ian and I are the closest of friends now. He tells me all about his trips up Arthur's Seat. Seems you too made it pretty far up with all the stories I hear!"

"Did-did ya... did ya find 'em, Kat? Did ya find Billy?" asked George, his head bobbed to his right side, causing his thick glasses to slide down his nose.

"No..." replied Kathryn sadly. "George, I've been away at school."

"She-She-liza told us, you found a way into 'da Mountain... she did! Is-is that true?" asked George excitedly with a grin on his face.

"George," said Kathryn softly, sitting down beside him and placing her hand on his back, "I did, but that was a long time ago..."

"So, you did find it!" exclaimed Sheliza, her eyes enlarged like golf balls. "The Raven's Gate! I knew it! I knew you found the Raven's Gate! I just knew you did! You must show it to me!"

"No, I won't Sheliza," replied Kathryn curtly. "That was a long time ago."

"Did you see Aählyéé?" she asked impulsively. "Did you make it to the other side?"

"I wanna go!" cried George longingly, lowering his head to his chin. "Kat! I do - I wanna go! I wanna see Billy again! I do!"

Eddie leapt to his feet; he pointed to himself and nodded his head up and down.

"Aye, Eddie - Eddie wants ta go too!" said George.

"George, Billy is dead," explained Peg.

"Noooo, no, he's not," said George curling his head down then pointing to Eddie. "Eddie - Eddie saw him... he did – he did!"

"That's - that's impossible, George," argued Kathryn.

"Saw him where?" asked Marie, her face had lost all its joy.

"In 'da fire..." replied George, "he saw him in 'da fire..."

"What fire, George?" asked Seamus. "Tell us where you saw him?"

"That fire," said George, pointing to the bright peat fire burning in the hearth. "I saw him too... I did-I did."

"Fire?" repeated Kathryn, bending down to the hearth and peered in. "This fire?"

"Aye..." replied George his torso now rocking back and forth. "I–I saw him in there. I did, I tell you! He looked scared, Billy."

"If he's there, trapped in Aählynéé and you let him rot there..." muttered Sheliza. "It's all your fault!"

"Excuse me?" said Kathryn with a hint of annoyance in her voice.

"Don't you see," said Sheliza observantly, "the only way is the Raven's Gate! It's the only way into Aählynéé! Where magic and power are at your beck and call and where men like George and Eddie are knights, riding into the sunset! Isn't that right, George?" Sheliza's eyes slanted towards Laurel's journal sticking out from Kathryn's backpack.

"Aye!" said George, holding up his arm with an imaginary sword, "I-I'm a knight! George 'da Dragon Tamer!!!"

Eddie grinned ear to ear, while Marie looked sad, scribbling on a piece of paper.

Peg slammed down her fist on to the table causing the sugar bowl to spill out and said, "Stop this insanity, Sheliza!"

"I-I-I wanna go..." whimpered George. "I-I-I wanna be a knight!"

"It's not even that, Peg," argued Sheliza. "Ian told me all about Aählynéé and what is going on the other side of Arthur's Seat!"

"I's did," mumbled Ian as his left eye twitched wildly.

"Oh, for heaven's sake!" said Peg disturbed.

"He's mad!" stated Seamus.

"There are healing powers there," said Sheliza single-mindedly. "It's the land of eternal youth, you know Tír na nÓg, think of what could be done for Marie?"

"Are you thick?" questioned Seamus pointing to Ian. "I think you've been hanging around this one far too long and he's rubbed all of his madness on you, Sheliza!"

"Seamus!" scolded Fiona.

"Then tell me, Seamus," said Sheliza craftily. "If you could do everything you possibly could do for your daughter, wouldn't you?"

"You're a right witch! Aren't you now?" snapped Peg cradling wee little Marie in her arms.

"Even her friend, John died," proclaimed Sheliza. "Shouldn't she be able to go into this magical world so she can find a cure?"

"Don't test me Sheliza!" warned Seamus.

"I-I-I don't wanna die, Seamus!" cried George slamming his leg onto the floor, he nestled his head into his arm and began rocking back and forth harder and harder, wailing, "I-I-I don't... I-I-I don't wanna die!"

"You're not going to die, George!" stated Seamus.

"I will not have this anymore!" interjected Peg. "Even if Aählyneé was real and Marie, George, and Eddie could benefit from it! Just the thought demeans them. They may have limitations in our world, Sheliza, but they are in no way, one bit less human! They can give and receive the same amount of love that you or I can. And they most certainly deserve the same respect. I will not have them think that they are less perfect or less worthy than you or I are..."

"I-I-I... don't... I-I-I don't..." whimpered George, his body swaying back and forth as if he was in a rocking chair, "wanna die!"

"See what you've done!" said Kathryn furiously; rubbing George's back to calm him down. She then turned to Sheliza. "Sheliza, you're still the same heartless selfish girl that was here so many years ago. I guess some things do remain the same, don't they?" Kathryn hugged George tightly. "It's OK, George. Sheliza tends to say the wrong things, all the time!"

"You are twisted girl," said Seamus.

Peg, Marie, and Eddie all went over to console George as he wailed over and over again, *'I don't wanna die.'*

It was just about that moment when Sheliza saw her chance. She shifted her arm out ever so slightly, just when they all weren't looking, pinched Laurel's journal and slipped it into her oversized magenta purse.

"Come on, Ian. Let's get away from here," said Sheliza. Turning to Kathryn, she smirked as she exited out the door with Ian wrapped around her. "Well, it's not much of a homecoming when one has no home to go to!"

Kathryn ignored Sheliza and focused on calming poor George down, who was still beside himself with fear.

The long walk home to the wee cottage below Arthur's Seat was a lonely one. Once she had traveled that road with Billy. Now it was just herself and the noisy sheep that dotted the passing fields. *What if he really is in Aählynéé?* she thought. She remembered what Maryanne had said about the Fire Crystal. When one possesses the teine criostal, they possess all of Aählyneé. *I need that Fire Crystal back! And I know exactly who will know where it is!*

She hesitated walking up the path to the cottage. It looked surreal to her, just sitting there, as it always has never changing, except for the extra layer of muck that covered the front door and the new stone wall with white daisies popping out. She took a deep breath, turned the handle on the old weathered red door, and entered into the main living area.

Grandpa was sitting at the aged, pine table with his hand on his forehead. For a moment, he appeared to be frail and weary to her. He raised his blue eyes to see her.

"Don't be gettin' too comfortable girl," he said agitated. "The Lott's just stopped by 'nd they're taken 'da house 'nd all 'da land!"

Kathryn looked at her Grandfather, the man who had sent her away for over five years. She cringed for a moment realizing all the anger that had built up inside of her. It hurt even more because it didn't seem to matter that she was home. He was more worried about the land and the house. She took a deep breath and let all her anger go; she needed to focus on why she was there and what she needed to do.

"Where's the Fire Crystal, Grandpa?" demanded Kathryn. Something inside her knew that he would know - he had to know!

"Geezzz... Didn't 'cha hear what I said?" grumbled Grandpa his eyes as red as tomatoes. "'Da house is gone! We're homeless girl! When I get me hands on that rancid wee leprechaun, I'm gonna..."

"I don't care, Grandpa," stated Kathryn. "Maybe if you cared more about your family than your possessions or your coin purse, maybe, maybe, I would care, but, I don't!"

"I don't care? I don't care?" cried Grandpa with his voice rising higher and higher. "Girl, I care more than 'yas think. You're ungrateful that's what you are!"

"You abandoned me, Grandpa!" griped Kathryn. "You threw me away, to be taken care of by some strangers. I'd say you don't care!"

Grandpa sighed and paused in quiet reflection. He bit his lower lip and peered straight into Kathryn's grassy, green eyes. "Sit! Sit down, girl," he said genially. Kathryn looked at him with spite. "Please... please, sit down. There're a few things I need 'ta tell 'yas." Kathryn seated herself down on one of the blonde chairs next to Grandpa. He continued, "You've got 'ta understand, I had 'ta send 'yas away!"

"Why?" she huffed, crossing her arms across her chest.

"Because, after ya touched the darn Fire Crystal they knew, don't 'cha see that?"

She examined his face, his eyes were now white, his face soft and cheery; after five years he hadn't aged much. In fact, he looked a bit younger.

"Who are they?" asked Kathryn, drilling him. "Knew what?"

"That 'da crystal was touched by you!" he said exhaustedly. His shoulders slumped down and he sighed wearily. "'Da Danyär are its protectors from ancient times, they sense it all 'da time, always searchin' for it. 'Ta join it together. You see, 'da stranger is part of 'da Danyär, 'da group who have sworn an oath 'ta protect 'da crystal and bring it back 'ta Nezroth." He paused for a moment, pursing his pudgy lips, and took a deep breath. "And since you are of royal blood, 'da crystal will do your bidding, and not theirs."

"Wait! Wait! *What?* What royal blood?" she said baffled. "You can't be serious? I'm from Brooklyn!"

"Yes, Kathryn," replied Grandpa. "You and Billy are of nobility."

"How can that be?"

Grandpa gazed down to the table, his fingers drummed on the soft pinewood. He cleared his throat and then grumbled a bit. He raised himself up slowing from his chair and he flared out his chest boldly pushing it forward. Kathryn gawked at him with her mouth open wide, for the eccentric old man was changing before her eyes into a strong and powerful man. Grandpa held his chin up high and said proudly, "For I am King Kendryck!"

Kathryn's jaw dropped down to the floor and her eyes grew to the size of ping-pong balls. She couldn't believe what he had just said.

"No! You're mad!" she said in utter disbelief. "You'd have to be a thousand years old! No, it can't be true!"

"Yes, yes it is true I'm afraid," said Grandpa, strolling around the cottage as if he was a young man; he needed no cane, he had no ailments, it was all just an act. Even his voice had changed as he pronounced his words more clearly. It was as if the man she thought she knew disappeared and was replaced by a changeling. "You see, I needed to keep you safe from them... from the Danyär. I myself escaped many, many moons ago, found the love of me life, and married. Had your mother who was such a blessing, but then she had to go off gallivanting up into Aählyneé on one of her crazy adventures, gone for years she was. When she finally returned the last time, she was pregnant with the two of you. She was barely here for a moment and then she was off to New York, always running away that one. I myself have been sneaking into Aählyneé searching for Billy, but I'm not as strong as I used to be... and I need your help to find him..."

"So, he is alive?" asked Kathryn amazed.

"Yes."

"I don't understand. Why didn't you go back to Aählyneé and stay there?" asked Kathryn, who was still in a state of complete and utter shock. Billy was alive and they were both of noble birth! "You would have been King, instead of a poor farmer."

"I didn't want to go back, it was too lonely being King," he said sorrowfully. "When I had your Mum and Grandmother about me, I had more than any magic could give me. But then when they were both gone, I grew accustomed to being alone and pushed everyone away. I don't want to be alone anymore, Kathryn. Will you help me find him? Will you help me go back to Aählyneé?"

"But Glubgrub couldn't find him," argued Kathryn.

"Who's Glubgrub?" said Grandpa confused.

"A woodland faery, I made a faery door! We figured out how to make one from Mom's journal," she said looking into her bag, but not finding any journal in there. "Where is it? But then..."

"But then what?" asked Grandpa, "go on, girl. What'd he say?"

"He couldn't find him at all," said Kathryn hopelessly. "But worse than that, we awoke Queen Maeve!"

"Queen Maeve?" shrieked Grandpa. "Oh no, did she cross 'da bridge?"

"No," answered Kathryn. "The nuns stopped her with the emerald Celtic Cross and Mother Superior's powerful glare."

"What'd she look like?" asked Grandpa curiously.

"She was *HUGE!*" said Kathryn animatedly, throwing her arms above her head, "covered in thick fur and leather, spikes, the skull of a tiger on her head! She was pretty scary! Wait a second, you said the Danyär were after me after I touched the Fire Crystal?"

"Yes," replied Grandpa.

"Well then," she asked candidly. "Why was one of them in town looking for me and Billy?"

"I'm afraid that when your mother was in Aählyneé, she had a run in with them," answered Grandpa. "I believe that's why she moved to Brooklyn to be as far away from them as possible. I'm not quite sure how they knew about the two of you, but she must've had something on her that made them chase her. When the three Nights of the Faeries comes, the veil between our two worlds gets lifted and all faeries can come in and out as often as they like."

"Well, what about two weeks after or before that?" asked Kathryn, still puzzled. "Can the veil be lifted?"

"No," said Grandpa decisively, "absolutely not!"

"Well, something happened," stated Kathryn, "because I had one of those Danyär's chasing me all the way to Mulleam's Ferry Crossing!"

"That's absurd!" said Grandpa scratching his fluffy white head of hair. "It can't be done!"

"It's true," said Kathryn.

"The Danyär stayed in our realm after the three Nights of the Faeries?" said Grandpa flabbergasted.

"Yup!"

"What sort of magic can allow them to stay longer?" he asked shocked and began walking around the room in circles.

Kathryn watched his face fall. He was now so removed from Aählyneé that he did not know what type of magic could bring faeries into our mortal world, outside of the three Nights of the Faeries veil. *How could he possibly know where Billy is when he doesn't understand Aählyneé's magic?* she thought. She needed to find Billy on her own and she needed to do it now!

"Now," she said forcefully, "where's the Fire Crystal Grandpa?"

"She has it..." he mumbled still in disbelief that the faeries could keep crossing over the threshold between our world and their own, "up on 'da Mountain."

"Who is she?" asked Kathryn.

"The one who fixed your leg," said Grandpa wearily, "one of the nine maidens of the Otherworld; she is the guardian of the Raven's Gate and of Arthur's Seat."

"She's kinda old to be a guardian," said Kathryn with a note of sarcasm to her voice.

"Oh by day she's a gruesome old hag," said Grandpa, "but by night, she turns into a beautiful wailing banshee."

"She was the banshee?" blared out Kathryn.

"Oh yes," said Grandpa a matter-of-factly. "She was sending you an omen that night. But, luckily she didn't hit you with her silver comb! Or perhaps one of us may not be here any longer, but enough of that! We need to rescue Billy!"

Kathryn's face flushed red and filled with anger. Grandpa had hidden so much from her and Billy. Why didn't he trust them? Or even warn them of the impending danger? He just filled their heads with stories. Kathryn huffed and then marched over to her Grandmother's portrait, yanked it open, reached in, and swiped the cursed necklace.

"So," said Grandpa watching her pack food into her backpack, "you'll be helping me to bring him back?"

Kathryn then climbed up the rickety ladder and snatched her book *The Legends of Arthur's Seat* by Peoke Thumbdill. "I don't think so, I'm doing this by myself," she said grimly as she shoved the book into her backpack. "I should've done this the day you told me he was gone."

"Kat!" cried Grandpa frantically, watching her open the weathered front door, "you can't do this by yourself!"

Kathryn turned to him, looked him in his crystal blue eyes and said, "Watch me!" She slammed the door and then stormed down the road.

"Kathryn!" called Grandpa. "Come back! I need your help!"

♦ CHAPTER TWENTY-ONE ♦
FINALLY, FOUND WHAT I'M LOOKING FOR

Indeed Kathryn Murphy was from the royal bloodline of King Kendryck, but at that moment there was nothing more important to her than to find her brother, Billy. She leapt onto Sheba's back, placing her feet snuggly into the leather stirrups. Sheba then bolted back on her hind legs into the cool air.

"Enough of that now, Sheba, settle down," said Kathryn, stroking her slender neck. She then thrashed her heels into her torso. *"Hah!"* she cried and off they galloped, riding high up the slopes of Arthur's Seat. Kathryn whispered in Sheba's ear, "I know you know the way, Sheba, let's go back to that shack."

Sheba pranced up the Mountain with the strength of a hundred horses, while her mane blew softly in the wind as she sprung over heavy rocks and wide ditches. Higher and higher she climbed up the steep slopes of Arthur's Seat without fear or hesitation.

"Seems you and Grandpa have found a bit of the fountain of youth?" laughed Kathryn as they trotted rapidly through the emerald tunnel and up to the old shack. Kathryn promptly dismounted and tied Sheba to a nearby post.

Then she very carefully pushed open the creaky door, almost causing the rusty hinge to break off. And what she saw made her eyes bulge out, like someone squeezing a water balloon. Immediately, she observed the changes on the inside of the aged shack. There were no more sticky cobwebs or ratty old chairs, the bookshelves were straightened, and the random squirming bugs in glass jars were organized and labeled. One jar which contained a million hairy, green squirming worms was labeled lazzôars. The place was clean and tidy and in some ways, it sparkled a bit. The back door flew open, causing Kathryn to jerk unexpectedly. The cloaked woman appeared, floating towards her as if she was floating on air. Slowly, she lowered her hood. To Kathryn's surprise, her face was soft and beautiful like an angel. She was no longer the deformed old hag that had told her and Billy the story of Aählynéé, no, her cheeks were warm and rosy, and her smile warmed Kathryn's heart.

"You want it back now? Don't you dear?" she said, her emerald eyes sparkled with excitement as she strolled over to the cauldron in the center of the room. "And you want to know where your brother is? Don't ya, dear?"

"Yes, I want the crystal back!" demanded Kathryn, not sure if she should be annoyed with the woman for having taken the Fire Crystal away from her.

"Awww... hush now, dear," she chirped, her wavy curls cascaded down into the cauldron, just barely touching its misty, hot brew. "Before you get upset, I wanted you to know, I needed the crystal for a few things."

"Where is it?" asked Kathryn, stepping towards the steamy cauldron.

"What's the magic word?" she giggled, waving her hand over the cauldron.

Kathryn threw her an angry look.

"Well, you couldn't have taken it with you anyway," she said and then lowered her voice to a deep, low whisper. "For you cannot take it past the boundaries of Aählynéé."

The cauldron bubbled up like an erupting volcano, swirls of mist formed high above it, creating a dark puffy cloud. The smoke faded and a bright red orb emerged from behind it. It hovered silently over the cauldron as if waiting for its next command.

"That's not the Fire Crystal!" snapped Kathryn.

"It's inside," she said, waving her delicate fingers at the red orb. "You have to ask it a question."

"Where's Billy?" said Kathryn loudly, and a bit annoyed.

The red orb began to rotate counter clockwise, while a dark smoldering plume of smoke billowed up from inside its glass-like walls. Kathryn's eyes began to sparkle as she watched baby flames lick up from inside its shell. Soon, a hazy picture began to materialize from within the crimson orb.

There in a dense forest, a silver waterfall crashed down from a hundred feet onto seven large stones into a river. Standing at the river's edge was a slim, young boy. It was Billy. He cradled a bow in his arm, while a barrel of arrows leaned against a nearby rock. Behind him was a thatched mud hut built with dirty stones, twigs, and dirt.

A hazy mist then blurred the vision. The red orb shook wildly, cracked open, and out dropped the Fire Crystal into the palm of Kathryn's hand. The Fire Crystal pulsed with a soft heartbeat. A soft tingling of goose bumps scurried up her arm and then throughout her whole body. Carefully, she bound a leather band securely around the Fire Crystal and hung it around her neck just like a necklace.

Suddenly, Kathryn felt the cursed necklace in her left pocket begin to lurch and jiggle around as if it were possessed. It took to flight swiftly, flying out of her pocket and into the air, slowly hovering before her eyes. And then strangely enough, the red orb, which was still open, swallowed it whole.

"Hey that's mine!" cried Kathryn, reaching for the necklace as it melted into the crimson orb. Its shiny outer casing then molded shut and the cursed necklace was no more.

"Sorry dear, those are the rules of the orbs! Ask a question and it will take something of value from you," said the cloaked woman. "Though, you do get whatever's inside it. So, I suppose that could be good too."

Kathryn didn't waste any time exiting the shack swiftly. She hurtled herself onto Sheba's muscular back, wrenched on the reins, and then dashed fearlessly up the hillside. The refreshing ride up the Mountain was not as long as she had remembered it to be with Billy. She passed the lonely dead tree markers, which lined the way to the Raven's Gate while rocky cliffs and sheer drops crashed down below her into gorges.

She turned around for a moment, looking over her shoulder. In the far distance, she could make out what appeared to be Sheliza and Ian climbing up the steep slopes of Arthur's Seat. Not far behind them were two other shadowy figures trailing far off near the Mountain's grassy edge.

Kathryn clicked her heels once again into Sheba's thick body and they galloped further up into the crags amongst the dense high trees, whose leaves seemed to whisper in the velvety breeze. The land cleared away and soon only bristly, purple heather bushes popped up between the rocks as she drew closer to the Raven's Gate.

In a small grassy clearing near the one tree hill, she dismounted from Sheba and patted her rump. "You're free to go!" she said.

And with that, Sheba raced back down the slopes of Arthur's Seat. Kathryn watched the white horse ride into the thick trees until she was consumed by their shadows.

The Fire Crystal flickered with the day's light as it rested tenderly around her neck. Kathryn scaled her way back up to the one tree hill, snatched up the weathered rope that she had lassoed around the last tree marker over five years ago, and hoisted herself up. It didn't take long for Kathryn to climb up the steep hill with her new upper body strength and rope skills, thanks to Sister Martin Marie. She easily shimmied herself back up and landed in the gorge before the Raven's Gate.

Standing before the great seven stones of the Raven's Gate, she heard a rustling noise coming from the crooked, gnarled tree above her. She twirled around; the seven red-winged ravens glided down from the clear blue sky, perched themselves on the tree's branches high above her, and peered down as if they were saying hello. The Fire Crystal burned brightly and a low pulverizing sound rippled against her eardrums. She whipped around; slowly the seven stones spiraled apart, creating a wide opening into the Raven's Gate.

Kathryn stepped into the dark mysterious labyrinth once again and soon was soon shrouded in complete darkness. Moving forward, her flashlight illuminated the way as she passed by the lone staircase that twisted high up into the Mountain. She continued on through the tunnel on her right. The only light was the one shooting out from her flashlight. To her left, colored cave paintings appeared on the tunnel's walls. They still looked as fresh as the day she saw them, over five years ago. Onward through the tricky tunnels, her feet wobbled as she passed the albino spiders that fled into the tiny cracks when her wand of light flashed across them.

Continuing on through the tunnel, she knew she'd have to pass by where the prisoner was chained to the wall. *Is he still alive?* she thought. She peered into the sunken dungeon. She could still see his weakened body bound to the rusty chains. *I need to set him free, but how?* Slowly she crept into the gloomy underground chamber. She could make out the prisoner's scratchings in the cavern's solid stone wall, it read: *Here lies a free man...*

She approached him cautiously and whispered into his ear, "William..."

His eyes popped open, causing her to jump back away from him. She could see his eyes were coated in a milky film and his crack lips quivered as he tried to speak. He shook his head and gasped, "It's-it's a trap, *run!*"

Kathryn pulled away from William and her ears immediately perked up as she heard a snap behind her. It was the grogochs!

Now wouldn't you know, Kathryn blasted out of that dungeon as quick as a fox, scrambling down the coiling tunnel, only to hear the sound of fat feet chasing after her? Finally, she found herself standing before the crystal-encrusted stalagmite, which divided the tunnel in two. To the left of her was that dooming tunnel she ran down all those years ago, which abruptly ended to a sheer drop into the dark lake where the peist lived.

Kathryn's heart drummed faster at the sound of chubby feet clambering down the tunnel. In the blink of an eye, she dashed down the other tunnel, not knowing where it led to, nor knowing where it ended. Deeper and deeper she ran into the belly of Arthur's Seat with the sound of pattering footsteps treading behind her. She ran for what seemed like hours, her legs soon began to cramp and her shoulders ached from carrying her heavy backpack. Even the air soon began to change, feeling lighter and more open. She could hear the sound of wind swishing, blowing not around her, but on the outside of the caverns. She slowed down for just a moment to listen to the whirling wind, which began to moan and wail like a banshee. Suddenly, her feet gave way below her, sliding on some wayward pebbles beneath her sneakers. Kathryn wobbled. Her flashlight beamed down to the ground, only to discover the path had ended, again, just like the other tunnel did. The pattering sound of running feet grew faster. Whoever it was, they were beginning to close in on her.

Now, what happened next to Kathryn was as quick as a match lighting or as quick as a snowflake melting on a hot summer's day; for her foot gave way unexpectedly and her body plunged down into a shadowy, deep cavern. It was a mighty fall she had, her body crashing down hundreds of feet on to the hard stones below. Her body laid there in the silence, torn and broken. Kathryn fell silent.

Above her, the cave's ceiling was lined with twisted roots clumped together in thickened mud. Before long, a tiny beam of light broke through a wee crack in the ceiling and then another, and still after that another, and another on top of that one, until the whole cavern was filled with millions of crisscrossing rays of light.

A booming voice echoed through the cavern, "Kathryn! Kathryn!" cried Grandpa, scooping up Kathryn's limp body. "Kathryn, child, wake up!" Kathryn's eyes slit open just for a brief second.

"Kathryn, *no*, please... don't *die,*" he cried, wiping the dirt off her face. "I'm so sorry for everything... I'm sorry I let ya down." Her eyes closed as he pulled her in tighter. "Can you ever forgive an old fool like me? Could ya, Kathryn? Could ya?"

Kathryn's mouth opened slightly releasing a trickle of warm blood down her chin. "Grandpa," she whispered. "Is - is that you?"

"Yes, it is child!" said Grandpa humbly. His eyes swelled with pools of tear. "It's me I'm so sorry for everything, child. Could you ever forgive me?"

Kathryn wheezed, "It's-it's all right. I-I f-forgive you... I..." Kathryn's eyes looked into Grandpa's blue eyes once again. "I – I love you, Grandpa..."

"I love you too, child," he said, wiping the tears from his eyes.

"I finally know it's all real... your stories," she said. "They were true... I finally can understand you..."

Kathryn's eyes rolled back into her head and closed gently. Her body was now dead weight. He laid her down tenderly on the icy, cold stones. Kathryn was motionless. Grandpa sat there in silence, staring at her lifeless body. She had grown so much these past years at St. Bernadette's. She had matured from a fumbling child into a beautiful young lady and he had missed it all.

"I would've liked to have known you more," he whimpered to himself. "What a stupid old man I am!" He took out a dirty handkerchief, pressed it to his nose, and blew like a loud bullfrog.

His brawny fingers ran over her pasty cheeks, brushing ever so slightly against her face. "You really turned into a feisty young lady," he mumbled to himself.

"*Sire!*" called a shadowy figure from behind. "I have retrieved your scabbard and some food for your journey," Raedan placed an aged leather belt with a long, slender pocket attached to it along with a burlap sack filled with food next to Kathryn's lifeless feet. "You must hurry! Koréna and the grogochs are on their way. You must leave now!"

"Raedan," said Grandpa, choking back his gushing tears. "Just a few moments with my Granddaughter now..."

Raedan looked down the shady tunnel, watching and listening for Koréna and her grogochs.

Now, with every good story there's a twist of fate and that's when the unthinkable happened! It just so happened, another shaft of light cracked through the dull, murky ceiling and struck the heart of the Fire Crystal and a bright light slowly began to pulse within the crystal like a heart beating. Slowly, it burned brighter, while swirling waves of golden light swelled over Kathryn, like a cocoon. It was at that precise moment, in which Kathryn's life would change forever and by a wondrous miracle, she opened her eyes and wiggled her thumb.

"You're - you're *alive*!" cried Grandpa, scooping her up and hugging her tightly. "I wouldn't believe it, if I didn't see it myself!"

"I was dead?" she asked oddly, staring at her hands, which were pumping red-hot. "I feel *great*!"

"It was the crystal!" he said mysteriously. "Yes - yes, it was.... wasn't it?"

"Sire!" said Raedan fearfully. "They're approaching!"

"Listen, we mustn't waste more time! We must find Billy," said Grandpa, punching his broad fist through one of the holes in the ceiling. He ripped out a chunk of dirt and green grass.

"Where are we?" she asked, brushing the dirt off her. "And who is that?"

"Aählynéé of course, and that is Raedan," said Grandpa, turning to Raedan. "Thank you my good friend." His fist burrowed through the same hole, this time he pulled out larger clumps of dirt and grass. "That should be large enough to crawl through." He wrapped the aged belt around his waist, buckling it firmly, and then he slid his old, gnarly cane into the slim leather compartment.

"*They're here!!!*" cried Raedan, vanishing back into the shadows.

"After you, dear," said Grandpa, raising her up to the opening. She wormed herself through to the other side. Grandpa, or should I say, King Kendryck followed.

It had finally come, the day that Kathryn Murphy had yearned for, for so long. Only just two lamb shakes away from removing the veil that had been keeping her away from the truth... Her eyes would remove the wispy mists, the dark shadows, and the misconceptions of Aählyéé would be removed. For in just a moment, she would see what was on the other side of Arthur's Seat and finally see what was real. No more drunken stories, no more legends, and myths, no more antidotes, no more hearsay. For the truth will be told now. The truth about Aählyéé and everyone, everything, every faery and every mortal, for the truth will be known, as of now and for all to hear and to see!

Kathryn climbed through the dirt hole as Grandpa lifted her body up. She wormed her way through the hollow space and rolled on to the grass. At first, the brilliant sun blinded her eyes as she coiled away, turning on to her stomach. A loud thud sounded next to her as Grandpa followed behind her. He stood up, wet his lips, drew two fingers to his mouth and whistled.

Far away in the distance, she heard a soft rumbling gallop that grew louder and louder. Soon, a large beast blocked the blinding sunlight and breathed its hot breath on her.

"Awww... Right, almost forgot ya can't handle the light just yet," said Grandpa, clasping onto Kathryn's hand and lifting her up to her feet.

"I think I need some serious shades," she said, shielding her eyes from the white light. She tried to focus on the beast before her. It was dazzling with the sunlight, it seemed to sparkle like diamonds and then it let out a hot breathy *'neigh,'* "Sheba?"

"Don't think I don't have my tricks and wits about me?" laughed Grandpa, heaving Kathryn up onto Sheba's burly back.

"When will I be able to see properly again?" asked Kathryn, still covering her eyes from the intense light.

Grandpa jumped up on top of Sheba with the ease of a young man, his knobby cane fastened securely to his side. "Hmmm... It'll come about in no time," he said. "Just be patient, all in good time."

A flood of wind blew across Kathryn's face as they began to trot through the magical land. Brilliant colors blurred across her eyes from flowered glades, emerald forests, lavender valleys, silver rivers, snow-covered mountains, and a sapphire sky as they rode into Aählyéé.

Her eyes gradually began to focus in on one golden object. At first, it was just a small speck of gold on the expansive horizon, but as they rode closer, it shot up into the sky like a massive molten gold umbrella. Soon, it was almost on top of them. Kathryn cocked her head upward and squinted hard. A tiny splash of gold began to lazily float down to the land, shifting ever so slightly with the wind and landed on the ground. Sheba slowed down as they rode under the canopy of the golden tree. It was the largest tree she had ever seen and the most beautiful.

"This is the golden tree of life," said Grandpa, picking off a golden leaf and handing it to Kathryn, "a very sacred place in Aählynéé."

Kathryn cradled the leaf in the palm of her hand. Her eyes began to focus back to normal now. "It's beautiful!" she said.

"Now, Kathryn," asked Grandpa. "What did you see in the red Orb of Fortune?"

"I saw a single waterfall that was about a hundred feet high crashing down onto seven large stones. There I saw Billy by a mud hut."

"He's in deeper than I thought," said Grandpa, as they continued riding under the sacred tree. "Good thing we darted under the tree," said Grandpa anxiously, "seems like we're already being followed."

"By who?" asked Kathryn.

"The Danyär," replied Grandpa. "They feel the presence of the crystal already." Grandpa turned around and looked at the Fire Crystal around Kathryn's neck. "Better tuck that under your shirt, don't want to encourage any thieves that may come our way."

"OK," said Kathryn, slipping the Fire Crystal below her shirt.

"Let's ride Sheba! *Hah!!!*" cried Grandpa, clicking his heels into her side.

They bolted off towards a shady and thick forest, but instead of entering, Grandpa shifted the reins on Sheba and rode fiercely alongside its borders.

"Wouldn't it be better to go into the forest?" asked Kathryn, her eyes almost fully normal now.

"You would think so, wouldn't 'cha? But that forest is a very bad part of the Forest of No Return. You'll be safe in the light. But there are creatures in there that no man or faery can see, they hide in its shadows, waiting for its next prey. Best head north towards the mountains. We'll cut over further up..."

"Do you know where Billy is?" asked Kathryn, hoping that he might actually have a clue where he was and where they were going.

"From what you described, I believe he's by the Feälin'aín Falls which is the start of the Erúdär River. It's on the edge of the most eastern part of the Forest of No Return. Besides, I have a leprechaun I must even a score with... *hah!*" he cried with a glint of vengeance in his eyes.

The two rode hard along the Forest of No Return's edge for quite some time. Kathryn took in all the beauty of the land that dazzled before her eyes. She thought to herself that she could never ever describe Aählyneé to anyone, for it was a beauty that only the beholder could know. She sighed happily as she clung tightly to Grandpa. She never realized that he smelled of a smoky campfire, but he did, and that made her grin from ear to ear.

Grandpa twisted his head back over his shoulder and growled into his snowy white beard, "Awww... Geezzz... they found us!"

Kathryn peered behind her left shoulder, only to see a lone, dark rider gaining on them. "Can't we outrun him?" she asked.

"I don't know," said Grandpa nervously. "There are two of us riding Sheba. Be my eyes, Kat! Let me know if he's gaining!!"

Kathryn steadily watched the dark cloaked rider aggressively gaining ground on them. "He's definitely catching up to us," she said disturbingly.

At first, the rider was just a mere speck of dust on the horizon, but he rode harder, and his horse quickened its pace and she watched him close in faster and faster than any normal mount could go.

"He's gaining! He's gaining!" she cried anxiously. "He's almost here!"

The mysterious rider, in just a mere second, was suddenly beside them. She could make out a pale pointy face, which was shadowed by its ruffling cloak as he raced ahead of them. Kathryn was perplexed to see him gallop past them a few yards; he then turned around and abruptly stopped, pulling out his polished sword high into the indigo sky. Sheba slammed her legs into the soft dirt, came to a dead stop, and reared back on her hind legs. Kathryn almost fell off as she clamped her arms tightly around Grandpa's waist with all her might. Sheba dropped back down to all fours and Grandpa swiftly veered the reins to his right. He then did the unthinkable and raced into the Forest of No Return. The dark cloaked rider pursued.

"I thought you said the forest was dangerous?" asked Kathryn, who was now starting to feel queasy from Sheba's quickened pace.

"It is," he replied uneasily. "Pin yourself to me and do as I say."

Sheba slowed down just before she entered the eerie forest and Grandpa let out a deep sigh as he pulled up on the reins tightly.

Now, for many Hawkmoons great men have feared this dark part of the Forest of No Return, all, of course, for very good reasons, indeed. Deep in its sinister shadows lived a presence in which no mortal man or a faery could see, for it was in the absence of light that the valmen-dûr lived. Some in the past have called them the shadow people and some even have called them the devil's hatchlings, for the valmen-dûr seek the refuge of the darkness and cannot tolerate the light. And, if one were to step inside its domain, one would cease to exist, for the valmen-dûr would devour one alive, along with any wild animal, man, or faery that would unfortunately step into their grasps.

Kathryn ears perked up, she could hear the shadows of the forest let out a fearful cry as they whispered around her in all directions.

"All right girl, you know what to do," said Grandpa, patting Sheba's neck as they entered into the disturbing forest. "Just stay in the light."

Kathryn gazed behind her, the dark rider halted at the edge of the forest, his eyes glowed red as she slipped her hand over the Fire Crystal for strength.

Kathryn's eyes searched the dimness of the forest, looking for an entity, a face, a body, but there was none to be found. *How can I not see these things?* she wondered.

Sheba's body clipped against the darkness. There were most definitely more shadows than light in that forest and strange chittering noises buzzed around the trees as they made their way through.

"Good girl you're doing fine," said Grandpa, guiding Sheba through the maze of sunlight.

"What are those noises?" asked Kathryn, shivering and then clinging herself closer to Grandpa.

"They are the valmen-dûr, creatures of the shadows, the shadow people. They live on anything that comes into their darkness," said Grandpa, tearing off a hard piece of leather which was flaking away from Sheba's saddle and tossing it into the shadow. In mere seconds, translucent creatures living in the darkness ravaged it, leaving not even a stitch left.

Kathryn watched in horror.

"But, where did they come from?" asked Kathryn, her heart throbbing with fear from the low, growling whispers.

"They stay in the shadows because they cannot bear the light,"

"But why?"

"The valmen-dûr come from a darker entity within this world. They only know how to destroy things. They will never change nor will they ever," said Grandpa. "Look there! The edge of the valmen-dûr's forest, we are almost out!"

Sheba shaved her way between the shadows of the Forest of No Return. Soon, they broke into a more open part of the woods, leaving the valmen-dûr behind.

"How do you know they're not living in the shadows here?" asked Kathryn, fearing if she moved any part of her body she may be the valmen-dûr's dinner.

"Do you hear whispers?"

"No."

"Do you see animals?"

Kathryn looked around the lush green forest, catching glimpses of golden-haired deer and beautiful songbirds. "Yes... but..." she said apprehensively.

Grandpa ripped off another strip of leather and threw it into the shadows. It landed in a sweet flowering meadow of bright pink and blue flowers that seemed to giggle in the wind. "Best test there is!" he said humorously. "Better now?"

They continued on through the dense forest, cutting their way through the thick brush, until they made their way to a rather small stream. Grandpa tugged the reins on Sheba and they began heading northeast along the side of the stream.

They traveled along the gurgling stream, stopping only for food and rest. The day changed into evening and then back into day again. Kathryn watched the landscape transform from dense forests into open fields of wild flowers. Grandpa would do a quick, *"Hah!"* clicking his heels into Sheba as they galloped through the fields as speedily as possible.

Sometimes, she would catch a glimpse of flittering faeries dancing on flowers as they trotted by. In the woods, she'd hear strange noises of animals that made her skin crawl. Even a few times, goose bumps would crawl up and down her spine. Somehow she knew that they were being watched, but by whom, or by what? The next day they passed by an abandoned campfire where someone or something had stayed the night before and still they rode on.

"Do you know where we're going?" asked Kathryn to Grandpa, hoping he had a plan.

Grandpa was strangely silent for a bit. "I have a feeling we're being followed again," he said apprehensively.

Kathryn scanned through thick, creepy trees covered with moss; they were at least ten times the size of any normal tree in Ireland, but in Aählynéé, they somehow fit.

"I agree," she said, pulling her hair out of her mouth, she scraped her cheek with her sharp nails. "I had that feeling for a day or so..." Kathryn held out her hand and studied her nails, which were strangely longer and stronger than she had ever seen, even somewhat talon-like. *Must be because I'm in Aählynéé,* she thought.

They continued galloping up the babbling brook, always a few strides ahead of whatever mysterious entity was behind them.

"I don't think it's the Danyär," she said informatively, staring through the misty trees. She could hear a deep guttural noise bouncing between them. "I think it's just watching us."

The morning's light had cracked through the canopy of the bulky leaves overhead. Sheba had not stopped riding through Aählynéé for over four days. *How is that possible? This horse had to sleep in the cottage when it rained. Now, she hasn't even closed her eyes. Just a few drinks from the stream, some grass, and now it's the Hercules of horses...* Kathryn was ever so bewildered. *It must be Aählynéé,* she thought.

Up ahead, a clearing became visible on the misty horizon. A powerful roar of water sounded into their ears as they came upon Feälin'ain Falls. Next to it, they could see a small round stone hut covered with thatch, mud, and prickly twigs. Kathryn couldn't believe her eyes. There he was, the pudgy greasy haired brother that she had missed for over five years. Strangely enough, he was no longer pudgy, but lean and strong. Even odder, he was still a twelve-year-old boy. *How could he have not aged?*

Billy stood at the edge of the falls, his hands waving furiously at some bugs flying in the air around him.

"There he is!" she cried, pointing to the mud covered Billy, swatting at what appeared to be wee flower faeries.

"Aye!" said Grandpa and rode up towards Billy.

"Get away from me! You - you little," screamed Billy, swiping at one faery that was pulling his long braided hair, another one tugged recklessly on his flimsy shirt, while another danced like a ballerina on his nose. "I said... leave me *alone*!"

Then, a wee white haired faery landed on an arrow that was nestled by the hut and raised it out of its case. She flew over to Billy, suspending the arrow in front of him, poking him in the chest with the sharp arrowhead, while a pudgier faery yanked on his ear and still yet another faery stuck a twig up his nose.

"Owww!" he cried, smacking the dancing faery off his nose and plucking the twig out of his nose, "for the last time! I don't have your *stupid* instrument!"

Grandpa, Kathryn, and Sheba rode in. To Kathryn's eyes, it looked like a swarm of angry bees flying around him. She giggled. *Billy finally is getting what he deserves from these angry bugs.*

"Billy!" cried Kathryn, leaping off Sheba and landing on the hard ground. Unfortunately, her legs had turned to jelly and she flopped down quickly to the ground.

"Kat? Grandpa? *What?*" replied Billy, still waving his hands wildly in the air at the angered flower faeries.

"Billy, me boy," said Grandpa joyfully, sliding off of Sheba's back. "What's the problem?"

"These stupid faeries think I have their precious violin," answered Billy.

Grandpa jerked the arrow away from Billy's chest along with the flower faery. "First, it's never a good idea to upset a flower faery!" he said firmly, opening up his hand.

The wee white haired faery fluttered its wings softly and landed on the palm of his hand. Grandpa raised the faery up to his ear as she whispered to him. Her whisper sounded like a beautiful song and Kathryn was amazed when Grandpa whispered back to her. The faery giggled at Billy. She then took flight, while the others swarmed around her before they buzzed away through the trees.

"What did you say to them?" asked Billy, rubbing his sore ear. One of the faeries had yanked at it too hard.

"Seems that the flower faeries have a crush on you!" laughed Grandpa.

"A crush?" said Billy, astonished, rolling his eyes.

"Yes," replied Grandpa, "a crush!"

Billy cocked his head to the side as he stared at Grandpa curiously. Grandpa had changed into a strong powerful man, which bewildered him quite a bit, and then he studied Kathryn, who was now a young woman.

"What the heck happened to you two?" asked Billy befuddled. "You're younger," pointing to Grandpa. "And you're older," gesturing to Kathryn.

"And you haven't aged, Billy," noted Kathryn. "Plus, you're as thin as a pole! You've been in Aählyéé for about five and a half years."

"I have?"

"Yes, Billy," said Grandpa sitting down on a rock. "Time is a funny thing here in Aählyéé. Years have passed in the mortal realm of man while you stayed youthful and young."

"And short," laughed Kathryn, who was now at least seven inches taller than him.

"But, I don't feel like five and a half years have gone by," said Billy.

"No one ever does," replied Grandpa. Hearing a rustling noise in the trees, he shifted his head quickly to the side and scanned the trees with a hawk's eye. Finding nothing, he continued, "This land is the land of eternal youth. I, on the other hand, am reaping the rewards of Aählyéé and the close proximity of the Fire Crystal."

"The Fire Crystal?" cried Billy excitedly.

"Yes, Kathryn is the bearer of one of the three parts of the Fire Crystal and now..." said Grandpa hesitantly.

A tree branch s*napped*!

"Get down!" cried Grandpa, yanking out his long blade from his cane, which glistened as he held it with two hands before him. Grandpa's eyes glanced from side to side. Another cracking branch pricked in his ears, causing him to look up. "There you are!" sneered Grandpa.

For what had eluded Grandpa for so many Hawkmoons was the feral leprechaun, which has been chasing him for all these years. Years back, when Grandpa was King Kendryck he came across a mortally wounded leprechaun in the Forest of No Return. He lay torn and twisted on one of the branches. The light was shifting over the canopy of trees and the valmen-dûr were quickly closing in on him. Grandpa rescued him just in the nick of time and in reward, the wild leprechaun gave him his two coin purses. One was the wee cowhide purse that was hinged to his belt, which magically produced a single silver coin each time it was emptied. The other was the tiny silver coin purse that was fastened by a silver rope around his neck.

Now, what makes the leprechaun so devious and mischievous as a creature is its ability to steal back his coin purses, whenever he likes. But, for this ferocious, savage-like faery, he underestimated the King's magical power and was unable to retrieve his fortune. For years, the fierce leprechaun stalked Grandpa until one day, the misty veil was lifted between our world and the faery world. This tricky faery snuck into Grandpa's cottage and stole back his riches. The faery may have retrieved his purses, but years of chasing after Grandpa made him truly bitter and his mind set on revenge.

Grandpa's eyes watched carefully at the dirty monkey-like man with orange hair. A sneer crawled across his face and he leapt from one tree branch on to another and then began to spin around wildly on its edge like a tornado. He stopped unexpectedly and growled at Grandpa. "I thinks I found you... again!" croaked the feral leprechaun, hurdling its shriveled body onto Grandpa's broad back.

Grandpa wrestled with the feisty creature, his body icy cold to the touch. Grandpa ripped him off and flung him down to the ground. The leprechaun hissed, and then flew on to Grandpa again, wiggling his way down his leg. The leprechaun's jaw opened wide, causing the light to glisten off his jagged teeth, and then he clamped down hard on Grandpa's leg. Grandpa howled in pain as the brazen leprechaun fastened his teeth deeper into his calf. Suddenly, out of nowhere, an arrow sliced through the air, striking the dirty faery in his arm. The leprechaun released his grip from Grandpa's leg. Turning around, he saw Billy aiming another razor-sharp arrow at him.

"Would you like another?" asked Billy, pulling the arrow back on his bow.

The leprechaun hissed at Billy, clasping his tiny withered hand around the arrow and then yanking it out from his murky flesh. A deep, burnt-colored ooze dripped down his arm. Grandpa swiftly clenched his hands onto the leprechaun's small leather bag around his shoulders. The leprechaun clawed at Grandpa with his dirty cat-like nails. Another arrow soared through the air, piercing the leprechaun in its buttocks. It squealed in pain as it collapsed to the ground. Grandpa ripped the battered bag off him and then the feral leprechaun scurried deep into the forest, leaving a trail of black inky blood.

"Grandpa!" screamed Kathryn, wrapping some cloth around his bleeding leg. "What the heck was that thing?"

"A wild leprechaun," said Grandpa as he fell to the ground, his leg oozing with blood and neon green pus. "But I got its bag!"

"That's not all you got," remarked Billy, pulling off the leather belt around his waist. "The bite of a feral leprechaun produces a paralyzing venom."

"Venom?" questioned Kathryn.

"Aye," said Grandpa groggily. "Billy, can you take me to Glubmar?"

"That's a day's journey by foot," replied Billy, fastening the belt tightly around Grandpa's upper thigh. "We need you to be there in a few hours!"

"Does Sheba know where Glubmar is?" asked Kathryn.

"Aye," said Grandpa sluggishly, the pupils of his eyes beginning to dilate.

"We'll put you on Sheba and she'll take you there," said Kathryn decisively.

"No," said Grandpa his eyes growing heavy. "I can't leave you by yourself - it's too dangerous."

"You have no time!" cried Billy, watching the putrid green ooze seep into Grandpa's leg. "The venom will paralyze you in an hour."

"Don't worry about me, Grandpa," said Kathryn, heaving him up on to Sheba's back with Billy's help. "You left me alone for over five years and I turned out all right!"

"But, the Danyär..." warned Grandpa. "If they find you... they'll...."

"I'll take her to Glubmar, Grandpa," said Billy. "I know my way around these parts."

"So, it's settled. Sheba will take you to Glubmar," said Kathryn, hitting Sheba on her behind and off she galloped into the thick, dark forest.

CHAPTER TWENTY-TWO
WOODLAND FAERIES

It was a grueling walk through the deep, lush forest and Billy was not good company at all. He was too busy hunting down some crazy thousand-legged bugs for when he goes fishing. Kathryn watched his hands plunge deep into a flaky pile of dirt, pulling out a handful of squiggly yellow insects with purple eyes. She thought it was strange that he found so much enjoyment from digging up creepy crawly things even though he was seventeen years old, living in a twelve year old's body.

Kathryn, of course, started to tell him the story of what happened to her when she found her way into Arthur's Seat all those years ago. She told him all about the red-winged ravens, the grogochs, Koréna, and the fearsome peist. She even told him about her time in St. Bernadette's, the Sisters of the True Cross, Mother Superior's evil glare, and learning how to be a "Warrior Queen" with Sister Martin Marie.

"Is that like being a true Indiana Jones apprentice?" asked Billy, picking up a fuzzy blonde snail the size of a golf ball.

"No, not at all," she replied, feeling her stomach squish around as he began to smell the slimy snail.

Kathryn continued on with absolutely everything she could think of; how she made a faery door, how she met Glubgrub, crossing the Devil's Bridge, the pooka, Queen Maeve and her two brutish bulls, and the grotesque goblins that had attacked her. She even told him about how Mother Superior stopped Queen Maeve from crossing the Devil's Bridge before she could make her way into the mortal realm of man.

"What do you think was in that emerald Celtic Cross she was wearing?" asked Billy, who finally lifted his head up from a damp mossy log, which had an array of wiggling worm-like bugs crawling on it and made eye contact with Kathryn.

"You've got me on that one," said Kathryn, shrugging her shoulders. "I'd assume it was something the faeries fear or at least Queen Maeve fears."

"Hey!" screamed Billy, holding up a fluffy white round insect with about a million skinny, orange legs waving in the air. "Can you believe I found a zarbugdin? These things are like extinct!"

Kathryn kept walking her eyes reflecting the sun's rays bursting through the high canopy of lush trees. "How much further?" she asked.

Billy placed his rare bug into a jar, sealing it up tightly with a few air holes poked into its golden lid and then tossed it into his bag. "A few more hours, Grandpa should be there by now," stated Billy.

"So, Billy," said Kathryn inquisitively. "I'm dying to know, how did you get into Aählynéé in the first place? You couldn't have gone through the Raven's Gate."

"Well," said Billy, his voice suddenly becoming very serious. "I was goofing around in the field. You know... chasin' after as many dragonflies as I could. Then, all of a sudden, I saw it!" Billy paused for a moment staring off into the distance, his eyes filled with awe from the memory.

"Saw what?" asked Kathryn.

"I saw the golden stag!" said Billy elatedly. "It was looking at me, like he wanted to tell me something. It was just the most beautiful animal I had ever seen. Something inside told me to walk up to him. He lowered his head down, like he was bowing to me and I just had this feeling he wanted me to go on his back. So, I did and then he took off like a bullet, running through the fields, up and down the crags further up the Mountain. Then, we entered this long, dark tunnel that seemed to go on forever. It was like a maze from what I remember. We were in the Mountain for what seemed like an eternity. And then, we came out into the bright sunlight. I couldn't see for hours. All I knew was - I needed to hang on as tightly as I could to the golden stag and then he brought me to Nyaïn."

"Nyaïn?" asked Kathryn.

"Yes, he is the wizard of the Forest of No Return," said Billy. "Remember, he was in the book *The Legends of Arthur's Seat?*"

"Vaguely, I remember," said Kathryn, trying to remember the million things she had read in that book.

"He took me in," said Billy, "taught me things, like how to shoot a bow and arrow."

"You know," added Kathryn. "There's a reason the golden stag was bowing to you."

"Because, we're nobility," said Billy.

"How'd you know?" said Kathryn, shocked.

"Nyaïn, told me," answered Billy. "He hid me from the Danyär."

"So, you know that Grandpa is King Kendryck?"

"Yeah," he replied. "Pretty cool, huh?"

"And you know that the Danyär are chasing me?" added Kathryn.

"Well," said Billy. "I know that they chase after whoever touches the Fire Crystal. But…"

Suddenly, out of the blue, a wee murky green creature with wings like a bat *zipped* between them, causing Kathryn's hair to drape over her face. Billy and Kathryn dropped down into a mossy green gully.

"What was that?" asked Kathryn, pulling her hair away from her face.

Billy peeked his head up slowly and looked to the left and then to the right, and then finally he looked up and then *zooooooommmm*, it whizzed right by them again!

"Here it comes again!" cried Billy tucking his head into lap, his hands covering his head as the winged creature seemed to dive-bomb them incessantly.

"Where'd it go?" asked Kathryn, raising her head up to see a green portly bat-like creature with two tusks protruding from his lower lip hovering over them. "*Shhh… Be very quiet… it's staring at me…*"

"What?" said Billy, raising his head up to see the chubby wee creature.

"*Gah'bun!!!*" it cried out loud, knocking them both back down to the wet mossy ground.

"Glubgrub?" smiled Kathryn, slapping her hands together and shaking the dirt off her hands. "It's Glubgrub!"

"You follow," said Glubgrub confidently, whizzing his little body down a small clearing in the forest covered in bright lavender flowers that sprung up like lollipops.

"You know him?" asked Billy gob-smacked. "You know a woodland faery?"

"Doesn't everybody?" she said, jumping to her feet and running after Glubgrub through the high purple flowers.

Oh, what a mystical view they saw as they both approached a large twisted, knobby tree. Lime green moss covered the majority of its bark, while large holes carved deep into its core made shady doorways. Glittering lights twinkled from top to bottom, exposing small living quarters.

Kathryn and Billy approached it in wonder. They could see slender rope-like vines pulling up and down an elevator made from soft stems and textured leaves.

It is known throughout all of Aählynéé that a woodland faery is the hardest and most dedicated worker of all the faeries. They are most particularly known for their carpentry skills of building anything with wood.

Kathryn stepped in closer to the plush moss covered tree. There, in the sunken wood knots, worked small gray woodland creatures hammering away at their daily chores. Some were tailoring old worn leather sandals or mending a torn trouser. Some were diligently tending to their lush vegetable gardens that were scattered about the tree. Whilst, still others were active cleaning their houses, sweeping the dusty floors, hanging out laundry, tending to their young, and still a few other woodland faeries soared in from the trees, just back from a scouting mission.

Glubgrub smoothly landed on the largest branch.

"You bring gah'bun?" asked Glubgrub hungrily.

"No, sorry Glubgrub," said Kathryn. "I didn't have time."

"No, gah'bun?" he whimpered, plumping out his lower lip.

"But I do have your hammer," said Kathryn, reaching into her pocket and pulling out the wee hammer. She handed it to Glubgrub.

Glubgrub cracked a smile through his two tusks and snatched up his hammer. "You here for Kendryck?" he asked.

"Yes," said Kathryn. "Yes, we are. Where is he?"

Glubgrub's eyes locked on to Billy and studied him up and down and then grinned from ear to ear. "Billy?" he asked whimsically.

Glubgrub sprung his oversized feet off the limb and glided down to a small glade covered with thick wooden vines. There, on a bed made of hay and leaves, was Grandpa resting. Kathryn immediately rushed to his side.

"Grandpa," said Kathryn, sitting beside him. His leg was bandaged up with some thin flat leaves.

"He fine," squeaked a female woodland faery, her body chubbier than Glubgrub and her eyes were bulged out like tennis balls. "He need rest," she said, stroking his pinky finger which lay haphazardly on the ground.

"He's OK?" said Kathryn.

"He fine, he restin'," said the wee female faery. "You stay, eat with us..."

It was always said the woodland faeries were the hardest workers in all of Aählyéé, but they were also the biggest eaters. A grand feast was laid out before Kathryn and Billy. They were even lucky enough to have Grandpa sit down beside them, now that he was feeling better. Tables lined around the tree as they brought out sweet honey wines, charred bugs, grilled vegetable roots, and a wee animal three times the size of a woodland faery was roasted and placed on the main table.

Kathryn, of course, was petrified of how much she was eating. She feared that one morsel for her would feed all of the woodland faeries for a month, but they did not care. They passed thimble-sized glasses of sweet honey wine to Kathryn, Billy, and Grandpa along with bits and pieces of what seemed to be barbequed worms.

"Cheers!" said Kathryn to Glubgrub, who was now minus his wings. "Tell me, Glubgrub, how did you have no wings... then wings... and then no wings again?"

"Portalilly berries," said Glubgrub as he began to sway side to side, no doubt from too much sweet honey wine. "Eat berry, grow wings," Glubgrub rubbed his roly-poly belly. "Flower faeries hate them, try to destroy crops."

"Really?" said Kathryn, watching Glubgrub's potbellied tummy begin to expand.

"Side affect though of berry is bad gas!" he said as one of his buttons popped off. "We smarter than flower faeries. We take instruments... make 'em mad! So, they no dance!" He chuckled with a quick hiccup. "Not so smart flower faeries and very, very lazy... they no work hard!"

"I see..." replied Kathryn.

"He's right," added Billy. "Flower faeries are very dumb and easily led astray."

"Glubgrub like, Billy," said Glubgrub. "Glubgrub say, he friend of woodland faeries." Glubgrub then pointed to Grandpa, "He King... King Kendryck... Feast for King!"

Grandpa soured his face. "True," he said puffing on his pipe while making shapes of flying banshees, dancing flower faeries, and fire breathing dragons with his white smoke. His leg was now healing nicely. "Once I was King, but that was a long time ago. I used to rule over this magical world, the heavens would open and the rains would fall down when I gave the command, but now, now, I'm an old man who just plants potatoes and searches for peace of mind."

"I can't believe you're King Kendryck, Grandpa," said Billy, popping a fat purple berry in his mouth. "After all these years, you really don't look like a King."

"That's because I'm no longer considered a King. I have no Fire Crystal, no Castle, and no subjects. I don't even know my people anymore, the faeries bow to no human and the humans left in this world seemed to be scattered to the wind. I'm afraid Queen Maeve and Dúcäin have weaved a web into the downfall of my kingdom."

"But we do have the Fire Crystal now," said Kathryn pulling out the brilliant Fire Crystal.

"Put that away, child!" said Grandpa hotly. He pushed down the crystal before any of the faeries saw what was tied around her neck. "There are friends and foes that lurk around. Best they not know about who has a part of the Fire Crystal. Besides, the Danyär can smell that thing from a hundred miles away. No one shall speak of this again," commanded Grandpa. "You two hear?"

Kathryn and Billy nodded yes, not quite sure knowing why they were nodding, but they did it anyway.

Kathryn gazed around the feast table and saw the woodland faeries were slumbering and snorting in their sleep. Their bellies were now filled and their belt buckles unhooked. A low grumbling sound of snoring and crickets echoed throughout the camp.

"Guess we should just sleep anywhere," yawned Kathryn.

The night air was sweet and perfumed with the pungent scent of portalilly berries. Kathryn and Billy slept deeply listening to the chirping sound of crickets. In the distance, the faint sound of chittering, laughing, and crunching leaves traveled from deep within the forest, and slick voices rolled off the tranquil trees.

Kathryn's body tossed and turned as her head raced with nightmarish images that flashed in her head: a dark stranger galloping behind her as she drove into Mulleam's Ferry Crossing; Queen Maeve, thunderous horned bulls, and her army of mad goblins chasing after her; crossing the Devil's Bridge; and then coming face to face with Mother Superior herself. She soon felt calm as she had visions of dragons flying across the Hawkmoon's light as they traveled north and her body soaring up high with them, floating on the wind like a feather. She felt free.

In the morning when they awoke, well now, that was a different story all together.

"*You there!*" said a stern voice, poking Kathryn in her arm with a glistening hard-edge sword. "*Arise!*"

Kathryn eyes flickered and then blinked lazily. She then turned over, smacked her lips together a few times, and fell back into a sweet blissful sleep.

"*I said arise!!!*" boomed the voice louder. This time, the voice tickled her eardrum.

Kathryn rubbed her eyes and then dug deep into her middle ear and wiggled her pointer finger wildly. Her vision was blurred at first, but when she could finally see, she saw a pasty tall man standing before her with dark blood-red braided hair. His left eye was encircled by a tattoo of strange circle shapes looping around larger sphere shaped circles.

"Kathryn, *get up!*" said Grandpa impatiently, standing above her with his arms pulled back behind his body. Next to him were ten other pale men with dark blood-red hair and disk shaped tattoos over their left eye.

It was the Danyär. Somehow, some way, they had found them. They bound Grandpa's, Kathryn's, and Billy's hands together with leathery vines and placed each one of them on horseback with another Danyär and began to ride off in a northwestern direction through the thickened brush.

Kathryn's head ached with the remnants of the sweet honey wine. The horses rode hard through floral fields popping with golden flowers, luscious purple heather, cherry red roses, lemon elf flowers, and creeping thistles. The journey continued throughout the day, passing glistening silver rivers with fish leaping through its waters and then past emerald glades filled with every shade of green. They only stopped a few times to rest properly.

The leader of the Danyär scanned the sky, searching for some sort of sign to lead them to their base camp. At last, he saw a streaming red light rise above the horizon high into the bright sky that transformed into a fiery red phoenix. Immediately their horses raced fiercely north towards misty purple mountains.

The powerful legs of the stallions sped into camp, scuffing up bits of mud and grass into the air, while the sheen of their brown fur glistened like cocoa in the sun's rays. The riders swift speed caused the red banner at the gate to ripple wildly in the wind, exposing the emblem of a silvery sword and a golden arrow crisscrossed over the heart of a double red-winged dragon. Cloth tents were spaced evenly across the campsite along with Danyär elves that were busy forging metal swords, shaping golden arrows, and molding slender breastplates. Kathryn's nose was filled with the scent of burning iron and a hint of lavender. The riders carrying the fugitives stopped abruptly.

The Danyär troopers dismounted taking Kathryn, Grandpa, and Billy along with them before securely tying them up to a tree on the edge of camp. Kathryn observed her surroundings and her capturers; she had never seen elves before. She had always thought they were peaceful faeries, at least from the tales that her mother had told her.

Indeed, the Danyär were once a peaceful kind of faery, but years ago when the Fire Crystal was ripped out of the double red-winged dragon, MääGord, they quickly changed and became rebellious elves who swore an oath to recapture the Fire Crystal and to return it back to the land of Nezroth.

For it was in Nezroth, the land of the fey or the faery-folk, where MääGord once lived and filled its land with splendid magic; it was MääGord who nurtured the land creating an Elven paradise. But when MääGord's egg was stolen, she created the land of Aählyneé with her fiery breath upon the raging sea. It was when all hope was lost that she landed on the island of Llangdon and died of a broken heart. Soon, a dark silhouette emerged from the darkness and cut her still beating heart out of her chest, thus stealing the Fire Crystal, which caused Nezroth to lose much of its splendid peace.

It was at that fateful moment, in which the Danyär broke all their relations with Danú and the other eleven tribes on Nezroth, to pursue their campaign in the search of the Fire Crystal. But unbeknownst to the Danyär, it was Danú who found the Fire Crystal first. Upon discovering the Fire Crystal once again after many Hawkmoons, Danú went in search of the greatest mortal King the world of man had ever known, but instead she only found his son, Kendryck. It was then that Danú extended the power of the Fire Crystal to Kendryck and all the inhabitants of Aählyneé as a peace offering. It was also Danú who created the mystical fountain on which it sat, for the Danyär could neither see it nor feel it when it floated upon that magical spout of water. Danú also made a powerful enchantment over Arthur's Seat so the Danyär could neither see nor sense the Fire Crystal, but if one were to take the Fire Crystal past the boundaries of the Mountain, surely the Danyär would know it.

"I thought elves were the good guys," said Kathryn, eyeing her capturers bitterly as they entered a large tent in the center of camp.

"Hmphh..." grunted Grandpa, trying to wiggle the unyielding vines loose. "The Danyär have allegiance to no one, not even to their Queen."

"Danú?" asked Kathryn.

"Yes," replied Grandpa.

"And," said Kathryn hesitantly and a bit perplexed, "why do they have a tattoo around their left eye and what's up with the dark red hair?"

"It is part of the Danyär ritual," answered Grandpa. "They dye their hair the color of blood to represent their eternal dedication for the Fire Crystal and the tattoo above their eye represents their continued search for it."

"Why the left one?" remarked Billy.

"It is the one closest to their heart," said Grandpa reluctantly.

A tall, wispy man with hollow cheeks stepped out of the main tent. His face was stern and cold. *He must be the leader,* she thought. His nostrils flared and his eyes were like icy stones as he glared at Kathryn.

"The Danyär," continued Grandpa in a low voice, "swore an oath, years ago, after MääGord's heart was ripped from her chest."

"*MääGord?*" asked Kathryn, bewildered.

"The double red-winged dragon who gave her life," said Grandpa. "Her heart is now the Fire Crystal. The Danyär's oath and quest for the crystal knows no bounds. They will stop for no man, no King, or any Queen. They seek to make the Fire Crystal whole again and to return it back to Nezroth, where MääGord was created."

The Danyär leader stood before them and addressed Grandpa in a firm voice, "Queen Maeve and Dúcäin are planning a war on our people. She is also planning a war on yours as well. It is imperative that we have what is rightfully ours!"

"You know I can't do that, Sain'óth," replied Grandpa looking up into his dark blood-red eyes. "It is ours now, it is part of us. Also, I cannot give you what I do not have."

"There is *no* cannot, Kendryck, it belongs to our people, those who created its essence," argued Sain'óth. "Or have you forgotten?"

"I'm warning you Sain'óth, the crystal cannot be taken away from our family, it is rightfully ours!" said Grandpa in a harsh voice. "It was bestowed to our family and that is a bond you can never break!"

Sain'óth slid out a silver blade from his scabbard and held it closely up to Grandpa's throat. "It was rightfully ours too," he growled through his crowded teeth, "or have you forgotten after all those years in the mortal realm?"

"Danú thinks differently, Sain'óth," choked Grandpa, the blade ever so close and ever so hot to his fragile skin.

"It was ours when Nezroth was forged many years ago, way before MääGord was even a thought," said Sain'óth contemptuously, pulling the blade away from his throat and aiming it at Kathryn. "She must relinquish the crystal Kendryck or we will relinquish her!"

"You can have it - if you want," said Kathryn, looking into Sain'óth's left eye, which began to glow red. "I - I don't really need it."

Sain'óth's lips curled into a grin.

"No!" yelled Grandpa, "Kathryn, there is much more to that crystal than you can ever imagine!"

Sain'óth eyes peered away from his prisoners, observing a scout rapidly riding into camp. The scout dismounted before his horse had even come to a full stop. Sain'óth turned to Grandpa with smite on his face. "You all became doomed when a *mortal* stole the heart of MääGord. That was the day you fell from grace and now you will be punished. The crystal will go back to Nezroth where it belongs," he said scathingly. He raised his sharp blade up and sliced his blade deep into Billy's leg.

"*Sugar booger!*" screamed Billy in agony.

"Billy!" cried Kathryn frightfully.

Billy writhed in pain as blood gushed forth from his leg.

"Billy! Are you OK?" cried Kathryn as she watched the Danyär scout speak with Sain'óth.

"Will you two hush?" whispered Grandpa. "I'm trying to listen!"

"Sain'óth, we stopped them at the glen, but they're coming down from the mountains in numerous numbers, they'll be here by nightfall. Also, from the west, there are strangers on horseback approaching. We do not know if they are faeries or mortals."

Sain'óth looked over the twenty-five or so Danyär that were at base camp. "Stupid beasts!" he said irreverently. "How many are at the glen now?"

"Just fewer than ten," answered the scout.

Sain'óth gazed at Grandpa, Kathryn, and Billy who was squirming with anguish. "They should be no trouble," he sneered confidently. "Take twenty of our best men to stop their advances."

The scout pounded his fist over his heart and said proudly, "For the heart of MääGord! We will triumph!" He then mounted his horse.

"Who are they talking about?" whispered Kathryn, watching Sain'óth return into his tent.

Twenty Danyär mounted their horses and charged off into the gloomy black forest.

"Nomad Fomorians. They're coming down from the mountains," said Grandpa. "The Danyär had flooded the valley where they lived. All their homes are now underwater. Just so the Danyär could sail their boats further into Aählynéé. The Fomorians, of course, fled into the mountains years ago. I guess they are finished living in the mountains and are ready to face the Danyär."

"Why do they think they own the Fire Crystal?" asked Billy.

"Nezroth is a land of pure magic, all faeries, no mortal men. The dragons fuel the magic and when MääGord left, chasing after her egg, she unintentionally created Aählynéé, a world where man can co-exist with faeries. Some faeries left Nezroth, while other just slowly migrated over here to stake their claim in this half-faery, half-mortal realm. But, Aählynéé fell into mayhem with men and faeries fighting for it. So, Danú appointed the greatest King man had ever known as the King of Aählynéé and that man was my father. Before he could take the throne, he was mortally wounded in battle. Danú sent scouts out, searching for his next of kin and then she found me. I was just a child when she gave me the Fire Crystal to rule over this land."

"My great grandfather was a great King?" said Kathryn, astounded.

"The greatest King of all mankind," replied Grandpa.

"What did Sain'óth mean when he said, 'It was ours when this land was forged many years ago before MääGord was even created?'" said Kathryn curiously.

"The Fire Crystal gives life, it gives magic, and it gives the faeries their strength. If one faery were to have any one of the Fire Crystals, they would be unstoppable," said Grandpa, wiggling his wrists around trying to break free. "So, Danú took all the Fire Crystals and placed them into the hearts of dragons."

"There's - there's more than one dragon?" grunted Billy, grinding his teeth together as he pressed his good leg on his wounded leg.

"Yes, I'm afraid there's more than one dragon. Each having a Fire Crystal giving it its life and power," said Grandpa, taking a deep breath. "Danú knew no faery would dare attack a dragon. They'd be dead before they got within a mile of one."

"How many are there?" asked Kathryn, watching the Danyär stand guard at their post.

"Can't say," said Grandpa loosening his vines slightly. "But there's definitely more than just MääGord."

Kathryn sniffed the air, leaning over as far as the vines would give, and whispered in Billy's ear. "I can smell you bleeding."

Billy rolled his eyes and crossed his legs even tighter trying to apply pressure on his deep cut.

"Now," said Grandpa, "we just have to figure out how to get out of this place."

Sain'óth stayed in his tent for a few more hours, they could hear him talking to someone about the nomadic tribe of Fomorians and his discovery of one part of the Fire Crystal. He was a bit self-righteous and boisterous as they overheard him talking of their capture. Luckily, one of the Danyär's men, Púmen, had come over to tend to Billy's wound, which put their minds at ease for at least a while.

"Thank you," said Kathryn kindly. She felt a warm, glowing light fill her heart as she observed Púmen wrap some thin cloth around Billy's leg and dress his wound.

"We are not all evil," said Púmen tying a knot firmly with the thick woolly cloth. "We seek to make the Fire Crystal whole again. Not just for us, but for all who inhabit these lands. Uniting the Fire Crystals will make all of us whole again and that is why we are bound to our oath 'til we die."

"Even if you kill innocent people or faeries!" said Kathryn intensely.

"It is of a higher power that guides us," said Púmen vaguely. "You would not understand."

"What if the Fire Crystal doesn't want to be with the Danyär in Nezroth? What if it wants to be with all of us here in Aählyéé?"

"That is not for me to say," said Púmen. He turned to Billy, who was resting. "This dressing will not hold for more than a day, it will need to be changed soon." Púmen stood up and turned to walk away; pausing for a moment he shifted around again and looked at Kathryn. "But, if it did, if the essence of the Fire Crystal did want something else, I would honor that, though others may not." And with that he walked away.

"We can take them!" roared Grandpa, still worming his body around in the stiff vines that bonded him. "If we could just break free from these dang vines…"

Kathryn lay still. *What did the Fire Crystal want? What was it searching for? Can a crystal want something?* She had too many questions in her head.

Suddenly, out of the dark forest, three riders on horseback burst into camp. Their steeds leapt through the misty air, catching the Danyär by surprise. The lead rider seized hold of the Danyär's red banner and straddled it closely to his side. He then struck a Danyär guard across his face with the pole, twirling him around tossing him down to the sodden ground. Sheba raced in behind them as the riders dashed around the tents, scuffing up dirt and stirring the Danyär to their feet. Two Danyär sprinted towards their mounts, but the lead rider rose up his pole, bopping one of them on his head and then clocking the other sideways with his sword. The fourth Danyär pulled out his bow and arrow, aiming it to the smaller rider who then leapt over him in midair, thumping him down with his blade. Strangely, the riders looked as if they were laughing as they knocked each one of the Danyär out cold.

"Sheba!" called Kathryn, watching the brilliant white horse approach.

Sain'óth pulled out his long sword and waved it around ferociously in the air, ready to destroy anyone who approached. The lead rider moved forward slowly, his horse fearful to move in any closer. Then, the lead rider dug his heels into the horse's side and the horse reared back on its hind legs. Sain'óth tossed his sword hand to hand, the rider charged, and then Sain'óth raised his sword, nicking the horse's back leg, causing the horse and rider to crash to the ground.

"Who's next?" yelled Sain'óth gloriously, watching the lead rider's horse clamber to its feet, leaving the lead rider on the ground, still and motionless.

The two other riders stayed in their place, silently watching their leader, immobile on the cold dirt.

Sain'óth waved his glinting sword in the air at the other two riders. "You dare come into my camp? You dare to fight me? Here I am!" he cried, swirling his sword around, taunting the two riders. "Here I am, come and get me!" he said smugly.

"Why aren't they doing anything?" asked Billy worriedly as he watched the two riders stare vacantly at Sain'óth.

"I don't know," replied Kathryn.

"So, you fear me?" cried Sain'óth. He walked over to the lead rider who still lay still on the ground. "Is that what it is? You don't have your fearless leader, so you cower away?" Sain'óth stood over the lead rider's limp body raised his long sword powerfully over it. "You'd never make it as a Danyär! Never in a thousand Hawkmoons could you ever be a Danyär!"

Sain'óth lifted his sword up higher and thrashed it down towards the lead riders body, only to pound it into the dewy earth below him. The lead rider quickly rolled away and kicked Sain'óth's legs away, tossing him on to his back. The lead rider then bopped him over his head, knocking Sain'óth out cold. The lead rider then jumped on top of his horse and journeyed towards the group.

Kathryn felt the vines release from her wrists as Grandpa jumped to his feet. He reached for his weathered cane, twisted the knobby top, and slid out a slender crystal edged sword.

"No time for heroics, Mr. Murphy! We need to get all three of you out of here," said Sheliza, wrapping some cloth around Billy's leg and helping him up onto Sheba's back.

Kathryn's mouth dropped open, gob-smacked. She could not believe her eyes... *Sheliza Lott is rescuing me?* But that was not all; the two other riders drew nearer. The lead rider moved towards Kathryn gradually, his face hidden by the bright blinding light behind him. Slowly, from behind the darkness, the light brushed against his face and Kathryn did not believe whom she saw.

"George?" gasped Kathryn in complete and utter shock.

George sat up proudly on his gallant steed, his eyes glimmering in sunlight. The second rider trotted up next to George, carrying a thick sword and a metal shield which covered most of his short body. "Eddie? But, how?" said Kathryn, astonished.

"No time for small talk now," said George, his rich chocolate horse kicking up his front legs up high into the air. "A knight's task is never done! Tie 'em up!" Directed George to Grandpa and Kathryn. "Make them as tight as you can and grab their swords and arrows while you're down there."

Grandpa and Kathryn dragged all of the Danyär together with the help of Sheliza and tied them tightly to the tree. Kathryn even made the knots extra taut, just in case.

"Everyone all right?" called out George from his steed, holding the reins steadily in his hands.

"Yes," said Grandpa and Kathryn mounting two of the Danyär's horses.

"Then let's be off!" commanded George and they journeyed deep into the mystical forest.

CHAPTER TWENTY-THREE
THE TRANSFORMATION

It was true George and Eddie along with Sheliza had overrun the Danyär in their base camp, tearing them away from their beloved Fire Crystal. And as for George and Eddie, it truly was a most peculiar and mysterious thing which occurred when they followed Sheliza Lott into Arthur's Seat. For you see, they found their way through the great labyrinth, past the grogochs, far away from the dungeon, and the inky-black lake with that menacing peist lurking in its deep waters. They had made it all the way to the other side because they had found another way into Arthur's Seat. The same exact entrance in which Billy and Kathryn had read about in the book, *The Legends of Arthur's Seat*. They had passed through the tandem gap of wonder...

> *By the light of the wind,*
> *By the beginning of the sea,*
> *Through the archway of the stone valley,*
> *Is the tandem gap of wonder.*

For that is how they made their way into Aählynéé and once they entered into this magical land, they found the air fresh and light and magically their minds and bodies were transformed. Where in the mortal realm George could not see well, but in Aählynéé, his eyesight was as sharp as a hawk. Where he once walked with a gait and stuttered, now he could stand up straight and speak with eloquence. Where in the mortal realm Eddie could not hear well, but in Aählynéé his ears were open to all sounds and where in the realm of man, Eddie was mute, now he spoke profoundly.

Their bodies pulled together as they stood tall and proud and deep down to the very core of their beings, they had finally had the strength of many men. For now, they had turned into true knights; knights of hope, knights of justice, knights of truth, and knights of valor.

The group traveled deep into the dense forest as they journeyed west, back towards Arthur's Seat. For they knew the Danyär would not be happy when they had awoken.

Eddie gleamed with pure happiness the whole way back to Arthur's Seat as his horse's shiny green tassels blew in the wind while they pranced up and down over the thick moss covered logs. George's chest was held high and a grin crawled over his face. Wisps of his golden hair blew with the breeze as he laughed the whole way back.

Night began to set in and they made camp as close as they could to the Forest of No Return without bothering the valmen-dûr.

"Set Billy down first," said George as he jumped off his horse, his body now towering over Kathryn as he stood up straight.

"Let me have a look there," said Grandpa, rolling up Billy's cloth pants, removing Pûmen's dressings carefully, and then examining his open wound. "Hand me the leprechaun's bag, will ya, love," he said to Kathryn.

Kathryn snatched up the filthy leprechaun bag and held it with just two fingers as it was as light as a feather. She thought it was odd that it was made of cracked dried leaves and leafy vines, but seemed to be as soft and smooth as silk as she handed it to Grandpa.

"I always wondered what leprechaun's kept in their bags," remarked Billy, clenching his teeth together.

"Me too!" said Kathryn curiously.

"Aye... me as well," answered George, bending down on one knee.

Kathryn, on the other hand, couldn't seem to stop looking at George's powerful form. He had not only just transformed into a strong and great knight, but he seemed in his own way, what he was truly meant to be.

Grandpa unlaced the earthy bag and poked his bulbous nose inside it and then quickly looked up. "Well, today's your lucky day," declared Grandpa. He rummaged his hand deep inside the bag for a bit and pulled out an emerald Celtic brooch, its brilliant gemstones glistened in the sun's rays.

Sheliza snatched the valuable brooch from Grandpa's hand. "It's exquisite!" she said, her eyes mesmerized with its glint. "I have never seen such a spectacular piece of jewelry. And it's made from *emeralds!* Do you know how much this is worth?"

"A lot of money," said Kathryn nonchalantly.

"It's more than *a lot* of money! This is a fortune! This whole land is a treasure. There must be millions, even billions to be made here!"

Grandpa then pulled out a polished silver flask and twisted the cap off, taking a strong whiff of its contents. "Here, pour this on his wound," he said, handing the flask to Eddie.

"What is it?" asked Billy, who was now sweating profusely from his brow.

"Leprechaun juice…"

Eddie took the flask from Grandpa and sniffed it deeply; he quickly squished his face together. Pulling back, he shook his head, causing his new thick curly hair to bounce around his pink ears. "Wow, that's some strong stuff. This may hurt you Billy," he said gently, pouring the thick orange liquid on his gash as it began to bubble up like an erupting volcano.

"Eddie!" cried Billy, "You can talk now!"

Eddie smiled at Billy and said, "Aye!"

George ripped off a piece of banner that was hanging from his saddle. "Here, Eddie, wrap it up tight. What else you got in there?"

Grandpa chuckled, "Oh, loads of stuff! Those leprechauns's always keep a mighty wealth on them! Let's see, we have a few gold coins," he dropped them into Eddie's hand.

"Surprise! Surprise!" chuckled Eddie, "a leprechaun having gold coins. It's like me not having my dentures in!"

Kathryn laughed along with the rest of them. She was so happy to finally have her friends back in her life and yet in some ways, they never really were that different after all.

"Well, we have a lovely copper key with some writing on it," he said, handing it to Billy, "a few silver buttons," spilling them into George's hand, "silver buckles," handing them to Kathryn, "some tobacco and a pipe… I think I'll be keeping that," and stuffed it in his coat pocket.

"How did you guys make your way here?" asked Kathryn playing around with her new silver buckle.

"Ian showed us the way," said Sheliza, still mesmerized by the emeralds flashing in her eyes.

"Then we followed the red-winged ravens just as you said Kathryn," stated Eddie.

"But then Ian got scared and ran back down the Mountain!"

"Did you find the gap?" asked Billy inquisitively.

"Aye, when we entered, we found ourselves traveling through the labyrinths for awhile."

"Until she helped us find our way out and into Aählynéé," replied Eddie.

"She?" questioned Kathryn.

"Koréna."

"You shouldn't trust her," said Kathryn, "she's evil!"

"No, she helped us find Aählynéé," said George.

"She tried to kill me! All she wants is the Fire Crystal, she'll stop at nothing to get it!"

"Aye, it's a foolish web we are weaving," said George, fidgeting with his sword.

"Do you have it?" asked Sheliza, "do you have the Fire Crystal?"

"Yes," replied Kathryn.

"Could I see it? I swear I won't try to take it," said Sheliza, "I just – I just want to see it."

Kathryn threw her a disbelieving look. "You just want to see it? That's all you want?"

"Please…" begged Sheliza, "I've waited so long. Please, it's the least you could do for me after rescuing you!"

"If you don't mind, Kathryn, I'd like to see it as well," said Eddie.

"Aye," said George, "me too, if you don't mind."

"Of course," said Kathryn.

"Now Kathryn," warned Grandpa, "I don't think that's a good idea."

"Let me show them," said Kathryn. "They've spent their whole lives not knowing, wondering, and hoping it was real. Let them see it for just a second."

"Well," sighed Grandpa, "maybe, just this once, but I'll warn ya to hide it away. All faeries – and all men will be wantin' to steal what's chained around your neck. And they might even be taking your neck off along with it – if they don't get it!"

Kathryn carefully unbuttoned the upper part of her shirt, exposing the Fire Crystal nestled just below her iridescent throat. It pulsed with an intense burning heat as Sheliza reached in with her skinny finger to touch it.

"Look, George," said Eddie, his mouth dropped wide open as his eyes became fixed upon the flaming necklace, "there it is… the heart of a dragon!"

"MääGord is the dragon's name," whispered Billy, the pain from his wound slowly leaving his face.

"It is truly beautiful," sighed George, as if he was in the presence of something divine.

"You don't know how lucky you are to have found it. The Fire Crystal ruled all of this magical land and now a part of it is strung around your neck," said Sheliza, running her icy, cold finger over the fiery hot crystal. Kathryn's pearly skin reflected its flame. "Such power it has over so many." Sheliza paused for a moment and then looked into Kathryn's eyes. "Your skin has changed around your chest, it's somewhat opalescent. Is the crystal affecting you? Have you felt a change being so close to it day and night?"

"I don't think so... I feel fine," stated Kathryn, holding out her hand and waving her long, sharp nails around before her, "my nails are really strong now, but my shoulder blades have been killing me. I think it's from the fall!"

"And your sense of smell has gotten better too," noted Billy, taking a wee sip of his syrupy leprechaun juice while Grandpa was busy rummaging through the leprechaun's bag.

"Hey! You don't know what that will do to you Billy!" cried Grandpa when he finally looked up.

"Things never are what they seem to be in Aählyneé are they? Kathryn, I have a letter for you from, Marie," said George sweetly, handing her a folded piece of purple paper.

Kathryn opened it up and began to read it:

Dear Kat,

Sheliza just came back into Flannery's and said she thinks you're heading up to the Raven's Gate right now to finally find Billy. She said George and Eddie could follow her and Ian, but I'm too small to make it. If you get this letter, Kat, if you really do find your way into Aählyneé, I want you to come get me!

Don't worry about Mum and Dad, they only want what's best for me. And what's best for me is to finally be in Aählyneé. That is my one wish before I die. Mum and Dad didn't want to tell you this, but Doc says I don't have much time left... So, promise me you'll come and get me - whatever it takes!
Hurry back!
Love, Marie

A salty tear dropped from Kathryn's cheek onto the lavender parchment, creating a darkened wet stain.

Kathryn looked up into George's concerned eyes. "She's dying?" she gasped.

"I'm afraid so," said George, holding back his own tears.

"Marie?" whimpered Billy, "she's – she's dying?"

"Her Progeria is causing her heart to weaken," said George, wiping away the leaking tears streaming down his stoic face, "we've heard Peg and Seamus discussing it. There's nothing they can do."

"It's only a matter of time," sniffed Eddie, as his red nose swelled and his eyes puffed with tears.

"Well, we'll just have to go and get her now, won't we?" declared Kathryn, rubbing her salty wet eyes.

"That's the spirit!" said Billy, jumping to his feet, "we'll take her back to Aählynéé."

"I told you this world can change them!" declared Sheliza snootily to Kathryn, "but you didn't want to listen to me!"

Kathryn stared coldly at Sheliza and flared her nostrils. For someone who seemed to have changed their ways, she was still far away from being kind; for the darker side of Sheliza still popped out and she revealed her ugly ways.

"Enough of that, Sheliza," said George bluntly, "this is neither the time nor the place."

"We have other things to worry about," stated Grandpa, "the Hawkmoon is almost upon us."

"What does that mean?" asked Billy.

"It is an omen," stated Grandpa. "Best get some rest now," said Grandpa lying on the ground, "the Danyär will be on our trail sooner than we think."

"Rest," said George, lying down on the cool, wet grass and stuffing a rolled up shirt under his head, "sounds like a good plan."

The entire camp laid their weary heads down on the ground and closed their eyes to sleep.

Kathryn's eyes lazily closed to rest and her head began to swirl with dreams. Air rushed over her face as she flew high above the trees; she could make out the landscape of Aählynéé. Twisting rivers carved their way through great mountains, lakes glistening with liquid silver, deep dark forests thickening the brush, fields of wildflowers painted the land, sugar covered mountains lined the northern sky which flickered in blue lights as the Hawkmoon began to rise over the horizon.

A lone island lingered in a wide vast sea, closer and closer she flew toward it. Its darkened rocky slopes glistened, then there at its peak, the shape of MääGord, lay still on its mountaintop. The echo of beating drums resonated in her ears as MääGord's eyes opened up before her, glowing with a bright red heat. A sense of longing pulled on her heart as she drew near the dragon. In her head she heard a deep growling voice say, *'Return to me'*. She could feel the Fire Crystal pull away from her chest as her eyes remained fixed on MääGord's.

When morning came, Billy cried, "She's gone!" He was now crouched up on a tree branch, like a leprechaun, "and I can see the Danyär approaching from the east!"

"Get down from there!" cried Grandpa, watching Billy jump from crooked tree branch to crooked tree branch, "I told you not to drink that dang juice!"

Billy somersaulted himself off of a thick high branch and landed in front of Kathryn and Grandpa. *"Rule Number Three! Always be alert and aware of your surroundings,"* laughed Billy.

Eddie smirked and said, *"This goes for when you are sleeping and eating as well!"*

"This leprechaun juice is simply amazing! I'm healed!" proclaimed Billy. "We need to bottle this stuff. We'd make a fortune!"

"Aye..." grumbled Grandpa, "and now the leprechauns will be after you as well."

"Wait, who's gone?" asked Kathryn.

"Sheliza," answered Billy, scratching his furry ginger colored forearm, "I could see her making her way towards Arthur's Seat."

Kathryn placed her hand over her chest "The Fire Crystal," she gasped, realizing it wasn't there anymore, "it's gone! She took it! I knew I should never have trusted her!"

"The Danyär are closing in," said George, jumping on his powerful horse and taking the leather reins, "No time to waste, Eddie and I will lead them away from you. You go after, Sheliza!"

"I know a back way in," said Grandpa, hopping on Sheba's back. "Let's ride! *Hah!*"

Chapter Twenty-Four

The Staff of Dúcäin

For it was the Fire Crystal which had vanished in the night and it was a hungry Sheliza Lott who had stolen it, her selfishness and hunger for power had enticed her to return to her old ways once again. The Fire Crystal, she believed could bear great things when given to the right person, which meant, her, of course. And who else would want the Fire Crystal more than the Danyär?

Into the Mountain she went in search for the one who could give her power, into the Mountain to find the one who desired it the most, into the Mountain to meet with Koréna once again. Sheliza Lott now had her own bargaining tool to use.

Grandpa's fingers wedged underneath a massive weathered stone and with strength greater than any mortal man, he lifted it up and cast it away. The boulder's entrance exposed a wee dirt staircase descending deep down into the labyrinth beneath the Mountain. Graciously, Grandpa stepped aside from the entrance and gestured cordially to Kathryn. "Ladies first!" he said.

Kathryn, Billy, and Grandpa moved cautiously, step by step, down into the pitch-black maze as they grasped at protruding gnarled roots, which jutted out from the cave's wall from a few nearby heather bushes. Kathryn wisely turned her flashlight on, which illuminated the dark, murky stairway. While Grandpa ripped a strip of cloth from his shirt and swaddled it around the tip of his sword, he then dug deep into his pocket, plucked out a match, and struck it against a stone, lighting his newly made torch.

"Now see, you're not the only ones who are creative now, eh?" chuckled Grandpa, as he began to lead the way through the labyrinth. "Come," he grunted, waving his hand forward.

"Are sure you know your way around?" whispered Kathryn. "I mean… it's been a long time for you, hasn't it?"

"Of course I do! I know that this is the way to the underground caverns of Loch Dorcha," said Grandpa, flashing his torch down a gloomy tunnel, nearly scorching Billy's shaggy head of hair. "Hmmm… You don't want to be going that way, if you know what's good for ya!"

The group made their way deeper and deeper into the belly of Arthur's Seat through lengthy passageways and looming tunnels.

Grandpa swung his torch from side to side, causing veins of marbled silver in the cave's wall to shimmer like diamonds.

"Bán damhán," said Grandpa warningly, as he stopped abruptly and studied the laced crystallized webs along the corridor. "Careful now..."

"What are bán damhán?" asked Billy, smelling the tips of his bushy hair, which were starting to change into a funky pumpkin color.

"That's a bán damhán," said Grandpa, gesturing to a thick ivory spider that crept along on a brilliant web.

"Wow!" said Billy elatedly. He moved in closer to study the colorless spider. "I've never seen an albino spider before!" Billy raised his dirty finger towards the bleached spider.

"Don't even think of it!" cried Grandpa, slamming down Billy's hand before he could even touch it. "Those things are killers! Watch and learn! Give me one of your bugs!"

Billy reached deep into his pocket and pulled out a squirming deep-blue beetle.

"How'd you know he had a bug on him?" asked Kathryn in a semi-mockingly way.

Grandpa smirked at Kathryn while she pinched the flailing beetle from Billy's hand and placed it upon the bán damhán's steel web. The bán damhán quickly scurried its legs, turning as black as midnight, and raced over to its prey, spinning its powerful sharp web around the beetle's body.

"Now see how the bán damhán has turned as black as coal? His body is now impenetrable, stronger than any stone fortress, and with only a mere bite from him, his poisonous venom would even paralyze a horse and he'd be dead in an hour, to boot!" remarked Grandpa.

"Really?" asked Kathryn.

"A poisonous spider that changes color!" gasped Billy, his eyes bulging with glee. "Can I bring him back with me?"

"No!" said Grandpa immediately, and took Kathryn's flashlight. "But, see here..." Grandpa beamed the light into the spider eyes and it bleached back to its pasty white color and scampered back into its den. "They don't particularly like the light! They will turn back into their harmless white shade, where ya can just step on 'em!"

"Cool!" said Billy.

"But, they do make a disgusting mess when ya do step on them. So, be forewarned," said Grandpa, and he continued down the passageway.

Kathryn gazed around the passageway and she began to sense a strong familiarity of her surroundings.

"I think I know where I am," said Kathryn happily, moving past Grandpa towards a longer passageway that jutted off to the left. "This is near the Raven's Gate."

"Aye! It is," replied Grandpa.

Kathryn walked toward the passageway; a prickling heat tingled up her body as she began to scratch repeatedly at her skin. "This damp air is making my skin feel like leather," she said, rubbing her arms and neck furiously up and down.

"We have to go this way, Kathryn. Come on, now," instructed Grandpa, and then he began to ascend the circular stone staircase.

The spiraling staircase went up for at least a thousand steps. Finally, when they had reached the landing, they could see it was still ravaged with debris; broken stone walls, collapsed turrets, blocked doorways, and missing ceilings were all they could see, until they heard her voice lingering through the rubble.

Grandpa crouched behind a large stone, which had fallen the day the Castle was consumed by the Mountain. Kathryn and Billy cozied up behind him as they all peered into the once grand Amethyst Court. They could see a brother and sister Fire Crystal floating on a trickling fountain that was more like a weak water fountain than a powerful conduit for the Fire Crystal's home. They could hear it gurgling loudly, trying to suspend the two Fire Crystals in mid-air. A frigid chill trickled over them as they peered inside and spied on Koréna sitting lazily upon Kendryck's old throne. Then a skin curdling voice arose from the silence.

With a soft *pop*, a half-sized man covered in coarse red hair appeared out of nowhere at the foot of the throne. "She'z back m'lady... she'z *back!*" said Earh hoarsely, spitting out some cream from his mouth as he spoke.

Kathryn let out a gasp and then hid her eyes as her pulse quickened.

"Who's back?" asked Koréna.

Earh peered out the doorway and saw no one there. Quickly he turned the corner and pulled in a frightened Sheliza.

"She'z come to make a peace offering," squealed Earh, twiddling the ends of his extra long ear-hairs and clenching Sheliza's delicate arm. "Mayz I have some cream now, m'lady?"

"What kind of peace offering?" questioned Koréna, pressing her red lips together, looking bitter and isolated.

"I-I have the Fire Crystal!" proclaimed Sheliza, holding up the brilliant crystal in front of Koréna's eyes.

"So... *you* have the Fire Crystal?" replied Koréna.

A deep glottal voice crackled behind Kathryn's right ear, startling her. "And now... I'z have you!" said another hairy half-sized man appearing out of the darkness.

The furry half-man captured all three of them. "I should havez the cream, m'lady," demanded Aldo, pushing Kathryn, Billy, and Grandpa into the grand Court. "Looky here... see who I've captured!"

"Welcome back home, Kendryck," said Koréna to Grandpa. "How many Hawkmoons has it been?"

"Not enough," answered Grandpa, grinding his teeth together as he looked at her dark eyes.

"Koréna, I am willing to give you this crystal in exchange for some of my own power!" demanded Sheliza, holding the powerful Fire Crystal up in the air as she snarled at Kathryn.

Koréna rose up from her ravaged throne and glided over to Sheliza and said, "You want power? Is that right?"

"Yes!" replied Sheliza.

"And what would a little girl want with power?" asked Koréna.

"I want to be the most beautiful woman in all of Aählynéé!" stated Sheliza, her fat mouth curling into a vicious grin. "I want to be able to change a thimble to gold! I want to be able to float on the air! I want everyone to adore me! And most of all, I want to make someone feel so much pain that they beg for my mercy!"

Koréna snatched the Fire Crystal from Sheliza's pale, white hand before she could say anymore. "Those are some very selfish requests you have asked for," replied Koréna. "These grogochs only work for barrels of cream and they've found two of the Fire Crystals already..."

Sheliza, who was shocked by Koréna's boldness, let out a

high-pitch whine, crossed her arms, and then huffed out a large amount of hot air.

Koréna glided up to the trickling waterspout where the two other crystals floated; gracefully she placed the third crystal beside the two. Her arms rose high into the air, as she began her chant to bind the three Fire Crystals together.

> *Heart of dragon forged by fire,*
> *Bound together by heart's desire,*
> *Strength of MääGord can't be undone,*
> *By forging these three into one.*

Crash! A thunderous roar bellowed throughout the Mountain.

"You still have not learned to change your ways," bellowed a wiry man wearing a long billowy robe. In his feeble right hand, he held a dark, thorny staff and at its pinnacle, it twisted into the shape of a cone and was covered in bright red diamonds. His ashy, sunken eyes glared at Koréna.

"Dúcäin!" muttered Grandpa.

Now, Dúcäin from the land of Llangdon was said to be the most powerful wizard in all of Aählynéé, though some say that Nyaïn was at the same level. Perhaps, it was all the dark deeds he had done that made his reputation precede him. They say, that at one time, he was a good natured wizard fathering the nine maidens of the Otherworld, and raising them up to protect this magical land of Aählyéé. But somewhere along the way, his eyes, which were milky white with a dash of scarlet behind them, grew blind from his search for power. That is about the same time the faery-folk said he met Queen Maeve. After the two forged an alliance to steal the Fire Crystal, a wrath of cruelty had diseased the land, turning faery against faery, faery against man, and man against man. Their evil began to consume the land, pulling it into a dark age of wrath, greed, and destruction. It was his sole purpose to acquire the Fire Crystal and use it to control all of Aählynéé. It is with his alliance with Queen Maeve that the two had decided to take control over Aählynéé first, then conquer Nezroth, and then the mortal realm of man.

Dúcäin raised his large thorny staff and slammed it down. Flittering dragonflies on the high arched ceiling flew down, swirling around Koréna like a mighty tornado.

"You were close, Koréna, if the Hawkmoon had arisen over the horizon, you would have been free and then you would have been able to finally join the Fire Crystals together. Had you known, only *one* thing; only one man can bind them together and that is the one who split them apart," said Dúcäin, his face showing no emotion as he stared at Grandpa. He tapped his thick staff two times and from its base it sprang alive with a wave of thorny vines slithering out and coiling their long, sharp thistles around Grandpa, Kathryn, Billy, and Sheliza. "Isn't that right, Kendryck? It was *you* who split the Fire Crystal into three. You wanted your freedom and most of all, you didn't want me to get my hands on it. That is why you stayed away all these years..."

"You split the Fire Crystal?" asked Kathryn, astonished as she wiggled her body within her barbed cocoon, trying to break free from the tight crippling vines.

"Yes *mortal,* he did. And now he will join them once again in Llangdon. Queen Maeve awaits us now outside these walls with her army of goblins. You grogochs take these mortals down into the dungeon and tie them up!" demanded Dúcäin, waving his crooked, lanky finger at Kathryn, Billy, and Sheliza.

Aldo and Earh paused for a moment and then Aldo scratched his wispy chin.

"Of course," said Dúcäin charmingly, waving his staff before their eyes. "You will be paid with a hundred barrels of the finest cream."

Aldo and Earh's meaty hands immediately lurched towards the three prisoners, gathered them together, and pushed them towards some shallow stairs.

Dúcäin then raised his staff and swirled it around and said, "Now off you go, Koréna, to a place where no one will ever find you!"

Koréna's body lifted in the air while a swarm of dragonflies raised her up. "Father, no!!!" she cried. A veil of pink and red swirled around her, higher and higher she rose, with a swarm of dragonflies whipping around her like a hurricane, and then she was no more.

"Grandpa!" cried Kathryn. As she watched, Dúcäin tapped his staff once, a puff of light flashed around them, and he was gone along with all three parts of the Fire Crystal, *"Grandpa!!!"*

The dungeon's air was slightly damp; a hint of mold scented the chamber as the two grogochs threw them down to the cold stone floor. The grogochs fumbled around with the gnarling vines, removing them rather quickly, scratching all of them badly as they chained them to the wall.

"Whyz we chaining them up?" growled Earh, shackling Kathryn's hand into a rusty iron ring bolted into the wall.

"We'z get cream... cream... for work," croaked Aldo. He fastened Billy into his chains and then strapped Sheliza into a wooden chair.

"You're not getting cream to tie us up!" cried Kathryn. "He put a spell on you! You just think you're getting some cream!"

"He'z to give us lotz of cream! *A hundred barrels of cream,"* sung Earh in a raspy crackling voice, *"on the wall, a hundred barrels of cream, take one down!"*

"Gulp it down!" sang Aldo.

"We'll be there to thank ya all!" sung the two grogochs.

"Loadz of cream," laughed Aldo, "more cream than this whole Mountain."

"We will swim in cream," they laughed, stepping out of the dungeon, their voices slowly softening as they walked away.

Kathryn looked over at William, she could see his kilt shredded near his dirty knees; years he has been there and still chained to the wall. Were they to be chained there forever too, slowly withering away while Queen Maeve and Dúcäin united the Fire Crystals together, and then took control of all of Aählynéé?

Kathryn continued to observe William, who was curled up against a stone wall, his hair mangled up like a bird's nest as he moaned in pain.

"Who's that?" asked Billy, as he twisted his wrist around in the shackle, trying to shimmy his hand through the iron cuff.

"It's William. He's been here for decades... Maybe, even centuries..." replied Kathryn wearily.

"Decades? Centuries? I want to go home!" whimpered Sheliza.

"Nice job, Sheliza Lott!" said Kathryn with a note of sarcasm in her voice, "once again your self-indulgent ways messed everything up!"

"Sheliza Lott," snickered Billy, "that sounds an awful lot like, *she lies a lot!* What a perfect name for you Sheliza. Wouldn't you say, Kat?"

"Perfect name," stated Kathryn.

"You can call me a liar all you want, but you're the stupid idiot, Kat," grumbled Sheliza, in her splintered wooden chair. "You had the Fire Crystal in your possession and you did what you're *not* supposed to do."

"And that was?"

"You trusted me," snipped Sheliza. "When that dum-dum Ian got scared off and ran down the Mountain, I had only George and Eddie to help me find you. I can't believe you actually thought I would save someone like you!"

"Yes, silly me for trying to see the good in someone like you, Sheliza," answered Kathryn humbly.

Billy wormed around on the floor, shifting his body left to right. "I can't sit here forever! *Helpppp!!!*" cried Billy.

"No one can hear you," snarled Sheliza, "you're still stupid as ever!"

Kathryn and Billy looked at one another with a smirk on their faces and yelled, "*Helpppp!!!*"

"Well, it beats crying Sheliza," muttered Billy.

William raised his head up and gave a soft, "*help!*"

"See.... he's been here forever and he still won't give up!" said Kathryn.

A rustling noise came from outside the dungeon's doorway. Sheliza immediately turned a pale white as all the blood escaped from her head. Billy and Kathryn froze up like statues and stared at the doorway, not knowing who was going to enter... the grogochs, Dúcäin, Queen Maeve? They nearly hopped out of their skin as a frail man appeared before them. At first, Kathryn did not recognize him, but as his shadowy figure slowly moved into the light, she smiled, "Raedan!"

"I heard your cries for help," said Raedan, quickly unlocking their rusty iron chains.

"Raedan, we have to get to Llangdon," said Kathryn, rubbing her wrists where the chains cut into her skin. "They're going to force Grandpa to forge the Fire Crystals together."

"I'll take you out of Arthur's Seat," he said releasing Billy's chains, "but I'm afraid I cannot leave the boundaries of this Mountain."

"Hey!" called Sheliza, wiggling around in her chair, "don't forget about me!"

Raedan walked over to Sheliza.

"No!" cried Kathryn, "not her! Release, William."

"But, she told me to keep him here," said Raedan vaguely.

"Raedan, I said release William," said Kathryn hotly.

"Yes, whatever you wish my lady," said Raedan softly, he changed direction and unlocked the withered old prisoner laying half dead on the icy floor.

"But, Kat!" questioned Billy, "she'll be chained down here in the dungeon for decades... centuries?"

"Wait until we get back, I don't trust her! Billy, give William some of that leprechaun juice you have," instructed Kathryn.

Billy poured the thick, orangey liquid into William's mouth. At first not much happened, William just fell to the ground and began to drool, but then his eyes popped open. And he sprang to his feet, whipped out a short knife from his high leather boots. "Where is she!" he demanded, his eyes wild and alert as he scouted the room, holding his knife firmly in his hand. "Where'd you take her?"

"Take who?" asked Billy.

William swayed as he gazed around the dungeon. "My wife, of course," he said, lowering his knife down slowly, "my wife..."

"We have to go!" cried Kathryn, "if we want to catch up with them!"

"This way," said Raedan, escorting them out of the dungeon.

"Don't leave me here!" cried Sheliza, bouncing up and down in her chair, fidgeting around in her leather bonds. "You can't do this to me! *Come back!* I promise I won't do it again... I swear!"

"Should've thought of that before you took the Fire Crystal!" yelled Kathryn, as they exited the dungeon. "And of course, *Rule Number Two! Always be one step ahead of your enemy.*"

"*If possible, two or three are better!*" laughed Billy.

Raedan took them through the dark and twisting labyrinth to the edge of the mountain. Before them a small opening was cut through the mountainside, the same hole Grandpa and Kathryn had used.

Billy stood on the outskirts of Arthur's Seat, looking off into the distance. "Great," he huffed, "we escaped, but how do we get to Llangdon to save Grandpa and stop Queen Maeve and Dúcäin from forging the Fire Crystals together and taking over Aählynéé?"

CHAPTER TWENTY-FIVE
MÄÄGORD

Kathryn slid two willowy fingers into her mouth and whistled as hard as she could, just like Grandpa did when she first stepped foot into Aählyneé. Along the emerald green horizon and beneath the puffy white clouds, Sheba galloped hard towards her, shimmering brightly in the sunlight.

"She can't carry all three of us, Kat," stated Billy, as he picked off a few wayward twigs poking out from his leather vest. "And we'll never make it in time!"

"No, she can't and we won't," said William, scanning the horizon, watching the swirling wind carry pink flower petals in the air. He then rummaged in his leather sporran which was adorned with grimy hair and dirty tassels and pulled out a crystal bell, which he gently rung seven times.

Now, before you start rubbing your eyes with disbelief, just remember that anything is possible in the land of Aählyneé. And it just so happened that seven red-winged ravens flew out of the heavens and landed before them. At first they were just oversized, burly ravens as black as coal with fiery crimson wings, but then they began to sparkle and twinkle with white and red lights popping out all around them. Before their eyes, they transformed into seven maidens. Their hair was wild and long like the leaves of a vine crawling down an ancient tree, their skin as bright as the sun, and their eyes flickered like flames.

"The nine maidens of the Otherworld will take us," said William, cuffing his glass-like bell and placing it back into his worn sporran.

"They're beautiful, but ummm..." said Billy curiously, scratching his woolly head, "I only see seven?"

The first maiden floated forward, her gown rippling in the wind, her skin glistened with a soft rosy hue as she raised her arm gracefully and said, "Two of our sisters are not here, for one guards our borders on the other side of Arthur's Seat, and the other was swept away by dragonflies by our father, Dúcäin. I am Rävauna. We are the keepers of the Raven's Gate and all of the portals in Aählyneé and all who enter here. What is it that you seek, William?"

"We seek passage to Llangdon, your home," said William, adjusting the red, gold, and black checkered tartan draped around his shoulder. "King Kendryck has been captured by Queen Maeve and your father, Dúcäin. They seek to bind the Fire Crystals once more... we have no time to lose!"

"We must make haste! We will take you to edge of the island," said Rävauna. A dazzling twinkling light covered her and then her slender body morphed into a sleek black raven with fiery wings along with the six other maidens of the Otherworld. One red-winged raven then hooked her talons deep into Billy's shirt by his shoulders while another clasped tightly onto Billy's trousers near his butt.

"Getting a little frisky there now, aren't you?" he asked as they rose up high into the air.

Kathryn followed with two red-winged ravens snatching hold of her, while the other three latched onto William's kilt and tartan. She was rising into the air steadily, her eyes streaming with tears as they met the cool, soft wind, and her wavy brown hair rippled off her face. Below her swaying feet, she could see Sheba racing along, until she hit the Forest of No Return. She then inched her way around the dark shadows and the ravenous grip of the valmen-dûr.

The trees high canopy whispered under their feet as they flew above the Forest of No Return. Dangling above the trees, Billy opened his mouth wide in hopes of catching a few grisly bugs in his teeth, while his feet brushed across a few rustling leaves. The chilled air filled their lungs with the sweet smell of flowers as they soared across great fields and valleys. Smaller golden birds took to flight darting in and out as they passed darkened mountain slopes. A flash of silver bubbled up below them in the form of grand lakes and rippling rivers. To the north, great snow-capped mountains shot up into the sapphire sky.

"I see them!" cried William, pointing down to a convoy moving swiftly below them in a dirty fog. "They're just before the Cliffs of Doom."

"There's Grandpa!" cried Kathryn, peering down at the dusty ground below them. "Bring us down!"

Slowly, without detection whatsoever, the red-winged ravens lowered Kathryn, Billy, and William just behind Dúcäin and Queen Maeve's army of dirty goblins. The army was moving at a rapid pace, causing puffy dirt clouds to encapsulate them like a cocoon.

Rävauna took flight again. She could see Queen Maeve below her through the dusty smog, riding on her brutish white horned bull with Grandpa straddled on the back of the bull's husky torso. Dúcäin followed a few yards behind, being carried by the burly brown bull. Rävauna descended down towards the convoy and landed in front of Dúcäin and the monstrous brown bull. She shifted into a willowy female, causing the brown bull to slam his thick hooves into the dirt, stopping abruptly. The brown bull then began to blow hot steam from its flaring nostrils.

"Where's Koréna, father?" demanded Rävauna, standing in front of the wild, savage bull and Dúcäin.

The army of ghastly goblins paused, sneering, and hissing at Rävauna's appearance. Dúcäin's head shifted towards Rävauna, showing his hollow, sunken cheeks, while his cold, black eyes were dead and still.

"She has been sent to her new home. Deep into the foulest, sinister, and darkest place I could find. She was cast down into the bowels of Häälaria!"

"You have been poisoned by Queen Maeve's wicked ways father!"

"You too can join her!" declared Dúcäin, swirling his staff in the air towards her. In a flash, a twisted bolt of lightning hurled towards Rävauna and she swiftly took flight as a red-winged raven.

"Kathryn!" called Grandpa, bound together with prickly, twisting vines.

"Let him go!" demanded Kathryn, stepping out from behind a large boulder covered in soft moss.

"Kathryn! No! Leave me!"

"I lost you before, Grandpa. I'm not going to lose you again!" said Kathryn, pulling out a sword she lifted off of one of the Danyär. "I can't let you take him or to take my crystal!"

"You're mad, Kat!" cried Billy, eyeing up the hundreds of sneering goblins covered in oozing boils.

Queen Maeve dismounted from her white bull and stepped forward in all her grandness. "The Fire Crystal is not yours! It is mine now!" she said, thumping her fist on her broad chest. "I own everything in Aählynéé... including you now!"

Billy trembling, pulled out his small Swiss army knife, and said boldly, "Just give him back! Go ahead and take the Fire Crystal!"

Queen Maeve lifted her chin up high and sneered. "We'll give him to you once he unites the Fire Crystals. Then... we'll return his *lifeless* corpse back to you!"

"To Llangdon!!!" called out Dúcäin, turning his back on them and riding onward.

The army of skeleton-like goblins then set off with fast, quick galloping strides as their shredded skin scraped along the ground. The two powerful beasts charged on towards Llangdon carrying Queen Maeve, Grandpa, and Dúcäin on their thick, burly torsos.

Streams of red and black ribbons riddled their eyes as the seven red-winged ravens landed before Queen Maeve and Dúcäin. Quickly they shifted into seven maidens, with William standing beside them. William clasped both his brawny fists on the hilt of his sword, raising it high over his shoulder, and cocking his head to his side, he said, "You're not going anywhere!"

The goblins let out a seething growl, causing white foam to seep from their mouths. Suddenly, the goblins leapt at their bodies, while flashes of swords and light streamed around them as they fought them off. Grossly outnumbered, they fought with all their strength, keeping the goblins back. The devilish goblins hissed and moaned as they slithered toward Kathryn and Billy.

"*Sugar booger!*" cried Billy, watching a dozen or so ghastly goblins crawl towards the two of them.

"Sugar booger is right," gulped Kathryn, as two goblins crept in closer, their hands scraping along the ground until they raised them up, reaching towards the two of them.

Out of nowhere, Sheba dashed in, catapulting in the air over a few frightened goblins in all her brilliance and landing down on a few, squishing them into dust.

"It's Sheba!" cried Billy happily.

Sheba pranced in as a beautiful snowy-white stallion and then, before their astonished eyes, she morphed into a pale, white Celtic tiger and pawed her way through the goblins, tossing two or three of them into the air at one time.

"What's going on?" questioned Billy, wrestling with a slimy goblin. "What happened to Sheba?"

"She's a pooka!" said Kathryn vibrantly, cutting down any approaching goblins, "obviously, you haven't been paying attention!"

The deformed, snarling goblins crawled in closer to Billy and Kathryn, their brittle bones protruding from their limbs as they hissed. Soon, the two realized there were more goblins than they could handle. Slowly, the bony goblins began to surround them, forcing them up against a mossy green boulder.

"What should we do?" asked Billy, his feet backing up to the stone with nowhere to go as hundreds of goblins slithered before them.

"I-I," hesitated Kathryn, "they don't prepare you for this stuff at St. Bernadette's!"

The goblin's eyes emitted a sulphurous yellow light and their grimy teeth snarled as they closed in on the two. One cunningly moved forward as the aggressor, his sharp claws flared to strike as he jumped into the air, hurtling himself at Kathryn. A high-pitch whistle strummed past Kathryn's ears as she watched a single golden arrow pierce into the goblins scrawny chest, he yelped, and then slammed down to the ground on his back. Quickly, over their heads a flurry of golden arrows ripped from the rocks above, raining down on the sneering goblins.

It was the Danyär! They hurtled themselves down from the rocks above them and advanced into the fight, striking at any grimy goblin that moved.

Queen Maeve shifted her leering gaze to Kathryn and Billy who were now standing alone beside the hefty boulder. Her body moved stealthy, striding forward as she pulled out her long, broad sword from the skin-like scabbard on her hip. She raised it in the air and stampeded towards Kathryn as if she was a charging bull.

"I remember you!" she growled, clenching tightly to her sword's hilt. "You escaped me once before! You will not escape me again!" Queen Maeve arched her sword high into the clear blue sky ready to strike and thrashed it down in the direction of Kathryn's head, only to meet Púmen's strong-edged Elven sword. *Clink!*

"Silly elf!" cried Queen Maeve, pulling her sword away, "You have just made your worst enemy!"

Queen Maeve throttled her blade towards Púmen's chest and he parried his body away from her assault. Her body straightened up and with her left hand she pulled out a lighter sword, which began to pulse white hot with lightning. She twirled the two swords above her head in a dizzying display and began to hack the two swords with great force towards Púmen's body. Her broad sword crashed down and then her lightning sword would crash down in a flash of blinding lights. Púmen rallied to his feet twisting, turning, and he then clinking his sword against hers, ducking and dodging from her advances. Finally, a golden arrow shot down from the rocks above, piercing Queen Maeve in her left shoulder.

Kathryn and Billy let out a quick, sharp cry as they watched Queen Maeve stop dead in her tracks. She glanced just for a moment at the arrow, and then clasped her thick, husky hands around the wooden shoot and snapped it in half. Her face filled with blood, her nostrils flared, and then her veins began to pop out. In a moment of rage, she let out a howling cry, thrusting her sword into Púmen's body, striking him dead-center.

"Púmen!" cried Kathryn, snatching hold of him before he dropped to the ground like a rag doll. Kathryn watched white blood gurgle up from his chest as his eyes became a pool of water.

At first, he began to choke on blood, but then he caught his breath.

"Take my sword!" wheezed Púmen, lifting up his sleek Elven sword to Kathryn.

"Púmen! No..." cried Kathryn.

"It is said..." gasped Púmen, tears dripping from his tattooed eye, "it is said... in legend, MääGord can live again..."

"The dragon?"

"If it lives... then there would be no more fighting... No more death..."

"How can that be?"

"There would be..." he sighed one last time and then began to drift off, *"peace."*

Púmen's eyes closed and his body fell limp.

"Kathryn!" cried Billy frantically, *"move!"*

Kathryn jolted around to see Queen Maeve standing above her, the point on her sword glistening as she hovered it over her head. Then Queen Maeve thrust the sword down at Kathryn's body, as she swiftly rolled away. Queen Maeve yanked on her sword, but it was now deeply embedded into the ground. Kathryn lurched herself around Queen Maeve's sword and seizing Púmen's sleek, shiny sword, she hopped to her feet.

Kathryn held the slender Elven sword firmly with her two hands and raised it up like a baseball bat over her shoulder. "You might be bigger than Sister Martin Marie," she cried, "but I whooped her butt and I can whoop yours too..." And with all her might, she hoisted the sword up over her head and swung it down towards Queen Maeve's burly elbows, catching the edge of her broad blade.

The two swords collided together, causing fiery sparks to rain down over Kathryn's head as she twirled between Queen Maeve's beefy legs, ~*swish,* ~*swish,* she murmured in her head. Queen Maeve spun around clumsily just as Kathryn cleverly scooped up a fistful of dirt and tossed it in her beady eyes, blinding her. Kathryn slid through Queen Maeve's legs again, this time slicing the back of her right knee. Queen Maeve shrilled in pain and crashed down to her knees.

"Good one, Kat!" called Billy.

"See you don't have to be big and bad - just fast and clever!" said Kathryn, slicing the laces off of Queen Maeve's timber boots.

Queen Maeve's brow dripped with sweat into her narrow, beetle eyes. Rubbing her eyes ferociously, she wiped the muck away. And then, with a mighty force, she discharged the hilt of her electrical sword at Kathryn's head. Kathryn stood frozen and mesmerized by the bright lightning bolt striking towards her. With a thunderous roar, Billy's Swiss army knife broke it down before it hit her. Queen Maeve let out a sneering growl as she arose back to her feet, her black eyes focused down at Kathryn and Billy.

As Queen Maeve glowered down at the two Brooklynites, Dúcäin lifted his thorny staff high into the patchy blue sky and with a mighty force, slammed it down hard into the earth. A tremendous crack of thunder bellowed out, which could be heard all the way to Ballyrun. A rippling wave of clear, misty clouds swelled from his staff. Kathryn's sword flew away from her hand as Billy and Kathryn crashed down to the earth from the shock wave caused by Dúcäin's staff. Kathryn's arm stretched out strenuously, trying to reach for her sword. Looking sideways, she could see Queen Maeve approaching. Kathryn's fingers floundered as she reached towards the shiny sword lying ever so close, but Queen Maeve's sharp sword pressed hard against Kathryn's chest.

"Once the Fire Crystals are united, they will all bow down to me – their Queen!" growled Queen Maeve with a note of anger in her deep voice.

"Never!" wheezed Kathryn, observing a large, dark shadow cast over Queen Maeve's raging eyes.

A fat, heavy brown club appeared out of nowhere, swooping down from the sky above, smashing Queen Maeve back ten feet, causing her to land harshly on her back.

There stood a massive stone-like giant with sticks and branches protruding out of his ears, along with small woodland trees poking out of his shoulders, clutching onto a wooden club made from what seemed like an old petrified oak tree.

"It's a Fomorian!" cried Billy elatedly, "and look there's George and Eddie!"

George and Eddie in their search to hold back the Danyär, had literally walked into these two nomadic giants and befriended them as they scoured the country side in search of the Danyär.

George and Eddie trampled through the crowds of goblins on horseback, like they were playing polo, knocking one after the other to the ground with their powerful swords.

Limping slightly, Queen Maeve retreated back to the white bull while Dúcäin cried, "To Llangdon!"

The convoy of remaining goblins set out in quick strides, following the two bulls carrying Queen Maeve, Dúcäin, and Grandpa, stirring up another puffy cloud of dirt that trailed behind them. Their journey continued on to the Cliffs of Doom where they made their way down a narrow stone staircase to a crystal lake at its base. From there, the convoy boarded golden boats which were manned by sea elves, the Trävakor. Their skin was a greenish blue, their watery eyes were just mere slits, and when they raised their long, slender webbed hands up to the sky, the golden boats set sail towards Llangdon.

Meanwhile, the two massive, granite Fomorians kicked around the straggling goblins that were left behind, stomping on them like they were little crunchy cockroaches scurrying about. The Danyär pulled away silently, trying not to be noticed by the Fomorians, and vanished into the thick, rocky forest. George and Eddie trotted towards Kathryn and dismounted before her in one swooping motion.

"They're getting away!" cried Kathryn, watching Grandpa disappear in the dusty fog of goblins.

Rävauna landed next to Kathryn and Billy along with her sisters and William. "They will forge the Fire Crystals on Llangdon," said Rävauna, "that is where its power will be strongest."

"But, how do we get there?" asked Billy.

Rävauna's fiery eyes scanned the group of Kathryn, Billy, William, George, and Eddie. "We cannot carry you all," she said apprehensively.

"No need to," declared George and then whistled, calling his new friends over, "Côrb! Tèthra!"

The two stone Fomorians stopped dead in their tracks, while horrified goblins scampered out from beneath their boulder sized feet. Turning around, they pounded the ground as they raced towards George.

Now long ago, before the Tuatha Dé Danann ever occupied Ireland, there were the Fomorians, a race of ancient giants who had been erased from the face of the emerald Isle many years ago. Once these beautiful creatures from Irish mythology had roamed the mountains and valleys of Ireland, building all the ancient towers, forts, and castles of Ireland, which are scattered throughout the hillsides of this beautiful emerald gem. Indeed, no human has seen a living, breathing Fomorian since the time of St. Patrick. Will wonders ever cease to amaze us, in this mysterious land of Aählynéé, where giants made of brilliant stone as large as an apartment complex in Brooklyn can roam freely in its glorious lands?

"My friends," said George, lifting his kind eyes up high and then shifting down to meet their bulging stone eyes properly, "will you take us across the crystal lake to Llangdon?"

"George," said Tèthra in a scratchy deep voice as she dangled a squirming goblin from her fingertips, it yelped in fear, "this lake is riddled with peists."

"Indeed," said George scratching his bare chin, "I see... and they will hear us, won't they?"

Côrb scrapped up a few creepy goblins, tossing them into the crystal lake at a horizontal angle so they skipped across like a rock, each one howling in pain as they bounced off the frigid lake's surface. "Peists are but annoying little worms for me," he growled, observing a slithering eel with the head of a bull drag one of the shrieking goblins down to the bone chilling depths of the lake. "I say we go!"

White foam bubbled up from the lake, churning wildly where a few of the goblins had landed; the peists were now feeding on their carcasses violently.

Billy gulped.

"But they will certainly see us coming," stated William.

"We have to get over there!" said Kathryn, gazing downward from a steep cliff. The sheer drop below her ended with wet tar covered rocks at the edge of a frosty lake, "Somehow."

"They'll be expecting us," mentioned Billy, observing Côrb swatting his hand in the air at some blue birds that were trying to nest in one of the trees nestled on his left shoulder.

"The peists in this lake do not like the wailing of banshees," said Tèthra, digging in her ear with one of the bony goblins.

"Rävauna, can you help us?" asked William hopefully.

"The Fomorians will take you across the lake," said Rävauna, her eyes bold and unyielding. "I know peists hate the wailing call of the banshee as you said. My sisters and I will wail as the banshee as Côrb and Tèthra carry you across. The peists' sonar will be disrupted and this will protect you from their assault."

"But we must not be seen as well," added Kathryn.

"We shall cloak you," said Rävauna, "so no eyes shall see you cross..."

The Fomorians scooped down and placed Kathryn, Billy, William, George, and Eddie on their broad shoulders. They all hooked their arms around the thick trees that sprouted out from their joints. Slowly, Côrb and Tèthra slid their stone bodies into the crystal lake, which chilled them to their stone core.

Rävauna lifted her arms up into the indigo sky and sung a few words in a harmonious voice, *"Dofheichthe, dofheichthe, dofheichthe."*

Soon, a shroud of flickering crystal covered the group as they began to wade into the lake. The seven maidens flew overhead wailing a sad song of the banshee as they wailed:

> *Cages will we be bound to,*
> *If the heart is not set free,*
> *This day all men will rue,*
> *If she does not truly see...*

The island of Llangdon arose on the horizon like a dark mass purging up out of the cold, dark water. They could hear the crashing thunder of ice crystals plunging deep into the water below as Côrb and Tèthra waded their way to the island. From the cool, misty waters, the spiked dark island jutted out from the lake. This was where MääGord died, where it all began, and where it all ended. Soon, they could see the silhouette of the double red-winged dragon frozen solid in stone, perched on the highest point of the coal island. It was MääGord, sleeping, silent, ever so still at her final resting place.

"Behold, Llangdon!" rumbled Côrb, breaking through the icy sheets. "Now, known as *the land of the dead!*"

Eddie shivered from the cold, his teeth chattering as they approached the bleak island, but Kathryn feared it might have been from something else.

"Take my hand," said Kathryn, extending her warm hand out to Eddie. He clasped it firmly with his, "your hand is ice cold."

"Your hand is burning hot!" said Eddie, taking hold of her fiery hand with his other hand to warm himself.

"Quiet," whispered George, "for we approach now..."

Côrb and Tèthra emerged from the lake, dripping crystallized water droplets the size of grapefruits that crashed down to the lake's surface below. The seven maidens hovered over the crystal lake, never approaching the island.

"We cannot enter Llangdon," stated Rävauna sadly, "our father will feel our presence."

"And these guys are way too big," said Billy, sliding down Tèthra's arm and onto the sharp rocks of Llangdon.

"We cannot hide our size," said Côrb, "so we shall wait for you here on the edge of the island."

Rävauna pointed her graceful finger to a winding passageway carved into the mountain. "Take that passageway into Llangdon. It will lead you to the Burning Crater where my father and Queen Maeve will try to unite the Fire Crystals."

"Burning Crater?" gulped Billy.

"Make haste!" cried William, clasping onto the hilt of his sword tightly, ready for battle.

"Let's go now!" cried George, and they began the ascent up the gloomy stone passageway.

Up they went into the shadows of Llangdon, *the land of the dead.* Higher and higher they climbed up the treacherous trail. Soon, they began to sweat profusely from the relenting heat as it slowly intensified with every step they took.

"Shhh..." said George, crouching down low behind a great stone. Peering over the boulder, they could see a small altar made from skeletons and above it, the three Fire Crystals hovered. Queen Maeve and Dúcäin stood behind it while grisly goblins strapped Grandpa back as he wiggled relentlessly to fight them off.

Two greasy goblins poked at Grandpa with a scorching hot poker, burning it deliberately into his arm. "I will *not* merge them for you!" hollered Grandpa.

"You will do as I say," demanded Queen Maeve.

"There he is..." whispered Kathryn, watching a slithering goblin sway the sizzling hot poker in front of his eyes.

"They're torturing him," yelped Billy.

"Look there," said Eddie, pointing his finger to the base of MääGord's body, rising up out of the island, and resting ever so still, "the dragon... It's real – there she is!"

A snarling laugh gurgled from behind them. All of them turned around to see a horde of seething goblins, snorting and sneering at them.

Queen Maeve snatched the searing hot poker from one of the goblin's twisted hands and held it up to Grandpa's neck; slowly she raised it up, his blue eyes narrowed at the searing white hot fire.

"How much pain... are you willing to endure?" sneered Queen Maeve, slowly gliding the sizzling hot poker over the bridge of his nose, between his eyes.

Grandpa took a deep breath as salty sweat streamed down his face. He stared fearlessly at the glowing pick before him. "I told you before and I'll tell ya again," he warned, "I won't do it! I'll *never* do it!"

Queen Maeve wrenched the red heated poker away from his face and pointed down to the burning crater to her right. "Would you do it for them?"

There, above the fierce Burning Crater was a pole with Kathryn and Billy bound to it, tied together by twisting, barbed vines, no doubt from Dúcäin's staff. They were suspended high above the scorching fires of the Burning Crater, its flames licked up at their dangling feet.

"Kathryn! Billy!" cried Grandpa, wrestling with his binds to no avail.

"Grandpa!" called out Billy, his feet beginning to sear from the heat, "don't do it!"

"Bind the Fire Crystals together Kendryck or your grandchildren will die a most horrific death," declared Dúcäin, holding up his staff, "one word, one command, separates them from flesh to the ashes that they will become. What will it be, Kendryck?"

"I... I..." said Grandpa hesitantly, watching the orange and red flames spark up from the crater below.

"Don't do it, Grandpa!" yelled Kathryn, the heat prickling at her feet while her eyes began to glow red.

"Oh... I think you will, Kendryck," said Queen Maeve slyly, tossing a few pieces of meat into the Burning Crater below, they immediately turned to dust as they hit the flames. "See, they are just one fall away from disintegration, complete and utter loss. No more family, Kendryck. All of them dead, turned to dust."

Grandpa watched Kathryn and Billy twist and turn on the pole, writhing in pain as the flames flared up.

Dúcäin escorted Grandpa, still imprisoned by his thorny vines, before the three Fire Crystals. "It is in times of doubt," bellowed Dúcäin pompously, "that one must concede to the inevitable, Kendryck. The Fire Crystals bound together or your family destroyed."

"In times of doubt," whispered Kathryn to herself, her skin crusting over, forming pearly scales in the intense heat.

Grandpa lowered his head down, and then he gazed at his grandchildren surrounded by burning flames, his heart sank, and his soul withered away from the pain. "Fine," he said defeated.

Dúcäin waved his magical staff in a circular motion. The rigid vines from Grandpa's body crashed down to the hard stone rocks below him. Setting him free from his bonds, he placed himself before the skeleton-like altar where the three Fire Crystals hovered silently above it, shimmering like diamonds. Grandpa raised his arms high over his head, closed his eyes, and began to chant.

Heart of dragon forged by fire,
Bound together by heart's desire,
Strength of MääGord can't be undone,

By forging these three into One.

The Fire Crystals trembled, then they quivered silently for a moment, and then slowly waves of clear white energy gushed up from their fiery red cores. Suddenly, like magnets, they slammed together into one, causing a brilliant blinding light to ripple throughout the island.

Queen Maeve and Dúcäin stood finally before the one united Fire Crystal. "Finally!" declared Queen Maeve, reaching her muscular hand towards the single Fire Crystal.

Kathryn felt anger bubbling up in her gut as her body writhed wildly on the suspended pole. *"Nooo!!!"* she roared, her eyes pulsating red hot, her sharp talon-like nails ripped through the vines, and then she plummeted down into the Burning Crater below, and vanished into the blazing fire.

"Kat!" bellowed Billy, shifting his head left to right searching to see his sister. "Where – where - where are you? Kat?!? *Kaaaaat!!!*"

"You first, my Queen," said Dúcäin, stepping away from the Fire Crystal as it throbbed above the altar.

Queen Maeve reached her thick, manly hands out just before the beating Fire Crystal, "I feel its power pulsating..." she said feverishly, "now all the faeries will bow down to me!" She drew her fingers in closer to its pounding heartbeat. Her fingers just barely grazed its tantalizing energy and then, in a blink of an eye, the Fire Crystal disappeared from her grasp.

Smoke spewed from Queen Maeve's flaring black nostrils. "Where is it!!!" she demanded.

Then across the flaming inferno of the Burning Crater, perched up high on the black rocks, at the foot of MääGord's petrified body, a voice called out, "Looking for this?" asked Kathryn confidently, holding up the throbbing Fire Crystal in her hand as she rested the soles of her shoes on MääGord's left claw.

"How?" said Grandpa, amazed as he observed Kathryn's new opalescent skin covered in dragon scales, her eyes glowed with a crimson hue like a dragon.

"Seize her!" cried Queen Maeve scathingly, and a flurry of spine-chilling goblins with twisted limbs began to charge towards Kathryn.

Kathryn scurried up the mountain where MääGord's cold, stone body laid dormant, passing the dragon's chiseled tail while heinous goblins clambered up the sharp edges of the mountain after her. Higher and higher she climbed, the Fire Crystal throbbing in her hand. Soon, she passed MääGord's massive belly, while snarling goblins chomped away at her shoes. The flames from the Burning Crater began to shrink as she continued her strenuous climb up MääGord's stone body, until she could not go any further.

"You're trapped, *mortal*," cried Dúcäin to Kathryn, his crooked staff raised in the air, ready to give the command, allowing the goblins to attack her, "you cannot go any further! Give up!"

The goblin's sulphurous eyes glimmered and their grimy sharp teeth hissed at her as they inched their way closer and closer to her body.

"Kathryn!" hollered Grandpa from down below, "It's OK. Let it go... Kathryn... Let it go!!"

"Let it go, Kat!" yelled Billy, his feet blistering from the blazing inferno below, which soon began to bubble up.

"Come back to us, Kathryn!" cried Grandpa, "It's not worth it!"

And then finally, as she stood next to MääGord's broad chest, she could see what she was looking for, a hole carved into MääGord's chest, the size of a bowling-ball.

The shrieking goblins mouths dripped with salvia as they slithered in closer, preparing to attack.

Kathryn stared down at Queen Maeve and Dúcäin. "Hey!" she hollered from above, "you forgot one very important thing!"

"What?" asked Billy, confused.

"And what is that, *mortal*?" asked Dúcäin contemptuously, lifting up his staff.

"You forgot, *Rule Number Nine! In times of doubt, do the unthinkable!*" cried Kathryn boldly. She tightened her grip on the Fire Crystal and shoved it back into MääGord's chest, "*And achieve it!*"

"*Exactly!*" cheered Billy, his legs raised up high from the scorching flames.

Now, what happened next is beyond any myth or legend you have ever been told before. What occurred next, was the most mystical and miraculous thing. For MääGord's heart began to beat once more! And its fierce drumming heart echoed throughout all the lands, *~thump, ~thump, ~thump*, it went.

Kathryn pulled away from MääGord and the coal-like shell of black stone, which had entombed it for all these years, began to slowly crack and split apart. Chunks of ashy stone rained down from its body as the goblins scampered away in fear, like cockroaches exposed to the light.

Kathryn stood back, watching in awe as MääGord began to breathe once again. Her eyes cracked open like eggshells and began to blaze red hot just like hers. Her body shuddered once more, the quake causing an avalanche of stone and mortar to cascade down the mountainside, finally setting her free. From underneath the rubble, MääGord arose high into the darkened night sky, her scales glistening like fire. Leaning back up on her hind legs, she roared her fierce flaming breath towards Queen Maeve and Dúcäin. Queen Maeve's eyes bulged in horror, while Dúcäin turned bleach white.

MääGord's thick, muscular forelegs stomped down into the broken mountain, her razor sharp claws piercing the rigged rocks. Her neck stretched out as she leaned down lower. White hot clouds of smoke steamed from her nostrils as her fiery eyes focused on Queen Maeve and Dúcäin. A whistling sound rung through Kathryn's ears and then MääGord spewed a river of flames once more at the two. Her mammoth double set of wings flapped wildly in the air as she took to the night's sky. MääGord circled around the island three times, shrieking a wailing cry. After the third loop, she cracked open her mouth, exposing her colossal, ivory teeth, and dove down towards Queen Maevè and Dúcäin, streaming out another river of flames.

Dúcäin raised his staff up high and in a flash, Queen Maeve and Dúcäin were gone, both vanishing into the night. The terrified goblins then one by one, plunged into the icy crystal lake, which was infested with peists; rigorously they tried to swim to shore without being gobbled up.

And so the great double red-winged dragon, MääGord's heart drummed once again in the land of Aählynéé, *~thump, ~thump, ~thump,* it went, as she soared high into the Hawkmoon's light, flying above the mountaintops and searching for her home.

♦ CHAPTER TWENTY-SIX ♦
DRAGON GIRL

It was only a three-day journey back to Arthur's Seat. Tèthra and Côrb had carried the group over the vast fields and emerald glens of Aählynéé and then they plowed their way through the Forest of No Return. For some reason, the valmen-dûr could not devour their stone feet. Even Tèthra and Côrb said the valmen-dûr felt like a million tiny flower faeries tickling their massive granite feet as they stomped through the Forest of No Return.

The seven red-winged ravens swooped down through the puffy white clouds, zigzagging between Tèthra and Côrb as they ripped through the thick canopy of trees, marching towards Arthur's Seat.

It just so happened that when Kathryn had finally set MääGord free, her thunderous flaming wings flapping hard in the darkened night sky, and all the scrawny goblins scurrying about, fleeing for their zombie-like lives, they had found Eddie hanging upside down over a white hot searing pit. He was somehow, in some way, to become dinner for the famished snarling goblins that prodded him with heated metal pitch-forks.

William and George, on the other hand, were still fighting it out against a dozen grisly goblins that had cornered them against the base of a towering cliff. Familiarly, the two men were in sync with one another as they thrashed their swords, cutting, slicing, and shredding as many menacing goblins as they could.

In the midst of battle, they heard the deafening roar of MääGord, which caused all the ghostly goblins to stop dead in their tracks. A spine-chilling shriek rippled from their mouths as they watched Queen Maeve and Dúcäin slip out of the shadows, disappearing into the velvety night, abandoning their minions to the wrath of MääGord. The goblins hissed fiercely, curled their long, pincer-like claws into fists, and then plunged themselves into the icy crystal lake, leaving William and George by themselves.

When they had sliced the thick vines to release Eddie, they had found that half of his new hair and part of his left eyebrow had been slightly singed off. But, no real harm had come to him, except for a few minor lacerations from the goblins' razor sharp nails on his face and arms, which would heal over time.

When they reached the edge of Llangdon, all of them found Côrb and Tèthra submerged below the frosty lake, holding their breath deep underwater. They played a game of peist origami while they waited, where they would twist one of these snake-like creatures into the shape of a flower faery or a banshee. It turned out, that it was quite natural, for Fomorians to go for long periods of time without breathing. When their stone-like bodies emerged from the freezing water, silver flecks of stone gleamed from the streaming water as it cascaded off their limbs causing small waterfalls to gush forth into the lake. Côrb placed his peist origami of a grogoch in a clown costume on the edge of Llangdon. He and Tèthra then scooped them all up, placing them on their garden-like shoulders bustling with small trees and bushes that grew within the dirt patches of their crevices.

The seven red-winged ravens flew out of the streaking red and orange horizon as the sun began to rise from its slumber. They did not transform, but soared overhead with the crisp wind rustling through their feathers, while Côrb and Tèthra journeyed back to Arthur's Seat.

Grandpa, Kathryn, Billy, George, Eddie, and William all laughed whole-heartedly as they told stories of how Queen Maeve's face turned as pale as a fish's belly when Kathryn put the Fire Crystal back into MääGord's chest.

"I never laughed so hard in all my life!" chortled Billy merrily, with a quick pig snort as he picked at the crusty scabs on his feet. "She never saw it coming! And then you... you with the, *Rule Number Nine!* That was hilarious!"

"A bit dramatic!" said Kathryn, as her mouth curled into a smile. She watched Arthur's Seat rise up over the horizon, growing closer to them as they traveled westward, "but it was worth it! I can't wait to tell Mr. Hewson about this!"

"He'd never believe that all his folklores, myths, and legends of Ireland were true! He'd keel over and have a heart attack!" remarked Billy, as he swayed back and forth while Tèthra squished her way through a muddy riverbed.

"I'm sure he'll want to know the truth," stated Kathryn, watching the shimmering yellow leaves from the golden tree of life float down like feathers, drifting softly in the wind, "the truth of what really is on the other side of Arthur's Seat."

"No doubt," stated Billy, "no doubt about it!"

George stared aimlessly into the distance, watching the swirling pink and sapphire clouds change colors in the sky. "This has been..." he said humbly, peering down at his powerful right hand, closing it into a fist and then flaring it open, feeling the blood surge through it, "the greatest adventure ever..."

"Aye," said Eddie sadly, looking gloomily at George, "I don't want it to end."

"Aye..." replied George despondently, and then they both stared off into the distant snow-capped mountains that lined the northern sky.

"Look, there!" said William, pointing his finger down at Sheba, who was now darting within the streams of golden sunlight behind them, followed by three of the Danyär's horses. They galloped in unison alongside them as they approached Arthur's Seat.

"Arthur's Seat," grumbled Côrb, lowering Grandpa to the earth below with his slightly damp moss covered hands.

"It is truly the most beautiful and mystical Mountain," said Grandpa, observing the wild mountain thyme growing around the blooming purple heather with awe and wonderment. "Is it not?"

"It is a prison to me," said William woundedly, stroking one of the Danyär's horses, "but it was your home, long ago, King." William clasped tightly onto one of the horse's saddle and then in one swift jump, he mounted it. "For that, you must understand why I must leave you now."

George and Eddie looked at one another with a knowing smile.

"I must be on my new quest," stated William, whose arms were still covered from sharp prickly cuts and red scratches from the goblins. "And that is to find my wife. I fear for her safety. It has been too long."

George, in a bold moment, took hold of one of the Danyär's horses and hopped on its back. Eddie, in turn, did the same thing mounting another one of the Danyär's fine steeds.

"George, Eddie, what are you doing?" asked Kathryn, not sure why her friends were looking as though they were about to embark on a long journey. "We're going home... back to Ballyrun, remember?"

"I'm sorry, Kathryn," said George boldly, the horse bustled back and then side to side, eager to ride, "but, I can't go back. You must understand. I can't go back to being," he paused for a moment as his eyes swelled, "to being handicapped."

"Here we are true knights!" said Eddie exuberantly, sliding his powerful steel sword out and clasping it firmly before his sturdy body, "we will honor the code. We will fight for justice, hope, and truth!"

"You can't blame them, Kat!" remarked Billy, who was pulverizing bits off charred clothing with his slightly carrot colored fingers tips, turning them into dust.

Kathryn looked at her friends smiling, healthy, and strong and said, "But what about Peg, Seamus, and Marie?"

"They will understand," said Grandpa.

"You must return and find Marie," implored George, "and bring her back to Aählyneé."

"I will," answered Kathryn, lowering her head down, she stared at her feet.

"Promise?" said George.

"I promise," replied Kathryn, digging into her pocket, pulling out Marie's crinkled lilac letter, "she asked me to in her letter."

"Just a moment," said Grandpa sternly, as he watched the three men ready to ride off.

"Is there something wrong?" asked Eddie.

"Yes," answered Grandpa, drawing out his crystal edged sword from his wooden cane, he raised it high in the air against the blue morning sky. "You truly are *not* real knights! Not until... I knight you! Gentlemen, please dismount from your horses."

William, George, and Eddie all dismounted from their high-spirited steeds, and went down on one knee before Grandpa.

The sun's rays glistened on Grandpa's sword as he lightly touched William's left shoulder and said bravely, "Be thou a knight!" He raised the sharp edge of his sword again and then lowered it down on George's wide left shoulder. "Be thou a knight!" he said gallantly, and then he gently tapped Eddie's left shoulder and said valiantly, "Be thou a knight!" Grandpa stood back, sliding his sword back into his aged knobby cane and looked at his three new knights, "Arise, knights!" All three shifted back onto their feet proudly as their chests expanded, raising their chins up high. "Go forth now... Knights of Aählynéé and honor its code to fight for justice, hope, and truth."

All three Knights of Aählynéé remounted their horses.

"It was nice," said George to Eddie, "to finally win... just once!"

"Aye," replied Eddie, "and that we did."

"What will you two do?" asked Kathryn.

George rubbed his chin. "I think I'll grow a beard," he laughed. "If it's alright with William, perhaps we will join him on his quest."

"You are most welcome my new friend!" said William. "We will ride north towards Snowden."

Côrb gazed towards the marshmallow dipped peaks in the north. "We will return to our tribe in the quarry," rumbled Côrb to Tèthra as a swarm of birds buzzed around the shady trees on her shoulders. "We will travel with you as far as we can."

"Then we are off!" cried Eddie, gleaming from ear to ear, *"hah!"*

"Hah!" cried George, riding off into the horizon. "I will see you again my friend!"

"Goodbye!" cried Kathryn, Billy, and Grandpa, waving happily as the first three official Knights of Aählynéé, trotted through the lush flowered fields with two stone Fomorian giants pounding after them as they made their way north towards the Snowden mountain peaks.

"It's a shame William thought of Arthur's Seat as a prison," said Grandpa, shaking his head side to side.

"Prison?" shrieked Kathryn. "Oh no, Sheliza!!!"

Now, by the time they released Sheliza from her bonded chair, she was as dirty as a rat and as white as the moon. Her eyes were glazed over as she muttered, "I'z have cream... for you... set me free...I'll give you cream."

Billy lifted her up from the rotting chair. *"Peee-uuu,"* he cried, "she's a ripe one!"

"Let's carry her to the Raven's Gate," urged Grandpa, leading the way down the tunnel.

"Cream... I havez cream for you!!" she mumbled to herself, as they carried her limp filthy body through the dark, winding labyrinth.

"I think we left her there too long," said Billy with a slight smirk on his young face.

"Perhaps," said Kathryn, her skin prickled unpleasantly as if a thousand tiny needles were poking up from underneath her skin. She began to scratch furiously.

"Right," said Grandpa, panting slightly from his travels and standing before the seven stones of the Raven's Gate, "are we ready?"

"Yeah, sure..." sighed Billy wearily, "just leaving a magical land to go back to...." Billy caught a glimpse of Kathryn's glowing red eyes. "Kat, are you okay? Your eyes... they look like..."

"Like what?" asked Kathryn curiously, scraping her forearm with sharp talon-like nails.

"Like," whispered Billy, *"MääGord's..."*

"Let me see..." said Grandpa worriedly. He clasped Kathryn's face with his chubby fingers and examined Kathryn's scorching red eyes. Her skin was now a pearly color, while scales began to pop up all over her opalescent skin. "Just as I had thought..."

"Thought what?" asked Kathryn fearfully, holding up her scale-like hands in front of her.

"Before, when you fell in the Mountain..." said Grandpa honestly, "the Fire Crystal..."

"What about," said Kathryn hesitantly, "the Fire Crystal?"

"You... *died*," answered Grandpa candidly.

"I died?" shrieked Kathryn; a soft burst of fire puffed out of her mouth as she spoke. She quickly clasped her hands over her mouth.

"And the Fire Crystal brought you back to life," noted Grandpa, "the blood of MääGord now flows in you, and if you cross back over..."

"What do you *mean?*" gasped Kathryn, terrified. "I can never go back to Ballyrun again?"

Grandpa tugged three times on the gnarled, grubby root that protruded from the wall and the seven stones of the Raven's Gate bloomed open once again. He took Kathryn's hand and passed it through the mystical portal and before their very eyes her hand changed form. Her skin transformed into sleek red scales, her sharp nails thickened and curled into a crescent shapes and transformed into dark talons, and where her human hand had been... there was now a scarlet red dragon's claw.

"You can go back," said Grandpa vaguely, "but if you do, you will turn into a dragon."

Kathryn clenched her claw into a reptilian fist. She could feel the Fire Crystal, the heart of MääGord, drumming in her own heart. "I'm a dragon?" she whispered.

"Kat! You're like... *dragon girl!*" laughed Billy. "That's awesome!"

"That's how you took the Fire Crystal from Queen Maeve and Dúcäin," said Grandpa informatively, "you swooped down like a dragon and took it from them!"

"Dragon girl..." mumbled Sheliza, her pupil-filled ebony eyes wobbled around in her head as she swayed uncontrollably in Billy's arms.

"In the mortal realm, you died," revealed Grandpa, "but you can still live here in Aählynéé."

"I can never go back?" said Kathryn sadly. "Never to see Peg, Seamus, Marie, Mr. Hewson, and the town's people... *ever again?*"

"I'm afraid not, if you did, you'd be in the form of a red double-winged dragon. You'd probably scare a lot of folks if they saw a dragon flying overhead in Ballyrun," uttered Grandpa, scratching his fuzzy white beard and pursing his fat red lips. "You'll have to stay here..."

"I'll stay with you, Kat!" said Billy cheerfully.

"No – No, I'll stay with her!" argued Grandpa.

"Both of you go back home to Ballyrun," said Kathryn firmly, pulling her hand away from the portal. She watched it collapse back into human form, and then it shrank, shriveling into a fleshy pink color along with her nails. "I can live here by myself," she said lamely, opening and closing her fingers, making sure it was truly her hand that had transformed into a real dragon's claw. "It'll be... you know... *fun!*"

"Nope, I'm staying with you," said Billy decisively, "Besides, I still look twelve years old. How am I going to explain to people that I'm seventeen when I look twelve?"

"Well, I'm staying too," added Grandpa, throwing a narrow look at Sheliza as saliva dribbled down her chin. "I don't have a home anymore, the Lott's took care of that! So, it's settled then. We all stay together!"

"I wanna go home..." moaned Sheliza, sliding down to the chilly stone floor.

"She'll never make it back in that condition," said Grandpa, shaking his head and turning to Billy. "Billy, do you have any of that leprechaun juice left?"

"Good idea," said Billy, quickly pulling out the silver flask and carefully dropping a few thick orange drops into her big mouth.

And before you could say, *'sugar booger,'* Sheliza Lott was back on her feet and alert. "Where am I?" she asked confused, staring at Kathryn's blazing red eyes and pearly skin, "and what the hell happened to you?"

"Sheliza, we can't go back with you to Ballyrun," said Kathryn, stepping away from the Raven's Gate. "But it's important that you tell Marie that we made it here."

"What the *hell* are you?" shrilled Sheliza, as she backed away from Kathryn, observing that her skin had an eerie milky-red iridescence to it.

"And you need to bring her to Aählynéé," implored Billy as he escorted her closer to the Raven's Gate.

"You're a *freak!*" screamed Sheliza at Kathryn, while her eyes began popping out of their sockets. "That's what you are!"

"Girl, you need to listen to me," said Grandpa calmingly, "when you go back to Ballyrun, it won't be a few days ago. It may be a few weeks or even a few months that have passed. You need to know that time has shifted in the mortal realm. Do you understand me, girl?

Sheliza just stood in the doorway, gawking at Kathryn like she had just swallowed a rotten egg.

"Time for you to leave now, Sheliza," said Kathryn.

"And don't come back unless you have Marie with you!" said Billy, pushing Sheliza through the Raven's Gate and out into the mortal realm of man, "Or I'll have Kat, breathe on ya!"

Sheliza stood on the other side of the Raven's Gate with her mouth hanging wide open and before she could say another word, the seven stones spiraled back together in a deep, heavy rumble and the Raven's Gate was closed again.

Grandpa, Billy, and Kathryn let out a deep sigh of relief and traveled up the secret spiral staircase near the Raven's Gate. When they exited the staircase, they entered into the Amethyst Court, which was now adorned with chunks of thick, granite stones and fallen debris. The threaded tapestries along the walls, displaying armored knights on horseback, chubby trolls dancing around a bonfire, and strange white bears with snowflakes dusting their heads, were now just mere rags, shredded, and covered with a deep layer of gray muck.

On the outside of Arthur's Seat, it was a magnificent day, but no ray of light pierced the dingy confines of the Amethyst Court. There was not one window allowing the sun's rays to shimmer on the dusty debris that was strewn about haphazardly on the cracked stone floor.

The two grogochs, Aldo and Earh, on the other hand, were still lurking within the dark, deep tunnels of Arthur's Seat. They tried the best they could to conceal themselves as they snuck about the Castle, vanishing out of sight when they saw Kathryn, fearing that she may charbroil them with her dragon breath and eat them for lunch.

Raedan appeared out of thin air, prim and proper in his formal attire of long, black stockings, silver buckled shoes, and a gold breasted jacket with tiny emerald buttons running up his chest to a feathery white ascot, to welcome his King back home, after oh so many Hawkmoons.

"Sire!" said Raedan joyfully, clicking his lacquered shoes together sharply. He then immediately threw formality aside and wrapped his arms around Grandpa, squeezing him tightly. "Sire, it is so good to see you and to have you back in the Amethyst Court!"

"And you too, my friend," replied Grandpa, tapping Raedan lightly on his back and then pulling away.

"You will forgive me for not having all things in order for your arrival," apologized Raedan, "since the Castle was swallowed by the Mountain there has been too many heavy stones to lift... even for a man of my caliber."

"No need to worry," said Grandpa, gazing around the dark and dingy court room.

"Sire, I was able to recover the sword of Arthur Seat's. I found it just recently after the Fire Crystals were forged back together. If you don't mind me saying, it seemed to just appear in the fountain mysteriously, out of nowhere," said Raedan. He held up a platinum sword with a silver pommel in the shape of a dragon's head with two glowing red eyes flanked by a set of dragon wings at the crossguard.

Grandpa grasped the sword firmly and held it aloft. A tear dribbled down his puffy cheek. "I had almost forgotten about her," he said proudly, "'Tis the sword of hope; fearsome, beautiful, and yet deadly."

"It's stunning," said Kathryn curiously. "I didn't know there was a sword to represent Arthur's Seat."

"There is," he said warmly, "and her name is Aláurián."

"Aláurián," said Billy, mystified.

"It was a gift to my father, and before he died it was taken away from him. For years I have searched for it. Oh, but that is another story, for another day," said Grandpa vaguely, gazing around the gloomy court. "Not a window in sight eh, Raedan?"

"We'll make do, Grandpa," said Kathryn, kicking away a few small pebbles still littering the floor. Her eyes were now back to their normal green color and her body even felt human again, not at all like a *dragon girl.*

"At least we are all together now," said Grandpa blissfully. "Family will always come first to me. Never again shall I let you two down."

"But, Sire!" said Raedan eagerly, "I have been preparing for your return! Look here..." Raedan pulled back a bulky, heavy tapestry covered with flying dragons and then yanked it away from the wall. A bright golden stream light poured into the Amethyst Court and they had to cover their eyes from the blinding light. "I burrowed this window out."

"It's a balcony," said Billy, lowering his hand down from his eyes and strolling out onto a veranda, which was carved into the Mountain's side. "Now, this is more like it!"

"Excellent job, Raedan," said Grandpa, with a genial nod of his fuzzy head. He and Kathryn followed Billy out into the brilliant day's sunlight.

"A pleasure, Sire," replied Raedan, raising his pointy chin up high.

"Look there," said Billy, waving his slender finger in the distance to a golden stag nibbling in the high grass below them.

"I don't believe it," said Kathryn, watching the magical stag raise his head quickly as if he had just heard a sound nearby. "That's the golden stag we saw all those years ago..."

"The one that brought me here?" remarked Billy, "It came back home, just like us!"

"So it did," said Kathryn, "so it did..."

"Finally, we are all back together again," sighed Grandpa, wrapping his arms around Kathryn and Billy's shoulders, "the circle is complete."

"Just like the mark of the Tuatha Dé Danann," stated Kathryn, "three circles intertwined together."

"Right, like a Celtic knot," murmured Billy.

They suddenly heard a low, soft drumming sound echo through the valley. The golden stag quickly ran off into the shady trees. The drumming sound grew stronger and louder.

"Do you hear that, Sire," said Raedan worriedly, scanning the horizon for drums.

"The drums echoing in the distance?" asked Billy, listening to the drums as they began to thump like a beating heart, "what are they?"

"I'm afraid I do hear them," said Grandpa wearily, "that is campaign drumming. It simulates the sound of a heartbeat... *~thump, ~thump, ~thump...* it goes. It is a call to war!"

"War?" gulped Kathryn.

"Yes, war," repeated Grandpa, taking a deep breath, "I foresee we will find out truly if I am King in the next few days..."

Kathryn felt a hot bubbling sensation rise up in the pit of her stomach.

"But, for now..." he continued, pulling Kathryn and Billy closer to him with his strong, burly arms, "for now... we are together and let it be known throughout all the lands, in every legend, and in every tale about this great day!" said Grandpa, nodding to Kathryn with a whimsical wink. "And about our new *Queen of the Mountain...*"

"Kathryn Murphy, *Queen of the Mountain!*" laughed Billy. "She's more like... *Dragon of the Mountain!*"

A cool, whispering breeze blew in from the north, sending goose bumps down Kathryn's back as one lone red-winged raven flew in front of them.

"One for sorrow," said Grandpa solemnly, his eyes fixed upon the fiery winged bird perched on the edge of the brown marbled stone fence that enclosed the ledge.

Another crisp breeze whipped Kathryn's hair, causing her brown locks to cover Billy's rosy face. This time, the cool wind brought another red-winged raven, which landed next to the first.

"Two for joy," cried Kathryn happily, pulling her tangled hair away from Billy's lips.

And then, before their widened eyes a third one landed.

"Three for marriage," muttered Billy, wiping his face from the feeling of scratchy hair.

Low and behold, still another red-winged landed on the rock wall.

"Four for boy!" said Grandpa elatedly. He puckered his red lips together and tapped his chubby finger continuously on them, trying to figure out what it meant, but, before a thought entered into his mind, a fifth blazing red-winged raven landed with the others.

"Five for silver," said Billy.

In the far distance near the snow capped mountains of Snowden, Kathryn could see the two stone Fomorians trudging through the fields. Then a quick flash of bright blue light popped into view. It was a small sapphire orb that seemed to be speeding towards them.

And then another swift, wintry gust of wind blew in and another red-winged glided down softly next to her five sisters.

"Six for gold," declared Kathryn. She narrowed her eyes, a large deep crinkle furrowing between her eyebrows as she watched the mystical sapphire orb hurdle to the ledge where they were standing. Its size enlarged quickly and before they knew it, it was nearly upon them. "What is that?" she asked.

"It's an orb!" cried Grandpa, as the deep, dark blue orb flickered with a pearly sheen and hovered over Billy's head.

A forceful blustering wind shifted around them, causing the air to change into a swirling icy mist. The last red-winged raven landed before all of them, rustling its feathers fiercely.

"And seven," said Billy mysteriously. *Crack!* The glassy blue orb cracked open like an egg, releasing a round slate disc with irregular oblique shapes carved into it. Around the holes were thimble sized stones jutting out of its center. Billy held the stone disc, which seemed older than the earth itself, and looked curiously down at it, "For the secret... that's never been told..."

Legend has it, that beyond that 'dere lone Mountain called Arthur's Seat, lays another world, a splendid world of endless mystery and bewilderment.

And so shall it be told in every story throughout the ages, in every myth that turns into a legend, about this land called Aählynéé; a land of faeries, myths, and legends, and without a doubt, untold magic. It is a land where believers dream and dreamers believe.

Through the darkness of the misty Mountain of Arthur's Seat, a new legend has awoken...

Who shall claim it for their own?

Now children... *that* is The Legend of Arthur's Seat!

GLOSSARY

AÄHLYNéé [al-len-nee] ♦ The magical land on the other side of Arthur's Seat.

AMETHYST COURT ♦ The throne room within Kendryck's Castle drenched with the finest jewels, gems, and richest tapestries. This has been Koréna's prison for almost a thousand Hawkmoons.

Aláurián [uh-lor-ree-an] ♦ The mystical and legendary sword of Arthur's Seat, which mysteriously appeared in the fountain where the Fire Crystal once called home.

ARTHUR'S SEAT ♦ The lone, dark legendary Mountain in Ballyrun that holds the Raven's Gate, the only known portal to man into Aählynéé.

BALLYRUN ♦ A charming idyllic Irish town on the edge of Arthur's Seat.

BANSHEE [ban-chee] ♦ An Irish mythological faery that comes in the form of a wailing woman, and whose cry is said to forewarn the death of a family member. The banshee is also said to be a messenger from the Otherworld, a fallen angel.

Bán Damhán [ban-duh-man] ♦ Thick, ivory spiders deep within the tunnels of Arthur's Seat. When they turn black, their bodies become impenetrable and with one bite, its poisonous venom will paralyze even a horse. They don't particularly like the light and will transform back into their harmless pasty white form when a speck of light hits them.

The Bridge of Diabhal [the bridge of dj-ow-al] ♦ Irish for the Devil's Bridge. It is the perilous bridge over the great ravine, which connects the mortal realm and faery realm on the mysterious Isle of Inishmara.

BURNING CRATER ♦ A roaring inferno in the center of Llangdon and at its base are the petrified remains of MääGord, the double red-winged dragon.

Bodhrán [baur-an] ♦ An Irish framed drum made of goatskin.

Cattle Raid of Cooley ♦ A legendary Irish folklore where Queen Maeve of Connacht gathers an army and leads an invasion into Ulster to steal the most famous bull in Ireland.

Changeling ♦ An offspring of a faery, which is switched with a human baby unbeknownst to their human parents.

Celtic Knot ♦ Three circles intertwined together depicting the Trinity.

Cliffs of Doom ♦ Treacherous cliffs which drop down into the crystal lake within Aählyneé.

Craic [crack] ♦ Irish term for merriment.

Córb [korb] ♦ a nomadic, male stone Fomorian.

Danyär [dan-yaer] ♦ A group of holy elves from Nezroth, who swore an oath to recapture the teine criostal, the dragon's heart.

Devil's Bridge ♦ A bridge over a great ravine that connects the two sides of Inishmara. Also known as the Bridge of Diabhal.

Dofheichthe [du-eck-ih-e] ♦ 'To turn invisible' in Irish.

Double Trouble Bubble Gum ♦ Do not eat or use this product at all costs! Very dangerous!

Dúcáin [du-cane] ♦ Koréna's father who entombed her within the Arthur's Seat and who is now the reigning wizard of Llangdon.

Danú [dan-nu] ♦ The oldest Celtic Goddess. She is the mother of all magic. All those who followed her are called the Tuatha Dé Danann (or the Sidhe) the children of Danú.

Eiri Mór [aye-ree more] ♦ 'To rise up' in Irish.

ERÚDÄR RIVER [E-ru-daer river] ♦ A mighty roaring river in Aählynéé.

FEÄLIN'AÍN FALLS [fel-in-an] ♦ A waterfall within Aählynéé that falls from a hundred feet onto seven stones emptying into the Erúdär River.

FIRE CRYSTAL ♦ The name mortal men gave the teine criostal, which was forged from the heart of a double red-winged dragon.

FLOWER FAERIES ♦ Pretty little winged faeries that like to sing and dance about on flowers. Not very smart though, they tend to have a bit of a temper if you were ever to steal their instruments or were ever to disrupt their merriments.

FOREST OF NO RETURN ♦ The cursed forest on the edge of Arthur's Seat within Aählynéé; where no man, faery, or animal can walk in its shadows without being eaten alive by the valmen-dûr.

FOMORIANS ♦ Irish mythological stone-like giants that live in Aählynéé.

GLUBGRUB ♦ A murky, green woodland faery who to his dismay, walked through Kathryn's faery door.

GLUBMAR ♦ A small village in Aählynéé where the woodland faeries live.

GROGOCHS ♦ Half sized furry men that lurk and live in caves, they work for cream and have the gift of invisibility. A sign that a grogoch is nearby is a strong scent of sour milk, while walking in a dark cave.

HÄÄLARIA [ha-lair-ee-ya] ♦ The foulest, most sinister, and darkest place where Koréna is exiled to.

HAWKMOON ♦ A measurement of the lunar time in Aählynéé when the moon is full.

KING KENDRYCK ♦ The reigning King in Aählynéé, until his Castle is swallowed by the mysterious Arthur's Seat.

Koréna ♦ The sorceress who is entombed in Arthur's Seat for a thousand Hawkmoons.

Leighaes cneá [layz-trey] ♦ 'Heal wound' in Irish.

Leprechaun ♦ Or should we say, 'feral leprechaun,' it is a stinky, wild faery that hoards many different treasures.

Leprechaun Juice ♦ A thick orangey liquid, which when drunk gives the imbiber great strength and agility. Side effects include: exhibiting the traits of a feral leprechaun by changing to an orangey color and becoming abundantly hairy.

Llangdon [lang-dun] ♦ A dark, lonely island in the middle of the crystal lake with a Burning Crater in its center. Dúcäin is the ruling wizard of the harsh island and it is the death place of MääGord, the double red-winged dragon, where she lies petrified on its slopes.

Lia Fáil [lee-ag fwel] ♦ Irish name of the Stone of Destiny. (See Stone of Destiny)

Loch Dorcha [luch dur-ch-a] ♦ 'Dark lake' in Irish. It is also, the loch within and on the other side of Arthur's Seat in the mortal realm.

MääGord [mah-gord] ♦ The name given to the double-red-winged dragon by Danú.

Nyaïn [nye-yun] ♦ The ruling wizard of the Forest of No Return.

Nezroth ♦ The magical land where Danú lives along with the Elven tribes. It is also, the land where MääGord originated from.

Nine Maidens of the Otherworld ♦ The nine maidens of the Otherworld are gate keepers and guardians of the magical land of Aählyneé.

Otherworld ♦ The land where the faery-folk live. In our story, it is the mystical world on the other side of Arthur's

Seat, the land known as Aählyéé is a part of this Otherworld.

Passage Tombs ♦ Believed to be mystical portals between the faery realm and the mortal realm.

Peist ♦ An Irish mythological lake-dwelling creature which guards a hidden treasure. It has a snake-like body and a head like a bull. They are known for their keen sense of sonar in the water and their powerful jaws which could snap a man in two.

Pookas ♦ Creatures from Irish folklore that are feared and revered at the same time. Pookas are shape-shifters and can change into the form of a rabbit, goat, dog, eagle, horse, goblin, or a Celtic tiger. Some of their features include dark, wild hair, and glowing yellow eyes. They often speak in rhymes and take their unsuspecting riders on wild rides through the dark night.

Portalilly Berries ♦ Berries which are found in Aählyéé and when eaten make a woodland faery grow bat-like wings. Only temporarily, of course, side effects include bloated belly and a very bad case of gas.

Progeria ♦ An extremely rare genetic condition causing rapid aging in children. Symptoms include: below average height and weight, narrowed face, beaked nose, hair loss, hardening of the skin, aged-looking skin, over-sized head, prominent scalp veins, high-pitched voice, loss of body fat and muscle, stiff joints, and hip dislocation. Children with Progeria have a life expectancy around thirteen years ~~old~~ young.

Queen Maeve ♦ A Queen from old Irish folklore. She strives to take over the land of Aählyéé so all the faeries and mortal men will bow down to her.

Rath Dé Ort ♦ [rath-de-or] A traditional Irish blessing meaning, the grace of God be with you!

Rav'ailín an Tulloch [ra-val-ee un tu-lah] ♦ A banshee expelled from Aählyéé who roams the cliffs of Arthur's Seat wailing night after night in search of her lost love.

Red Orb ♦ Orb of Fortune.

Red-Winged Ravens ♦ Guardians of the Raven's Gate. If one were to see one red-winged raven it would stand for sorrow, two for joy, three for marriage, four for a boy, five for silver, six for gold, and seven for the secret that's never been told!

Sain'óth [san-auth] ♦ The leader of the Danyär.

Seanachai [sh-anna-ch-ee] ♦ A traditional Irish storyteller.

Sheba ♦ An old, pasty horse owned by Grandpa.

Selkies ♦ Creatures that appear as seals, but they are really half-faery and half-man. They are said to bathe on the rocks, in the sun's warmth they will peel off their hides and emerge as a beautiful woman.

The Sidhe [the sid] ♦ The Sidhe were a supernatural race, comparable to faeries or elves. They have been said to live in the faery mounds, across the western sea. The Sidhe is also known as an invisible world that coexists with the mortal realm.

Snowden ♦ A land of white snow-capped mountains in Aählynéé.

Stone of Destiny ♦ Lia Fáil in Irish. The Stone of Destiny is the inauguration stone of all the High Kings of Ireland. It is said that when the rightful High King of Ireland places his feet upon the stone, the stone will roar with joy. It is also said, that the Stone of Destiny contains the soul of Rav'ailín an Tulloch, a banshee expelled from Aählynéé who roams the forbidding cliffs and crags of Arthur's Seat, wailing night after night, in search of her long lost love.

Soilsigh [sol-chee] ♦ 'Illuminate' in Irish.

Teine Criostal [tyne kris-tol] ♦ The name the faery-folk gave to the Fire Crystal, which was forged from the heart of a double red-winged dragon.

Three Nights of the Faeries ♦ A three day festival celebrated by the townsfolk in Ballyrun, where all sorts of peculiar faeries seem to pop out of nowhere!

Tirana [tir-an-a] ♦ The ruler of Snowden.

Téigh [ty-eeh] ♦ 'Go' in Irish.

Tèthra [teth-ra] ♦ A nomadic, female stone Fomorian.

Tír na nOg [tj-ee-rr nu n-og] ♦ The land of 'eternal youth,' a part of the Otherworld.

The Crone ♦ The name of Captain Seaneen's ferry that travels from Mulleam's Ferry Crossing to the Isle of Inishmara.

Tuatha Dé Danann [tu-ah-tha dee dan-ann] ♦ A race of people from Irish mythology who are known as the children of Danú.

Valmen-dûr [val-men-dur] ♦ The shadow people or even the devil's hatchlings, they seek refuge within the darkness of the Forest of No Return. If any animal, man, or faery were to step into its domain, a dreadful and awful thing would occur.

Woodland Faeries ♦ Little pudgy faeries that live in the forest. They have a great love for working hard and an even greater passion for eating!